Advance Praise for *New Millennium Boyz*

"There's no way a robot wrote this book. **A no-holds-barred tour of the Millennial mindset's spiritual DNA.** Anything goes."

—Douglas Coupland

"**There is some twisted shit in this book that will likely fuck with your head and break your heart.** Remember Woodstock '99, and how a sick, profit-driven media culture pushed boys to their worst impulses? Think Larry Clark or Bret Easton Ellis by way of Charles Bukowski or J.G. Ballard. **These kids are not all right.** Kazemi's prose produces the same visceral response as an early Tarantino movie. **Proceed with caution.**"

—Douglas Rushkoff

"**I walked a path parallel to my own, and it was honest, authentic and awful.** *New Millennium Boyz* is an intrusively intimate narration of someone who lived in familiar coordinates yet a different social stratum. That wholly un-unique alienation and emptiness is one that fills me with a nostalgia for a past that was, and was not, my own."

—Brooks Brown, Columbine Survivor and Author

"In *New Millennium Boyz*, Alex **Kazemi dissects the post-Columbine generation with wit and a sharp scalpel.** His characters are damaged products of their time. While this is **a dark chronicle**, there's also a cozy *High School Confidential* feel to the tale and the various media Kazemi employs to tell it, resulting in **a compulsively readable novel.**"

—Poppy Z. Brite

"*New Millennium Boyz*, the debut novel by Alex Kazemi, reveals a group of American boys for everyone to see, and does so with a driving, honest, and almost frightening narrative style. **Readers are immersed in the minds and hearts of American teen boyz who are trying to understand—and live—in our desperate adult world.** Kazemi's almost musical dialogue, and his novelist's craft capture the potential loneliness of these boyz with passionate intensity. While certain graphic aspects of the novel require that I do not recommend it for our youngest readers, I highly recommend it for middle and older teens and all adults who are raising boys."

—Michael Gurian, *New York Times* bestselling author of *Saving Our Sons* and *The Stone Boys*

"*New Millennium Boyz* is **a glimpse into the raunchiest and most deranged aspects of bro culture, a culture where women are one-dimensionalized and subordinated for men's sexual cravings.** While bro culture creates serious problems in numerous ways for both women and men, Kazemi focuses on some of the most toxic masculine elements in the culture, where women are treated as props in a pornified world of their creation, a world where men are sexual sociopaths taken from the darkest *SVU* episode imaginable. **This book should be read with caution and understood within the context of a patriarchal society gone mad**, where #metoo is considered to be a joke and where men are abusive deviants and perps. What may be the most disturbing thing of all is that elements of real-life society actually condition boys to become like the men in this book so that at the end of the day, it's less shocking when something like the Steubenville or Richmond High School gang rapes takes place. While *New Millennium Boyz* may be a troublesome book to read, we ignore the issues raised at our own risk."

—Dr. Thomas Keith, Author, Filmmaker, Educator

"This book is **raucous, raunchy, and sure to offend**, and there are readers who'll appreciate those things. **I will forever defend Kazemi's ability to write this book** and entertain his intended audience against those who'd torch all three."

—Ellen Hopkins, author of *Crank* and a dozen other banned books

"'90s' yesterbation, or molesting time for the sake of historical revisionism, is not what *New Millennium Boyz* has to offer. What it gives us is an honest query about how we can all change the world one book, one poem, one show, one picture, or one song at a time—but can we really without disastrous results? We need writers to challenge us, to wake us from our collective somnambulist dread. Books have a way of holding us in their pages with unmean-spirited, courageous arms. **Kazemi's writing of *New Millennium Boyz* is so critical to our need to communicate with one another about shit that, essentially, no one ever wants to speak about.** That is his job well done."

—Kembra Pfahler

"With this **dreamlike dialogue tale** of bored privileged boys, Alex **Kazemi collides pop culture with the burgeoning accessibility of internet notoriety**—the ultimate blend for our epidemic of sickness unto death, spinning through cyberspace."

—Laura Albert (aka JT LeRoy), author of *Sarah* and *The Heart Is Deceitful Above All Things*

New Millennium Boyz

ALEX KAZEMI

A PERMUTED PRESS BOOK
ISBN: 978-1-63758-391-3
ISBN (eBook): 978-1-63758-392-0

New Millennium Boyz
© 2023 by Alex Kazemi
All Rights Reserved

Cover art by Mikel Benhaim
Author photo by Lauren D. Zbarsky

PERMUTED
PRESS

Permuted Press, LLC
New York • Nashville
permutedpress.com

Published in the United States of America
1 2 3 4 5 6 7 8 9 10

Note to Reader

This book contains scenes that some readers may find disturbing or upsetting, including descriptions and depictions of self-harm, sexual abuse, drug consumption, offensive language, and violence.

To anyone in this world who was born a boy

"Good wombs have borne bad sons..."
—*The Tempest*, Shakespeare

*"The only thing necessary for the triumph of evil
is for good men to do nothing."*
—Unknown

*"you know what maybe I just need to get laid.
maybe that'll just change some shit around."*
—Eric Harris

☆ 01 ☆

"This is the summer of 1999 you can't see on The WB." This chorus of a new rap-metal track that's been all over the airwaves this month is bouncing in my Discman as I make my way to the back of the bus. I love the glitches in the song's production, the purple tint of the music video. I adjust my headphones, maxing out the volume. Lit plays next. A hunched over dude with blue streaks in his hair wearing a "DESTROY ALL SKA BANDS" shirt reads *Kerrang!* with the Deftones on the cover. The headline: "The revenge of the anti-heroes."

I take the window seat beside him. "Nice shirt."

"Sublime is a cancer to this earth." He laughs.

"I'm into the chain too."

"Thanks, buddy! I just got it from the gumball machine at the pool."

"Oh, shit. I was gonna get one. I want a silver one. Those are sick."

"I would way rather rock a silver chain than puka shells. Puka shells are for boyband butt bandits." He fist bumps me. "I'm Daniel."

"I'm Brad."

"Want a Slim Jim, Brad?"

"Sure, thanks." I lift the headphones off my ears and take a bite. "What are you listening to?"

"Tricky. I don't know, it's trip-hop. My bro gave me the CD when I was packing last night. He went to Europe this summer with all his college buddies and now he's like obsessed with MTV UK and this movie, *Human Traffic*."

"Every dude who comes back from Europe tries to act so evolved and cultured. Douches."

"He's all pissed about how cheap techno CDs are in the UK. Costs a fortune to import that shit here."

"I like Moby. I listen to that shit when I try to study."

"I love *Play*. What a fucking monster of an album. What about you? Do you fuck with techno?"

"I'm not a big techno guy. I've been trying to get into Fatboy Slim and Jamiroquai."

He picks up his Discman. "You want to listen? What's in yours?"

"It's a comp, but Lit is playing now."

"Dude, I fucking love them so much. It's fucked. I wish that I was at Woodstock this month. I think the Chili Peppers are playing."

"Could you imagine being there?"

"My bro promised he'd buy it off pay-per-view, tape it for me while I'm here. Live, no censorship."

"There's going to be so many fucking bare titties on those tapes."

"Fuck, I know! The best part of rock shows is when the girls take their tops off."

"Can you imagine being a rock star today? The hottest girls throwing themselves at you 'cause you got a video on MTV?"

He makes an hourglass with his hands. "Oh, you fucking know those groupie sluts in the audience are just begging for rock star seed to drip all over their jugs."

"You get an all-access pass to hot pussy when you're famous. Girls let you do anything to them. Can you imagine having all that power? Dude, there's this chick at my school, Candice Cotton… If you saw her… No other girls look like that."

"Nice tits?" He makes an orgasm face before motorboating his lips.

"Huge tits. You know who she kind of looks like? Jaime Pressly."

"The *Poison Ivy 3* slut?"

"Oh, yeah!" Daniel does an air-handjob. I stick my tongue out.

"Switch?" I hold up my Discman.

Daniel nods and we swap. "*Angels With Dirty Faces*."

"What?"

"That's what the album is called. In case you like it."

I put my headphones on, hit play, and stare out the window, looking back at what I'm leaving. A fantasy of me sitting shirtless on my bed, resting between pushups. I pass out as Tricky whisper-growls "Talk to Me."

Something wakes me up, Daniel's head is on my shoulder. Rows of Douglas firs flash past. I hit play and return to sleep.

In my dreams: *Marilyn Manson feeding Slim Jims to big-titty strippers in white-face Juggalo paint and devil-horned robes, down on all fours. "Waterboard me, MM!" "Pistol whip me, MM." "Kill me in a bathtub, MM." MM in a black suit and red tie. "There's a new moon tonight. Be careful what you dream. Brad, you can't leave this room until you nut on her butt and spill your seed in her mouth." Buff men in cloaks chant, "Spill your seed! Spill your seed! Spill your seed!"*

I wake up as the bus pulls to a stop. The camp counselor jets out of his seat, clapping. "Is everyone ready for W-E-S-T C-A-N-Y-O-N?"

Daniel and I return our Discmans to each other and make our way off the bus into the parking lot. I look at Daniel. "What kind of crystal meth is he on?"

"I want whatever semi-charmed-life he's on."

The counselor cheers. "Are you ready for W-E-S-T C-A-N-Y-O-N?"

I see the cabin ahead of us and walk toward it. The door opens onto a group of shirtless boys with perfect pecs, huge biceps, six-pack abs, and bubble butts whipping their towels, taking off their long socks, jumping on each other, high-fiving, shorts dropping beneath their knees, nipple-dancing, smacking the air, screaming, "Boo ya!" One crouches in his white CK briefs to turn up the radio. Sports scores blast into the room. The boys unzip their bags and put their clothes away.

I look at Daniel. "Oh, just wait until they start body-piling and ripping each other's clothes off."

"Like that creepy Abercrombie shower rape ad?"

"Do you honestly think that girls find those catalogs hot? All that gay shit? ...Daniel?" He's in a trance watching the boys. "Don't stare."

"Huh?"

I hit his shoulder. "It's...like...they are in some fucking cult."

"Yeah, it's called the cult of being born hot."

Daniel pulls a spray out of his bag. I grab the bottle out of his hands. "What the fuck is that? Do you also happen to have a knife in that bag that I can stab myself with?"

Daniel grabs it back. "Bug Juice."

"For what?"

"In case I get a mosquito bite on my dick, you asshole."

I fake a gasp. "Oh, no! I'm just so upset! My dad forgot to pack my limited-edition WWF cup that I got at the movies last week. What will I ever do?"

Daniel fake gasps. "Oh, no! I might have forgotten my Garth Brooks CD. I swear it was on my floor while I was packing." He tapes *X-Files* and *Buffy* ads onto the wall. "Can someone please lead me to the nearest Hellmouth?"

I laugh. "Oh, you would. You fucking would. You're like one of the only people who probably watched that *Dark Skies* show before NBC canceled it."

"I was devastated! I started a petition to try to get it back on the air!"

"Yup. I knew it. Well, you do kind of have the whole Angel thing going on."

"You hitting on me now?"

I make an orgasm face and twist my tongue. "Can't you tell? I'm just so down for your diiiiick."

Daniel laughs. "Dude, what's the best thing that you've seen at the movies this year? Mine was watching Willow from *Buffy* talk about sticking a flute up her pussy. The whole theater was dying."

"Fuck you! You snuck in? I still haven't seen *American Pie* yet."

"Yo, did you pack any extra batteries for your Discman? Can I borrow some?"

"Sure thing! My mom got me a super-size pack of double A's." I climb up, unpack my running shoes, a bar of soap, shampoo, toothpaste, clothes, and a "have fun, Brad!" sticky note that my mom snuck in. I set up my sleeping bag and pillow. I go back down and pass a handful of batteries to Daniel, then climb back up to make my bed.

The camp counselor opens the door, making West Coast gang signs. "Yo, home skillets, come with us to the lake-hizzay."

I eyeroll. "Do we need our swimsuits?"

Daniel's tone goes dryer. "It's some kind of meeting. Maybe we have to hold some hands and pray to Jesus Crust or something. They on some Jesus camp shit. Let's go, lil n****!"

We follow the group downhill between the trees to the lake.

"Are you on AOL or ICQ yet?" Daniel sucks on and spits out a Warhead.

"No."

"Why?"

"I just don't care. You know, why use your time surfing the web when you can be hanging out in real places?"

"I'm a total net-head. I'm online all the time. I've got my own Tripod site."

"Oh, yeah? What's your site?"

"It's an *X-Files* fansite. I've got a hit counter and everything."

"For fuck's sake, man. You need to get laid!"

"Buddy, I'm a horndog. By the end of summer, all the pages of my Britney *Rolling Stone* are gonna be stuck together."

"There's a pic of her in there where she's standing in her bedroom. Her tits look so huge. I want to bury my face in them tig ol' bitties. Boomin' upstairs."

He slaps my back. "I think about that pic all the time, my boy."

"Britney's cover is why man was gifted with *Rolling Stone*."

"Why didn't I steal some of my brother's *Penthouses* and rent them to all of the horny retards in our cabin?"

I put my hand over his shoulder. "We could have run a bootleg *Playboy* ring all summer. Ringleaders, man…you and I. Full-on gangstahhhhs."

"Let's break into our counselor's cabin and steal some porno mags… if they have any…"

"Oh, they would be 'mos to not have any."

"Talking about Britney right now is taking me back to the school dance where all the girls were dancing like she does in the video. They kept singing 'show me how you wanna do me.' It was so fucking hot. It was like being in a porno. All the guys loved it…" Daniel winks.

I smile. "And that's who they were doing it for…for the boys."

Everybody lines up behind the camp leaders. The shore is filled with bodies. I stare ahead at a small island. A middle-aged lady in yellow wears a fanny pack and shouts into a megaphone. Two male leaders beside her hold unlit torches.

"Daniel, is this some southern evangelist extremist ritual?"

"I think so, but I don't remember my mom telling me about this part."

"The least our parents could have done was warn us that we were all about to be inducted into a cult! What if we never see them again? Getting kidnapped by Christian cult leaders was so not the summer that I was planning for."

"Shush. You don't want them to hear us."

"My family isn't even Christian! My mom is like a total blood oath new ager who watches Oprah. Why in the living duck fuck would she send her son to a Christian summer camp?"

"Shhh! CCD is about to begin."

Dana waves. "Welcome to West Canyon, fellow campers, where dreams become realities and life becomes a dream. My name is Dana, and I'm here to warn you that ahead of us is Nixie Island. No one is allowed to swim over there. If we find out that any of you…"

A guy in khaki board shorts cuts her off. "Why? Is it haunted? Is it a piece of the Bermuda Triangle? Were people sacrificed on it or something?"

"No, it isn't haunted. You know, it's rude to interrupt someone while they're speaking. If we find out that any of you have gone there, we will call your parents. You will not be sent home; however, all your privileges will be suspended. You will also be expected to check in every night at 9:30 to do whatever it is that counselor Marc deems sufficient punishment. Imagine lots of physical labor and unpleasant chores. But we're not here to lay down the rules. You should know them already since you were told them as soon as you got off the bus. Who likes surprises? In the order in which you are all standing, each and every one of you will not leave our sight until your head is dunked below the water. Do not remove your clothing. Simply line up between the torches." She points to Sean and Cody, who light the torches. "State your name, and while your fellow camper is dunking their head, you all repeat the words and clap: 'I belong to the water. You belong to me! Unleash your inner polar bear! It's cold in there!' Sean and Cody, your counselors, will be the ones giving you the dunking."

I watch everyone take their turn, but it's so boring. I shut my eyes and fantasize: I'm in the back of a limousine with a red leather interior, watching a blonde with huge fake tits pour Absolut into a daiquiri glass. She grins at me.

Chants in the background: "I belong to the water! You belong to me! I belong to the water! You belong to me! I belong to the water! You belong to me!"

The last brunette chick in line, face in her hands: "I'm not doing this. I'm not messing up my hair. Sorry, I can't. You wish! I am not taking out my vintage Chanel hair clip that I got in LA for this. It's just not happening!"

Sean winks at me. "It's your turn. Now say your name as if you're kneeling in front of Jesus himself."

"Brad." I walk into the water between two lit torches, kneel down. A techno song spins in my mind. *I'm a superstar. I'm a superstar. Baby, I'm a superstar.* Sean dunks my head. *I'm a superstar. I'm a superstar. Baby, I'm a superstar.* Cody dunks my head.

"Great job, everyone! You are all now officially West Canyon camp members! Now go dry off! We have dinner in the mess hall at six p.m. Singing, games, and God! Wow! What a summer we have for you all! Our lord and savior, Jesus Christ, is good to us! Enjoy your first night!"

We walk back to our cabins in our wet clothes. Daniel catches up to me.

"You look—"

A long pause, then, at the same time, we say back and forth:
"Drenched."

"Drrrencheedddd."

"I feel like I swallowed the jizz of a lake monster."

Daniel laughs. "They say that the lake here is totally bottomless."

"Like your black heart."

"How did you know?"

"Did you see the girls in the white shirts getting dunked?"

"The pop-punk gods are looking after us because we can't be at Woodstock."

"Did you see the tits on the blonde in the butterfly shirt? God fucking damn."

"She's going right in the spank bank. I would let her suck on my Ring Pop anytime. How does a man jerk off at summer camp, anyway?"

I air jerk-off. "After those afternoon titty teasers, I'm thinking about busting a nut on some tree bark tonight. Father nature, buddy."

I walk into the cabin and climb up to the top bunk to grab my blink-182 towel. I climb down, take my wet clothes off under my towel, put them on the floor, and wrap myself up. The boys are taking their underwear off and throwing their clothes on the floor. Under my breath, "Don't make eye contact, look ahead." Daniel sits on the bottom bunk in his *X-Files* towel. I shoot a middle finger at him. "You're the fucking worst... Mr. What Would Mulder Do."

"Oh, eat a chode. Mr. Rags had a sale and this was the last one that they had in stock. This is an expensive towel, alright?"

"You might be worse than the *Star Trek* people."

Daniel jumps up and down, punches my arm. "I shouldn't have to defend myself to the guy in a blink-182 towel. I bet you fantasize about Tom and Mark running around naked." He punches my arm again. "I bet that video gives you a woody. Oh yeah, Mark! Wash me up. Oh, yeahhhh. Do a bad TLC cover for me on *Unplugged*, Mark... Oh, yeahhh. Fuck me, Mark! Stick your Hoppus up my cornhole!"

I punch him back. "This is not just a blink-182 towel, you fucking cocksucker, this is a limited edition fan club only blink-182 towel that my dad ordered for me online."

He punches me back. "I bet your fan club membership came with an exclusive limited-edition dildo with Tom's face to stick up your ass, plus the chance to win front-row tickets...or maybe the chance to win backstage passes to meet them in the flesh! And I'm sure if you're extra lucky, it'll come with a calendar..."

I push him onto his bunk. "Bite me."

Daniel gets back up. "We get it, bro. You like to listen to KROK and play air hockey in your basement with your dad. You're such a real original, groundbreaking young American man."

I stand in front of him. "I know that losing is hard for you to like, process, but you're a total gayboy for having an X-*Files* towel."

He smacks my ass as I walk away. I pick my wet clothes up off the cabin floor, walk out to the deck in my towel, and put the clothes on the ledge to dry in the sunlight.

Back inside the cabin, a boy stands in front of a boombox with a CD between his teeth as he lifts his tank top over his head. He takes the CD out of his mouth, puts it on, and hits play. The chorus of Eminem's "My Name Is" adds heat as I scan. Another shirtless boy pulls down his briefs and rubs his pubes. Another is on all-fours on his bed while another in a plastic cowboy hat rides him. "Yee-haw!" Another puts his hand on the wall, sticks his tongue out, arches his butt, and shakes it as another shirtless boy spanks him. Fruit of the Loom, Hanes, Calvin Klein, Tommy, Joe Boxers, Dockers waistbands... I make eye contact with a guy who has the same pair that I'm wearing. A shirtless boy balances a 7UP bottle cap on his nose, another does squats, and another on the floor spoons Creatine into a water bottle and shakes it. Another shirtless boy with a tribal arm tat and a nipple ring walks over, stands in his Calvins, and holds out a bag of Doritos. "You want some Ritos, boys?"

"No thanks, bro."

He takes a munch. "You need to borrow one of my backwards caps? I brought two just in case a fellow cabin bro needs one."

"What?"

"You aren't wearing one… How you gonna look like a pimp and throw that mack on the honeys, my n****?"

"Uh, well…"

"Why don't you boys stop being weirdos? Man the fuck up and come meet the rest of the boys on our side of the cabin."

"Sick invite, man, but we're doing fine over here on our side."

"Yeah, in your little corner with your little *X-Fag* poster."

"I mean, well, uhhhh."

"Wow."

"Suit yourself, cupcakes, and make sure to use a rubber. Have fun talking about your feelings, or whatever felchers like you two like to do with each other for fun. And hey, before I dip…I wanted to ask you homos. How many do you see?"

"What are you talking about?"

He grabs my fingertips and rubs them along his abs. "1…2…3…4…5…6…" He spits on his stomach, then my fingers. "Look at all that spit just swimming down these washboards, baby. Later, tools!" He gives two middle fingers.

I lie down on Daniel's bunk and rub on the cabin walls.

He stands in front of me. "Why do you look like you're about to pull a Cobain?"

"I don't know. We've been here for what, two fucking hours? Why am I surprised that some ESPN-monster-cocksucker-lacrosse-fucko has already made me feel like shit?"

"There's a ninety-nine percent chance that we just got inducted into some kind of fucking brainwashed Baptist cult. I get it."

"Do you expect me to sport a Kodak?"

"The Aberbitch didn't get his daily sword fight in with his buttbuddies and you're the one who has to pay for it… It's kind of funny."

"What's so fucking funny about this?"

Daniel traces his fingers in the air. "You got…finger…raped."

I bang my head back against the wall. "Why does this fucking cult have a ban on handheld electronics? I want my Gameboy, man. I want to play *Pokémon Blue*. My dad just got me a cool clear case from GameStop."

"Barf me out. Can you shut the fuck up about your dad?"

"So, how old were you when your parents got divorced?"

"Seven."

"Thought so."

I get up and stand in front of him. He reaches out and touches my shoulders.

"Listen, man," he says. "We are two men cut off from the world in the wild, wild wilderness."

"Yeah. This is going to be okay. Let's just be super chill."

Daniel nods. "We need to stop this before we become like total '99 summer camp suicide statistics."

"We're Americans. How do you expect me to be chill without a 7-Eleven in walking fucking distance?"

"No *MTV News*. No AOL. No Deja. No *Hercules* cartoon on Saturday mornings. No PlayStation. No *X-Files* message boards. No new episodes of *Low Days*… No…no Nag Champa!"

"A hot Mandy Moore video could be premiering on *TRL* right now and we're missing out…and that's okay."

He looks me in the eye. "I'd hug you right now if it wasn't gay."

"I'd hug you too, man. I'd hug you too."

I go up to the top bunk, grab my bag, and bring it down the ladder. Daniel sits on the bed as I hold up two shirts. "Should I wear my Columbia house shirt or the Ralph Lauren polo?"

"Shit, I should have brought my BMG shirt. We could have been matching."

I make a peace sign. "Matching corporate whores owned by the machine worshipping the AOL pyramid."

"You got it."

"I don't want to wear the polo."

"Why not? It'd look sick on you."

"It's too much."

"It's not too much."

I grab the cK One out of my bag and spray it on myself, then grab my Dep gel and rub it through my hair.

"Can I borrow some?"

"Yeah, sure." I toss over the gel.

"Can I borrow your Adidas slides?"

"No, I need to wear them."

"Ok, fine."

"Don't be a lame ass and tell me you brought Birkenstocks."

He smirks. "Maybe I did."

"You don't have Adidas slides?"

"My mom got me these." Daniel holds up his Birks.

"Have you ever noticed that if you say Adidas in a spic accent, it sounds like 'adios'?"

"Adidos, Adidos, Adidos."

"Fucked. That's so fucking sick."

I put on my Ralph Lauren polo and Umbro shorts. Daniel, shirtless, whips me with his shirt.

I whip him with mine. "I'm going to get you bad when you're asleep."

"I'm too lazy to get dressed."

"We have to get dressed."

"Can't we just stay here?"

"Can you give me that spooky Tricky CD? I want to take it for another ride."

Daniel picks up his Discman, hits eject, takes out the CD, and passes it to me.

I salute him, then climb up to the top bunk, get in a fetal position, stare at the wall, put my headphones on, put in the CD that Daniel just gave to me, and hit play. *Angels with Dirty Faces* starts to spin. I close my eyes as I play with the strings on my shorts and grab my dick. *I am at Burger King in an employees' bathroom. A knockoff J. Hewitt brunette is pushing my face into her tits as I undo her Burger King polo. She grabs my finger and sucks on it. I grab her tits. "Please! Please! Titty fuck me!" Splice. In Vegas, spinning on a heart-shaped bed, a blonde sits on my lap in a candy necklace thong, shaking her big ass. I lick the* Playboy *bunny logo on her cheek. I look to each side… Two men in "Buttman" black suits and aviators grin at me. "Young man, we have served you what you want." She looks at me. "You are just so buff… I bet you love this big fat ass in your face, don't you?" I eat the candy off her thong. Strawberry. Splice. I look into the distance down an empty street and see a cardboard cutout of the* Dixie Chicks *Wide Open Spaces. A man holds up a protest sign and yells about how much he hates "Everybody's Free (To Wear Sunscreen)." I start to hear the song in my head, but sped up a hundred times. Splice. A hooded man starts to carry—*

Daniel climbs on top of me and slaps my forehead. I open my eyes and shake my head. "Whoa! You didn't just see me—"

"Wake up, tardo!"

I sweat. "Whoa, hold up. You didn't just see anything, right?"

"What?"

"Like my hand wasn't on your dick. Fuck, I mean…my dick."

"No, because when you're on the bottom bunk reading *Archie* comics, you thankfully cannot hear the sound of someone touching their dick."

"Fortunately."

"Come on, we have to fucking go to dinner. Everyone is leaving."

I look at the open door—all of the boys from the cabin are dressed up, standing on the deck. I grab my wallet.

☆ 02 ☆

The lights in the distance lead me and Daniel to the mess hall.

"They better sell Surge at the concession or I'm going to be very fucking pissed off. I want it right now. I need to get some Surge in me before I break down. I'm going to make a fuckin scene and go *Real World* crazy if I don't get some fuckin Surge. I'll hang myself. I'm not fucking scared."

Daniel sneers. "Relax, freakazoid. I'm sure they have it."

"Surge brings up a lot of trust issues for me. My mom's cousin visited last spring break, and he would drink all of mine. Ever since that happened, I feel like there is never enough Surge in this world."

"Meanwhile there's like actual starving, dying children in Africa. Have you never seen those ads about helping starving Blacks, or are you completely retarded?"

"What if one day I wake up and Surge is extinct? That'll really be the time to end it all."

Inside the mess hall, I look around the wooden walls, then up at the roof and a painted banner. "WELCOME TO WEST CANYON SUMMER CAMP." A group of boys from my cabin wear matching backwards caps and Tommy and Ralph Lauren polos. They're sitting on circular wooden benches with hot blondes in slutty tank tops, butterfly clips in their hair, and elastic chokers on their necks.

I tap Daniel's shoulder. "Where's the concession stand?"

"I can't fucking hear you. It's too loud."

I get close to his ear. "I said, where is the concession stand?"

"Fuck. Use your fucking eyes, you braindead retard. It says right there: 'concession.'"

"It's game time, boys. Let's crush a fuckin Surge." I walk over and wait in line. "Is everything we eat going to taste as strong as all this wood?"

He points to his crotch. "That's what my ex-girlfriend said to her friends after she finished tasting this diiiick."

"Seriously. I've literally never smelt such strong wood in my life."

He shakes his head. "You aren't helping yourself here, bud."

I look around for the blonde with huge tits from the lake baptism, who I swear kind of looks like Denise Richards. *Maybe I'll stop being a bitch tonight and actually talk to a girl who looks like that. Mark and Tom would want that for me.* My eyes scan a boy from my cabin in a backwards cap flexing his muscles as a girl beside him feels his biceps. I land on a blonde girl in a white dress sitting alone with a can of orange Minute Maid soda, her hair in pigtails, arms folded over her stomach. *Where is she? Do I wait for her to come back? Those sad eyes are unwinding. Should*

I go a little closer? I don't remember seeing this one. Follow the sound of her.

As I walk over to her table and see her gap teeth, an anime sequence of the two of us enters my mind. *A techno-trance song plays in the background of a Sailor Moon–type scene where she and I are sucking face on a park bench, then kissing underwater with heart eyes and sparkles surrounding us. I don't want anyone else here. This is the one I want tonight.*

I make my move. "Is anybody sitting here?"

"No."

I sit down. "So, what's your name?"

"Call me Aurora."

"That's a cool name."

"Yeah, I think so too."

"What's on your necklace?"

"It's the tree of life. If you hold down the spheres, these orbs light up in my soul and I can astral travel to different dimensions. You may not see it lit, but I do. I think only I can see it."

"Is that one of those Hare Krishna things?"

"It's Kabbalah."

"So, are you a big Madonna fan? My mom always rewatches her *Oprah* performance on full blast and dances in front of the TV. It's so humiliating. What is it with moms and *Oprah*?"

"Kabbalah is the portal and wisdom that transports you to higher dimensions, into the ascension of the soul. Kabbalah has nothing to do with Madonna."

"This sounds like some woo-woo stuff."

"What is your star sign?"

"You really believe in that star sign garbage? When people talk about anything mystical, I just feel fucking sick due to the level of stupidity… It's just not real. People are so desperate to believe in anything. I bet you and my mother would get along. She's like a blood-oath new ager that has never missed an episode of *Oprah* in her life."

"I do believe it because I truly think we are all star children, made of the cosmos… Who would have thought some boy in a Ralph Lauren polo was the Mister Know It All authority on the whole wide universe?"

"Oh, so this is the part where you're going to try to judge me by how you think I am? Are we really going to do this stupid shit right now? FYI, I'm a Cancer."

"I thought so. You look like a Cancer."

"What does that even mean? You are so reaching right now."

"Well, you're wearing a silver chain, and in the Linda Goodman book of astrology, she always says that you can spot a Cancer wearing silver jewelry out on a summer night."

"Well, you can tell Miss Linda Goodman to suck it. That's just called a coincidence."

"You do know that there is no such thing as coincidence, right?"

"Well—"

She cuts me off. "So, when are you going to ask me about my sign? You haven't asked one question about me! You aren't doing so well. Awww, look at you…such a selfish little Cancer." She pinches my cheeks.

"I'm not selfish! And I'm not a 'selfish Cancer' because being a Cancer means nothing."

"Wow! Look at you go! Typical Cancer! So sensitive."

"Would you stop that? Let me guess, you're a Cancer too?"

"I'm a Pisces. Cancer and Pisces are water signs. We are prone to over-dreaming, over-feeling, over-empathy, over-everything."

"Okay, fine. I will neither confirm nor deny that I have such girly traits, but I still think that this is fraudulent and has nothing to do with real science. There is no proof, no evidence that the stars affect our personality, or anything stupid like that. It's just mind-blowing to me that people would even entertain this bullshit."

She rubs her fingertips on her collarbones. I look at her bra strap. *If I looked under the table right now, would her underwear be showing? God, this girl's talking voice is so hot.*

She flicks the charm on her velvet choker. "What do you think of my eyes?"

"Your eyes? They're cool."

"They're too far apart. They aren't the ones I want to have."

"If you can't change something about yourself, you might as well learn how to love it! I think they're cool, like those dolls from the seventies."

"Yeah, I guess. I don't know."

"Have you done anything cool lately?"

She pats her neck. "You know, just last week, when I woke up, I found a dead dragonfly by my window. I put it above my rib cage, hoping that its soul would make a hole in me and break through, using my body as a vessel, giving it a second chance at life."

"Wow. Well, I used to cut worms that I found in the dirt when I was little."

"I did that too. I put them in the freezer. My mom used to put slugs in the freezer on full moons. She said that they'd bring me good luck."

"Slugs in the freezer?"

"My mom was weird. Do you want to try to catch some salamanders this week?"

I drag my words. "Totally. I'm such a great salamander catcher."

"I think salamanders are friends of the fairies, so we have to be nice to them. You can hold my fluorite stone to activate them."

"Okay, yeah. Sure."

"Why do you keep staring at my eyeshadow?"

"I am?"

"Uh, yeah. You know you are."

"Close your eyes. Your eyelids are so blue. They're so glittery, so blue. So shiny."

"Do you think I'm pretty?"

"Yeah, you're pretty."

She rubs her fingertips on her collarbones. "Do you like water? I just love water. Sometimes I can feel my hands drying up, even when I'm on land. It's crazy to say it, but it's true."

"Water is nice. In my neighborhood, we have a duck pond and a swamp with a bridge. I go there sometimes to sit and when I look into the water, I think about all of the places that I could be. It's kind of like looking into a future that doesn't exist."

"I want to go to a secret creek one day, but it has to be far away, and you'd have to drive hours to get there, so no one can know that I'm there." She rubs her foot on mine under the table. "I want you to come with me. I want you to come with me to spray my perfume on tree bark while we're out here. So, can we summon the water faes sometime this week?"

"I'm down."

"Sometimes I wish the bottom of my bathtub was the bottom of a swimming pool. I always hold my breath, close my eyes, and put my head underwater, knowing that I'm on my way to a different place than here, but I reach a dead end that stops my journey. Ever do that?"

"Wow, I used to do that a lot when I was a kid. I haven't been to the bottom of a swimming pool in such a long, long time. It's one of my favorite places to be."

"I just think the sound of who we are underwater is the closest thing that we have to the truth."

"Yeah."

"Be honest with me, Brad. Do you even want to be here?"

"My parents said that summertime is a time to make new memories with new people who aren't from your neighborhood. I guess they're right. I'm not getting anything out of my friends back at home. I'm bored of them. I want something new, so here I am."

"You probably made all of those friends at school."

"Every guy meets their friends at school."

"I can't imagine what that's like. I've been homeschooled my entire life."

"So you must be a Jehovah's Witness?"

"No, I already told you. I practice Kabbalah."

"Whoa, okay. That must be so fucked. What's that like? That would make me crazy. I wouldn't know how to get away."

"It is what it is. I don't know anything different. My neighbor is my teacher and he paid for the train ride for me to come down here and everything. It was his little treat."

"God, I'm just fucking annoyed right now. Just talking about my neighborhood makes me so pissed."

"About what?"

"None of my friends back home ever want to do anything other than what we do all the time. We don't do anything, we don't talk about anything. It's all nothing."

"What does that even mean?"

"What does *what* mean?"

"Like, 'it's all nothing.'"

"Being in my house, walking around the neighborhood, even just being alive and living there… It just gives me this constant fear of not doing enough, like there are all of these places, parties, or things that I could be doing outside with other people, new friends, not just with the same boys that I've known and hung out with every day since the third grade. It's this constant knowing that, deep inside my heart, I'm missing out on something. Even if I can't exactly say what it is, I know that I'm missing out on it. I can feel it."

"I know what you mean. I have so many memories of the things that I see on TV or in magazines, but I don't know if there are many exciting things happening in my life. It's like, when is it my turn? When are things ever going to end up becoming fun? What's outside of the fantasy?"

"Yeah, exactly. I feel the same."

"What do you and your boys do back at home?"

"The same thing every day. We rotate hanging out in each other's basements, talk at school about the same stupid shit, walk in circles around the grass field by my house, play PlayStation, go to McDonald's, or sit in Dunkin' Donuts. We go to the movies. A lot. We're always at the movies. We walk around the drugstore. We shoot bottle rockets. Where I live, at night, nothing happens."

"And that's not enough for you?"

"It's so fucking boring seeing the same things all the time, the same people at the store, the same streets, the same gas station with the same bags of candy and Slurpees. You start to get all dizzy in a place where everyone recognizes you."

"There's no privacy."

"There's no freedom, no privacy. The worst part is that nobody ever talks about it. Everyone is so chill living this way. You're just supposed to be okay with it, smile, stay there, and never leave."

"It must be nice to go home to a place that never changes, though."

"I guess?"

"Well, guess what? It's summer now, and not just any summer. This is the last summer before the turn of the millennium, the future. All the cool magazines are saying that 2000 is going to feel like this big dance party with lots of metallics and opportunities, and you're here right now with me. This is your chance to experience something new that you'll maybe never get the chance to experience again."

"Do you want to get out of here?"

"I went into the girls' counselor's cabin and stole some smokes. She's old, like twenty-one. I've never smoked before."

"Won't we get caught? Did you find any alcohol in there?"

"Who's going to tell on us? The trees? I left the box, silly. I only took two. Just enough for her not to notice. Let's go!"

"Where can we go?"

"It's summer camp. If you want to do something bad, you go into the woods."

☆ 03 ☆

The chorus of Everclear's "I Will Buy You a New Life" drizzles from the boombox on the table. Out on the grass, staring at the archery target, a brunette in a dragon tee crawls her fingers up my back and kisses my neck.

"Do it again!"

I grab another arrow from the sling on my back, place it in the bow, and shoot it.

"Boom! That's what I'm talking about, baby! Boom!"

"This was your fourth in a row! You're so amazing."

"Hey, thanks!"

The beginning of Heather Nova's "London Rain" plays as I leave. A guy in a black beaded necklace nods. "Dude, you did so good out there. I'm blown away. You have to teach me your skills."

"Thanks, bud."

I high-five him, then look back at the brunette's tits and fantasize about giving her a pearl necklace in the woods. I take my shirt off and rub my face on it before walking between the bushes. A group of girls in Abercrombie shirts with flowers taped to their cheeks ask me to snap a pic of them against the cabin wall, but I ignore them. I put my shirt back on, look out at people rolling down hills in tires, and flash back to roasting smores by the fire last night, Daniel and I fighting with our sticks, how I can't wait to see *American Pie* when it's out on video. I imagine waiting in the Blockbuster parking lot, watching through the window as an older guy buys it for me. I go to the cooler on the porch and grab a blue Fla-Vor-Ice, rip off the top with my teeth, and spit it out. I suck on it while rocking on the porch chair. I bite my lip and conjure another fantasy about titty-fucking the dragon-teed brunette while she lays on the dirt moaning, eyes rolling back, but in this one, she's telling me how big my dick is when Aurora and Daniel come running up. Green and blue scales are dabbed on the side of Aurora's cheeks. She's dressed in a baby blue butterfly shirt tucked into daisy dukes. Daniel is in a bucket hat, 311 shirt, camo Oakley swim shorts, and an orange and white tiger mask.

"What's with the queer bucket hat? You guys look crazy, but so fucking amazing!"

"All the girls have been taping dandelions and flowers to their faces. I want to do it too, but they didn't match my face paint."

"Yeah, they were asking me to take Polaroids of them. I didn't do it, though."

Daniel pats my back. "Atta boy. Girls are so retarded."

Aurora eyerolls. "Well, whatever. It wouldn't match my silver nails."

"It's weird. What if someone mails the trend to *Teen People* and Britney Spears does it in a photoshoot, and then every girl in America goes to school with flowers taped to their faces?"

"Pollen on their faces, that's all I have to say, my man. Pollen."

Aurora hits Daniel's arm. "Ew! Ew! Ew!"

Aurora grabs my hand and Daniel follows behind as we run to the shore and onto the pier. I lean over the edge, twirl my fingers in the water, slides off, hot feet on the wooden planks. As I look up, Aurora takes off her shirt, revealing a white bikini top. I watch her pull down her daisy dukes, revealing a matching white bottom. She throws her shirt and jelly sandals onto the dock. I whistle at her. She giggles back. Daniel takes off his shirt.

"You ready?"

Aurora and Daniel hold hands and jump into the water. I watch the lake ripple and spin into the idea that this is all happening—hallucinations of myself forming in the water…being six years old, looking into the chain link fence out at the Port Nells public pool. I look at Daniel's and Aurora's tote bags: Garbage, *X-Files*, Alien Workshop, Kate Moss, and *House of Style* pins, a Lit patch, flower embroidery. I take my shirt off and throw it onto the dock.

Daniel splashes. "Oooh, look at that sexy beast! Now come in, nut-licker!"

I take a second to lay my body on the hot wood, eyes roaming around, checking out everyone else on the shore, and in my own silence, I watch Aurora and Daniel swim.

"Can you grab the i-Zone out of my bag and snap a pic of us?" Daniel asks.

"Yeah, sure."

I take out the cam and snap Aurora and Daniel holding peace signs up against their eyes. I watch the pic spit out and put it into his bag to develop. I jump into the water and swim toward them. "The water looks like glass."

Aurora holds onto the back of my neck. "You don't know how bad I want something to grab me and pull me under."

"That's what's so weird about lakes. They're so murky. It's like something is always ready to pull you down, but that's what I love about it."

I smile. "Aurora, put your head underwater. Daniel and I are going to count how long you can stay under." I watch her go down. "…fifty, fifty-one, fifty-two, fifty-three, fifty-four."

Her head shoots up, wet hair flowing down her shoulders as the colors from the fake scales smudge and drip down her face. I grab a lily pad and throw it at Daniel. He grabs some and throws them at me. I swim alone to the mini dock in the middle of the lake. Underwater, I can't see much, but reach out to feel what seems like mini poles. I crawl up the ladder onto the dock, jump back into the water, and swim to Daniel and Aurora.

Daniel spits water, then says, "Where are all of the water angels?"

Aurora smiles. "I'm the water angel."

I point out the view. "Look how visible the mountains are."

Daniel asks, "What time is it?"

"We've been swimming here forever. Everyone is gone."

"Who cares? What is time anyway? If you'd never seen a clock before, none of this would even matter."

"You're right. Time is whatever we make it up to be in our heads. There is no time underwater."

"You can just look up at the sky to see if it's night or day and that's all that matters. All of us right now, splashing around."

"You guys, I never want to leave. This, right here, is all I want."

Daniel sucks lake water into his mouth and spits it onto my face. "Okay, dream over. Time to get out."

Aurora suggests, "Let's go to that hill to dry off in the sun, the one that I was talking about, where no one ever goes. It doesn't even feel like it's part of here."

I follow Daniel and Aurora through the trees to the hill. When we arrive, I take my slides off, barefoot on the warm grass. Daniel and Aurora put their bags down. I look at Aurora lying on her stomach in her bikini, picking the grass. I shoulder Daniel.

"Nice, right?"

"Very nice."

She doesn't notice.

I ask her, "What do you think about love?"

"I think that boys have more fun dreaming about love but are afraid of feeling it because that would hurt too much."

"Daniel, do your dolphin voice."

"EHHHHHKKKK EHHHKK."

"Wow, that is so...weird."

Daniel tosses Aurora the Polaroids that I took of them. She holds one up. "This one is so good. I love it."

Daniel throws me a Sunny D. I take a sip and pour some onto the grass.

He's stoked. "There's this new song on the Go soundtrack, 'Steal My Sunshine.' I wish we were listening to it right now because it would fit the vibe so well."

"What about that new LFO song that's been blowing up? The 'Chinese food makes me sick' song."

"Aurora, you don't like LFO, right?"

She makes a yucked-out face. "Ew, no. I don't listen to that kind of bubblegum music."

I put my arm around her shoulder. "What a gem. You hear that? She doesn't listen to LFO. We got a keeper here."

"I feel like we're in a music video on MTV."

"If it's summertime and it feels like you're on MTV, that's a sign that everything in your life is going right."

"Or you're doing everything right."

"Like the Mariah Carey video where she's swinging and they're at summer camp, the baby one."

"Aren't all of her songs about baby? She's always singing 'baybehhh.'"

"Mariah Carey has a great rack. I would nut on those jugs. True story. Those guys in the video who kidnap her are lucky." Daniel pulls a package of Pokémon temporary tattoos out of his bag. "Brad, can you do the Bulbasaur on my arm?"

I grab the package. "I want that one."

"Okay, I'll do it for you."

I turn to Aurora. "Do you have a water bottle we can use?"

"It's fine. I have one, as well as this." Daniel pulls out a mini towel. "I got this. I take temporary tattoos very seriously. I am a prepared man." He pours water onto the cloth, peels off the plastic, and presses the paper sheet against my skin. He grabs my hand. "You have to wait thirty seconds. Just think of the chorus of 'Dammit' and it'll be done by then."

I close my eyes as Daniel presses the corners of the tat with the wet cloth over and over again. I think of blink playing "Dammit" while I'm in the front row headbanging, holding up rock-ons, a hot blonde grinding on me as I'm holding her from behind, grabbing her tits. He peels off the paper and I look down at the Bulbasaur tat. "Dude, this looks fucking sick. Thanks, man!"

"You got it, bro. I feel bad or kind of weird saying this, and I know, I know it's going to sound crazy because it's not an actual place, but I miss posting on the X-Files bulletin board, being in the X-Files chat rooms."

Aurora picks the grass. "That's so weird to me. You know, sitting on the computer, talking to strangers about your interests."

I nod. "Yeah, that is fucking weird."

"It's fun. It doesn't bother me."

"What doesn't bother you?"

"I already told you, spending time on the internet. It doesn't mean much to me. I still spend more time in real life."

"You think there's a balance?"

Daniel mocks Neo's voice. "That balance is called *The Matrix*, baby."

"Okay. What do you love most about being at home in your bedroom?"

Daniel smiles. "It's a place that never changes."

He takes out his silver wraparound Oakleys, but I grab them before he can put them on. "Let me try these on."

He grabs them back. "No."

"Dude, your Oakleys are tuff as fuck."

"Are you making fun of them?"

I grab them again. "No, I love them. I want a pair so fucking bad. I love the blue lenses with the black." Daniel puts them on. I gasp. "You look like an actual rock star in those."

Aurora laughs. "He looks like he's in Hanson!"

"Take that back. I'm nothing like those fags. I thought I'd be over my Oakleys because I saw Freddie Prinze Jr. in them and I wouldn't wanna seem like a butt crusher like him, but I still love them."

"Just let me try them on."

"You were making fun of my bucket hat."

"Yeah, because your bucket hat looks so fucking gay. You should take it off."

"No."

"You seriously look like a flaming homosexual. It looks bad, dude. Take it off. OshKosh kids wear bucket hats." I take off his hat. He puts it back on. "Dude, if you want to look like the retarded bald New Radicals guy, that's on you. That motherfucker literally looks like a Down syndrome Mr. Clean in that video."

Daniel puts his shirt over his head. "Guess who I am? Heh. Heh. Heh. Heh."

Aurora cuts us off. "Do you have any Skittles in your bag?"

"I fucking love the episode when Beavis chainsaws the praying mantis. That was so fucking hilarious."

Aurora lies on my chest. I put my hand on her shoulder and feel her hair in my mouth as she leans over to take lipstick out of her bag. She puts it on, then takes out a shell mirror to look at herself. I look over and see a ginger girl who kind of looks like Katie Holmes approaching us with a video camera.

"Oh look, Ginger Spice has come to see us."

"Talk in a British accent. Cheerio. Cup of tea. Cheerio."

She scoffs. "You don't think I get that all the time? Think of something more original, loser."

Daniel fake coughs. "Achoo, firecrotch."

"Excuse me? Uh, anyway, I'm the head of the WCTV committee and we want to tape some footage of you guys for this week's WCTV update."

"Can you flip the screen around so we can see ourselves while we're taping?"

"No, this Handycam doesn't have mirror mode."

"Wow, that's gay."

"Okay, are you guys ready? I'm going to hit record. I'll say 'action' when I hit the red button. Ready? Action! Hey, West Canyon campers. This is Erin here with your weekly WCTV update. I'm here sitting with…"

The camera falls on me. "Sup, I'm Brad."

The camera moves over to Daniel. "Yo, this is Daniel."

The camera pans over to Aurora. "Hi! I'm Aurora."

"Aurora, what do you think of the fashion trend going around camp of girls wearing flowers taped to their faces?"

"I think it's, you know, beautiful and creative. It'd be really pretty to see it on the runways of Paris or in *Vogue*. I could totally see Kate Moss doing it. I would be doing it if it matched my look today."

Erin lights up. "I love the way that you've been doing your makeup. It's so cute. Just so you know, a lot of the girls at camp think you're really mysterious and pretty. I just wanted to tell you that."

"Aww, thanks, baby doll. I love your necklace."

"Awww, thank you! What would you say is your must-have beauty product this summer?"

"I'm obsessed with the Maybelline metallic silver lipliner and lipstick right now. I think it's going to be a big thing that we're going to see a lot more of in 2000. I just love it. It makes me feel like a new millennium princess, and that's kind of the vibe that all of us girls should be striving for, to be as pretty and futuristic as possible. I really hope that by like 2020, we can clone all of the endangered animals to keep them from going extinct."

"I can't wait to buy that when I'm home!" The camera pans to Daniel and me. "And boys? What would you say your most memorable moment of camp has been so far?"

"Well, dude, skateboarding up that ramp was sick. I scraped my knees a bunch, and I bailed like thirty times."

The camera returns to Aurora. "You guys, cut it out. Don't be mean to her."

I snap out of it. "Okay, sorry. You don't have to use that."

"Wasn't planning to."

"I love all of the Fla-Vor-Ice. I feel like I'm going to become mister Fla-Vor-Ice because I've eaten so many."

Daniel spits on his hand and rubs it all over his face, then spits down his chest and rubs it in.

"Ew! We have to edit that out."

"What? I'm trying to cool down."

I deflect. "I just love to walk around and swim."

Erin changes the topic. "What do you think could be so special about this summer?"

"This summer has a feeling to it. This is something more. This is special."

Aurora smiles. "Summertime. The concept is like a dream. Sometimes it's better to lose yourself in the expectations of this season, but this year...this year—"

"Daniel, remember how much I hated camp when we got here and now I'm like obsessed and don't want to leave?"

"Talk about how fun it was the night that we all played lantern on the dirt hill."

"That was soooooo fun."

I look at the redhead. "You should be taping Aurora. She'll say something beautiful."

The camera moves back to Aurora. "Okay, Aurora. Say something beautiful for the camera."

"We all sound the same underwater. And when the lights are off, we all look the same."

"Wow, that was so authentic and deep. Thank you so much! I think we've got enough. Thanks, guys! You can watch it on Friday. It's going to be part of this week's WCTV update on the TV in the mess hall."

Daniel cuts in. "Can you make me a copy of it?"

"No!"

"I want to see the footage again, though."

"Too bad. So sad." Erin puts her Handycam back in her sling bag and leaves.

Aurora puts her hands over her eyes. "Oh no, you guys, I don't want to see myself on TV!"

"I should take a pic of my hard dick and put the sticker onto the male counselor's cabin door. Wouldn't that be so fucking funny?" Daniel grabs his i-Zone and snaps pics of Aurora and me pushing our eyelids down, laying our heads on each other's shoulders and putting up peace signs. He gives three to me and three to her.

"We look half asleep and half awake. Can we lay here all day and do nothing forever, please?"

Aurora walks her fingers up my arms. "Don't lose the Polaroids or you'll never remember this."

☆ 04 ☆

A hanging lantern glows on the porch of the female counselor's cabin. In the blue dark, a greasy brunette in a Rainforest Cafe shirt and khaki shorts plays guitar and sings the chorus of Marcy Playground's "Sex and Candy."

There's a knock at the window. I look in at Aurora making funny faces. I tell the girl, "Wow, you're doing a great job with the song. I love it. *Unplugged* vibes."

She stops playing. "Are you making fun of me?"

"No."

"Why don't you just admit that you're being mean? You think I'm gross and dirty, a crack whore like Courtney Love! Be honest!"

"Huh?"

"Guys who look like you don't pay attention to girls like me unless they're making fun of me. You don't think I'm aware of that after all these years? Leave me alone."

"I don't understand. I really like your version of this song. I said it sounds like *Unplugged*. That's a compliment."

"I'm sorry. I'm not being a drama queen, it's just, at my school, the guys call me and my friends 'the dirty girls' because we're grungy and not as polished as the chicks in their Prada backpacks and MAC makeup. The guys who bully me look like you, even dress like you. I never thought that someone like you would ever notice me."

"It sucks that people do that to you."

"Yeah, well, thank you for speaking up and complimenting me, for being nice to me."

"Yeah, sure. No problem. So, you like Rainforest Cafe?"

"I love the thunder and lighting effects. It's like not having to deal with real life. It's different from every other part of the mall."

"The Amazon Natural Burger is pretty sick."

Aurora comes out in a baby pink tank top and daisy dukes.

"You look…stunning."

She turns to me. "So… guess what?"

"What?"

"I have a surprise for you."

I put my hands up. "No, no, no. Stop. I'm not good with surprises. Just tell me!"

She takes a white and red beaded bracelet out of her back pocket and dangles it in front of my face. "Daniel and I made this for you this morning. And we blessed it with good intentions. We soaked it in the lake and I visualized white light being infused into it so it can bring you good luck and protection. You can always remember us, even when we leave."

"I—"

"You'll always be reminded of the safety of this summer." She takes my hand and pulls it toward her, then slips the bracelet onto my wrist.

"I love it. Wow!"

"It's got your name on it. The letter beads are special just for you."

"I mean…"

"I think the red represents your passion, but Daniel says that the white represents your 'boringness.' I'm not saying that to be mean, I don't know. I guess you'll have to figure out what the white means by yourself."

"It's so sick. Like it's really dope. This bracelet rips hard. Seriously, thank you."

She leans in to kiss me. I look up at the lantern and hear the sound of the greasy brunette singing the chorus of "Sex and Candy" again. *For once in my life, everything is making sense.*

☆ 05 ☆

I grab Aurora's hand and lead her to a small clearing in the woods, the light of the full moon rippling on the water. I push her against a tree and French kiss her, sucking on her tongue. She takes out a grape Push Pop, bites off the top, and puts it into her mouth before pushing it into mine. We both bite down on the shards. I put my hands into her jean shorts, then up her tank top, and grab her tits.

"Fuck yeah!"

"Can you lick my eyelid?"

"Sure."

She closes her eyes and I lick her eyelid. I move my head down, eyes pressed against her neck, then put my fingers down her underwear while I grab her tits. I push my fingers into her pussy, then take them out and suck on them. The feeling reminds me of sticking my fingers in a McDonald's apple pie. *My first taste of girl.* I lift her shirt.

"No, wait."

I move back. "What? You said you wanted to do this."

"I'm sorry. I'm sorry. I'm so sorry!"

"What are you talking about? Can we please just do this? Let's do this right now. This is going to be fun, you're going to feel so good. Don't you want me to make you feel good? Didn't that just feel so fucking good?"

"You were great, and that was great. It's just—"

"We are going to make each other feel good. Everyone wins."

"I just want it to feel perfect."

"I'm sorry, but I don't know what you want from me right now. Candles and Savage Garden in the background?"

"Whoa." She pushes me. "You don't need to be a meanie."

"Come on. The full moon isn't romantic enough for you? It's right there! Look. I'm not Brandon Walsh. I don't know how to be like the guys in the shows that you watch. I'm not Dawson or mister *She's All That*. I'm just a guy."

"Wow, you aren't helping yourself at all right now."

"I don't get what changed."

"What changed is that there's a difference between thinking about sex in your head and when it's actually happening. I'm just a little overwhelmed. Am I not allowed to feel overwhelmed?"

"You shouldn't be overwhelmed. You should feel excited."

"That's so easy for you to say as a guy, but, for me, I'm letting someone into my body, inside of me, for the first time ever."

"I'm not just someone. I'm someone who likes you, someone who likes you so much. Here, maybe a little candy kink could make this more fun." I take a Ring Pop from my pocket, unwrap it, put it on my finger, and hold it up to her nose. "Cherry."

"Yeah, cherry."

I put the Ring Pop near her mouth. She licks on it, then sucks it.

"See? Sex is going to be fun. Now I want you to do what you're doing right there, exactly like that, only somewhere else." I unbuckle my shorts, waiting for her to pull them down. She drops down to her knees and I look up to the sky making prayer hands. She stands up.

"Why did you stop? What's going on?"

"I just don't know if I want to do that."

"You don't want to blow me?"

"Brad!"

"Well, that's what it is, and girls like doing it. It feels good and warm apparently in their mouths. I'm not just saying that. Don't they teach girls that stuff in *Cosmo*? This is what I've heard!"

"I've never even taken my clothes off in front of a boy before." Aurora gets on the ground and leans against a tree with her arms folded before picking at the bark.

I lend her a hand. "Sorry if I sound like an asshole, or immature or whatever. I just really want to do this. There isn't any other girl as beautiful or as special as you, who sees the world in the way that you do, and I couldn't imagine having our first times with anyone else. I feel all fizzy in my heart for you. It's so lame to say that, but it's how I feel."

She kisses me on the cheek. "Do you like me?"

"I like you. I like you so much. I have such a huge crush on you, it's crazy."

"Well, I like you, and I have such a huge crush on you too."

"No one even knows that we're here. This is the other side of the lake, it's super quiet right now. No one is going to catch us. Just trust. Trust."

"Do you have a condom?"

"No."

"What?"

"Should I go back and look for a Ziploc bag or Saran wrap? I've never had sex with anyone. I'm completely clean from any STDs and so are you. We're not gays, we're not going to get AIDS. I promise I'll pull out."

Aurora gets up from the dirt. "Fine. Okay, okay. I'll do it. I'm ready."

I bite my lip and do a boo-ya dance. *Boom! Got her! Daniel's going to flip when I tell him.* "I promise that you're going to love it. You won't regret this."

She lays down on the dirt and her hair disappears in the dark. I pull down her jeans and lift up her tank top. She leans up. "I'll do it, don't worry." She unclasps her bra and throws it onto the dirt. She leans back down. I take off my shorts and shirt. I'm so hard.

"There's dirt in my hair."

33

"It's fine."

"Why are you laughing?"

"I don't know!"

"Your hair is in my mouth."

"Sorry."

"Fuck."

She pushes down her lips. "Are my lips purple because of the Push Pop?"

"I can't really tell, but I think so."

"Can you lick my thighs?"

I lean over her, rubbing my hands on her tits, sucking on her neck, licking across her nipples.

"Go slower."

"Yes! I told you you'd like it."

"Shut up, keep going."

She grabs my hands on her tits and puts them into her mouth, sucking on my fingers. I try to put my dick in, but it lands on her belly. I put my dick in her pussy. "Can you feel me inside of you yet?"

"Yeah, it's in."

I thrust, thinking that this is the warmest place I've ever been. I want to be locked up in her forever because it's so fucked how good and warm my dick feels. How is this even possible? Holy fuck. "Fuuuuuuuck yeah! Fuuuuck yeah!" I grab her tits and thrust, thinking about how my dick could be drenched in virgin blood after this, or if the branches are going to hit me, or if garter snakes are going to crawl into her. I want to flip her over, fuck her doggystyle. I close my eyes and pretend the tits that I'm grabbing are Carmen Electra's. Splice. I think about a Britney Spears lookalike sucking my dick in a park bathroom, then I flash to a girl biting on tulip petals and flowers being grated in anime on a screen, flowers being washed in sinks. I open my eyes and look down. Aurora moans, "Oh yeah, yes. Yes. Yes. Oh, yeah. Keep doing that." I cut to the phat ass in blue jeans that I saw on this chick at Ross last month. I think about her bending over in front of me and teasing me with her curves. I keep thrusting, holding onto her thighs. I put my hand over Aurora's mouth

34

and think of pulling myself out to eat her pussy in the dirt. I'm ready to blow. As the nut is about to release, I see in my mind a group of guys on a sports field holding me up in the air. "Champion! Champion! Champion!" I keep thrusting, rubbing her tits as I'm fucking her. Boom, just like that, I pull out and cum on the dirt. "Fuuuucccckkkk yeaaahhhh!" I hold onto her tits for balance. I look at Aurora, breathing heavily, then back to our clothes, then out at the full moon on the water, then down to my dick. There is no blood.

☆ 06 ☆

Aurora rides on my back as we come back from the plywood signee wall where I carved "B. Sela + A. Luna Summer '99." We sit on a log, holding hands and rocking them in the air. Aurora, in a white dress, takes her Lip Smacker out. "It's a shiny roll-on one. I love them right now. They're my fave! But I ordered the Bonne Bell Lip Lix and I didn't like it."

I shake my head.

"You have no idea what I'm talking about."

"I don't, but you sound pretty when you talk about it, so I'm just going to nod and keep listening."

She laughs. "Oh, good. That's what you're supposed to do. That just means you're a normal guy."

I nod. "Thank God for being a normal guy."

"Okay! So guess what? I did something crazy. I put on Cinnamon Sugar, Vanilla Frosting, *and* Bubble Gum." She kisses me. "Does it taste yummy?"

"It tastes so yummy, but I like the Dr Pepper flavor the best."

"Wow, but don't they make my lips look shiny?"

I look out across the shore: the pines, the sunlight on the water, the swing on the tree. "This is the last time that we're ever going to be here. That's hitting me, and it's not fair. I don't want to feel this right now. I don't."

"How can I make this all go slow?"

"Isn't it so weird, how we only go to some places once in our life?"

She grabs my arm and we rock back and forth. "This happened outside of time."

I shake my head. "You only ever get to feel the things you feel once. Then they disappear. It's not fair."

"We can come back here whenever we want. We just have to close our eyes. Who knows? What if, right now, we're reliving a dream that we'd forgotten?"

"Every day is a different scene in the same movie, and I'm so over it. I don't want to go back to that. Why can't you live on my street? Or in my neighborhood?"

"Summer camp can't last forever, but even when we go home, we don't have to leave this place."

I touch her arm. "I know. I listen to blink-182 a lot and they sing these over-emotional songs about girls. I always felt like I didn't know what they were talking about but now I do. I've finally felt the emotions that I always listen to in songs. I'm really experiencing this. It's not an abstract thing. I'm sorry if this sounds super retarded."

She holds my hand. "I'm so grateful for the time the universe gave to us, for me to meet someone like you, to have had this much fun with you. I had the best time being inside this dream. Do you want to know what I love? About earth? About this place?"

"Yeah. What is it?"

"We may change, but the sky and the moon will always stay the same. Whenever we feel alone, we can look up at the same moon, the same sky, and feel that oneness, that connection, that magic. It's always there for us."

"Yeah."

"Why are you afraid of going back home?"

"If I were to answer that, and be totally honest with you, something that I really want more than anything in this world is to evolve, to grow, to experience myself, to become who I am, but I don't know how to kickstart that process. I just don't know how to make it happen. I don't want to go home and have to face all my bullshit worries about getting into Berkeley."

"You'll figure it out. You will, I know it. You just need to stop thinking. Why think about something when you can feel instead?"

"It makes me so sad that sometimes you're going to be hurting. I wish I could stop you from feeling anything bad ever, but even if I can't control what you feel, I don't want to *believe* that summer flings aren't real. I just want to see you longer, to be closer to you. I don't want to go home. This fucking sucks, dude. This is shit. I just want to be someplace that I don't feel like I have to run away from. I thought I finally found it."

Aurora takes a milky gel pen and pink stationery out of her bag. "Do you promise to write me letters?" She holds the pen cap in her mouth and writes her address on the paper, slips it into my bag, then grabs my hand and draws hearts on my wrist.

"I promise."

She kisses my cheek. "You'll dream about me. I'll make sure of it. We've both been here before. The dream went too fast. It's like we have no memory that it even happened."

"Aurora."

"Yeah?"

I take a long breath and shiver. "Maybe there will be a time when we're all grown up that these fast moments will start to make sense."

"No, I don't think that will ever happen. Life is a series of images and clips that flash and burst into nothing."

Daniel runs up and motions for us to go to the parking lot. "Dude, what the fuck? We have to go. They're loading the bus and everyone is waiting for you." Daniel hugs Aurora goodbye.

As I walk out through the lake entrance, it all comes back to me in a flash: Daniel and I sitting on the lower bunk flipping through our CD wallets, girls in bandanas and tie-dye shirts with their hands around each other skipping and singing, everyone cheering for the older male counselors playing soccer, rock climbing on the rainbow pebbles, the rush of zip lining through the trees, hands dangling in the water while canoeing, i-Zone sticker Polaroids of swimming in the lake, the dirty girl

37

and her guitar singing "Sex and Candy," the smell of cK One, the footage of us on the grass airing on the mess hall TVs, the flash bursting after the camp photo, Sunny D pouring into paper cups, the trails we got lost on, shadowboxing matches in the wooden ring, the three of us singing "My Sharona" into one mic on karaoke night, fist pumping to Third Eye Blind, slow dancing with Aurora to Sixpence, the Doritos and milk chugging contest, marshmallows melting into the fire, spinning down the hills in tires, the taste of her pussy on my fingers, my dick inside of her, nutting on the dirt. I climb onto the bus and look over at Aurora standing in front of hers.

Is this the summer I got the closest to the 13th hour?

☆ 07 ☆

"Mom, can you just *not* right now?"

I pop a Flintstone vitamin and tap my fingers on the counter as I stare at the toaster. I grab a bottle of Nesquik, squeeze it into my milk, and spin my spoon as a *Brokedown Palace* trailer plays on TV: "It was the perfect summer…with the perfect stranger…until it became the perfect setup." Sitting on the kitchen island chair, I side-eye the radio across from me, "Bills, Bills, Bills" by Destiny's Child floating out at middle volume, my mom in her overalls singing along to the chorus, sending me back to the TV where Chris Rock, Janeane Garofalo, and Method Man star in a *Blair Witch* parody promoting this week's VMAs.

"Can I not *what?*"

The toaster dings. I grab my Pop-Tart and put it onto a plate.

"I don't know, you singing along to this song while I'm trying to eat my breakfast? It's uncomfortable for me."

"Oh, it's fine. I'm sorry."

"I don't mean to be mean, it's just, like… Do you even know who sings this?"

"TLC?"

"No."

"Janet Jackson?"

"No, Mom. It's Destiny's Child."

I go to the radio and turn the dial. "Big scoop just in from Hollywood... Movie mogul and Miramax chairman Harvey Weinstein is said to have angered his neighbors in Martha's Vineyard by—get this—planting trees and shrubs to block them from driving across his property. I know! Crazy!" I turn the radio off and sit on the couch, grab the remote, and watch a Live video on *Dawn Patrol*. *It's too bad Miramax is not producing my life and I'm not about to start shooting the back-to-school opening scene where I walk through the halls with The Offspring blasting in the background.*

Mom hands me a clear Jansport. Disappointed, I hold it up.

"Mom, you don't think it's kind of ridiculous that I have to wear a plastic backpack to school and look like some PLUR'd-out raver try-hard just because of Columbine? Eric and Kev told me their moms got them mesh Jansports."

My mom rubs my cheeks. "Everyone wants a safe school. I told you that they were all sold out of the mesh ones. Don't you think Kevin looks kind of dorky wearing those short sleeve shirts on top of long sleeves?"

"He looks dope! Wait. Do you remember that woman in line with us at Walgreens who said that the Columbine killers learned about natural selection from *Blade* and we got into that huge argument on the ride home because you agreed with her?"

"You do know that some people your age walk out of movies like *Scream 2* and think of making their own real-life sequels, and it's all the—"

"You really think that the people my age who saw *Blade* wanted to leave the theater and join a secret society vampire cult? I mean, it's ridiculous how you think that entertainment creates violence and influences the youth of America."

"I'm never going to stop believing that *Scream* is dangerous."

"Mom! They used the real-life sequel tagline to market the movie so they could spook teenyboppers into buying tickets! Also, you know that leaving Tony Robbins tapes on my bed with a 'Love Yourself' sticky note does not motivate me. It does the total opposite, like want-to-dive-into-a-pool-of-alligators opposite."

"If you could just take one second off from your eye-rolling, skeptical mindset towards the world and just watch an episode of *Thinking Allowed* with me to learn about the secrets of manifesting your own destiny—"

"You have not been forgiven for forcing me to listen to Doctor Laura in the car after school in ninth grade! I mean, not everyone is fortunate enough to experience a spiritual transformation sponsored by Nag Champa and Oprah! When are you going to accept that the new age industry is full of guru thought leaders who need more help than we do?"

"It works!"

"Maybe the whole b.s. self-help industry should accept that the cruel things we say to ourselves when we're alone might just be things called facts, and not 'negativity' or whatever nonsense those woo-woo peddlers are selling these days."

"Oh, Brad, come on. You don't really think that about yourself, do you?"

"You don't need to guilt me about my skepticism making me an awful person. I've figured that out all on my own."

"You are—"

"A *guy*? I'm just a guy, not a new age woman who discovered yoga and thinks that she's enlightened now. I'm just a dude and that's all I'll ever be." I shove my books into my new backpack.

"I found stuff in your room," she says as she puts dishes in the sink.

"What? What stuff?"

"Cups. You have lots of cups and cans. You never bring them back downstairs when you are finished with them. We are going to be late!"

"I could walk. I told you all week that I'm fine walking to school."

"You won't make it in time."

"Okay, Mom. I'm not meaning to be rude, and this has nothing to do with you, but can you drop me off near the gas station? I don't want people to see me being dropped off in front of school. It's just not sick to do that."

"I'm so nervous. I'm sorry, Brad, I am."

"What are you nervous about? You seriously think a crazy gunman who saw *Heathers* one too many times is going to shoot up my school?"

"You have to think about what this feels like for me. The country feels different now. Metal detectors at the entrance? And the newsletters that your teachers gave out to parents before the summer?"

"Nobody is going to shoot me. It's going to be fine. This is not a Dimension Films movie. A school massacre could never happen in a place like this."

Mom holds me tight. "I want you to listen to me. This is your senior year; no matter how much something appears to be exhilarating, pleasurable, and intimate, it's a deception. Do not separate yourself from who you are."

I shake out of her embrace. "Mom, we gotta go."

That Everything but the Girl video is ending. I chug the Nesquik as my mom checks the time.

"We are going to be late."

☆ 08 ☆

As I look out Kev's computer room window to the empty driveway, the recurring daydream of the week comes back for another swirl: Discman clipped to my belt, I skate down an empty California boardwalk. Hole's "Malibu" plays as I take off my blades, rest my feet in the hot sand, and take in the rolling ocean waves.

Eric slaps my back. "Back to earth, space case."

Kev pushes Eric. "What is going on with the Evil Angel catalog situation? A dude on my team told me the big asses on those tapes are unreal. All oiled up and shit."

"Dude, I fucking told you. I'm working on it. I'll get you *Buttman In Budapest*, don't you worry."

I'm leaning on the wall, sipping from my Burger King cup as Eric and Kev huddle around the computer screen and tap their fingers on the table, waiting for the pics on BigJugsXXX.com to load.

Kev hits the tower and yells, "Why won't this fucking gay ass computer hurry the fuck up? I want to see some big fuckin titties!"

The pictures load one line at a time, revealing side-by-side images of platinum blondes with nice nips and dick-sucking faces grabbing their tits.

I look at the door, sweating through my shirt. "Are you sure no one is going to come home?"

Kev chuckles. "Dude, the house is empty. Everyone left like thirty minutes ago. I planned it perfectly. Chill."

Eric's eyes dim. "These jugs are nothing that you haven't seen in *Score*."

"I'm a man. I need something new to keep me stimulated. Don't be a fag," Kev snaps.

I ask, "Who told you about this site again? Your older bro?"

"No, there was some porn slut on *Loveline* last night and Carolla was all like, 'You gotta see this Caroline's boobs, boys.'"

The page loads as Eric points out Caroline. "See? I told you she would be as hot as her talking voice. This was worth the wait. It was all that I could think about at school. Now, go home so I can abuse myself."

"You serious?" I giggle.

"No." He laughs.

Eric grins as he taps a box of CD-Rs. "Dude, I'm definitely ordering her porno CD. There's over fifty pics of her on them!"

I shake my head at Kev. "I can't believe that you don't give a shit about keeping porn on your family computer. You're seriously a man-imal."

He shrugs. "I don't give a shit if my parents find my folders. I think they'd just be happy that their son isn't a fudge packer. All I'd say to them is 'Would you rather me have folders of dong pics?' I like to look at beautiful naked women, fuckin sue me."

Eric hits Kev on the shoulder. "The man has a point."

I move toward the door. "Alright, can we leave already? I want to go to the park."

☆ 09 ☆

The sign hanging over me in Blockbuster says "$1.99/5 Day Rentals. Go Home Happy." *Heathers* plays on a mini TV. I'm standing in the comedy aisle, checking the new releases rack. An employee in a bucket hat rides by on a rolling cart. He tugs his puka shells and smiles at me.

I go outside to an AT&T payphone and dial 1-800-COLLECT. I listen to the operator and punch in my house number. The automated voice: *"Please state your name."* I respond, "DadPickMeUpAtBlockbuster."

☆ 10 ☆

I walk between the bushes, down the paved path to the smoke pit, headphones on, Duncan Sheik's "Barely Breathing" spinning. A punk with spiked hair in a brown leather jacket is talking to a white trash girl with chopsticks in her hair and an anime gun-girl shirt. I grab at the berries in the bushes, stare into the swamp water in front of the path, and think of Aurora rubbing her fingertips on her collarbones.

The girl says, "I do that, I do. I create conspiracies of what people are thinking about me all day. Maybe it's like a total hallucination or a perceived feeling, but it doesn't even fucking matter at this point because I feel it, and I don't want anyone to be thinking about me."

"You gotta cut this out," he says, grabbing her arm. "You've been really freaking me out lately. It must be your Venus in Aquarius."

"No, I can't. Ever since we did those Scooby snacks at Jess's pool party last week, I've been fucked. Do you want to skip and go to the movies? I'm already getting annoyed thinking about freshmen who stop while I'm walking in the hallways. I just want to gut those mindless retards."

"I told you already that we would be skipping the first week. That's such an us thing to do."

"Mescaline and acid together. How could we be so dumb?"

"You have to admit, it was fun watching—"

I tap the punk guy's shoulder. "Yo. Can I grab a light?"

"Get your own fucking BIC."

"Dude, chill. I forgot it."

She glares at me and slices her finger across her neck. "Why are you still talking to him? Leave us alone."

"Whatever, whatever."

Eric is running up from behind, shouting my name.

☆ 11 ☆

A goth boy with devil horns on his head in a Slipknot shirt stands at the cashier as I look through the Dunkin' Donuts window. I turn around. We're shotgunning soda cans under the front lights looking across the strip mall parking lot. An "OPEN" sign on the liquor store glows in red and blue above Kev's car. Eric is sitting on the ground in a B.U.M. sweater as Kevin stands in a Starter varsity jacket.

I fold my arms. "I'm supposed to be volunteering for a teen crisis hotline right now. You know, actually giving back to society instead of rotting in a fucking Dunkin' parking lot? I actually have purpose and direction. I have a future."

Kev laughs. "Oh, come on, man, you ditched out on playing the new *Worms Armageddon* with the boys to read to retarded kids last week. You gotta take the pressure off of yourself. You're going to get into Berkeley. Can you stop the bitchy PMS Meredith Brooks vibe and have some fun? You owe us. Just chill out."

Eric pats Kev's shoulder, then sighs. "When have you never gotten what you wanted? You'll get into college. If your dad can't pull the strings, I got an uncle in California who probably knows someone. Chill. This is senior fucking year. We get to be kings." Eric gets on all fours and pretends to get fucked doggystyle by Kev against the wall. "Please, Kevin! Don't do it! I'm so, so, so, scared."

"Let me tell you something, you little slut! You are going to take this dick!" Kev roars.

Eric is rubbing his ass on Kev's dick, laughing, mock-orgasm eye rolls. "Oh, yeah! Fuck yeah! Kevin! Fuck me! Kevin! Yeah."

Kev turns to me. "Brad… Can I get an *oh yeah*? Brad?"

Eric laughs. "Fuck it, Kev. I'll do it again. Oh, yeah! Oh, yeah! Oh, yeah!"

The goth in the devil horns is walking out with his order. I scan the black eyeliner drops underneath his eyes. Kev screams, "You fucking queer." The goth kid shakes his head.

Eric steps in front of him, tugs on his shirt, and says, "You fucking creep. You fucking listen to Slipknot? You're proud of that? What kind of man are you? Look at you! You're a fucking horror show." Eric shines his laser pointer on the kid's face.

Kev corners the other side of his body. "Are you going to fucking shoot up the Dunkin' Donuts? Where's your purse?" The boy tries to speak but can't. The boys let him go and, when he's freed, he looks at me with disappointed eyes, a kind of hurt gaze like our moms know each other, like he knows who I am and he expects something of me. Kev punches my arm. "You were a buzzkill. That was the perfect one to fuck with. You could've given that kid a bloody sucker."

Eric agrees. "Assert your fucking dominance. How could you be such a pussy? What a perfect target."

I take my BIC out and light it under my palm "I don't care."

Kev and Eric's conversation about last summer, sex, and girls is null and void as I put a Dunkin' Donuts box on the hood of a car. I take it off, throw it on the ground, and jump on it. A fantasy of mine is coming out of this. There I am, sitting on the carpet of a strange basement watching footage of myself on a TV in this same parking lot but it's now a Sony Discman commercial. Everything is flashing fast as a fucked-up techno beat blares. Next thing I know, I'm sitting crouched in a grocery store cart being pushed around by a faceless man in a silver Sony hoodie as he holds a silver Discman with silver headphones. The commercial ends on me with manga bug eyes and text below that reads: "LET YOUR MIND PLAY."

☆ 12 ☆

A student hall pass around my neck and the sound of guys pissing in the urinals, I'm in a stall pulling out my hard dick after seeing Candice's tits in a tight blue shirt. I pull up a curvy blonde in a *Slap* logo bikini in my mind. She's doing the "come fuck me" dance poolside at a Beverly Hills Mansion. I'm suave, lying on my beach chair, watching, pretending I'm working on my PalmPilot. Now the chick is licking a lollipop. Opening her legs, she pushes my head between her thick thighs. I undo her bikini. Now I'm shirtless in an Adidas visor, Calvin Briefs, long socks, and Nike Airs. I can feel her warm hands on my dick. She jerks me off as I pull on a silver elephant tooth necklace. I reach out and grab her big natural tits. My knees shake. It's coming. I look at my load shot on the door.

☆ 13 ☆

I put the Handycam on top of the TV, flip the screen to mirror mode, hit the record button, sit on my bed, and stare into the lens.

"VMA Recap: now this is the kind of shit you can't see on MTV, a real everyday guy's opinion. First off, let's just say that the pre-show was absolutely incredible. Blink's performances were perfect. I'm stoked that they played 'What's My Age Again?' I will fucking die if they ever come here. Seriously, I will blow a hobo for tickets if I have to.

"Now, let's get a look at my blink wall…fucking legendary." I lift the Handycam and scan the wall of blink-182 cut-outs.

"Alright, so let's get into the facts, boys. Chris Rock is not funny. I don't like the guy. I don't know if it's 'cause Black people just try so hard to be funny that it ends up being annoying, but he annoyed me. Tom Green also annoyed the hell out of me. What a punchable face. How is that man even a real person? How did we, the American public, allow Tom Green to happen? His stupid show has been on since I was like twelve and it needs to get the chop. Ax him off MTV! Boycott Tom Green! I fucking barfed in my mouth every time the camera was on him.

"*NSYNC and Backstreet Boys suck dick. They blow chunks! Those faggot boybands should all move to a fucking island and never come back! They're just puppets! These faggots make music for ballpits!

"I gotta say, Aaliyah deserved Best R&B Video. And, holy fuck, what was with those trannies during the Madonna tribute? Grandma is too fucking weird for this world, man. I don't want to see trannies! We had enough of her ethnic, Indian bullshit last year. I seriously feel sick anytime I see that clown RuPaul on VH1 or *Spring Break*. Trannies should find their own planet. That stuff should not be on TV because it's not normal. It's just weird. We don't need to see that shit. I'm not even a church guy, I'm just a dude who knows that shit is gross.

"But I gotta say, the highlight of the night—and I just got off the phone with my buds talking about this 'cause they called me to make sure I was watching, looking out like real friends, but wow—the Britney Spears performance was crazy. Wow! It was on mute, of course, but I wish the camera zoomed in more on her titties so we could get a closer look at those jugs. I can't believe how hot she is. I can't believe we're the same age. You never see tens like that at the mall or school. You only see bitches that sexy on MTV.

"Anyway, that's my wrap-up. Remember: this world gave man the VCR so we can tape slutty pop stars for the spank bank. You heard it here first. Now you know why MTV calls it Spankin' New Music."

I get up, stop the recording, grab my Discman off the floor, put on my headphones, fall onto my bed, and stare at my wall as the Blur album begins.

☆ 14 ☆

On a wooden bench in the locker room, rubbing sweat off my face with my gym shirt, I look down at Brody pulling up his socks, and then up at his biceps. I flash back to the black and white Abercrombie ad I saw this morning of boys wrestling in a high school gym.

John hugs Brandon from behind, grabs his nipples, and spanks his butt. *I bet he's enjoying the feel of Brandon's Calvin boxer briefs.*

"I know why all the girls keep grabbing it in the halls now, fag." Brandon sticks his tongue out, presses his hands against a locker, arches his back, and shakes his ass as John pretends to throw dollar bills at him. The other boys whip rolled-up shirts at each other's asses. I take my shorts off and look over at the showers, watching a couple of guys rotate in and out. I unlock my locker, grab my clothes, and put them on fast. Cam from my math class lifts his gym bag, smiles at me, and walks out, the scent of A&F's Woods. I go over to the sink and splash water on my face. In the mirror, I see Tyson, shirtless, stand on the bench and flex.

"I'm a fucking lion up here."

"Bro, you're like the MGM lion."

"Do a roar."

"Roaaaaarrr!" His fists beat his chest. "Boys! Can you believe it? Senior year. This is going to be the best year of our lives—house parties, senior camping, pranks, booze, bitches. This is going to be so fucking dope, n****."

"N****, this is going to be fuckin on some shit, bro…on…some…shit."

"Bro, I know…and you fags know I got the VIP pass to Candice's bod all summer long. I'm talking all…summer…long."

"You are like a god."

"Like? I *am* a god."

"You are a total god…"

"Candice is sexy as hell and a good fuck, but she doesn't know that I'm fucking some of her friends on the squad right now too."

"That's what a pimp does. That's why you're the best."

"I know, I know."

"You know who is looking fucking hot right now? The blonde junior… I don't know her name, but her jugs got bigger over the summer, and I'm gonna jizz all over them."

"I wish I could connect my PlayStation remote into one of those freshman bitch's pussy, and just make her do whatever I want."

"Hit Triangle for blowies, Square for all-fours…"

"X for mute…"

"Someone get this man a Rated R sticker for his forehead. Class of 2000, boys! Let's get explicit."

"You gotta start passing Cassie around, bro."

"Dude, I need the mute button for Cassie. She talks too much. She's so fucking annoying. I don't want to hear about her weird ass incense shit or the gay ass book she's reading all of a sudden to seem deep."

"I hear Cassie gives great burn."

"She does, but who told you that?"

"She's blown the whole lacrosse team, bro. That's facts. But if she didn't, she'd be an idiot."

"Dude, what the fuck? When is my turn? I'd pay good money to have her suck my dick, n****."

"How much?"

"Fifty cents."

"That's my man, my n****!"

"What about that big-titted Spanish bitch from the Glencoe party last weekend? Now, she was nice. She was a good time."

"Oh dude, remember when I told that girl I wouldn't let her suck my dick until she undid the ugly ass bun in her hair?"

"Dude, the Glencoe ginger who sucked my dick at your BBQ last week did the craziest thing after I jizzed in her mouth. There was still leftover jizz and, wait for it… She slurped it up, like, off the tip. It was so dope. I felt like a fucking king. That's wifey material."

"Legendary. Glencoe girls are so hot. When they come over for volleyball games I just want to pound 'em all."

"You know how I got Candice to get so good at fucking? I stole one of my dad's pornos and made her watch it with me. I was like, 'This is what you need to do. This is where you learn how to fuuuuck.'"

"That's the new millennium man right there. That's so fucking sick. Stern was just saying that the other night, that girls need to watch porn and take notes."

"Girls love it too. They finger themselves, like in *American Pie* when that European bitch is going through his porn. They love that shit."

"Dude, my buddy was saying that he was fucking this girl and she said that it felt like she could feel his dick in her stomach, that's how fucking inside of her he was."

"I just want to find some bad freshman bitches to be like, 'Turn around for me, baby—shake that ass like you do on *Spring Break*, you slut.'"

"Freshman *Girls Gone Wild*, North Douglas Edition."

"Rob the cradle, baybey! That's what my older bro always says!"

"We could make bank off that shit from all the horny loser guys in our school. And there's some dirty, slutty girls who'd be into that kinky shit."

"Tyson, you need to make a tape of you fucking Candice. Hide the camera next time you're banging and make copies for us so we can see that perfect ass in action."

"Yeah. Do it, you pussy. Tyson knows I always jerk it thinking of his girl's ass riding me... I just want my face buried in those cheeks. Fuck, her ass is as nice as Pamela's."

"You boys just want to see this monster cock in action!" Tyson takes off his towel and spins his dick around in circles.

The boys cheer. "Woof! Woof! Woof! Woof!"

I push through the gym door and exit to the halls.

☆ 15 ☆

On my desk, my mom has left a handwritten card from my neighbor, thanking me for mowing their lawn. I smile as I pick it up.

I grab my tape recorder and speak into it. "Sometimes when the house is empty, I'll cry alone in my room. For a second, the world starts to spin in that ice-green tint in all the music videos these days, like Third Eye Blind's 'Jumper.'"

☆ 16 ☆

A tape of blink-182 MTV interviews and commercials is playing. Shirtless in my Hanes briefs, I get ready to get up. The phone rings, but I let it go to voicemail.

"Dude, what the fuck?" says Eric. "Where are you? Pick up. I know you're there beating your dick. I told you to come to the pool today. Kevin and I met these slutty, fresh juniors from Glencoe. One has massive—"

I pick up. "Yo!"

"Yo, fag. What are you doing? You have to see the jugs on this Glencoe chick. I made sure we took a group Polaroid so I could get a pic of her in her bathing suit to show you."

"Sick. I'm just bored."

"Why are you being weird?"

"I'm not being weird."

"Well, you could've met some hot junior pussy today, and you know the rule… if you're a senior and you go to a different school than a junior girl, you can fuck her, no problem. Dude, these rules apply to us for the first time. We can fucking do this."

"Let's see if you fuck her."

"I will, dude. I'll make you watch."

"Alrighty then."

"Do you want to come to my basement? I told the girls that we could play a sesh of *Super Smash* tonight. I got the crib to myself. Just come over and meet these bitches. Let's get them drunk and yucky."

"I don't really feel like hanging tonight, dude. I'm like thinking about shit."

"Thinking about what? Get out of your feelings, pussy boy."

"I don't know, like, remember in seventh grade when you'd call all the time, and, you know, something that excited us was like a new Green Day music video, and we'd turn it on at the same time, and that was enough to make us happy?"

"I don't get it."

"I just feel like everyone is so different now and everyone's changing so quickly, and now everything is about fucking and getting high."

"Dude, that's what's sick about being our age right now. We get to fuck and get high as much as we want. We get to go out there and hunt for girls. Come on, man. What would this neighborhood be without your wolfpack? Your day-one boys? Stop being gay."

"I feel like you're implying that I don't want to live my life."

"Well, that's how it's coming off. You can't just bug out on MTV and Doritos all day."

"I'm not—"

"How many times have you jerked off tonight?"

"Once."

"Brad."

"Okay, three times."

"Brad!"

"I'm serious."

☆ 17 ☆

Santana's "Smooth" plays outside my window. I slide the blinds to the side and look down on the backyard deck. My mom's Tupperware group is gathered around the table, passing around a bottle of wine. I grab my TV remote, rub the buttons, and think about turning on MTV, but don't. I look down at my school planner and open to my homework assignments.

☆ 18 ☆

I'm taking the sidewalk route home from school when a BMW slows down and rides alongside me. Tyson, wearing puka shells and a white Nike hat, sticks his head out the passenger window as "Semi-Charmed Life" booms.

"Faggot!" he yells.

I look ahead and keep walking.

"Do you have any empty bottles that we can throw at him?" Tyson says to his friend.

"Nope, not today!"

He turns back to me. "You're lucky, super-homo shitbag! Do you need a ride to Dairy Queer to grab a cumsicle?"

He curls his tongue in a V. I walk on as the car speeds off.

☆ 19 ☆

In the Spencer's mini disco ball glow, I pass through the seventies' dangling bead door. Kristen's walls are plastered in magazine cut-outs of Shirley Manson, Janet Jackson, and Madonna. *Romy and Michele's High School Reunion*, *The Last Days of Disco* and *Buffalo '66* posters hang above the plastic flowers that decorate the head of her bed. An orange iMac with stickers sits on her desk. Kodak film rolls and faerie statues sit on the dresser next to framed pictures of herself and a half-full bottle of Dior's Hypnotic Poison. A View-Master lays on the carpet beside a *Kama Sutra* paperback and a pink phone and Walgreens photo envelope rest by a digital clock on her bedside table. Across from her bed is a VHS slot TV and Blockbuster rental cases. I process the pictures of her and her friends tacked on the wall — drinking coolers at the beach, in line at a concert, sitting in the grass sticking middle fingers up, out clubbing, her face buried in a friend's tits while she wears a plastic glitter cowboy hat, smiling in a classroom, a laughing boy with a pierced and bloody nose, the same boy with an ice pack on his face, pouting. A stacked CD tower stands near a purple CD player and a matching purple blow-up couch.

Kristen is sitting on the bed in a red dress, white choker, and ripped nylons. She leans over and taps her cigarette into a Dairy Queen ashtray.

"My boyfriend made me take down all of the pics of the guys on the wall. This is when I was attempting to look like Sibyl Buck, trying so hard to be this alien babe goddess. Don't worry — Leo was up there. I had a whole shrine to him in *The Basketball Diaries*. That was my ultimate type in high school, a guy who looks like he just left a heroin detox clinic. Ugh! So fucking hot! Oh my God, fuck, and Ewan McGregor in *Trainspotting*. So hot. I don't get why my boyfriend thinks I'm weird because I only want to fuck using the Garbage *Version 2.0* condoms. I mean, I only ever wear orange Garbage nail polish. Is that, like, obsessive? Do you think that's weird?"

I sit on the bed and read the sticker on her mirror, watching the disco light glow on her face. "What's nerve.com?"

Kristen makes a mocking face. "Do you even know what salon.com is?"

"No."

She pinches my cheeks. "Of course you don't. You're not intellectual enough."

"I don't get it."

"You're not *supposed* to get it. It's a smart, older people, college kind of thing. We got nerve.com stickers at the end of our class from a speaker who was talking to us about dating and sex in the modern world."

I push her shoulder. "Wow… Looks like someone's post-adolescent idealistic phase is getting to their fucking head…"

"What? It's the truth. Do you even know who Baudrillard is? Douglas Rushkoff? Camille Paglia?"

"Triple hard no."

She gives me a stunned face. "Oh my God. Camille Paglia is a super cool feminist. She came to talk about feminism and I'm just really into world issues right now, like women's empowerment. I love *her* version of feminism because it's more modern, not the boring kind from the sixties. I saved the flier—she means so much to me. She had this whole talk on how *Sex and the City* and porn becoming more mainstream is empowering for women."

"Uh, cool. Sounds really boring."

"Wow."

"What?"

Kristen looks heated. "You've never even had any rights to fight for. You are straight, white, and a man. That's the top of the pyramid."

"I wouldn't say so. It's hard being straight, white, and a man. You have to impress everyone—literally everyone—actually, mostly other guys, and you have to get the hottest girl while doing it."

She rolls her eyes. "Those aren't real problems."

"For me, right now, in my life, it *is* a real problem. You shouldn't be such a bitch about it."

"Who are you calling a bitch?" she shouts.

"I'm not calling you a bitch. I just mean, like, I'm not going to stop my life and start thinking of every decision I make as a luxury because I think that there's a lot of shitty things about being a guy. It's just that nobody talks about it. There's no TV show about how hard it is to be a guy because nobody cares about male issues."

"Wah wah wah. It's all the same. You sound like my boyfriend when I want to watch these tapes of Camille Paglia on *Politically Incorrect*. He's always like, 'Turn off that stupid old feminazi.'"

"Guys understand other guys and a lot of guys think the same. I don't see what your point is."

"You've never had anything to fight for."

"I've never had anything to fight for because that's a waste of my time. I'm not going to, you know, stop listening to Eminem or stop looking at pictures of hot girls in bikinis or stop being who I am, all because a k.d. lang-loving carpet muncher lesbian is on TV trying to tell me that I'm doing something wrong, or that it's offensive. I'm not doing anything wrong. I'm having fun, and if me having fun, you know, a good fucking time, offends you, then…"

"Whatever." She rolls her eyes again, only this time she could probably see her brain. "Apathy. So so typical."

"I think one of the most beautiful words in this language is 'whatever.' It captures how I feel about everything. I don't have to care. I don't have to be involved. I don't have to participate. Caring is so embarrassing. It's for total losers."

She sighs. "The whole nature of having privilege is that you don't know you have it. The entire point is that you can turn off the news and the world and be like, 'That's too negative.' Not everyone can do that.

Some people need to know if they might be getting slaughtered in the streets tomorrow. There are killers out there that want to kill my Black and gay friends. Don't you remember the murder last summer outside of the gay bar? Where the drag queen's body was found?"

I respond, "You and I get different news. We are plugged into different parts of the fucking world. I watch something called MTV, and that's the only news that I need. I don't care what's happening on CNN or what smart college kids going through their annoying-ass deep existential phases are watching to feel part of the world. The only news that I care about is if blink-182 is coming on tour or if Lit is releasing a new album."

"I don't know why I even bother with men. You don't understand anything because the world has been designed for you. I just can't wait until the day my generation takes over and we have more diverse perspectives in mainstream media."

"I really really don't give two fucks."

"Two fucks, huh? You are so hopeless."

"Sorry, seven fucks. One hundred fucks. There's a billion fucks that I don't give about these issues. I like hot women, I like rock music, I like my life. And like I fuckin said, if feminists hate Eminem and make fun of him on MTV during those *educational* moments where they get someone smart to make a comment on what's going on in pop culture today or whatever, then fuck that shit. I'm living my life."

"Eminem is disgusting. There is no hope for young men in America today."

"Well, thanks. Real nice of you."

"I'm being harsh." Her eyes soften. "I'm sorry."

"I don't know what's gotten into me. I just want to nap all day, and it's not like I want to die but I—"

She touches my arm. "Everyone is like that at your age. I was like that too."

I slink backwards. "Okay, but look, everyone always saying that they felt how I felt at my age doesn't really help the fact that I'm living through this right now. It's not like I fucking care what everyone else has gone through."

"You're right. People in their thirties do that to me and it feels like condescending bullshit. Sorry. It's weird…when you're in high school you have all of these feelings, all this euphoria, and then you leave and it's all gone because none of that stuff matters anymore. But it's absolutely impossible to explain that to anyone who is going through it because it's real…right now, what's happening in your life is real."

"Do you ever wonder what your old friends from high school are doing?"

"Sometimes, but it's not like there's a way that I could see into their lives. It's harder to care when you've been so disengaged."

"You don't ever miss high school? Shocking."

She laughs. "Do ex-convicts ever miss jail? Have you been smoking crystal fucking meth?"

"Do Doritos and Surge count as crystal fucking meth? What does it even feel like to be in your twenties?"

"Looking back at being a teenager, I think about how I only knew how to be who I was back then. I didn't know how to be anyone else and I did all that I could. That's all I knew. Now that I'm in my twenties I'm doing all that I can to be who I am. I will fuck up and make mistakes, but I can't control everything that happens."

"Noboddddy lykes yew when yurrr twenneh-thwwee."

She lets out a sigh. "Shut up."

"I need your advice, some girl advice."

She pushes me. "Spill."

"What do you think would be something that isn't considered boring in a love letter?"

"Hold on. Do you own the *Romeo + Juliet* soundtrack?"

"No."

Kristen grabs her tote bag, takes out the *Romeo + Juliet* soundtrack, walks over to her CD player, puts the disc in, and hits play. Garbage's "#1 Crush" haunts the room. I think about Aurora rubbing her fingertips on her collarbones, putting our clothes back on in the woods, sitting on the log with her on the last day of summer camp.

"This song…"

"I know," she nods. "I immediately think of Leo in his Hawaiian shirt and cream."

"Some songs can say the things that we are feeling and thinking but could never express ourselves. Go back to what you were going to say about the love letters." Mirrored light moves along the walls.

She comes closer. "Girls want access to something intimate, secret, totally trippy, something about you that's unseen by everyone else. You have to think of the letters you write as gifts."

☆ 20 ☆

Jenny McCarthy sucking me off on her knees under my desk is a fantasy I've been having ever since I got to my seat. I eyeball the classroom: an American flag, a "HAVE THE DESIRE TO SUCCEED" banner above the whiteboard, the ceiling tiles. Clips play nonstop in my mind: the previews that MTV has been playing all week teasing blink-182's *Making the Video* episode, the Columbia House order that I forgot to drop in my mailbox, the 1-800 ad of a purple computer graphic alien creature that I saw last night before bed. Around me, rows of people sleep on their rolled-up sweaters. I stare at the blank screen of the hanging TV monitor, hoping to hypnotize myself, but nothing changes.

A knock startles me. The door opens, and a boy in a black "ANTI-SPICE SUPERSTAR" t-shirt, chipped nail polish, and wraparound shades walks through, Sony headphones wrapped around his neck, a Discman in his hand. I study his padlock choker, baggy goth pants, and the mesh Jansport slung over his shoulder as he hands the English teacher a slip.

"Class! We have a new student transferring from Glencoe High. Please welcome—" She's confused. "I'm sorry, your name is scratched out."

"Lusif."

"You have one name?"

"Sure do."

58

"Wow! Like Bono, like Madonna, like Sade, like—"

"Like Satan."

A spiky-haired redhead behind me yells, "Great! Let's pollute more people in this nightmare. That's just what this hole needs!"

"Jordan! Do not speak that way in my class."

"Whatever."

"Please welcome Lusif."

He takes the empty seat behind me and I feel something on my neck, moving down my back. He's dragging a pen on my skin and then under my shirt. I turn around.

"What are you doing, dude? Lay the fuck off."

"Want to chill after class?"

"I have class. My academic schedule is packed. I'm not cutting."

"Let's skip. Don't be a pussy."

"Right, okay. This guy is calling me a pussy? The guy who walked into my English class wearing his sunglasses inside like this is a goddamn fucking Movie Awards red carpet pre-show? The guy who looks like he put on black nail polish while hanging out with the Columbine killers is calling *me* a pussy?"

"That is seriously the nicest thing anyone has ever said to me. I'm almost in tears."

"Well, I'm happy we got to have our Lifetime moment. Now fuck off."

"Dude, please, let's just chill. I only know one other guy at this school who transferred with me from Glencoe and you're like the first person I've talked to. I fuck with you. I fuck with your energy."

"If I do, do you promise to cut my body up, throw it into the duck pond, and feed my flesh to the crows so I don't have to go through the rest of this semester?"

He puts out his fist to bump. Our knuckles touch.

"I want you to use a machete. No pussy-ass steak knife. I want some blood, west coast gangsta shit, hard slits deep in the skin."

He shakes my hand. "Done deal, dickhead."

The bell rings and we walk out of class and through the crowded hall together.

Lusif nudges me. "We have to go pick up my buddy by the guidance counselor's room."

"Oh God, there's another one? Are you like the Trenchcoat Mafia of new freaks coming to ruin ND?"

"Watch your mouth. I know Glencoe girls. You don't fuck with the man with the connects."

"I'm sure all the babes at your old school must love a man with black nail polish and a Hot Topic shirt."

"Watch it! Unless you want our slaughter deal to happen faster than you can say 'Kodak,' bitch!"

"Resist drugs and violence" says the D.A.R.E. sign on the wall of the guidance counselor's office. Lusif is making drugged-out faces trying to make me laugh.

"What is that?" I ask, pointing to the numbers on his hands.

"My new locker code."

I move closer to him. "Can I ask you something?"

"Sure."

"Why were you sitting in the back of class?"

"I like to slam my head on my desk in peace."

"Put your textbook up and hide your face. They'll never know what you do back there."

His buddy walks out in red Converse high-tops and a Led Zeppelin shirt tucked into his Levi's. His greasy shoulder-length hair covers his face.

I think about what to say. "Uh, you look like you just walked out of the preview for *Detroit Rock City* that they keep fucking playing."

He doesn't make eye contact. "Nice to meet you, too."

"I mean seriously, dude, did Goodwill sponsor your outfit? Do you shop at Army Surplus?"

He looks me right in the eyes. "Suck a dick, you air-hockey-and-ping-pong-in-the-basement-with-his-daddy looking motherfucker. Where's your wallet chain and 311 shirt?"

Lusif smiles. "This is Shane." Turning to me, Lu facepalms. "I didn't get your name. Sorry. Fuck."

"Brad."

"Shane, this is Brad."

"Where do you want to hang?"

"Let's go to Pedo Park."

"Pedo Park?"

"You don't know Pedo Park? It's where this pedophile used to lure kids into his white van with American Girl dolls."

Shane says back to Lu, "Isn't that the balcony rapist that they were doing protests against last week?"

I tilt my head. "I've lived here all my life and never heard this story."

"It's just up the street."

I lead us out the back door. We take the sidewalks by the strip mall and Lusif leads us down a path through the trees to the park. Shane drops his bag, runs up to a swing, and twists his body around. I lean against a metal pole on the other swing set. Shane tosses a pack of Camels to Lu. He lights a cig. "Did you do anything chopped this summer?"

"Chopped?"

"It's, like, a word I made up because it sounds sick."

"I went to summer camp."

"You actually went to a summer camp? Like a real-life summer camp? Are you a virgin?"

"I'm not a virgin. I fucked like three chicks at camp. I don't even remember their names. Girls couldn't get off my dick, dude. I got so much neck. All the older cabin counselor guys nicknamed me Mack Daddy."

"Dude, that's my boy!" Lu fist-bumps me. "That's sick!"

"Did you get any pussy this summer?" I ask him.

"I got AIM pussy, man, all summer long."

"AIM pussy?"

"Oh, bro, AIM pussy is the future. Now when you go out, you can be anywhere and meet a girl: a rave, a party, the mall, wherever. You get her screen name and talk to her. You just add her to your buddy list, send her winky faces and hearts. She knows what you want."

"You get right to the point, I guess. No small talk."

"When she gives you her screen name, she's agreeing to fuck you. You know she wants the dick because why else would she spend all night chatting with you?"

"True, true."

Shane exhales. "Tell him the Angelgurl666 story."

Lusif lights up. "I fucked this freshman chick that I met off AIM in my friend's shed. Everyone was upstairs moshing to Nine Inch Nails and I was banging her head against the fence. She said it was so fucking kinky." He makes prayer hands. "AngelGurl666, please come back for seconds."

"You want to know a charm that an older dude gave me?" I ask Lu. "You take a girl to the park and pull out your dick. She's going to love seeing it so much that she will just start sucking you off and doing shit with it. I've had no problems with that technique."

Shane says, "Men don't have a wall. God put a wall in girls' pussies for a reason… to be broken."

I laugh. "Deflower power, buddy. But yo, I bet these girls are all goth types, not blondes. You know the black hair chick? The one in *The Craft*?"

"Fairuza Balk?"

"Yeah."

"Oh, fuck *The Craft*! Fucking trash. There are so many stupid girls who watch that and then go buy a pentagram necklace and start telling people that they know how to hex their boyfriends."

"All women are braindead," Shane jokes.

"Let's talk about all the trash and terrible movies out right now, all of these stupid fucking goddamn teen movies."

Lu goes, "You know, it's just for creepy old guys so they can watch teenagers have sex."

Shane laughs. "I'm sorry, but when do girls our age ever walk out naked in whipped cream with cherries on their tits? But you see it happen in *Varsity Blues*."

I pause, then light up. "You guys don't know how fucking happy I am right now to be talking about this with someone. People don't understand how angry this shit makes me. It's just sick."

Lu says, "What about the 'Kiss Me' song and all the fucking fake prom scenes that try so hard to make a high school that we can recognize? That shit makes my stomach sick."

"It's not fantasies, it's lies," Shane agrees.

"If sluts act slutty, it's because they copied the movies. Girls think that we're dumb, that we don't see through all of that."

Lusif's eyes dart at me. "We are being groomed by corporate America to believe in this fantasy that once we turn twenty-one and can go out to clubs and to Miami for spring break, then everything is going to be okay, like once you arrive in your fantasy, you'll be inside of it, but—"

I cut him off. "The fantasy can't fix things, and it will not make you or your life better, that I *know*."

Lusif smiles. "I hate MTV, but I can't stop watching or thinking about it all the time—"

Shane interjects. "MTV is the opiate of the masses, as Nietzsche would say."

"I have no idea who Nietzsche is. Is that a German band like Ministry?"

Lusif turns to me in disbelief. "Ministry is not from Germany, dummy. And Nietzsche is this French philosopher that Marilyn Manson always talks about. On this message board that I go on, all of these cooler older college people quote his work and say that everything Niet says is cool and true."

"Maybe every man in America needs a dream to believe in, but sorry Green Day, I'm not fucking having the time of my life—that's for sure!"

"I think about this kind of thing a lot, Brad," Shane says. "Us always seeing these images of how things are *supposed* to be. It's not like I'm ever going out of my way to fit into this whole idea of what being young means, like I see in the movies."

Lusif agrees. "*She's All That* is trash."

"*Idle Hands* is trash," Shane adds.

"*Disturbing Behavior* is trash," I say.

"*10 Things I Hate About You* is trash."

I can't stop, I scream. "*Dawson's Creek* is trash!"

"*I Know What You Did Last Summer* is trash!" Shane tacks on.

Lusif raises his voice. "*Dawson's Creek* is the worst fucking show, and I swear the worst people watch it. Anytime I'm at Tower and see someone buying that soundtrack, all I think about is how the world could really do without their bad taste."

"Why is it like that?" Shane asks. "It's like all the people who listen to this garbage bubblegum pop are the same people who watch *Dawson's Creek* and shop at Abercrombie."

"The media is trying so hard to glamorize being a teenager," I tell them. "It's like, no, I just want this shit to fucking end."

Lusif says, pissed, "The darker Kevin Williamson movies are just another excuse for Hot Topic to sell more 'I hear voices in my head' shirts to teenyboppers. Kevin Williamson is so hated on alt.horror."

Shane agrees. "And now there's that new show *Popular* premiering on The WB, and then the other new one, *Get Real*, on FOX. It's like, how fucking dumb are these people?"

I punch the air. "Yes! How much more garbage can they assault our brains with? People our age watch those high school shows and want life to feel like that, to be that intense and dramatic, and it's just never going to be."

Lusif agrees. "And now you open *Rolling Stone* and in the Nike ad there's some guy our age with a lip piercing and orange shirt trying to look all badass and alternative."

I pause. "I never even think about what it means to be a teenager until someone brings up my age and then I have to be reminded of it. I want to be an adult. I'm ready to be an adult."

Shane turns to me. "This is not dope. This is not like the MTV ads where they try so hard to show us a reflection of who we are."

"When I see that," I add, "I'm just like, 'Nice try, but your Viacom brainwash doesn't work on me.' I hate that Hollywood wants to try to convince me that I'm like a character in *The Faculty*."

Lusif looks hopeless. "I hate everything." He turns to me. "Wait…
Do you do drugs? I love drugs. Drugs are so chopped."

"No."

Shane's in shock. "Wait, you don't robotrip?"

Lu laughs. "Oh my God, Shane. He doesn't even know how to
robotrip. Remember when we robotripped that whole period and I wrote
Ministry lyrics all over my scantron? That was so fucking funny."

"Dude, scantron is sick." I light up. "I passed so many tests last year
just because I sat beside an Asian who let me copy off him. I got the best
grades and my parents were like, 'What the fuck?'"

Shane can't stop laughing. "Gung Hay Fat Choi happened, baby."

Lu turns back to Shane. "Remember when we did those drugs that
the creepy skater gave us and we cut class to walk around the pharmacy
and you thought that Herbal Essences bottle was talking to you? That was
fucked up."

Shane's eyes light up. "Then we went to Hamish's and watched *The
Doom Generation* and ate that really fucking good pizza. I can't believe
ninth grade was three years ago."

"What is robotrippin?" I ask, two topics behind.

Lu looks at me. "It's when you trip off of Robitussin. I'd do it in the
school bathroom all the time last year. I put it in this cool flask and this
dollar store water gun that I kept in my locker. I'd squirt it in my mouth. It
was my aesthetic."

I say, nervous, "The worst thing I've ever done is probably use my
water bottle to steal from the McDonald's soda fountain."

Lu turns to me. "Wait. Do you want to come robbing with us
tonight? I want to try to walk into people's houses."

"Dude, what the fuck? No. That's fucked. I know a lot of people here
and their families and shit. I don't want to do that."

Lu pushes my shoulder. "Are your parents at work right now? We
should go to your place and chill. Do you have the keys?"

"Duh, dickbait."

Lu lights up. "Let's get wasted at your place. Your dad probably has
lots of beers that we can steal. If the school calls your house, I can just

delete the message from your answering machine before your mom comes home."

"There's the rest of the school day, dude. I already have a project due, and I'm using next period to work on it."

Lu stares at me, maybe mocking me. "Why not, puss puss? They did it in this movie that I rented the other night, *Black Circle Boys*, and they never got caught! The guys were checking people's doors, going into their houses, and drinking. I think it'd be so chopped if we went and did that right now. Have you rented *Black Circle Boys* yet? There was one scene where the main guy bit off a frog's head in bio class in front of everyone and I was like, 'Wow, that's so me.'"

"Stress. So stress."

Lu asks, "What do you like to do for fun?"

"Walk around. All me and my buddies ever do is walk around."

"If you want to start hanging out with us boys, everything could totally change."

☆ 21 ☆

I run into Lu in the hall.

"Oh, wow," he says. "We take bathroom breaks at the same time. This must be true love."

I smile and flash him a middle finger. He smirks and middle fingers me back.

"You want my number?" He winks.

I take out a pen and Lu writes his digits on my arm.

☆ 22 ☆

Kev and Eric are playing games in the arcade. I zone out on the alien heads on top of the fast lane automatic ticket machines, then try to find some hot girls to look at in the lineups. I'm about to order a large popcorn with extra butter and a Surge. I pace around the movie theater, hoping to bump into Lu and Shane.

☆ 23 ☆

Mountain Dew and Pepsi vending machines sit beside each other in the distance. I watch a boy in a Fat Albert shirt tucked into his 501s kick the Pepsi machine and pull his hair. I think he's in my math class. I'm holding my Jansport between my legs beneath the table. The loudspeakers blare announcements in the background. Lusif sits across from me in a Beautiful Monsters Tour shirt and leather choker spinning an empty Fruitopia in his hands.

I hold up a *Friends* Coke bottle. "Do you know where I can enter a sweepstakes to get guillotined?"

Lusif laughs. "If you do that, you won't be able to nut to the new *Making the Video* episode that stars your boyfriends, blink-182!"

"It's torture being in school right now. I want time to speed up. I'm so fucking excited for tonight."

"You know, 'All the Small Things' is called that because Mark Hoppus has a small cock?"

"Bite my dick!"

"I knew you'd be upset about the news of his shrinkly dinklie, but hey! Maybe if you're lucky like the rest of the unnecessary shitty pop-punks on this planet, blink will do an AOL live chat this month and you'll get the chance to ask Mark or Tom what butt-fucking position they prefer. You can get your asshole prepared for when they come here for a concert again."

I get ready to whip him with the bottle. "I'm going to shank you! blink is not gay! blink is not the Backdoor Boys! I know this new video is going to do so well on *TRL*. I'm rooting for the boys with this one."

"I get that you're excited. This is how I felt the day 'The Dope Show' premiered. I faked being sick because I just couldn't focus on anything but the marathon leading up to the premiere. Wait. I've never asked you. Do you like Marilyn Manson?"

"He's okay. I caved and taped 'Mechanical Animals' off the radio 'cause I fuck with it. I just think he's kind of a sellout."

"That's not the name of the song, that's the album. How is he a sellout?"

"What happened to the badass Manson from a few years ago who had candles and doves on his shoulders and was making creepy satanic videos? When 'Sweet Dreams' came on the TV, the whole fucking room changed. That was some graphic shit and now he's some gross little transsexual alien bitch. You can tell with this newer sound that he's sold out to be more mainstream and get more famous."

Lu looks stunned. "Watch your fucking mouth. Before I'm an American, I'm a Marilyn Manson fan."

"You don't think I realized that the first second I saw you? You have Manson-blood-oath written all over you."

"I would let The Reverend stab me with an HIV-infected needle if it meant I got to become his friend."

"Now, that's what I like to call fan loyalty."

He pulls on his shirt. "I saw Hole and Manson in March. I wore the shirt to school for a week straight. We all had to chant 'We hate love, we love hate' before he came on stage. It was like a black magick ritual. I lost my voice for two days from screaming so loud and Manson was making all of these funny ass jokes about Courtney Love."

"What'd he say?"

"That she was in the back playing with her dirty snatch. Then Courtney stormed right on stage, lifted her skirt, and jumped on him. It didn't even fucking feel real. It was seriously like a dream seeing my worlds collide. I love them both so much."

"MTV covered that concert like it was a part of the Gulf War."

"How many times do I have to say it this year? You can love both Hole and Marilyn Manson. You don't have to choose."

"I hope he made a joke about Courtney murdering Kurt! That'd be so fucking priceless."

"I don't think he did, but that day, we all waited in line and chanted satanic shit just to piss off all of the retarded Christian conservative nut-jobs. I got in a brawl with this old guy and I swear I'm still buzzed over it. I spat on the face of this Christian protester who had a 'Sodomy isn't a human right' sign." I can't hold back my laughter. "Why are you laughing?"

"That's a fucking funny ass sign."

"I know, but I just like the idea of performing. I was standing up for something just so I could piss people off. I liked the feeling of everyone in line looking at me. I felt like a leader in the lineup. It's not like I meant it."

"Why didn't you try to stalk his tour bus? Did he kill any chickens at this show?"

"Dude, I fucking tried. I brought Twiggy a box of Dunkaroos 'cause I read in *Metal Mouth* that he loved them, but they wouldn't let any guys inside, only girls. Yesterday I saw these girls who posted online about meeting Twiggy at a signing in their city and it made me so filled with rage. It ruined my fucking night. I want him to sign my *Rolling Stone* cover of him so bad. When I see him signing other fans' magazine covers on MTV, I get so jealous."

"What was the mosh pit like?"

"It was so fucked. This gross fat goth bitch poser scratched my face and I was bleeding. There were also retarded little twelve-year-old try-hards, like, why are you even here? You don't even know who Anton Lavey is. Go home and play with your tubbies!'"

"How can you tell that someone's a try-hard?"

"You just feel it in your bones when someone is a poser-ass bitch. You just know they don't even know anything off of *Smells Like Children*. People like that just make us real fans look bad. We call them randoms— stupid fucking one-songers, dope-showers, sweet-dreamers. There's no one in the world who understands him like I do. Most people who live here are way too stupid to get him."

"I heard that Marilyn Manson had his lower ribs removed so he could suck his own dick."

"I bet you also heard that Lil' Kim got her stomach pumped 'cause she swallowed too much cum."

I laugh. "How'd you know?"

"Rumors are always so much more fun than the truth and, you know, the best place nowadays to start rumors is on the internet."

The school bell rings.

☆ 24 ☆

Lusif and I are smoking cigarettes far out on the school field, leaning against a chain link fence. It's break and Shane is running toward us. "Yo! Dick-nut bag!" I yell.

Lu pushes him when he stops in front of us. "Where have you been, fag? Were you sucking your boyfriend's dick out back again? We told you that you can't be doing that on school grounds or you'll be suspended, young man!"

Shane ignores him. "Dude, what the fuck is wrong with this fucking piece of shit school? Do you know who Mr. Karrington is?"

"Do not get me started, I hate him! Karrington is a men-seeking-men section faggot. He's fucking horrible. He gave me a C minus because he had some kind of vendetta against me last year."

Shane nods. "Fuck him so hard. He was talking to me like I was a little kid. I fucking hate teachers who treat me that way. I fucking hate him, dude. I want to switch out."

"Oh, you're fucked now. You won't be able to get out of the class."

Lusif agrees. "Shane, it's simple, just don't go to his class. You don't even have to go to school."

I change the topic. "Do you guys wanna chill on the grass?"

"Fuck no. I don't feel like getting up right now." Lu pushes the plush keychain that Shane has on his bag into the air. "Uhh, why do you have a fucking *Daria* plush doll thing ringed to your bag now?"

"You don't think it looks chopped? I just got it."

"No, it looks so gay, like a middle school girl. You couldn't have at least gotten Trent?"

"You fucking fuck, they were sold out of Trents at Tower. Besides, you were just saying last night how cool it would be to have a *Cat in the Hat* plush on your bag!"

"Yeah, but that's different because that's actually creepy and chopped, sick, and weird, cool, and gives big Manson vibes. *Daria* is just bogus!"

"Dude, shut up," I cut in. "*Daria* is funny as fuck. The new season of *Daria* was chopped. The world is a fun place because of mean and sarcastic people like that. I fuck with your push doll, Shane. I support you in this purchase."

He lights up. "See? This guy gets me! And yes, it sure as hell came with an exclusive twenty percent off coupon on the brand-new *Daria's Sick, Sad Life Planner* CD-ROM that's available this November. Fucking eat it."

I knock his shoulder. "Boo ya! Slam dunk!"

Lu makes a serious, commercial-like voice. "Rated T for Teen."

Shane turns to me. "Brad, let's go for a Blockbuster bin-dive sesh together sometime this week. I want to get to know your tastes and shit."

"Oh, you trying to judge me now?"

"You say judgment, I say getting to know the real you."

"You guys are such losers," Lusif interjects. "*Daria* is for people who think they are so much smarter than everyone else but are normal as fuck and just don't see it."

I continue, "Shane, are you going to hang with us or what?"

Lu refuses. "I can't hang with either of you. I'm busy today. I have to go to Panda Photo to pick up a pic CD. It's a lot of prep work to post a photo of yourself on the internet."

"No, I'm going home. I'm in a bad mood 'cause of that Karrington dick-eating son of a bitch cunt. But wait, I need to do something."

I look at him. "Wait…what is that?"

"This is my psychiatric medicine for my depression…"

I stare back at the little round pill. "Uh, okay? Prozac?"

"No, Luvox."

Lu interrupts, "You are doing this for the aesthetic and the drama, for the cameras."

"You of all people fucking know that I was on suicide watch, how serious and severe my depression is, yet here you are sitting here and trying to tell me that I want to be depressed, or that I enjoy this. Fuck you!"

I come between them. "Dude, dude…"

Shane snaps. "No, no, no. Fuck this. I'm going home!"

Lu pushes on me and moves us forward. "Why don't you just give your new little *Daria* keychain to your lesbian girlfriend? I'm sure she'd love it."

"She was not a lesbian, for the five-hundredth fucking time!"

"Shane, she was the only girl in our school who wore a *South Park* sweater. She was a lesbian. A k.d. lang-loving, Lilith Fair-attending, pussy-licking dyke!"

"Dude, she sucked my dick. You were at my fucking house when she was doing it. She likes dick!"

"Look! I'm not feeding your retarded-little *Chasing Amy* delusional bullshit right now. For fuck's sake, the girl is gayer than Pepper Ann. Shane! After you're done with your little special-ed mental tantrum, remember you have to go to fucking Walgreens and pick up the pics that we snapped last week. They've been ready since yesterday, so stop being a lazy fuck and do something productive with your day. I want to see the snaps."

Shane storms off. "Arrrrrghhh!!!!!"

Lu looks at me. "Tcht, tcht, tcht…Pisces…Pisces Iscariot!"

"What do you mean by 'Pisces Iscariot?'"

"Oh, it's code. It's what I call Shane when he's being over-emotional and annoying."

"Uhh? I don't follow."

"The Smashing Pumpkins album. Wow, listening to Pit, Shit Eye Blind, and dick-182 is really rotting your brain."

"I fucking hate The Smashing Pumpkins whenever they come on the TV with their stupid fucking weird uber gawf goggle glasses with the yellow lenses. I see Billy Corgan's punchable face and it makes me so fucking annoyed."

"Don't say that around Shane. He's obsessed with *Pisces Iscariot*, but I know that he only loves Billy Corgan so much because they are both depressed little victims of life—poor-me crybaby, 'where's my daddy' bitches."

"Wah, wah, wah. I can't listen to the whining and complaining in their music. Plus I just hate Billy's voice."

"Don't ever tell Shane that I'm telling you this, but when we were thirteen, his mom wouldn't let him get *In Utero* because of the song 'Rape Me.' He ran away to my house for three days, pretended to commit suicide, and left a fake suicide note in his room on his tape recorder. The authorities got involved, it was a whole thing. I honestly think he was totally trying to get on the five o'clock news."

"Holy fuck, what a dummy. This kid sounds so messed up. Did he end up getting the album?"

"Yeah. His mom got it for him that week, when he got her worried enough."

"Chopped."

"So, do you want to go draw swastikas in the boys' bathroom?"

"Why?"

"I'm so bored. We could do it with red lipstick on the mirrors so it looks like blood."

"You like to do anything to piss people off, huh? You are just that kind of dude."

"I don't care what it is. I don't even know what some things mean but if I know it's bad and it makes a lot of people shocked, then I'll just do it to fuck with everyone. I troll like that, no shame."

"There were Confederate flag stickers in the boys' bathroom last year and the principal didn't even care. Before summer break some guys wrote 'watch out until we gonna Columbine this place, summa 99' in the stalls and signed it off as a fake mafia. It ended up being a joke and a dare from the guys on our lacrosse team. It wasn't serious, and they ended up turning themselves into the principal."

Lusif turns to me and smirks. "What's more offensive, a Confederate flag or a Hanson sticker?"

"You know my answer."

☆ 25 ☆

Sitting on the slanted roof, I look out across the grid of sandpaper clay tiles to the backyard: the satellite dish on the roof next door, the barbecue on the deck, a trampoline, screwdriver sounds, the pine trees, cars speeding past. Lu is sitting in a Baphomet hoodie, Sony Discman on his lap. Shane is standing in a Smashing Pumpkins shirt, sipping a plastic jug of chocolate milk. He takes out a pen and draws eyes above the scab on his pinky, holding it up: "Doesn't it look like a smiley face?"

I put an orange glass pipe in my mouth. "Wait, so what do I do with this?"

Lu taps my shoulder. "Do not suck it until I light the bowl. Inhale until your throat burns, then lift your thumb off the hole, and suck it in. You'll know what it feels like."

Thumb on the hole, Lu lights the bowl. I inhale, throat burning, coughing, eyes watering. A clarity washes over me, slow, heavy. A vision of me on the floor of a white padded room surrounded by shark tank walls. Lu hits my shoulder. I pass it to him. He takes a hit, embers in the bowl, breathes the smoke clouds in front of his face. Shane bites into the smoke. I cough. "So did I do it right? Did I toke properly?"

"Yes. Yo, so what about that bullshit about Scott from STP being hospitalized for his heroin overdose in July? It's so disgusting not knowing what it's like to be a part of a public drug scandal."

Shane shakes his head. "Lu, shut the fuck up and roll me a fucking joint."

"The wind is going to blow out your fucking joint, asshole. Remember last time? You always n**** lip my joints. I'm over it."

I nod. "I have to say, that was actually fucking disgusting. The fucking Black dude in the orange Atari shirt—"

Lu chips in. "The one outside the arcade?"

"Ew. Yeah, did you see how hot his girlfriend was? She was at least an eight, and I was just like, what the fuck is wrong with the world for a hot chick like that to be hanging out with some ugly fucking Black dude?"

Lu goes through his bag, takes out a Kodak disposable, snaps a shot of me. I pose. He passes me his Discman, I hit eject, and see the Sneaker Pimps *Becoming* X CD.

Lu taps me. "Put on track three."

I put the headphones on, hit play, close my eyes, and look deep into the blue sky. The sound of "6 Underground" plays; the song's chorus feels like a fairy speaking in a secret language only I can understand. Under my breath, a deep tone. "I can feel myself diving…into the music…and never…coming back…up…to the surface. This song…crucifying…my soul."

I open my eyes and take the headphones off. Shane is leaning his head back as Lu drops Visine into his eyes. "How fucking weird is it that pickles are cucumbers? Like why don't we fucking talk about that more? Like how fucking insane, that is like, so fucking weird."

Shane is cry-laughing.

"He's two seconds away from throwing up Nesquik chocolate cake and drawing peace signs on his balls."

"Chocolate cake? Oh my God, Shane, I love you, my squirtle-fungus baby." Shane tosses a Mason jar with a slug in it back and forth between his hands. I start singing. "Let's go buy lavahhhh lamps, man!"

Shane taps Lu's shoulder. "Can you stay stoned forever? This is classic. I wish we were taping his first time."

I laugh. "Can you think of anything worse than being inside of a *Road Rules* van?"

Shane looks over to Lu. "He's so funny. I love this kid."

"Snap a chopped pic of me blowing smoke out of my mouth." I blow out and pose. Lu snaps.

"Calm down there, *High Times*'s Model of the Month."

"Brrrr. You know? It's all, like, brrr right now." I rub my jeans. "Who is the chick from the Lenny Kravitz video, the one in the American flag pants? What's her fucking name? She'd give good burn."

Lu rolls his eyes. "For God fucking sake, it's Heather fucking Graham."

I shrug. "Shane, do you have the *Juggs* college girl issue that just came out? I might need to lock myself in your bathroom. This weed is getting me horny."

Lu tries to whisper to Shane, "Just when I fucking thought the kid couldn't get even more annoying, let's add weed into the mix."

I laugh. "Hey! I heard that!"

Thumb on the bowl, I light up again. ...*Bend time to fit your will, slow it all down... This works. This is how you get quiet. This is how you get slow... It all can just melt and fade out...this is how. One day, can I get so high I'll finally feel like myself?*

Shane tells me, "You know there's a tree underneath one of the doors at the elementary school? You can use the branches to climb to the top. I've always heard about it but never had anyone to go up there with."

"Wow."

Shane stares at the sky. "Do you ever feel like you feel things for other people before they get a chance to experience them for themselves? You have to sort through what is real and what's imagined."

"Shane, that's too trippy for me. Get me some ice. I want to chew ice." Shane returns inside through his window. I follow Lu, pushing himself through. "I want to watch *Doug*. I want to watch *Daria*. I want all the cartoons right now. Fuck it, let's watch *Hey Arnold*! I just want to hug people. People are so nice."

☆ 26 ☆

My head on the carpet, I think about shooting hoops on my door's basketball hoop. I find a bottle cap under my desk, press it against my palm, and watch the imprint appear. My phone rings and I pick it up. Lu is on the line.

"Have you heard about AT&T's new teen talk plan that includes three-way calling?"

"Sure have."

"What do they say in the ad again?"

I pause. "The thing about Friday nights."

"Oh, yeah. 'Are you ready to make sure to plan your Friday nights easy with your new teen talk three-way calling plan?'"

"God, I fucking hate commercials. If people were as happy and faggy as they are in commercials—"

Lu laughs. "On the real, though, I want the new cordless red VTech clear phone."

"I have the new cordless silver clear VTech. I'm on it right now."

"That one is chopped. It matches your vibe."

"I haven't seen the red one yet. I can go to RadioShack with you if you want to get it this weekend."

"Yeah, maybe. Put on MTV. Let's roast the bullshit that's on right now."

"Game on, baby. Sound-off time!"

I grab my remote and turn on the TV. *MTV News* is on and the lead singer of Silverchair, Daniel Johns, is in a cherry t-shirt, being interviewed by John Norris. "I had a lot of troubles with anxiety and had to take medication because every time I left the house, I would think people had conspiracies and people were after me, and every time I left the house I thought I was going to get beaten up."

A rage hits. "I'm going to spit on my screen. I swear. I'm about to do it."

"Dude, you hate him too?"

John Norris's voice plays over a Silverchair video clip. "And while living away from the watchful eyes of his family and friends, Daniel's eating disorder intensified."

"You know, it must be real fucking nice to be famous and complain all the fucking time about your made-up, delusional problems and act

77

like us regular people give a shit about your fucking attention-seeking bullshit."

Lu's voice grows angry. "Oh, Daniel, it must be sooooo hard being in a successful band and having your fucking face replayed on MTV all day in everyone's bedrooms and living rooms. I'm sure it was a big booboo on your entire life to become a famous rock star. Wah. Why don't you just call up Damon Albarn and you two can complain to each other about how it's sooooo fucking hard to be famous rock stars?"

"And all the girls that he must've gotten for being a little baby bitch in a try-hard teenybopper band? That Hanson-outdated-grunge-edition-fuck of a band, fucking faggot. I always hated him. I want to crush his fucking skull."

"He's going to come back again in two years, only vegan this time with new revelations about caring for the environment, on some barefoot, pussy-ass Pearl Jam shit."

"No, even better, he'll come back with a fucking boyfriend—look at how queer he is. That's why they have that song 'Abuse Me,' 'cause that's what he wants: a dick in his hole. He's a little fairy-looking bitch. And I hate 'Ana's Song.' It ruins my day every time it comes on the radio."

A clip of Daniel playing "Ana's Song" on acoustic guitar plays. "When you get letters that say, 'You've helped me admit to anorexia,' and… 'I was gonna kill myself until I heard this album,' that makes people that say, 'You're exploiting your problems,' just seem like such a little speck in the dirt. You just don't worry about it…"

Lu screams. "Okay, that's it. Turn it off. That's enough abuse for the day."

I grab the remote and flip my TV off. "Is it off now?"

Lu's voice changes tone. "All I can see is my reflection in the black of the screen. It's like a total abyss."

"What movie character are you trying to sound like?"

"Someone from *The Doom Generation*."

"Oh, word. I read somewhere that you can see Rose McGowan's bare tits in that movie."

"You can. They're nice and hot, but she's wearing a butch dyke bob the whole film, so it's not as sexy."

"Boner kill."

"Hot girls should always have long hair. Always."

I pause. "Wait, let me add Shane to the call."

Shane clicks in. "Yo."

"Shane, you in?" I ask.

"Yeah, I can hear Shane."

"Yeah, guys, I'm here."

He sounds weird. "Shane, why do you sound sad?"

Lu says, "That's his natural voice. It's called the sound of attention seeking."

"Fuck you, dog dick. I was just watching MTV and they were interviewing—"

Lu yells, "Oh, do not do it, Shane. Do not do it."

Shane, even louder, "Let me fucking finish. Daniel Johns from Silverchair was opening up about depression and it was so relatable and so real. It was almost cathartic for me to hear that on MTV. Every word he said felt so fucking real. You know, to see that on EmpTV, the wretched world of illusion and vapidness, like to see something that real, I really needed to hear this today. It's almost like, for a second there, I believed the universe had my back."

Lu is repulsed. "Are you smoking crystal fucking meth? That was a drama-class-level performance that made my skin crawl."

Shane yells over him, "Lu, you don't understand that the more you invalidate people's depression and psychiatric issues, the more you make us feel crazy and like we aren't going through it. You say all of this now but you could totally wake up one morning and I could be dead. That could actually happen, you know. That could be a real situation in your life."

Lu laughs. "Depressed people are all primadonna drama queens who need everything to be about them and their feelings. Depression isn't real."

"Silverchair blows fucking monkey chunks. Shane, I'm not with you on this one. That was painful to watch. Painful."

Lu cuts in. "What are you going to do, go outside, make a fucking sign, and march on the streets? Start a help-teenage-boys-with-depression club at school? Do you want to get kidnapped in the middle of the night and get sent to some fucking troubled teen camp in middle-of-nowhere, Utah? Maybe then you'll feel like people care about your stupid fucking feelings. News flash! No one in this fucking world cares about your problems. Just go on the internet. There's probably hundreds of people on the world wide web who are just as obsessed with themselves and their quote-unquote depression who will happily circle-jerk post about their feelings. Then all you guys can gather round and share your suicide attempt stories."

I check in. "Shane? You there?"

Lu laughs. "Pisces Iscariot. Pisces Iscariot."

"I heard him hang up, Lu. Don't you think that was kind of harsh? I don't know shit about mental health problems but he seems very sure of himself."

"No, he just needs to toughen up, harden up, and man up. It's fucking pathetic to be his friend and have to deal with his psychiatric problems, his depression, and his obsession with his own sadness. It's exhausting to listen to his feelings all the time."

"I get that one hundred percent."

☆ 27 ☆

Limp Bizkit's "Nookie" leads out of Gadzooks. I'm ripping a Wrigley wrapper. A guy in a *Girls Gone Wild* shirt whistles and shouts "dammmmn" at a group of junior girls in plaid miniskirts and cut up Korn, Manson, and Slipknot shirts, their belly buttons showing. Lu elbows my side.

"AOL Keyword: GothPussySlayer. Watch this." Lu goes up to one with blue hair and grabs his dick. "Come get this dick, baby."

"Buzz off, Luke! You need to stop IM'ing her! She's never going to fuck you. You look so pathetic and desperate."

"Yeah! I'm never going to fuck you, Luke."

"Yeah, Luke, she's never going to fuck you. Get over it."

"Why not? Why not!" Lu grabs the blue hair's ass.

She hits his hand. "Luke! The guy that I'm seeing right now, he's like twenty-seven and he works in the music biz. You're not going to believe this, but he says that he knows Manson's manager. They go way back."

"You really are just a dumb slut if you think that anyone who lives here knows anyone who knows *the* reverend." Lu grabs his dick again. "Come on, baby. I can keep you hydrated. You like Frost Gatorade? I know you want to be my slave."

"Stop! Stop! Stop!"

"You're a bad girl. Everyone knows you have pictures of the Columbine killers in your locker."

"What's your point? Eric and Dylan are my babes. You are not my babes. Besides, my boyfriend's dick is ginormous and he knows how to do satanic sex magick, something that you know nothing about. Oh yeah, and that picture of your dick you emailed me? Well, all of the girls with me right now know what your dick looks like." The girls walk in the direction of the escalators.

Lu megaphones his hands. "Come on, Claire. Everyone knows that you're a slut. Everyone knows you sucked Amber Wachowski's dad's dick in the bathroom at the Tool concert." Lu takes a dime and hurls it their way. "That's what you're worth to me. That's what you're worth to everyone, you sluts."

☆ 28 ☆

A "MISSION HILL PRMRE" tape sits on the floor, and I'm about to put in my VCR to watch it, but I pull back. I grab my baseball cap, toss it in the air, and catch it. The Blockbuster Favorites case on my desk reminds me that I was supposed to return *Doug's 1st Movie* on Sunday. *I could walk, but it's always better when someone gives you a ride.* All of these thoughts wipe out when I glance over to my bedroom table and see Britney in those little polka dot shorts and a black bra on the cover of *Rolling Stone*. Dinner is soon and a sui-wank isn't worth the risk right now, so I grab my phone and call Kristen.

She picks up. "So what do you think of the Silverchair interview that MTV has been playing all week? There are so many people shit-talking it on the message board I'm on."

"No, no, no, not this again."

"What?"

"I just don't give a dick about Silverchair or Daniel. This is '99, there is no more grunge."

"But don't you think it's kind of punk that he's talking about male anorexia on national television? It's just so taboo. This feminist in my class said that it was a revolutionary act to see something with so much substance on EmpTV."

"I'm sure that's the exact reaction the suits at the record label who are trying to sell records to uber-depressed fifteen-year-old teenyboppers want."

"Do you smoke weed yet? I found this old stack of *High Times* from junior high. I used to write the bad things that I did on the weekend all over the cover girl spreads in Sharpie. You'd throw up if you read it, like I can't believe I thought it was important enough to describe how I felt the first time I saw a schlong in the flesh."

I lie. "I don't give a shit about weed, right now, at least."

"True, true."

"Can you boot for me some Marlboro Lights and a 40 of Captains? Also, you have officially been hired. You are getting me any Rated R movies I want."

She laughs. "Look, it's sacrilege, but I'll help you out. I remember when people my age helped me when I was your age. Are you going to a party?"

"No, I just want to go down to the woods. There's this pathway by my house and I just want to smoke and be alone."

"You're a cutie. I'd pinch your cheeks right now."

"Projectile vomiting. Can you pick me up in like fifteen? I need to go drop off a tape that's overdue at Blockbuster."

"Only if you go inside and buy me a pack of Twizzlers while I wait in the car."

"Fine."

☆ 29 ☆

Sitting on my bed, I take the *Title of Record* Filter CD out of the Sam Goody bag, ripping the plastic off with my teeth. I jump up and down.

"Oh my fucking God! It's beautiful!" I open the CD case and a mailing coupon for a Filter shirt drops onto my lap. I look at the shirt, run to the hall, lean over the banister, and call out to my dad.

"Yeah, bud?"

"Can I borrow your Visa? I just got the new Filter CD and I want to order a shirt."

"Filter?"

"Yeah, I love them right now."

"Are you allowed to wear Filter shirts? Hayden's mom was at a parent's council meeting and a lot of band t-shirts were banned after Columbine. I don't want you to get profiled."

"Oh, who cares! I'll be fine." I hold up the coupon. "The shirt is chopped."

"Chopped? That's a new one."

"Yeah, it's like my fave word right now."

"I've never heard Eric and Kev or the rest of the boys use it."

"Well, uh, it's a new one!"

Dad comes up the stairs and hands me his Visa.

"You're the king!"

Dad slaps me on the back. "That's you, champ."

I make "rock on" hands.

☆ 30 ☆

Trying to read someone's Sharpie writing on the bathroom wall, I sit on the edge of the sink, dangling my feet. Lu leans into me, puts a Camel in my mouth, and lights it with his BIC. He takes out his Polaroid and offers it to me.

"Take a picture of me against the white tiles."

I shake my head. "No, I don't want to see these white tiles ever again. I am so sick of this school."

"The white tiles are cursed." Lu grabs the cigarette and blows smoke into the mirror. An Asian freshman in a 311 shirt walks in.

I hit Lu on the shoulder. "Let's fuck with this fag." I turn to him. "Hey, Ching-Chang! Who says you can come in here?"

Lu knocks his shoulder. "Ew, a 311 shirt? You fag."

"Hey, little faggot. I said hey, little faggot. You no speak English, you fucking retarded egg roller? You gonna shit egg rolls?"

The freshman walks into the stall with his head down and locks it. Lu holds onto the top of the stall door, pulls his body up, looks down at him, and spits.

The Asian kid tears up. "Please stop."

"Look at the small Asian dick! You want me to smack that hot chinker ass until you're black and blue?" He spits again. "Hail Satan!"

☆ 31 ☆

Tall grass fields surround us on an empty path by the river. Lu and I take turns sipping a bottle of Surge as we continue to walk into endlessness, wasting away our lunch hour.

I turn and look at him. "Would you go paintballing with me sometime?"

Lu tosses pebbles between his hands. "Oh yeah, for sure. I think that would be fun."

84

"I'd rather stick a McDick's straw up Matt Damon's cornhole and suck his queefs out than be at school right now."

His eyes widen. "Have you ever tried scarfing?"

"What the fuck is that?"

"Scarfing is this new sexual trend that I read about on alt.fetish last night. You choke yourself while you jerk off and get this intense euphoria. You have to use something to obstruct the blood flow to the head. It increases the pleasure when you climax."

"Okay, well, if I see on the news this week that a seventeen-year-old who went to North Douglas High was caught hanging from a closet rod surrounded by porno mags and a bottle of Jergens, then I think I'll have an idea of who it was."

He laughs. "You don't have a private world of dangerous sexual fantasies that you'd never act upon?"

"Well, I never discover anything new about myself when I masturbate."

"*Clueless* was on TV yesterday and I turned it on right at the perfect time—the scene where Alicia is in that gray dress."

"The only memory I have from '95 is jerking off to Alicia Silverstone in *Clueless*, my preteen sexual awakening."

"You've seen *The Crush*, right? She's so sexy in that movie."

"Oh, yeah. *The Crush* is a huge life lesson for all men. Flush your used condoms and all hot girls are fucking crazy and can scream rape or assault at any point in time."

"You're avoiding what I was asking you about. I want to know if there are any fantasies you've ever had where you felt ashamed after you nutted."

"No, there's none. Are you implying that I've—"

"Gay thoughts."

"DiCaprio, Affleck, and Pitt could all be lined up in front of me with their hard dicks out and I wouldn't feel a thing. That's how straight I am."

"Are you afraid that if you fantasized about another guy in the privacy of your own mind, then you would like it too much?"

"Can you stop? Are you only saying all this shit to me because this is your way of telling me that you're curious about fucking guys?"

"I'm saying that you should give the unnatural, the disgusting, and the boundary-pushing a chance."

"Do you like dick? Do you wanna get fucked by dick? Do you wanna suck dick? If the answer is no, then you aren't gay. You aren't a queer. Find a new shock antic. This one is boring me."

"I'm transparent with you. I get excited when I'm embodying something that upsets people. I like reactions. Look, I like to see you sweat. I remember reading in *Time* that after Eric Harris's ex-girlfriend broke up with him, he splashed fake blood and faked suicide. I thought that was the coolest thing ever."

"You didn't answer my question. Are you a butt-fucker in denial?"

"Does every person who fantasizes about shooting up their school just because they wonder what it would feel like end up doing it? You're ridiculous. It's not illegal to have thoughts. You can't arrest someone for wondering about what something could feel like." I shake my head as he hits my shoulder. "Oh, come on. What are you saying with that face, Brad? That the macho man police are going to come and arrest me? Are Carrola, Stern, and Kimmel going to come revoke my man card because I had private thoughts?"

"One of the best parts of a sexual fantasy is that the girls you're thinking about don't say no. You have total control over the entire scenario."

"I want you to answer me right now. If I was a real queer, which I'm not, but if I was, what would make it so difficult for you to be my friend? I'm trying to understand."

"I don't want to deal with all the Gay Straight Alliance tolerance bullshit. I don't want to feel uncomfortable and think that you're checking me out in the summer. Oh, and if you get gay-bashed, then going and visiting you in the hospital will take a lot of work. Everything gay just ruins the vibe. I couldn't relate to you anymore, and I need to be around guys that I can relate to. There's nothing we have in common if you can't get an erection from a topless Carmen Electra, so what business would you have being my friend?"

"What about bisexual men?"

"Bisexual just means you're gay and closeted. It's not real. Bisexual means you don't want to accept your true self."

"Twiggy Ramirez is bisexual."

"Twiggy Ramirez can shave off his eyebrows and wear dollar store blood and call himself bisexual in magazines all he wants, but you still see the guy on MTV doing whiskey shots with big titty blonde strippers sitting on his lap, acting out the same desires that any meathead football player would have if they were in his position."

"So you think he's straight?"

"The way I see it is like this: you can have a nipple piercing if you are masculine. You can wear sex chokers if you are dominating chicks. You can do all of the edgy stuff in the world as long as you aren't an actual homo, as long as you're a man about it, as long as you get some pussy out of it."

"Rock 'n' roll in the new millennium is all about offending people and challenging the world around you. This is not just a lifestyle, but a 24/7 state of mind, my friend."

I laugh. "I just want you to know that I'm not the totally oblivious guy in the straight-to-video teen movie who meets the satanic psychopath and goes into some never-ending downward spiral that includes mutilating animals and homosexual experimentation. You wish!"

"Isn't the whole point of making new friends to reveal things about ourselves we never saw coming?"

"Columbine, the war in Kosovo, the Oklahoma City Bombing, Princess Di's death, the Clinton impeachment trial, the O.J. Simpson trial, the Rodney King riots, the Lewinsky scandal, the fall of the Berlin Wall, oh, and now you and I becoming friends. What's next? The end of the fucking world."

☆ 32 ☆

Garbage's "#1 Crush" plays through the empty house as I lie on the wood floor and rub the smooth boards. I stand and look out my window to the streetlight illuminating the road. I peek at my neighbor's rosebush, rip the letter I'm writing to Aurora out of my notebook, and place it into my hoodie pocket. I walk out the front door and approach the bush, find a thorn, prick my finger, and press the blood onto the letter. *I hope this shows how much I care.*

♡ L1 ♡

Aurora,

    I know you had that Garbage patch on the bag that you always slung around your shoulder at camp. Do you appreciate this symbol of my feelings for you? This music and these words say something better than I ever could about the lightspeed emotions rushing through my body every second of the day. Do you remember spooning on the lake dock, Kool-Aid on the beach, talking about moon shells? Our red Ring Pop tongues? I loved when you told me to go look in the mirror to see my sunlight streaks. I think I'm obsessed with you! I miss you so much.

Yours truly,
Brad Sela

♡ L2 ♡

Brad,

    There is something that hurts so badly about this summer ending. I'm not sure if it's because you and I met, but God, I get so sad that you aren't in my arms right now. There's this haunting emptiness in every room I go into 'cause you aren't around. Goodbye to the season of no order! Chaos, sparks, bursts. Wasn't it so beautiful, baby boy? At least it'll be easier to sleep in the next few weeks 'cause the heat is fading away. I told you, I'm a sun-chaser. Ugh, I just love thinking about the water droplets glistening on your arms as you're about to get out of the lake.

I look at my life as a split: before I met you and after I met you. I have been forever changed by you, this magical person who has given me back what I want to give. It's lightning!

Let's not date these letters. I want our closeness to exist in a place outside of space and time, where you and I can be in love without the clocks watching us.

Oh, how I wish you could see that dumb schoolboy grin you had walking back to the bus. It made the ride home so sweet for me.

Write me whenever. Write me everything that you're going through. Don't laugh at me, but I've already started working on a scrapbook of your letters that I'll keep under my bed. The short amount of time that the universe gave us is just not enough. I'm so selfish. I want more of you!

A girl can sit around and dream about what real love is going to feel like all she wants, but I think I found it at West Canyon. You've been the best summer camp boyfriend that a girl could ever have! MWAH!

Your girl,
Aurora

P.S. A blood-stained letter with Garbage lyrics on the envelope? The perfect hilarious way to start my September...

☆ 33 ☆

A *Girls Gone Wild* Mardi Gras commercial plays during a rerun of James King on *Howard Stern*. Lu and I are on the phone, an open pack of Fruit Gushers on my bed.

"You need to keep asking your dad for your own computer," he says.

"My mom is paranoid I'm going to become part of the Screenager epidemic," I sigh.

"Your parents are being so homo about that."

"PBS. Parents bullshitting."

"You're missing out on a lot of fake nudie pics. You ever wonder what Christina Aguilera's pussy looks like? The internet can make that happen for you."

"It's not that simple. I can't just tell my dad that I want my own computer so I can jerk off to internet porn in the privacy of my own room, chat with my friends, and surf the web."

"You can, you can. Every teen male lead in the movies these days has one."

"Whatever. I've tried. It's just not happening, alright? Don't make me feel even worse."

"Look, I was on alt.satanism last night reading about this new book Jay-Z loves called *The 48 Laws of Power*. It's about how men can unlock total control over people and the world around them. Before you say anything, when we get off the phone, don't fucking call me because I won't pick up. I'm downloading some secret next-level occult type shit."

"Alright, alright. I got it."

"I am so sick of weak people. I want to wipe them out. Social Darwinism 101. I'm done living around all of these idiots. Let's get back to that survival of the fittest shit."

I nod. "Have you heard of *Six*, the new zine going around school? It's got all these scandalous dirty rumors and shocking stories about people who go to N.D."

"A scandalous sex stories zine made by some loser at our school who is taking her love of *Cruel Intentions* a little too far is the least of my fucking concerns."

"Don't get all butthurt! The only reason you don't care about it is because there's nothing about you in it yet."

"Why don't we make a rumor that you and I killed an animal in a satanic ritual and live streamed it to the internet on some secret website?"

"You have to be low-key in life. You have to make fun of everything and everyone and not participate. That's real power."

"All I want is to create a mythology around myself. This is the chance to do that at a new school. A new school means a new audience."

"Look! Outside of your huge fucking idea of yourself that veers on megalofuckingmania, you aren't thinking of how a rumor like that could damage my reputation, you know? A run-in with the local authorities after school could spoil my image."

Lu chuckles. "Oooh, I got you now. It's all coming together. You're one of *those* guys."

"What do you mean?"

"You're as cold and calculating as they come. You're a production of yourself."

"What the fuck did you just say to me?" My hand forms a fist. "Are you calling me a phony?"

"You're deceptive. You're fake. Let's hold off on hanging out until you learn how to stop being such a control freak, princess."

"I am not calculated. What is there even to be calculated about? I'm the least manipulative person that I know."

"You exposed yourself on this call. You showed me just how safe you play it. You want to protect your public image, and I don't trust you at all now."

"Meet me outside of Subway in fifteen. I'll fucking knock your teeth out." My voice shakes.

Lu laughs. "So angry! Look at you! You got caught!"

"You're twisting me out. I'm not a Twizzler!"

"You did this yesterday! You talked about how you'd react to something all to fit an image because you need to control how people see you."

"Oh, okay! So, now I'm calculated because I'm thoughtful? I think intentionally in order to make the best decisions in my life—to respect my parents and the friends that I grew up with. I'm sorry that I'm a good person and that I'm considerate of others. I don't like messes! I don't like accidents!"

"I'm about to hang up."

"All I said is that I don't support you spreading lies about yourself that could jeopardize my reputation."

"Enjoy your boring, clean-cut, *Mickey Mouse Club* life. God, I can't believe that someone who is going to be eight-fucking-teen in a year is thinking this way. You're pathetic. You're so good at creating propaganda about yourself now, aren't you? Why don't you just accept that you're fake?"

"Eat my hole, you bastard."

"You can dish out heat to some celeb on MTV, but you can't take real criticism. Noted. This is not some closeted gay relationship, this is a friendship. You should want to be seen with me everywhere and anywhere. Let it all loose. Do whatever you want in the moment. I'm the same on and off camera."

"You're an asshole to make me feel like this right now. This is disgusting."

"Your manufactured, corporate-calculated good-boy image is never going to be real. You can put in all the work that you want to create this fantasy for everyone in your life, but something you don't understand is the more hard work and intention you put in to sustain this image, the higher the stakes become that you're going to fuck everything up. At some point, you are going to slip, embarrass yourself, and it's going to hurt so much worse than if you were honest from the start. You can't be good, pure, and innocent all the time. You have to realize right now that it's a pose. That's all it'll ever be."

"Maybe I don't want to be a myth! Maybe I want to be myself! This is who I am! I am good! How could you do this to me? This is who I am? How could you attack me like this?"

"The only way to free yourself and become who you are is to stop giving a shit about what anyone thinks. The second you start to care, you give your soul over to an image. You might as well be fucking dead. Really, Brad. Who gives a shit what other people think? Everyone is going to find out who you really are when you slip up at some point anyway."

☆ 34 ☆

Hand out the window, I look down at the *Being John Malkovich* cups, then back at my dad's face, as we drive home from the movie theater.

"That was a beautiful young woman, that blonde girl, wouldn't you say, Dad?"

"One of a kind. Feels like they don't make girls like that anymore."

"She's in another movie that I really, really want to see…"

My dad pats my shoulder. "So, what'd you think, pal? Did you like it more than *Eyes Wide Shut*?"

"*Eyes Wide Shut* was cool, but I thought *American Beauty* was kind of special."

"Your mother is saying this is absolutely going to sweep the Oscars."

"I don't know why, but *The Thomas Crown Affair* poster bothers me so much. I kept thinking about how much I hate that poster. There were some good previews, though."

"The *Fight Club* poster is interesting, hey? I wonder what the soap means. I hope it's not anything gay. Brad Pitt was dressed up like a queer in that preview. Did you see that coat?"

"I hope not either. Gays are fucking weird. There's nothing worse than when you're watching a great movie and shit turns gay."

My dad laughs. "That's my boy! Remember when I took you to *Interview with the Vampire*? You loved it so much that I got worried for a second. Remember how you used to always talk about how much you loved Bush? Do you still listen to them?" He laughs. "The band, not the president."

"Yeah, I know."

"You wore your Filter shirt tonight, so I guess Bush is out and Filter is in with the kids today."

"I've changed a lot since I was thirteen, Dad. I don't even listen to Bush anymore."

"Wow, I can't believe that was so long ago."

"Time goes quickly when you grow up in the house together, I guess."

"You know, some parents don't even get to watch their kids grow up. I'm a blessed man."

"And I'm a blessed son because you know what? I love getting to go to the movies with you, Dad. I love it."

"And I'm happy that I got to have a son. If you ever heard the stories from people at work who've read this book *Reviving Ophelia* about damaged teen girls… I thank God every day that I never got a daughter, and instead I got you."

I nod. "The movie made you feel that way too, huh? 'Cause Angela was pretty slutty."

My dad smirks. "Did you have a crush on her?"

"Oh, yeah."

"Look, son. She's your age! You're allowed to. Me? I'm not allowed to think of her like that, if you know what I mean. Mena Suvari's a little too young for me."

"Yeah, I know what you mean."

"But Howard Stern wouldn't give a shit about thinking about her like that."

I laugh. "He's famous and can say and do whatever he wants. It's the whole Hollywood shock thing. You're going to ask me what I think of the movie, right? I like our discussions on the ride home. I like hearing your thoughts."

"Sure. What did you think of the movie?"

"Okay, so I kind of didn't know what to expect because I watched the VH1 special last week and was a little confused by what was going on. The movie kind of reminded me of what it's like to grow up in a neighborhood, all of the stuff that goes on that we never get to see. All of the things that we don't even tape on home video. It got me all charged up with this feeling of, maybe there's something lurking where we live that we can't ever see."

My dad's voice raises. "Life isn't like *American Beauty*. I've never met anyone like those characters."

"That's not true! We don't know every single person that lives here. Who knows their lives, or what they do? We just drive past these rows of houses and think we know what's happening inside, but we don't."

He glares at me. "Look, we know most, son, and I can tell you most anything about everyone who lives here because I've talked about their lives with them at dinner parties."

"I'm not talking about this anymore."

"Why are you being pissy like a girl? I didn't know I had a daughter. This is news to me."

I feel my hands spazzing. "I'm angry with you and Mom. You're too controlling. I mean, not allowing me to get a car until I turn nineteen? No computer in my room?"

"I told you! Families with our kind of money go off the rails when their kids get cars. It's too much freedom. There's a dozen eighties movies about this. We don't want to lose our little boy to something dark brewing outside of this neighborhood."

I raise my voice. "Did you not see the movie we just watched? It's all happening right here, Dad! There just isn't a network that airs all the twisted things I bet people do here."

He roars, "Do not get emotional, young man. You know better than that."

I cross my arms. "It's fine! Maybe I'll be less disappointed if I don't speak my thoughts out loud."

"Do not be sensitive!"

"What do you not understand about the fact that I'm growing up, Dad? I'm trying to learn how to like the mystery of living where we live, okay?"

"But there is no mystery about the things around you. There is only a mystery because you want to experience it and feel that way about the world. That's all on you."

My body is about to hit a breaking point. "Wow, Dad. That was low. That was so low."

"Who has been disappointing you? Were you just talking about me?"

"No, no! It's not about you. It's just that I don't think anyone cares about the things I have to say! I'm trying so hard to accept that, but sometimes I don't want to accept it because I would like to, for just one second, feel like someone is listening to me, and that I matter."

The car pulls into our driveway. I look at the beam of the house lights above my garage. The car stops, the headlights click off. *What if things are how they are rather than what we choose to see them as?* I roll up the window and get out.

☆ 35 ☆

Moshing in the crowd, a metal band I've never heard of, Jason's Vigil, is playing at The Alligator, some seedy concert venue that Lu's taken me to. There's goths and creeps here, not a lot of people dressed pop-punk like me. Lu is smash dancing, sticking his tongue out and making "rock on" hands while Shane is outside looking to score some drugs from his friend in the opening band. I'm trying to find this girl in lace who talked to me about PM5K by the merch table between sets. An older guy is grabbing my shoulders. Beer spills all over my new Filter shirt.

☆ 36 ☆

Marilyn Manson's "Antichrist Superstar" plays at mid-volume as we swerve into the Burger King drive-thru. The crackled voice says, "Give us a sec, please."

Lu punches the wheel of his '86 Honda Prelude as I grab his Handycam off the dashboard and start taping. "Welcome to Burger King. We are only serving breakfast right now." Lu looks into the Handycam lens. "What do you fags want?"

I turn to the backseat. "Shane, what do you want?"

"Oh, fuck. Just get us Cini Minis."

Lu starts, "I'm going to get a number one with a Dr Pepper and an order of Cini Minis."

The voice through the intercom returns, "Ham or sausage with your number one?"

"Sausage!" I scream.

"Homo!" says Shane.

Lu turns around. "Fuck my dick."

"Can I get you anything else?"

"Nope, that's it."

Lu speeds up to the drive-thru window behind a gray Volvo with a Coast to Coast AM decal on its bumper.

"Lusif… Do you have anything to say to the camera?"

"Fuck off! Stop taping me."

"Why are you smiling so big? Is it because you love attention? Because you think that you're some big rock star, some big legend in your own mind? Aww. Someone's a little camera shy!"

"Oh my God, Brad. Fuck off."

Shane grabs the top of the headrest and looks into the lens.

"What's in the water bottle that you got in the back?" I ask.

"Vodka."

I mock him. "Vodkuhhhh."

He tosses the bottle back and forth in his hands. "I don't want to go to class," he moans.

I nod. "We literally have school in thirty minutes. Isn't that fucked?"

"I would rather light my pubes on fire with my BIC than go to that school." Shane takes a swig of the vodka and crawls his fingers toward the lens.

"Tell the camera what we did yesterday," I instruct him.

"This guy, like, my neighbor, okay, he left a broken computer by his driveway for someone to take, and we did something so fucked. We took it into the woods and Lu, like, made all these pipe bombs because he was learning how to make them from this book…"

"*The Anarchist Cookbook*, by the way!" I say into the camera.

"Yeah, so, it was fucked. We threw these little Molotov cocktails onto the computer and there was fire and everything, and then we started kicking a TV on the street."

I turn to the lens again. "And I smashed the screen with my Doc Martens."

The drive-thru dude hands Lu his bag, and we leave. I film the windshield as we cruise to school and put the camera back on Lu as he's driving. "Tell the camera why you're wearing a shirt that says '100% evil.' Did you get that at Hot Topic, mister razor-edge?"

"I am Lusif, the angel of death, the god of chaos. And, oh, I can promise that you will see this footage on MTV one day. I am one of the Scorpio prophets. I am one of the Antichrist Superstars here to terrorize the new millennium, CNN, and Fox News! See this face? This face should be on a Burger King bag!"

I turn to him. "CNN is so fucking retarded. Yesterday they were doing this whole segment on how teen boys are prone to the business of hate."

Lu grabs his cup and sips the soda in one shot. "And what business is that?"

"I don't remember—"

Shane cuts me off. "Did you hear about the webpage going around with jokes about Black people? This freshman, Seth, made it."

I laugh. "Oh, wow. That's so fucked up."

"Am I racist for not finding *Half Baked* funny?"

Lu smiles. "I don't watch any shows on UPN, but I still have Black friends." He turns to the camera. "Wait, so Shane, tell our audience what we were debating yesterday."

I tape a Marilyn Manson shock-symbol sticker on Lu's dashboard and return the camera to Shane's face. "The debate was, when you finger a chick, does she prefer three fingers or one?"

"I say three," says Lu. "You just jam it up. It's more pleasure for her."

Shane looks concerned. "I've been doing one finger."

I laugh. "Yeah, right. You've been doing one finger up your own butthole."

"You guys!" Lu shouts. "You guys!" I tape Lu's face as school appears in the distance. "I really need to shoot up heroin. I've even been practicing making a fat vein with my fist like those meth heads on *True Life* the other night. I just want to go do it, like, I'm so bored."

I push his arm. "Are you serious?"

"I'm serious. My dealer is twenty-six and he's so cool. He lives downtown on Lawson and goes to all these cool metal shows. He was telling me how there's this new mix of mesc and E called Timex. Apparently the high lasts for hours and feels so good. I just love the aesthetic of tourniquets, shooting up in dirty bathrooms at the mall. It's such a fucking vibe. Besides, he said we can get it super cheap. I want the look of the needle marks so bad."

I cut in, "I would way rather jump someone than do heroin. That's way more chopped. Like if we jumped a bunch of junior dudes, but we don't, like, take anything, just beat the shit out of them."

"You've never gotten beaten by seniors?" Shane asks.

I turn to him. "I did when I was a junior all the damn time, even when I was walking to the park at night just to get my mind off shit."

"I'm the suicidal one. You all should be worried about me if I end up overdosing," Shane says.

Lu pulls into the student lot, turns off the car, and looks ahead. Shane and I get out.

"Uhhh, you gonna come with us?" I ask.

"No, no. You guys go. I'll see you later."

☆ 37 ☆

On the grass, our heads pressed against the chain link fence, Shane and I look out across the school field. He slips *Prozac Nation* into his bag as Filter's "Take a Picture" ripples out of my Discman headphones at full blast.

Shredding a Kit Kat wrapper, I tell him, "Seriously, if a camera crew was following us around and we were famous actors playing teens in some Dimension Films production, do you think every other scene would be us sitting on the grass, smoking cigarettes, bitching about pop culture and hating the world?"

"Doesn't that sort of thing ever hypnotize you?"

"*Hypnotize?*"

"How much we are always in the same places, doing the same things, and nothing ever interrupts this boring pace of our lives?"

"Are you saying we don't know how lucky we are? That maybe one day life won't be this boring?"

"I sometimes wonder if the voice that tells me that no one understands me will get stronger as I get older, or if it'll fade away."

"This isn't to upset you but I just don't understand your whole psychiatric thing. I don't believe life out here is so bad. Have you seen how big the houses are in this neighborhood?"

"I live in one, and that doesn't change my daily fantasies of overdosing on Advil and dish soap. All I ask for is one day, just one fucking day, without infinite darkness."

"Is that what depression feels like?"

"You carry this shame inside your heart like you're holding onto something that you know doesn't belong to you anymore. It's constant. You wait around wondering if the feeling has an end."

"You wonder when you'll be able to let go."

"Yeah."

I push him and chug a bottle of water. "Open your mouth."

Shane laughs. "I don't want to choke."

"I can't believe that Lu pussied out."

He opens his mouth. I spit the water in, and he swallows. We're laughing so hard as Lu appears, walking toward us in a glittery Marilyn Manson "Dope Fiend" shirt. I get up and he tickles me.

Lu knocks my shoulder. "I heard you put a lil Jesse Camp poster in your locker."

"What the fuck are you talking about, dude? Shut the fuck up."

He flashes a wide grin. "You're blushing. You have a thing for JC. Wow. You want Jesse Camp's huge kleptomaniac dick down your throat."

"I don't have a fucking poster of Jesse Camp. Shut the fuck up. I'm not in the mood for this, okay?"

He pulls my t-shirt over my head and puts me in a headlock. "I should never underestimate your bottomless human capacity for missing a joke." Lu pushes my shoulder and a baby blue holographic flier covered in hearts, pumpkins, and female silhouettes slips out of his pocket. It looks like a screensaver. I pick it up and read it.

hYpErReAl eNtErTaInMeNt iS PrOuD To pReSeNt tHe sExIeSt eRoTiC ElEcTrOnIcA hAlLoWeEn afTeRhOuRs iN ThE CiTy. If yOu lIkEd "cYbErInG" ThEn yOu dEfInItElY NeEd tO CoMe oUt tO OuR FoLlOw uP EvEnT! tHiS Is tHe hArDeSt, MoSt hArDcOrE HaLlOwEeN 1999 bAsH WiTh a sUrE FiRe eXpLoSiOn oF HeAvY BaSs, ApOcAlYpTiC SoUnD, oRgAsMiC ViSuAlS, aNd sExY Go-gO DaNcErS... ArE YoU ReAdY FoR BoDy pUlSiNg lAsErS, aNd a nIgHt oF GlObAl mUsIc? CoMe aNd lEt yOuR EnDoRpHiNs fLy sUpEr hIgH.

"What is this?" I ask him.

"It's nothing. Don't worry about it."

"Just tell him." Shane glares at Lu.

"Have you heard of Volt, that new all-ages club opening on Halloween night? This is the flier for the afterhours rave happening at this warehouse downtown."

"Whoa. So you guys planned on going without me?"

Lu chuckles. "You can't handle sweating on the dance floor, a night on X, your jaw jumping up and down, and making out with as many strangers as possible. It's a one hundred percent blackout state."

Shane nods. "This is way hardcore. Not your scene, Brad. Trust."

"What the fuck? You guys aren't inviting me? I swear to God, dude, you are such a fucking dick. Like, why do you fucking do this?"

Lu rolls his eyes. "You're doing it again, pretending that you want to come hang out and do fun things with us, but you're really more interested in the approval of being included just so you can feel good about yourself. Next."

"Oh, okay. Did I not do fat weed tokes right in front of your eyes? Did I not pocket the Backstreet Boys bubblegum right in front of you last Friday when you told me that I was too pussy to steal?"

"You think you can handle a night with goths, punks, faggots, queers, ravers, wiggers, witches, druggies, crackheads, weirdos, and club kids? I don't see this for you. I mean, you in big baggy raver pants?"

Shane cuts him off. "That's not true, Lu. The rave scene is changing. Didn't you see that thing on MTV about how rave purists are pissed off that rich Hilfiger kids are showing up in camo pants and gas masks? The scene is full of fakers now."

"Shane, I just had a flashback to that DJ Demigod spring rave that we went to. Remember the girl in the Saran Wrap shirt sucking on that light-up soother?"

"Holding the Teletubby with the banged-up bloody knees? She was eating out the tubby and rolling face so hard while I was smoking and you were getting the hand job from the one in the big puffy silver coat and angel wings."

"I know what raves are like," I yell. "I've seen Go!"

"That's a movie," Lu says. "A movie about L.A. This is not the movies and we are not in Hollywood. There is real chaos at a rave. Nothing in the night can create order."

Shane laughs. "How about instead of going to Volt, we all hang in Brad's basement and watch Go?"

"Oh yeah, My Halloween '99 night sponsored by Columbia Tristar Home Video. That's a hard fucking pass!"

Shane changes the topic. "This week I'm going to grab the Vitamin E, Tryptophan, and Ephedrine."

I'm confused. "What is all of that for?"

Lu puts his hand on my shoulder. "You wouldn't understand."

Shane hits Lu's knee. "Let's meet up with Frog Shirt and get the Mitsubishi X before they sell out."

I stare at them. "Frog shirt?"

Lu ignores me. "I heard from this Aquarius girl who knows Frog Shirt that the best X on the market right now are the pink ones with the three-diamonds M logo."

"A girl online was telling me it's better than the Playboy X from the start of summer."

"I don't want fakes. I want the real Mitsubishi X. The Mitsu X has crystal in it!"

Shane shakes his head. "How the fuck are we going to pay for this? It's so expensive!"

"Brad, do you wanna come to the rave with us? If you pitch in for drug money, you'll get the door password and location address. Be a thug, steal cash from your dad's wallet, and yeah, you'll also have to do the X with us."

Shane gets super stoked. "This one is encrypted?"

"Password-protected parties are so chopped. 'Shareware' was my fave door pass this year. You have to be worthy to get inside."

"I liked 'solve et coagula.'"

"I'm not doing X. Do I look like a cracked-out freak?"

Shane nudges me. "I would want to be around you the day after when you're totally divorced from reality."

"Huh? What happens?"

"Well, the comedown is not a consequence. It's the best kind of punishment. I get off on the pain. I love it."

Lu nods with approval. "You're missing out on overflowing, being so obliterated that every sensation is gone except for pleasure."

Shane's eyes light up. "You don't ever get curious about certain emotions, feelings, or states of euphoria that you can't access without drugs?"

"I'm not coming."

Lu shakes his head. "You prove my point over and over again. You just got caught in another one of your manipulative, dishonest schemes. You baited us so hard right there."

"So that's it? You guys aren't going to let me come with you all because I won't do fucking X? What kind of WB peer pressure bullshit is this?" I look down at my Timex. The bell signals the end of lunch, and Lu and I start walking to English. "You don't think that was a little fucking weird? It's just disrespectful, dude. It's messed up to do that to your friend."

Lu raises his voice. "Jesus fucking Christ, what are you going on about now?"

"This is so low of you. I'm actually a good person. I don't treat people the way you do. I would never talk about a pizza night that I'm having in front of a friend who wasn't invited. That's inhumane. It's truly evil. I can't believe that I just listened to you brag your face off about all the fun times that you've had without me, like we were on Donahue's couch. This was fucking cruel."

"Uh, since when are your sensitivities toward the world *my* responsibility?"

"You treat me like I'm beneath you. You act like I'm a pledge. It's worse than if we were enemies. You don't think that I know I represent everything that you hate about guys our age? And yeah, maybe you are more mature, you party with older people and you've seen crazy shit that I know nothing about, but why can't I come? I can feel that shit, dude."

"What do you want me to fucking do with this information? Invest in a diary, leakage!"

"Lu, I'm never going to be part of those past shared memories that you and Shane have together. I don't want it to be about the two of you anymore. I want it to be us three. I want to be in the circle."

"Oh, so now it's my fault that you can't be authentic and chill, that you have to calculate all of your decisions? It's my fault that you have some paranoid complex that doing X once is going to make you some dirty junkie?"

"Are you calling me a buzzkill?"

"I was thinking of an anchor. Your need for acceptance right now is disgusting."

"All this week I have listened to you guys talk about your flashbacks: the first time you did drugs, the first time you fucked the same girl, the first time you watched *Spice World* together on shrooms and called the cops freaking out thinking there were aliens in your TV. I have none of that with either of you."

"You make it one hundred percent transparent that you play yourself in this made-for-TV movie about your life. I'm sorry to break it to you, but the character is not interesting. He's not fun. He's suburban. We've seen this before."

"So, you're embarrassed of me? That's why you're so sure that your older friends would hate me? You think I'm uncool?"

"Let's do a test. What if we are around one of my older friends and he asks you, 'Where is the cool place to buy gear right now?'"

"I don't know. Spencer's?"

"Wrong! The 99 cent store. Everyone cool is getting glitter 99 cent store cowboy hats right now. Jesus fuck, a coolhunter would ignore you on the street, that's for sure."

"A coolhunter?"

"Soulless college students paid by corporations to do market research on teenagers. Culture vultures who sell photos of your individual style for cash. Who would want to see their concert outfit worn by some model in *The Face*?"

"I don't follow."

"You have no originality to protect."

"This is what I'm talking about! Why do you think that you can say this shit to me?"

"What are you going to do? Show up in a Freshjive sweater with an old pair of LA Lights? You're so out of place with me and my older friends."

"I think I fucking hate you."

"You don't hate me. You hate that I can see the true desires you hide from yourself. You don't seem to get that living a life of manufactured moments is only going to end up disappointing you."

"Please, can you just tell me where I can get the address and door pass to the rave on Halloween? I want to get into this party so badly. I'll wear an orange camo suit with a gas mask. I don't care. I'll be a raver."

"Listen, you aren't coming with us. I'm not telling you the password. You aren't getting what you want this time."

☆ 38 ☆

A breeze glides through my half-open window as my neighbor drags his garbage can across the sidewalk. I'm sitting on my bed, talking on the phone with Eric and Kev.

"Do you boys want to go to the corn maze?" Eric asks. "Halloween plans. Spit options."

"Nah!" says Kev. "Let's walk around the hood and shoot Roman candles."

"We should get a Unicef box and pretend we're collecting money for starving African kids but lock it away in a fund for our eighteenth birthdays at the titty bar."

"That'd be so sick. What do you think, Brad?"

"Yeah, sure. Dope."

"Alls I know is I'm not fucking down to watch *The Simpsons* treehouse marathon again," Eric continues. "I want to do some fun shit this year. And no Potters either. We're getting too old for the haunted-house-in-a-garden-nursery thing."

"Brad, did you hear? Tyler Benz used his dad's credit card and mail-ordered the Pam and Tommy tape off the *Playboy* ad. He's been making copies and selling them at school."

"Guess who got a fresh copy, baby! This is way better than waiting two hundred years for it to finish downloading on the internet. Put that shit into the VCR and you're good to fucking go, boys."

"Tommy Lee's dick is ginormous."

"I heard he's packing eight and a half inches."

"Can you believe it, Brad? This isn't your usual Cinemax/Spice type shit. This is hardcore. It's what every American man has been waiting for since *Baywatch*. Pam sucking dick and getting fucked on a boat. Uncensored. Real footage."

"Dope."

"Wow, you're being a fag," Kev sighs. "Don't be like this. You don't want to borrow a copy? How are you not more excited?"

"You're in one of your moods again, Alanis."

"You fucking want to know how I really feel? Right now, I couldn't give a shit about Pam and Tommy's sex tape. I don't give a fuck about going to the corn maze with you guys, and I would prefer someone light a bottle rocket up my asshole so my insides can burn, and I don't have to exist any longer."

I slam down the phone, pick it up, and dial Lu.

"Lu?"

"I was just about to leave. What do you want?"

"Do you think you could change your mind about me coming to the rave? I mean, I want the address. I want the password."

"You want those things because you aren't just being handed them. Exclusion is the key to happiness. Exclusivity is where fulfillment is."

"Could I pay you to get access? My dad could give me some money."

"See? This is the kind of behind-the-scenes deal that is ruining the quality of people at underground parties today. You can't accept you aren't cool enough to come with me and my older friends. I've earned getting into this party, I have the right connections. I worked for this. You didn't."

"Are you calling me pathetic for another round of shooting my shot? There's this yucky feeling that I could be missing out on some essential event, that this party could show me a new part of myself that I couldn't access anywhere else."

"Your *yucky* feelings are nothing I can help you with. Maybe go eat a Snack Pack and calm down. Why are you so bugged out?"

"I'm afraid I can hide my true desires so deep from myself that I won't ever be able to access them."

"You're putting this on yourself. You're lucky I'm not taking the money because I have integrity. I do want the Mitsu X, but I'd rather stick to my guns than let someone like you into this party. I'm leaving. See you tomorrow."

"Wait!"

"What?"

"I've never gone to a club all night with friends. I've never even hung out at Denny's until the sun was up. I've only ever heard about it."

"For your Halloween '99, why not stay in for a night of digital violence? Torment roleplaying chat room freaks on AOL with your butt buddies and a six-pack of Natty Lights."

"You know, that's not going to make me feel better."

"I gotta go. Later."

As he hangs up, I cover my mouth, scream, and throw my phone across the bed.

♡ L3 ♡

Aurora,

What about all the musicians and poets in the world who have written songs or poems in fevers of deep young love? They thought that it was going to last forever, but now they're completely different people, all grown up. This is what scares me—the constant torturous future-trips in my mind of who I'll be when I'm older. I don't know how to just relax and exist. But with you, when I was finger-twirling your hair or as I was in your arms looking out onto the lake, your head on my chest, I could feel time moving at a different speed. For the first time in my life, I found a place where I could just…be. Our slow kisses won't leave my brain.

Maybe it was just the idea of us that felt so intoxicating, the location, the heat, meeting someone new, but do I really know what I'm doing? I'm only seventeen. I know nothing about how to be a girl's lover, let alone from miles away.

I know that this is one of my worst qualities, but sometimes I wonder if going through life with the earth-shattering pain of not experiencing anything and never being hurt is easier than throwing yourself into situations where you can end up burned. I know I'm getting scared of all these intense feelings bubbling up because what if I'll never experience anything so kismet again?

Want to know something strange about me? I've got this weird thing where I'm always looking back at something as if it's over while it's still happening.

Sometimes I think you might be the only person on this entire planet who gets to see the real me, just another terrified American boy.

Yours truly,
Brad Sela

P.S. Last night I said to you in a dream: "I would be wild and free if I hadn't met you." I woke up not knowing what it means.

$\heartsuit$ L4 $\heartsuit$

Baby boy,

That's not what it's about! Love is about continuing to feel these mysterious things that we can't understand even if we're afraid they're going to disappear. It's about being strong enough to be grateful that we met and to continue to write these letters to nourish the flames of our bond. This is the work you don't get to see in movies. I would never have had sex with you if I didn't feel what I felt. Souls united. I never even knew that I was waiting to meet you. Do you know how many older guys have tried to get in my pants? At the pool, on my walks? Something just felt right about you. It's strange. Love is the highest point. Why would you be so stupid to ever want to come down?

Wow! How sad it must be to view special moments as if they're already gone while they're still unfolding. I think a big problem with you is that you weigh every decision you want to make on a scale. You move too much with your mind and not enough with your heart.

Remember at camp, how I used to laugh about the way you overthink everything? You have to giggle at yourself in the same way. Take more risks!

Remember this: we don't want to be like the rest, people who find beautiful things out in the world and do nothing with their discoveries.

Your girl,
Aurora

☆ 39 ☆

The new issue of *Spin* just came in the mail. It's opened on my bed to a Pauly Shore interview. I flip back to the Kahlúa ad with this big-tittied blonde on a mountain looking like some kind of fuckable snow bunny, then flip back to the Candies ad with Carmen Electra, mouth wide open while she's on her knees opening Dennis Rodman's pants. I go over to my desk, rip a piece of paper out of my journal, and write:

"I miss Aurora. Aurora is like a spinning top, everything I'm not. Girls like that are so hot and cool and dreamy. You feel like they are hiding something, which only makes them hotter. I really like Aurora. Whenever I'm in a crowded place, I always fall in lust with the face of a beautiful stranger. That same night I find myself lying in bed dreaming about the person I saw earlier, but by the time I wake up in the morning, they're gone. It's an endless cycle."

I flip the page over and write: "We find those magnetic people who make us feel like we've found a missing piece of our puzzle, and then we love them until the feeling wears off." I grab an *Animorphs* book and put the paper inside.

☆ 40 ☆

At a CD stand by Mr. Rags, Lu's fingers rub the plastic on Slowdive's *Souvlaki*. He turns it over to read the track list.

A girl beside him with hot pink dreads, in an Aphex Twin baby tee and JNCOs, muses, "You should get that one."

"Oh, yeah?"

She looks over to me and grabs my arm. "I'm picking up on something. Oh my fuck! I'm picking up on something. Wow! There's a lot of water in your chart!"

She has one cat eye contact lens. "In my whata?"

"I can read the Akashic records."

"I don't speak *Tank Girl*, sorry." I zone out on her lime green eyeshadow.

"The Akashic records, silly. I was born with this special gift of being able to access this library of unlimited souls. I can read people's souls."

"First, my dodo-bird friend here believes that witchcraft is an actual thing and not a concept created by the movies, and now this. Has everyone lost their fucking minds all because the new millennium is about to hit? Is this how we're going to go into this decade?"

"How many times do I have to say this?" Shane interjects. "Spirits are not real. Souls are not real."

She grabs Lu's arm. "Have you ever seen the footage of Björk beating up the reporter in Bangkok? My friend is, like, obsessed with Björk, and she's selling a bunch of bootlegged tapes of rare interviews, concert footage, and stuff. She's spent the past few years recording this rare content. Do you want one?"

"No. Wait. What logo is that on your shirt? It's so fucking familiar."

"Aphex Twin!"

"Oh, I knew that. Sorry. Fuck. I'm dumb."

"If you can find it somewhere, you should get *Music Has the Right to Children*. It's by this group Boards of Canada. They're on Warp Records. This guy in Sam Goody told me about it the other day when I was cutting class and it's like a total automatic OBE! I wanted to pass along the secret to you, if you can hunt it down. Do you have a pen?"

"No."

She bites the cap off a Sharpie and writes the title on Lu's arm. I look over at the "How to Use the Internet" kiosk and the plants by the spiral chairs. Two boys pass by in Alonzo Mourning and Chris Webber jerseys, their arms over each other's shoulders.

"Hey, thanks!"

I look at the girl's belly button chain as she takes out a pack of smokes and walks away.

Shane nudges his elbow into me. "Doesn't that bitch look like she shoots some fucked up shit into her arm?"

"I want whatever she's on. Look at her, she just makes me want to be on a lot of drugs. Goth goggles and pink dreads mean she's a slut who likes to get freaky. I'd shoot all sorts of magic into her. I mean…"

"There was this cracked-out dude outside McDonald's the other day and he was talking about how he's obsessed with this New Order remix, like, Pump Panel or something. I don't know. It was fucked, but he totally reminds me of her."

"Do you ever help out crackheads? Like, give them money?"

"Last time I checked, there is no law that says I have to make this world a better place."

Lu walks over to me. "That girl has that seconds-before-the-gangbang permanent look on her face." He points to the ground. "Look at all this checkered floor shit. This shit, it's all a plan, a plot, a scheme. It's the masonic elite brainwashing us."

"Checkered floors mean nothing," Shane responds. "Everything is meaningless."

Lu smirks. "Fuck. I wish we were all on G right now. That'd be so fucking chopped. Being on G at the mall is my aesthetic."

I pat him on the back. "This mall was made for you to tweak in."

☆ 41 ☆

"Call us by our stripper names," says Cassie as she and Charlotte grind on each other in the glow of the streetlamp.

"What are those?" Lu asks, smiling.

"Dark Moon and Cherry Ivy."

KMFDM is blaring out of Lu's car at the far end of the lot. Lu and I sit on a bench watching them kiss each other's necks, grab each other's tits, and rub each other's thighs.

Lu takes out a piece of Doublemint gum and laughs. "There's acid in this."

I knock his shoulder. "You were out of date-rape chewies? You gotta give it to her. She's already so wasted."

"No, just wait. Goth chicks are so dumb. Watch this." Lu gestures for Charlotte to come over. She does and sits on his lap. Cassie is so drunk that she keeps humping the air. I look over to Lu and we laugh. Cassie doesn't get it.

Lu puts his arm around her. "Remember when we were IM'ing about how you wanted me to teach you how to evoke Asmodeus, that satanic entity?"

"How could I forget? I read alt.satanism every chance I get. At the library, at school, at home, at my friend's house. Whenever I'm online!" She hits him, giggling. "Are you going to teach me how to conjure a demon?"

Lu holds up the gum. "Well, this is Asmodeus-charged gum that I bought off the black market. I wanted to give it to you."

She covers her face. "Oh my God, Lu. I'm so flattered. What is it going to do?"

"It's going to turn you into a goddess of lust. You'll have access to powers beyond your belief."

She grabs the gum and starts chewing. I'm laughing so hard, and so is Lu, as we exchange eye contact. Cassie stumbles over and sits by me. She goes for my neck but I push her away. "I'm not in the mood." She folds her arms and watches Lu and Charlotte.

Lu grabs his bag and takes out a Mason jar with a live garter snake in it. I take out his Handycam. Lu holds the jar up to Charlotte's face. "I want you to take this river-plucked garter snake, cut it with my ritual knife, and rub the blood on your titties."

"What? Is this part of evoking Asmodeus?"

"Sure is. We want to videotape it."

113

She sees me starting up the cam. "Your face isn't going to be in the video," I assure her. "No one is ever going to know it's you."

Cassie is trying to rap Lil' Kim, oblivious to what's going on. Charlotte's face melts into fear and paranoia.

Lu walks over and zips my zipper up and down. "Wouldn't you say my friend Brad looks sexy tonight?"

"I never signed up to play your homo-torture-psycho-sex-role-playing-occult game at the park."

"You consented to joining the game when you messaged me on AOL asking if you could hang with me and Brad tonight. There's no logging out now."

"Come on," I laugh. "Look at you, sweetie. You're hanging with the cool senior guys now. You're getting what you wanted. Why act all afraid?"

"Didn't you tell me that you loved the backstage torture chapter in Manson's book?" Lu teases. "I know it turned you on."

"But that's a fantasy I'm in control of."

"It could be real if you stop being a little bitch! You aren't rock 'n' roll. You have to live and die for this shit. You think Twiggy would ever bring a scared lil' preppy Abercrombie bitch backstage? Don't you wanna be different and special?" He opens the jar and pulls a blade out of his pocket.

Pointing the camera at her, I say, "Come on, lay on the ground."

"Maybe you'll be so turned on seeing all that snake blood on your tits. We will make you a copy so you can finger yourself."

I nod. "You'll be faceless, totally anonymous."

She walks over to Cassie as Lu grabs her arm. "Don't fucking touch me!"

Lu pushes her hard. "All you're proving to me right now is that you're a poser stuck-up little bitch who wears Baphomet necklaces but isn't ready to be the bad girl you portray. Where are you when the opportunities come up to play with real-life demons?"

She snipes, "I thought we were going to talk about Poppy Z. Brite and our favorite moments off the *God Is in the T.V.* tape. Maybe I was going to suck your dick."

Lu unbuckles his jeans. "You still can, sweetheart."

Charlotte grabs Cassie and leads her away. Lu puts the Mason jar back in his bag.

"The fear in her eyes. I haven't felt that alive in so long," I say to Lu. "Pushing someone to that place and feeding off of their pain is something I didn't even know was available. So do you think the soundtrack in the background helped the aesthetic of the scene?"

"One hundred percent." Lu puts his arm on my shoulder. "Fear is the most powerful state to put a girl in. Even if she doesn't know she wants it, she's asking for it."

"She doesn't even know the LSD is about to hit. What a dumb little whore. So what are we going to do with the snake?"

"I'm going to make vials of its blood on the next New Moon." Lu opens his arms. "Bring it in."

We hug on the bench.

☆ 42 ☆

The dandelion dust is on fire. It's disappearing fast. Shane puts his BIC back in his pocket. He's in a "Screw this! I'm moving to Mars!" shirt and plaid pajama pants, crouching down on the sidewalk. I'm throwing sour keys onto the grass by the metal fence.

"Do you know what BSTL is?" Shane asks.

I cut him off. "Wait. Does your mom ever freak out because you always smell like smoke?"

"Yeah, but I just tell her that we've been burning dandelion dust and leaves."

"This is true. That's all we do."

Shane gets up and sits beside me, takes out a Push Pop, and cracks it in his mouth. I ponder. "BSTL. I know this."

Shane laughs. "Balls stuck to leg."

"Why are you laughing?"

"'Cause you have BSTL right now."

115

I knock his shoulder. "You and I haven't walked home together in a while."

"I know. I never go to school. I've been hotboxing my room and watching *Slums of Beverly Hills* over and over. I'm not ding-dong ditching or kicking the can or a hackysack, sorry to break it to you, FOX!"

I nod. "Did you hear on *Loveline* last night that some girl from Dallas just got gangbanged and she was talking about how she queefed?"

"Now that'd be a hard *Loveline* episode to masturbate to."

"Ask me some questions. I'm so fucking bored."

Shane plays with his hands. "Do you think you can have a first love with someone who doesn't love you back?"

"No."

"Would you rather have someone see you cry or see you naked?"

I think about it. "I don't know. What a weird question, you fucking weirdo."

"I would rather have someone see me cry."

My eyes roll. "I'll take Teen Suicide for three hundred, Alex."

"Anyone can see you naked, but can anyone ever see you cry? I think it'd turn me on a lot to watch a girl cry, but it can't be forced. The girl has to be upset about something, have her heart broken or something."

"Yeah, I guess it is kind of hot when girls cry."

"Howard Stern was talking about Woodstock '99 and how guys our age are so frustrated by girls being able to show their bellies and have their tits out that rape is all about getting back for what's unfair to us. What do you think of that?"

"I don't know. I mean, a girl gets to choose if I get a boner, she gets to control my dick. I get how that can fill you up with rage, but it's not worth putting all that work into raping someone. That's just being dumb. Fuck Howard Stern. Fuck these guys from those *Girls Gone Wild* infomercials. I'm fucking sitting in my bedroom watching E! and these random dudes are with tens who are flashing them and shit. Why do they even show us this shit?"

Shane shakes his head. "Howard Stern is an asshole. He was talking about how the Columbine killers should have fucked the chicks before they killed them because they died virgins."

"Whatever. It's Howard Stern. He says shit like that all the time. It's not serious. I think those kids hated how aimless their lives were. I heard on the news Dylan had depression like you do."

"It's not glamorous being depressed like me, hanging out in my pajamas, not changing my clothes, not brushing my teeth. I've totally given up on myself, yet some people love this shit. It's not a *Detour Magazine* shoot. My life isn't sad chic. Misery is what I feel all the time."

I mumble, "We know, Shane. We fucking know."

"And now you go into a diner and people are reading books with 'teen angst' on the cover, jerking off that market. And then you have Daniel from Silverchair on MTV talking about depression, you think it's going to help, and maybe it did for a split second, but there's no solution. Shit never ever changes. It's a constantly redone presentation of the same fucking problem over and over again. I won't ever grow out of this."

I put my hand on his shoulder. "I mean, I have this feeling the fucked-up part about growing up will be losing parts of yourself over and over again and having to win your lost parts back through new people you meet as you get older. I don't like that. That scares me."

"Dude, that scares me so much. That's the scariest part because what if when you do you arrive and find out who you are, there is no more discovering left? What if the journey just ends? You'll lose your wonder and curiosity. That would hurt."

"What if, in your twenties, you grow up to be happy? I mean, is that impossible?"

Shane laughs. "But then what? I'm going to be in my twenties, just partying downtown every night and doing nothing? Trying to indoctrinate myself into some kind of social scene and climb up the ranks just to look down on people because I know more about Ian Curtis and own more Joy Division records than the guy in the Ralph Lauren polo shirt who watches Comedy Central and then pretend that it all means something other than being a narcissistic asshole who is obsessed with image? Like, yeah, no. Fuck that. I hate selfish people."

"You're only making things more difficult for yourself. You love that shit. You love all of this tragic bullshit."

Shane shrugs. "Whatever. Maybe I'm allowed to, maybe it's my right to not want to get better."

"Can I tell you something else that's kind of weird?"

"Spill."

I take a deep breath. "I've got this haunting in my body that I'm meeting everyone at the wrong time and there's nothing I can do to stop it. I feel like this version of me is going to be left behind with everyone, and I'm this disappointment. I could be a better person, but I don't know how to do that. I feel like I'm fucking up just by being who I am right now, and yet I can't control any of it. I can't stop it. I can't fix it."

"I feel that way all the time. The idea of meeting new people who awaken something that exists within me is terrifying because it's almost like once someone does that, then those parts of you belong to the person who awakens you. I don't know. I sound fucked."

"Something that's fucked is that I was watching Disney Channel the other night and there was this movie, *The Thirteenth Year*, about this kid who finds out that he's a mermaid and he's different than all the other guys. It's like, fuck, I relate to that kid."

Shane laughs. "That's kind of gay."

"You're right. That's very fucking homosexual!"

☆ 43 ☆

Natalie Imbruglia's "Torn" blasts from the mall speakers. In the smoking section of the food court, I middle-finger the CCTV camera. Lu has a Hot Topic bag hanging off his chair. He's leaning back with his feet on the table, smoking.

"I've always wanted to shoot up this mall."

My eyes roll. "Save this talk for tonight's slumber party."

"I would start by Kmart, make my way down to Hot Topic, and then the big finale: the food court!" He makes finger guns. "Pew, pew, pew."

"Today was so fucked. In the locker room after gym, Tyson's friends were talking about how Candice has been telling him to try all of these different fruits so she can swallow his jizz in different flavors. They were talking about how fuckin stoked they were for him, and I was just so fucking angry about it all day, like I've had a crush on that girl my whole life."

Lu's eyes widen. "If you can't get her, then let's fuck with her and get even."

"How?"

"Don't worry about it."

"Whatever."

Lu's mind wanders. "Do terms ever get stuck in your head? Like the aesthetic of terms?"

"I don't get it."

"I'm obsessed with the terms 'masochist,' 'sadist,' 'dom'… like it's so fucking cool to me. All of these older guys on the MM message board are always posting about them, acting out rape fantasies with their girlfriends, using fake blood, and it's just such a vibe. I already want to change my screen name."

I change the topic. "Do you want to go downtown later?"

"It's so fucking hard to find parking and I don't want to go on the train. I want to get a tattoo that says 'sadist.' Sadist would be so hardcore."

"Uber hardcore."

"Did I tell you? I took out this new book on Hitler at the library, but I got too hard reading it. I ended up just jerking off all night. When they were talking about the concentration camps, I was like, 'Wow, I'll never be soft again.'"

I laugh. "Try again. Your butt buddies on message boards or maybe some random Hilfiger prep might act all shocked, but that does nothing to me. I'm your friend, and news flash, fake goth shock doesn't work on friends in 2000."

Lu gets louder. "I wouldn't give a shit if people saw what files I have on my hard drive or the things I look at on the internet. I'm not ashamed."

I take the free "CHOOSE APATHY" sticker out of my Mr. Rags bag and hold it up to Lu. I peel off the sticker and stick it on the table. I look around at the lit-up logos: Taco Bell, Pizzeria Party, Cinnabon, Panda Express, The Gyros Place, A&W, KFC, McDonald's Express. I look at the silver gates, the plants, the palm trees, the standing ashtrays. Shane is walking over from Orange Julius holding a drink tray. I grab one, then Lu grabs one. I sip.

"I'm going to RadioShack," Shane says.

I turn to him. "Why?"

"I just wanna look at shit and numb out." Shane walks off, sipping his drink. I read the back of his shirt: "I SHOULD BE IN THE 70s."

I look over and see a mall security cop. Buff, he looks like Brendan Fraser, someone I'd want to be. I think of him plowing the blondes that I've seen all day in some secret part of the mall, unzipping his uniform so they can suck his dick.

I light up. "Burger King lets you smoke inside."

Lu takes a drag. "I know, but how much longer are we actually going to have this with all the fucking environmentalist mentally ill retards boycotting this part of the mall? It's disgusting."

"Enjoy it while it lasts, or whatever gay cliché shit they say."

Lu knocks my shoulder. "I can't believe you're so obsessed with Mr. Rags."

"I just love all of the sex shirts and raunchy stuff. There's nothing else like it."

"It's so fucked up how fucking quick the trends are going right now. Like, how will I ever be able to keep up and fight against it all?"

I wince. "It disturbs my soul that you can't go to this mall without seeing someone you know. It's horrific."

Lu points out a guy in a *Girls Gone Wild* shirt. "Fag!" A girl in an "Our Pussys, Our Choice" shirt: "Retard." A guy in an NC-17 shirt: "Fucked my friend." A girl in a Hole shirt: "Cokehead." A guy in a

Hercules Mega Mall Tour top: "Asked me to do heroin with him at a house party in '96." I get ready to get up and Lu grabs my shirt. "I dare you to look at a hot guy in this mall without thinking of him fucking a hot girl that you want to fuck."

I sit back down, lean over my chair, and look over at a guy in a backwards cap and a Hooters shirt. *He's decent, seems like a good-looking dude.* Splice. I think of him in my bedroom, on my bed, fucking a hot blonde hooker doggystyle, slapping cheeks, moaning, orgasming.

Lu grabs my shirt. "So? Did you?"

"Fuck! Fuck! Fuck!"

"Told you. Every guy who plays this game always loses."

"Why?"

Lu stubs out his cig. "Well, if I tell you to not think of a guy fucking a hot girl, you are going to want to do it, because you're telling your mind that you don't want to think about it."

"I did not sign up for this, Morpheus! Get me out!"

"Have you ever played the death stare game?"

I shake my head. "What's that?"

"It's this game I made up. You can play it in public anywhere. You find someone to stare down and—"

I cut him off. "But how do you win the game?"

"It's all about making them react, making them freak out. You want them to feel like a demon is sucking away their soul. I usually feel like I've won when someone tells me to fuck off."

I find someone sitting across from me, an Asian chick, maybe from our school, in a blue bandana triangle shirt with rhinestone letters spelling "Headless" glued to it. I look at the "DVD VIDEO" logo temp tat on her shoulders as she eats chow mein out of a Panda Express box. I look into her eyes.

She looks right at me. "Fuh off, you fuhka!"

Lu stands up. "What did you just say to my friend?"

"Piss off. You fuhkin cwazee."

Lu laughs. "Sorry, I speak English."

"Go to hell. Stop staring me."

"Oh, I just did before I got here. Satan's huge dick down my throat, his pubes in my fucking teeth. I finished him off."

"Fukh awf! Leave alone!"

Lu starts pushing the dELiA*'s store bag hanging on her chair. "You are ugly and Asian. You're never going to be a dELiA*s model, so give it up. Stop trying to look pretty and cool. You'll never be pretty and cool."

The girl's mouth drops as she puts her head into her sweater on the table. She tears up, dragging her fingers up and down her arms. I get up, pull Lu's shirt, and hold him back. "Stop. Just stop. Leave her alone."

☆ 44 ☆

Shane is downstairs grabbing a snack as Lu and I sit on his bed. Lu picks up Shane's fishbowl with a Betta fish and spits in it. "I want you to do something that'd be so Nine Inch Nails vibes. I'm talking like the 'Closer' video level of fucked. Some real ass industrial art."

"What are you fucking talking about?"

"Don't be a pussy. I dare you to put the fighting fish on your tongue." He leans over his bag and pulls out a Polaroid camera. He takes the flopping fish out of the bowl. "Stick your tongue out." I stick my tongue out. "Now take your shirt off. Come on, pretend this is your *Spin* cover shoot."

I'm shirtless. A demonic pulse takes me. There is freedom in listening to him instruct me. I put the fighting fish on my tongue, stick it out, and pose into the flash.

♡ L5 ♡

Aurora,

You're totally right. You aren't supposed to create the rapid montage in your head about an event until it ends, and from the looks of it, babe, you and I are still happening! Thank you for calming me down and for getting me outside of my head. This is what makes you so special to me!

I'm so frustrated. The year is almost over and all I can think about is how every moment living without you in this place is wasted—all of this unused time that could have been spent learning more about each other.

Can you imagine if we both had AOL? I would wait for hours just to see you online. I'd chat with you all night long. We should seriously kill our parents for not letting us have our own computers. IM'ing was made for lovers to feel each other faster and neither of us can. Futuristic torture.

I crave videotapes, photo albums, journal entries. I want to be consumed by everything about you. I want to flip through the magazines in your room, read your favorite books, watch all of your cherished movies. Anything to get closer to you.

Oh, and the notes I would hide in your bathroom cabinet when you're downstairs and I'm still in your bedroom, just waiting for you to come back so I can give you more kisses.

Why don't you ever call me? You never leave messages on my machine. I wrote my number beside my address on our last day.

Do you want to tease me? How long do I have to wait to hear your voice again outside of my daydreams?

How are you doing? Tell me everything. The stupid details of your day, the ones that you're convinced have no interest or meaning to anyone else. I want to know all of these things. I want to feel it all.

Yours truly,
Brad Sela

♡ L6 ♡

Baby boy,

First off, this letter is so, so sweet. I've been reading it every hour since its arrival. I can feel how much you miss me. I love how important it is for *you to learn new things about me. I often have the same frustrating thoughts about how time is moving at a new pace that I've never felt before every time I realize you're not here with me. Please! Keep expressing all of these feelings.*

You ask why I don't call. I've never told you about how controlling my dad is, and in the past few years, his obsession with security cameras and surveillance has heightened. There's always RadioShack bags around the house. He tracks my phone calls on the bill every month. He's made it clear, there's a "no boys allowed" policy. He'd be devastated if he ever found our letters. I could get in the worst trouble of my life. This is why I'm not allowed to have my own phone or computer.

I mean, I see him all the time. Let's just say that I'm used to being taped...monitored.

When my mom passed, he started a black market tape business out of our basement: Godhead Video. All different types of people, all kinds of ages, come and buy bootleg videos from him, stuff you can't buy at Blockbuster. He's very specific, organized, even. There's labels, catalogs. It's all coordinated but I'm not allowed down there. Some of the symbols I've seen on the front page of the Godhead Video catalog seriously look like they've been stolen from my nightmares. I don't know what he's selling.

My dad's rage is something I've never seen in anyone else, a quality I swear only exists inside of him. He's a total weirdo, too. There's a stash of expired Twin Peaks *log candy from 1991 in a bowl in his bedroom. Beats me.*

I don't even have a key to the basement. Sometimes I dream of having that space back to myself again. I have so many memories of me and my mom down there dancing.

Won't it be more special for you anyway when you get to hear my voice again in the flesh?

Your girl,
Aurora

☆ 45 ☆

Lu leans against the school gym door in ski pants, kicking the snow. Shane is making snowballs and singing a parody of "Hey Leonardo." "She likes me for my D." I sing back a stupid parody of "She's So High."

Lu hits me on the back with a rolled-up copy of *Entertainment Weekly*. "If Marilyn Manson could find a way out of his shit life in Ohio and used *The Satanic Bible* to manifest being one of the most famous people on the planet right now, then why can't I?"

"You aren't ever going to experience anything glamorous in this world unless you move to New York or Hollywood, mister delusional."

"Who says that I won't one day?" Lu flips through the mag. "You flip through an *Enter-taint-ment Weekly*, you see snaps of Tom Cruise and Nicole Kidman at a movie premiere, and then you realize, 'Oh look, Neve fucking Campbell is there too.' You feel this distant empty space between you and the pages. Life's not fair. What am I supposed to do when I encounter the void?"

"Sometimes I think the simple things about growing up here are better than being on the other side of the empty fantasies you're talking about."

Shane comes in. "I read in that issue MGM bought the rights to *The Munchies*, an upcoming horror movie about a bunch of anorexic models that eat their victims."

I laugh. "And people said that Kate Moss couldn't star in movies."

Lu stomps. "You guys! I feel like my time is running out. I turned on VH1 yesterday and one of the hosts was talking about how Bret Easton Ellis wrote *Less Than Zero* at seventeen. He skyrocketed to worldwide fame in the eighties by twenty-one."

"Since when are you a writer?"

"It's not about that. It's about the fame. I just have to discover my stratospheric talent. Maybe I'll make it big being a director? I've been thinking that I could be the next Gregg Araki."

"If that Rebecca Gayheart chick could go from Noxzema commercials to the big screen, I guess there's hope for all of us."

Shane beams. "Oh my God, dude. Talk about twelve-year-old lust."

"You guys aren't listening to me." Lu raises his voice and slaps my back. "You have to watch *Nowhere* or we can't be friends. The whole reason I killed off Luke and gave myself the name Lusif is because of Gregg's movies."

Shane chuckles. "You sure try *so* hard to produce your life to feel like a Gregg Araki movie."

The last lunch bell rings.

☆ 46 ☆

Mariah Carey's "All I Want for Christmas Is You" blares out of the mall speakers. Lu and I stand in line, waiting to get pictures with Santa. Lu is in black lipstick and eyeliner, wearing a black choker, fur coat, platform sneakers, and a Baphomet shirt. He holds a Manson lunchbox. A mom behind us covers her son's eyes. Lu rubs on my Santa Claus hat as I look around at the decorations: plastic reindeer, fences with blinking lights, a tree drowning in decorations. I look back at the "Santa's Entry" sign, then over at the "Welcome" script scrawled on the bricks.

A man dressed as an elf approaches. "It's your turn, boys!"

We go up and sit on Santa's lap. "Have you been good boys this year?" He holds both of us and we both answer in unison. "Santa, we've both been very, very good boys."

We make blank stares at the camera, the flash bursts, and we get up and walk out as an *NSYNC Christmas song starts. I look at a little boy in overalls holding a Game Boy, who reminds me of my childhood self. I think of how alone I felt waiting in the food court as a kid, and how peaceful this boy's mind must be. That euphoria of opening gifts on Christmas day as a little kid hits me. A group of moms in blazers walk ahead of us holding Victoria's Secret bags. *Will anything ever be that easy* *again? Will I ever be as free as a child? Was everything good about my childhood a total fucking lie?*

☆ 47 ☆

A soundtrack booklet flipped over on the table, a black and white photo of Patricia Arquette. The *Lost Highway* credits play on the TV as Lu passes me the Pizza Hut box. I take a slice and pass it to Shane, who grabs a Sharpie off the table and writes inside the box. Shane bites on the cap. Lu is wearing a *Lost Highway* shirt.

"Got Meta?"

Shane laughs. "Be like…Meta!"

I turn to Lu. "David Lynch is one of the worst directors alive. The movie had no plot, no story, and some weird dwarf…"

He cuts me off. "Our consciousness levels are too low to understand the high plane that David Lynch operates on. He's a movie god."

"Yeah, sure, bud. Well, next sleepover, I'm choosing what we rent."

"You aren't questioning the surfaces around you hard enough. Manson wouldn't have associated himself with this movie if it wasn't brilliant."

"You're such a hypocrite. You said that *American Beauty* is for 'stupid people who need to try to think of their wasteful suburban lives in a newer, deeper way.'"

"Why don't we watch an episode of *Twin Peaks*?"

Shane chimes in. "I hate *Twin Peaks*."

"Oh God, my dad loved that show when I was a kid."

Lu faces me with a snarl. "Your dad watched a show about dead little teenage girls and prostitutes? Your dad is a pervert."

I laugh. "Now you know where I get it from!"

I leap up from the couch and Lu grabs my arm. "Where are you going?"

"Oh, I'm sorry. So now I'm on prison watch?"

"If you were on prison watch, that ass would've been raped. Your hole would be bleeding 'cause of some six-foot-five Black brother."

"I'm going upstairs to grab a Coke. Do you have any other useless questions I can answer?"

I go up to the kitchen, grab a *Cruel Intentions* cup, and pour some Coke. I read the red text on the front: "What you can't have, you can't resist." I walk down the basement steps and Lu blocks the entrance, standing with his hands touching the walls.

"What's the password to the cellar?"

"Shut the fuck up and let me through."

"No!"

"I'm serious. I'm about to throw this Coke all over your face."

"Do you want to know what love smells like?"

"Tell me. I'm dying to know."

"The crawlspace, the cellar. Tell me, Brad, are you going to make it to the sequel?"

"I'm the final boy of the night. I can feel it."

"Tonight you'll be…terrorized…pursued…gutted…crossed… erased…totally toyed with…"

Lu lets me pass and I put my cup down on the table. I get on my knees and bend over to eject the VCR. Lu whistles. "Damn, boy! Look at that phat ass. That's a bubble butt!" He comes behind me and smacks it as I turn around. I give him a middle finger and put the tape on top of the VCR. Shane takes a mini jar, a syringe, and a paper cup out of his bag, and goes to the bathroom to fill up the cup with water. He comes back and hands the cup to Lu.

My jaw drops. "Is that… Is that fucking heroin?"

Lu looks at me as if I'm handicapped. "No, you absolute fucking retard. Heroin is a powder. This is a liquid."

Shane's eyes light up. "It's G. You never build a tolerance. It's liquid ecstasy. Well, that's what people are calling it right now. It's the drug of the millennium."

Lu puts the syringe into the jar, fills it up, and squirts it into the paper cup. "Wait. Andrew said two mL for the G, right?"

"Yeah, two mL is good."

"But what about fifteen mL?"

"You fucking idiot, fifteen mL is how Andrew V's fat friend got put in an ambulance. His heart stopped and he was in the hospital for three days."

"Oh, shit. But wasn't that because he's morbidly overweight? Wait. I want to snap pics before you do it."

Lu grabs a Kodak Max disposable from his bag. Shane holds up the G jar, pouting his lips, and the flash bursts. Lu winds the cam and I listen to it grind as I open the flap of the Pizza Hut box and see what Shane wrote inside: "B.L.S. H8 Dec 99" with alien heads, peace signs, and stick figures.

I close the box and turn to Lu. "How did you guys even get this stuff? Don't gay people buy video head cleaner from sex shops and snort this shit?"

Shane shakes his head. "I'm confused. Are poppers GHB?"

Lu shrugs. "Isn't RUSH poppers?"

"I don't fucking know what RUSH is!"

"Stop distracting us with butt sex talk. Shane, take the G."

Shane takes the shot and makes a grossed-out face. I ask him what it tastes like. "Like salt and soap. So fucking gross."

Lu turns to him. "You are going to start to get all unconscious soon."

"I just wanna forget where I am, forget who I am, forget this moment."

Lu grabs a *Rolling Stone* with Marilyn Manson on the cover, takes pills from his pocket, and crushes them with the bottom of his keys. He grabs a straw out of the empty Burger King cup on the table, cuts it with scissors, and does lines off of MM's face. He whips his head up. "Woohoo! Fuck yeah." He leans down and does another. "Oh, yeah!"

Shane is on the couch with his legs open, eyes rolling back, drooling. "I'm just, fuck-a, faza, fuchgh. I'm all fuggin drugginnn, fuggin flawhhhzeeeedahhhhh. Woo!"

Lu faces me. "Brad."

"Yeah?"

"You're going to help us make a home movie tonight."

"What are you talking about?"

"I need you to get your demons working."

"*Huh?*"

"See my video camera over there?" Lu rummages through his *101 Dalmations* bag, talking to himself. "Knife. MA CD in the boombox. Sugar packet, Shane on G. We're ready to shoot." He passes me an AV cable. "Put these into the yellow and white inputs on the TV and then turn on the camera."

I insert the cords and turn on the camera. The video feed starts up with Lu on the screen. Shane brings a straw chair over as I tape Lu sitting on the floor with his bag.

"Wait, look!" Lu holds up a pink candy cane. "Can you guys see this? I love this flavor." He chews, opens his mouth wide, and reveals the shards on his tongue. "Yummy!"

I turn to Lu. "Are you going to say something to the camera about the movie we're about to make?"

"Ever since I got my own video camera, I don't want to live off-camera. This is all I want to do."

I fake cough. "Attention whore."

Lu fake coughs back. "Dicksucker. Get your Kurt Loder voice going. You have the backstage all-access VIP pass to the hardest-to-get-into gore slumber party on the block. Cameras were never permitted… until now."

I start. "Hello all, Carson Daly from *TRL* here. We're in the studio with Occult Starz, who will be opening up for Marilyn Manson at Madison Square Garden tonight. Lusif, we have a fan question for you via email: Jason, fifteen, from Nevada, asks, 'Can you tell us something controversial that you did during your freshman year?'"

"The week I found out Twiggy Ramirez brought a naked twelve-year-old boy on stage, I sent him nudie Polaroids of my underage schlong."

"Do you have any advice for the teenage boys at home?"

"Boys, if it doesn't scare you and make your dick hard at the same time, don't do it."

Shane is on the couch with his legs open, eyes rolling back, pushing his cheeks in with his thumbs. Lusif leans over him, unzips Shane's jeans, and begins to pull them down.

Shane screams. "No! Don't!"

Lu laughs. "You're wearing Fruit of the Loom tighty-whities from the pack I boned from Walgreens, right?"

"Yeah, I remembered. Jesus."

"Well, take your jeans off then."

"I don't want you guys to see me change. Sorry!" Shane ducks behind the couch and takes off his jeans before returning. Lu rubs Shane's bare thighs. "Ewie! Don't touch me, fag."

"Ice out. Why would that make you uncomfortable if you weren't a fag?"

"Can I have more G before we shoot? Pwease!"

I turn to Shane as he whines. "No."

"We should have gotten you the Buzz Lightyear kids undies. That would have been sexy."

"The American Family Association was saying that the current pop culture of 1999 is a 'disturbing mix of childhood innocence and adult sexuality.'"

"I was thinking more Wes Craven presents *Kiddie Porn Vampires* in suburban basements."

I smile at Lu. "So what do I need to know about your vision, mister director?"

"Pretend you're a pedophile billionaire on a private island and you bought us for your entertainment. I want to do a whole black-market-illegal-human-trafficking-kidnapped aesthetic."

"Like we're making a music video at Neverland Ranch."

Shane cuts in. "Pretend you're part of some secret sex society in Hollywood and a huge movie star like Kevin Spacey is here, watching us."

"This is like going on the internet and seeing something you didn't plan to see, but you clicked on it anyway, and now it's going to haunt you forever. I want to harm and scar your mind."

I nod. "I feel nothing. Good luck trying to change that with your movie."

"We told you you'd find out who you really are if you came to our slumber party."

"I don't remember that on the invite." I hold the cam and look back at the TV.

Shane walks over to Lu, who is sitting on the straw chair with a knife. Lu lifts off Shane's shirt and I tape it on the floor. Lu says, "Twist the screen. I want to look at myself." I flip it for him. "I am so fuckiiiiiing good looking."

I turn the lights off and turn on the camera's video light. "Okay, that looks fucking insane. Stay like that."

I twist the screen back and hit record. "Action!"

Lu looks into the camera. "Welcome to my private party."

Shane crawls to Lu on his knees, and Lu lifts his chin. "Tell me how much of an embarrassment you are for wanting to be my twelve-year-old boy slave."

"I'm so humiliated, sir. I'm so ashamed of handing all of my power over to you, sir."

Lu breaks character, then nods. "Okay, that was good. Now say something more fucked up, like your parents wouldn't ever buy you something, so you had to come see me for it. Sound super fake in your voice."

"'My parents wouldn't ever buy me the Oreo O's cereal that you have at your house, master.' Like that?"

"Yes! Back on."

I hit record and Lu slaps Shane in the face. "I own you for the next hour."

"Master would like to watch me sin?"

"Sin is in!"

"Sin is in, master. You are so powerful."

"Well, little boy, what's the point of having power if you don't abuse it? Okay, Brad, zoom out and film Shane's face."

I stand over them, zoom out, and film. Lu continues. "I'm going to get angry with you, boy! Are you not having a good time at our playdate?"

"Throw me on the ground, babysitter. Get blood all over my face. Fucking knock me out. Please. I need it."

"Okay, Brad, quick, hurry! Go over to the boombox, put on track two, and blast it."

Shane screams. "Let the blood bender begin!"

I go over to the boombox, hit the track, and crank the volume. "The Dope Show" screams from the speakers. I point the camera as Lu slaps Shane hard in the face.

"Harder!" Lu slaps Shane in the face again. "Fucking harder!" Shane starts blowing into Lu's belly button. Lu puts his fingers into Shane's mouth as Shane bites down.

Lu turns to me. "Get him biting my nipple ring." Shane bites on Lu's nipple ring and pulls it with his teeth. Lu, moaning, holds the back of Shane's head and pushes him down as he spits on his stomach and rubs on it. Shane moves out of the shot and I shoot Lu's eyes rolling back. Shane grabs the knife and a sugar packet off the table and comes back into the frame. Lu's arm is turned over, facing the camera.

Shane carves an S into Lu's arm as he screams, "Hail Satan!" Blood pulses out and moves along his skin. "Fuck yeah."

These attempts, you are going to make, when you get older, to numb, to hypnotize yourself. Shane carves an A. *Ever sit around, to wonder, about all the things that have gone on here that we will never be able to see?* Shane carves a T. *You get off on it. No one knows you are here. Sometimes it's like it has to happen first, before I get to experience it.* Shane carves an A. *You don't really want to know that you made that tape, do you?* The knife carves an N. *To nummmb, to hyp-hyp-notize these attempts you, when, you...are, when you...to numb, to hypnotize yourself.*

The camera scans the carved "SATAN," bleeding fast. Blood drips on the concrete. Shane smiles wide into the camera before dabbing blood from Lu's arm all over his face, streaking it down his cheeks with his fingers. Shane opens the sugar packet and pours it onto his arm and rubs it into the blood. He licks the blood and sugar and gurgles it in his mouth before spitting it out onto his arm.

"We love fear! We hate love!" they scream in unison.

Lu points. "Get a shot of him spitting the blood on my chest. You love this blood feast."

"One hundred percent maximum pleasure. Give it to me."

I pan the camera to Shane spitting blood onto Lu's stomach. Lu yells at me. "Brad, there's only twenty seconds left in the song."

"What's something we can do?"

"Shane, bite my ear! Quick, Brad. Film it like the 'Criminal' video. Bodies only, no faces."

Shane bites Lu's ear and pulls it with his teeth. "The Dope Show" ends.

Lu smiles. "Ladies and gentlemen, that's a wrap! Holy shit. My heart is beating so fucking fast right now! I was so into character."

"Ew! There's so much blood. It's all down my throat. This is so fucked." Shane gets up from his knees and runs to the bathroom. I hear him throwing up.

I look over at Lu. "SATAN" is still bleeding on his arm. "Can you grab me that bag? There's a mini towel and some band-aids."

I throw the bag to Lu. He dabs the towel on the cuts and bandages himself up. He stares at the *Rolling Stone* and winks at me. I bring it over to him with a straw and the pill bag.

"I don't even want to wait to make a line. I'm just snorting." He crushes the pills and snorts. "How was your time in the underage sex chamber?"

I laugh. "You could say it was chopped."

Lu fist-pumps. "Suck on that, Rod Ferrell! Did we shock you? You're super traumatized now, right?"

"I mean, Drew Barrymore hanging with her guts bursting in the opening sequence of *Scream* did nothing to me. I was like, whatever, next. Your sick flick didn't shock me."

"Tonight was tame. At the MM concert, there was a guy who cut a shock bolt on his arm in the crowd and everyone started licking it."

"Cool."

Lu shrugs. "Are you mad?"

"Feelings are for losers."

"You can't handle all of my god-of-fuck dark power. This isn't on a bootleg black market catalog, not even alt.snuff. You could never get this shit by mail order."

"I don't know what a newer low for my life could be after this."

"You could start watching *7th Heaven?*"

"Low, but not that low."

"Someone who sees this is going to feel how I felt when I saw the Nine Inch Nails *Broken* tape."

"Watching is not going to feel as filthy as making it did. What are you planning to do with the footage?"

"I might make copies and hide them in people's bushes. Or leave them on their doorsteps. We could put them in McDonald's or around the mall, or in the school bathrooms."

"But your faces are in it."

"Shane doesn't give a shit about his life. Why would someone who did put himself in a clip like this in the first place, you know?"

Shane comes up behind me, the blood washed from his face. I turn to him. "What are you going to say if your mom finds those towels?"

"That I tried to dye my hair red using Kool-Aid because they were sold out of Manic Panic."

"What did his blood taste like?"

"Metal. Hardcore metal. Like licking a metal pole."

"What was going through your mind while you were licking all the blood and stuff?"

"A Mariah Carey song."

"Huh?"

"Yeah. 'Bliss,' off her new album. It's so sedative."

"You can't get AIDS from licking someone's blood, right?"

"You think that we're bug chasers? What do you think this is, a gift-giver faggot convention?"

Lu laughs. "Well, if you were going to catch HIV, I'd want you to do it in the house!"

I put my arm around Shane's shoulders. "You did such a good job, Shane. Like you full-on changed into a little kid."

"Eat your heart out, Hollywood."

I tense up. "You guys, I feel like the tape would be more special if only we knew it existed."

Lu sighs. "Does anything even happen these days if you don't tape it and share it with your friends?"

Shane smiles. "Maybe nothing is real unless it's captured on camera."

"Be honest, Brad. What did tonight feel like for you?"

"The only real way I could describe it is that it felt like remembering images destroyed on videotapes that I can never see again."

I walk upstairs to Shane's bathroom as Lu and Shane follow behind. I brush my teeth, watching my reflection in the medicine cabinet mirror. I go into Shane's room. Lu and Shane are passed out, spooning in their underwear. I take off my jeans and shirt and get on my knees beneath the windowsill. I look out through the blinds to the streetlights lighting up the cul-de-sac. The trees beyond the houses shake in the wind.

I grab a pen off Shane's desk and write on my hand: "Sometimes all you can do is forget. We are beasts."

☆ 48 ☆

I finish *Tony Hawk* with a 50/50 grind and turn off the PlayStation. I look at my desk: a Hershey's bar, my Timex wristwatch, the Blockbuster holiday newspaper flier, gift bags, my Game Boy Color, a Rochas Man cologne box, and Christmas cracker wrappers. I sit on my bed and start a three-way call with Lu and Shane.

"How's your Christmas going, queers?"

Shane says, "I'm in bed watching a movie about a dog that thinks he's a reindeer, so that's where I'm at in my life. This is my lowest low, and I'm proud to be here, alive in the year 1999."

"For fuck's sake, man."

"What did you guys get?"

Lu answers, "I didn't get a call from my dad."

Shane follows. "I didn't get a call from my dad either."

"Oh."

"Yeah."

I reply, "Are you pissed?"

Shane's voice rises. "I don't get pissed at people who only know how to disappoint me."

"Same."

"But did you get any gifts?"

Lu answers, "My mom offered to pay for me to go to a mental health treatment center, but I told her to fuck off. I kicked the door, and have been chilling on IRC ever since."

"Gross. Justin Fagerlake just came on my TV."

"Shane, what did you get?"

"Books and shit. Computer games. I don't care about this day at all."

"True."

Lu laughs. "Did you get a computer so you can finally beat your meat to internet porn?"

"I didn't. I got *Tony Hawk* and some blink-182 stuff. I'm playing right now. It's fun. The soundtrack is dope. My dad said the guy at GameStop told him the PlayStation 2 is coming out next year, and that you'll be able to play DVDs on it. Do you guys know anything about it?"

"I don't even play my Game Boy anymore. I'm so bored of it. Now that I have a computer in my room, I just don't give a shit."

"They're so childish and retarded now. I feel like now that I'm actually doing more shit and hanging with new people, I just don't give a fuck."

"Yeah."

I sigh. "The snow is so loud right now."

"I know. It's fucked."

"Do you guys wanna go sledding or, like, push ourselves down some hills tomorrow?" I ask.

"Uhhh, no?"

"Whatever. Sue me for trying to have some fun during the holidaze."

Lu scoffs. "I want to be in some den smoking crystal meth in a Santa hat and blasting Nine Inch Nails. I don't want to be part of society."

"Oh! My mom's calling me. She needs help cleaning up the wrapping paper." I hang up.

☆ 49 ☆

Tori Spelling's face looks like a genetic mistake in this made-for-TV movie from the early nineties. I'm about to change the channel when the doorbell rings.

I open the door to Shane in a Crash Bandicoot hoodie, holding a Virgin Megastore bag.

"What are you doing here? Are you here to sell me a Dianetics book?"

He dangles a TDK VHS tape. "I bought these *Spawn* bootlegs off this goth guy last night after that poetry slam at Starlight."

"You know I've had trust issues with adult cartoons ever since MTV canceled *Downtown*."

"Well, are you going to invite me inside or what?"

"Uh, no. I'm not comfortable that you're at my house right now."

"What the fuck is that supposed to mean?"

"I don't want my parents to know that I know you. You're fucking lucky they aren't home right now because if you showed up unannounced while they were here, I would've completely pretended that I didn't know you."

Shane's face shivers. He bites his lip. "So, your other friends, Eric and Kev, they can come over, but Lu and I can't? How can you hide me and split? What kind of person are you?"

138

"I've known Eric and Kev since I was in the second grade."

"You're ashamed of me."

"No."

He holds his throat. "You don't know how bad this hurts, to know that someone feels so much disgust about being seen with me that they won't even let me into their house. I just wanted to watch cartoons with you."

"You aren't even letting me explain myself. You're jumping to these conclusions in your head."

"You don't even feel bad about it! You're standing there with no reaction, all calm and cool. You treat us like we have the key to some twisted, dark secret world, like that's our only value to you. You're a straight-up user. We aren't your friends to be a part of your private life. We want to be a part of your real life."

"You aren't even willing to listen to my reasoning. I'm trying to protect this. You don't get it."

"Why should I believe anything that you say? Why are you being so fake?" He takes a thumbtack out of his jacket and pricks his finger. Blood drips out. "This is what rejection feels like."

"Stop!" I face-palm. "You don't have to hurt yourself! Stop!" He pricks another finger. "Why are you fucking doing this? Oh my God. This is not what being a teenager is supposed to feel like."

"Oh, I'm sorry. Do you want to go jump the fence and break into your neighbor's pool? This isn't a Smashing Pumpkins music video, Brad Sela. This is real life."

"Like you know anything about real life, you fuck up. At least I'll never be as fucked up as you!"

Shane shakes his head. "Oh, you'll be the only one who fucks yourself up way before anyone else gets the chance to. I can promise you that." He rubs his teary eyes with the back of his hand.

"You're a man with a dick. You aren't on the Lilith Fair lineup. Stop this shit. I've never met a guy who acts like this. Stop making me feel like I'm a bad person! I'm not!"

"You need to realize that the truest parts of you don't disappear just because you try so hard to convince yourself that they don't exist."

He dabs the blood from his finger, puts it on his tongue, licks it, and runs off.

What have I done?

☆ 50 ☆

A poster with Japanese symbols is on the wall. I study it and try to imagine what it means—*All celebrities were once human? Pain is life's limbs? Once a god, always a god?* I think of how big the rack on this Asian waitress is. I don't have yellow fever, but there's something about the chopsticks in her hair paired with those jugs. A soundbite in my mind of Adam Carolla talking about how big Minka's tits are—"number one big boob Asian queen." I zone out and wait for the waitress to come back so I can stare at her rack again.

My dad looks over the menu as he decides on an entrée. I admire the way he drinks his Asahi. The shine when I'm around him almost gives me this kind of rush that shoots through my body. It's love. I twirl my chopstick in the miso soup and watch as the water drops from our cups collect on the table.

"Dad, I don't know how to do the whole being-seventeen thing right. There's all of this pressure in the media with all of these portrayals of what it's like to be a teenager today. I don't frickin' know what to do. I only know how to be myself, and for some reason, that doesn't seem like enough. It just doesn't cut it."

"But that's you. *You* are saying that you're not enough. Stop saying that. Women don't find that attractive."

"To me, being young is like being handed this weapon, and I have absolutely no idea what to do with it or how to operate it."

"That's the point."

"I'm not saying I'm not enough. I'm confident. It's just that having youth, and knowing that I have it right now, is almost too much to handle."

"You were always so concerned about people as a child. You were this little boy who just cared so much about what was going on around him."

"Oh God, don't tell me that. I don't want to know that."

"I remember we were walking downtown and you pointed out this young homeless boy who was shivering on the streets. You kept nagging me all day asking, 'Is he okay? Is he okay, Daddy? How can we help him?'"

"Yikes."

"You were always putting everyone before yourself."

"I just have this need to be seen as good. I want you and Mom to be proud of me. I don't want to make a mistake and not be the son you want, ever."

"That's one of your best traits."

"I feel ashamed when I do something I shouldn't. Do you think the past can define us forever?"

"People say you can't change the past, but that's not true. You can become the evolved person you should've been in the moments you regret."

"So, just become the person you wish you were back then?"

"Sounds like it. Look, I'm just happy you don't act like the kids in PBS documentaries. You're not like one of those *Rockdale County* kids."

"I'll never be white trash."

"It's nerve-racking as a parent. There's always stuff in the news, all this fear in *Newsweek*, all the goddamn headlines: 'Is your teen boy doing drugs?' 'Is your teen boy in crisis?' 'Is your teen boy abusing ADHD medication?' And all these things about binge drinking games, now screenagers."

"Oh, that's what they are calling us now? Last week we were school shooters, this week we're screenagers. Great."

"Your mother and I still don't want you to have your own computer in your bedroom. This is better for you."

"I've never even done drugs."

"Your mother and I call those boys who stay up all night playing disturbing video games 'dead eyes.'"

"You don't need to worry about me. I don't even have one friend who listens to Marilyn Manson."

"Marilyn Manson is one of the sickest bands ever promoted by a mainstream company. These are freaks who smoke human bones and burn the pockets of mentally unwell teenagers. You know—"

"Dad, I know you don't want to hear this from me, but I do feel like I'm alone in my own world."

"That's what being young is, son."

"Is it, though?"

"Everyone is in their own world. The biggest challenge you'll ever have is bringing someone into it."

"You're right. Maybe there is no right or wrong way to experience the world around you, but there is something that really does bother me about life. Why is it that the things that feel so good disappear quickly? It's like I'm trying to make the nice feelings stay with me, but they slip so—"

"Brad, I learned the hard way that life is a never-ending hunt for substitutes of the things that once made us happy."

♡ L7 ♡

Aurora!

I'm sure your dad is selling concerts, rare TV specials, the type of stuff my friends buy online. Nothing for you to worry about or anything that's worth digging into. Lots of people run video rings out of their basements. I mean, the corporate selections from Blockbuster and Hollywood Video can get a little tiresome. We need businessmen like your dad to shake things up with less commercial content. Yeah, it sure sucks that he's such a dick, but a man being protective of his daughter is nothing new. At least I don't have to feel my voice shake as I call your line and ask: "Can I talk to Aurora?" So yeah, I can wait to hear your voice when we meet up again.

I have this one friend, Lu, who is obsessed with taping everything. Little does this guy know that it's impossible to share a real intimate moment in front of battery-charged, soul-sucking video cameras. It was nice at camp. All of my favorite moments with you weren't recorded. He and I are like cavities in the teeth of this place.

It's the holidaze and I'm depressed. This time of the year always sucks for me. I mean, I've never had an Xmas where I haven't gotten whatever I wanted. It fills me with dread and shame, getting everything I want all the time. I mean, I know I'm not getting a computer or a car, which is just so ridiculous and absurd, if you want to talk about controlling parents. Ha-ha!

I feel like maybe I lack purpose, meaning, direction. Sorry for the sad thoughts.

You should be sitting on my front doorstep with me right now, smoking, talking about nothing. You should see my neighborhood at midnight. When you visit, I want you to wear one of my t-shirts to bed. That'd be so hot.

Hey… isn't it crazy how when you meet someone new, you can't help but wonder about all the moments you missed out on when you weren't in their life? You try to make up who you think they were before you met them? All the memories you didn't get a chance to create? Please tell me that you know this feeling!

Merry Xmas, I guess.

Yours truly,
Brad Sela

P.S. Do you like the amethyst necklace? I saw it in one of my mom's new age catalogs. It's the Pisces stone. Anything for you.

♡ L8 ♡

Oh, Brad!

I do know this feeling! Sometimes when I can't sleep after the lights go out and I'm staring at my wall, I imagine all the days I never got to spend with you 'cause you weren't in my life yet. I'm wearing your necklace as I write—it's so beautiful and thoughtful of you. Maybe you're right about my dad. Maybe you aren't. It's a hopeless situation with him.

I don't want to upset you, Brad, but just to give you some perspective outside of your own sadness… lots of people would love to have a family to spend the holiday season with. I get that you feel upset right now, but this time of year I really really miss my mom. When I see all of the moms outside with their kids, I feel the little girl inside of me aching for her. I still shadow-dance in front of my wall by my nightlight. Sometimes I wish I could time travel back to my childhood and be the angel I needed.

Mom's music box has been spinning a lot this week. I do this thing where I lay in her walk-in closet and smell her old clothes. I dance to her favorite Kate Bush tape as I put her dresses over my face. My mom used to say that there's a place that exists inside of everyone's heart where "you can feel yourself missing people you'll never meet." Do you know this space? I have her words written on my arms right now: "the moon is your mirror— you wane and you wax as you wait for yourself to come back."

I remember hearing about guardian angels on The Montel Williams Show, *how spirits communicate with us through repeating numbers that we see throughout our day. An hour doesn't go by without me seeing the number twenty-two.*

Some beautiful flashbacks I have about her: the sound of her shower coming through the window when I'd sit in the backyard in the morning, our water hose in hanging flowers, the safety of just knowing that she was down the hall from my bedroom. Bone broth steaming in the kitchen! The short drive to the liquor store to stock the house for her dinner parties—God, everyone loved her.

It's never not hard to think about the reality that I won't be able to create new memories with my mother. You don't want to have to wait for tragedy or celebration to bring people together—you should search for love in the room everywhere you go. I hope that's what you can learn from my loss. Feel all the love!

Mom always told me a secret: "angels are fueled by people dancing." Maybe you and I will be gifted something divine when we reunite and spin around on the grass.

Right now, I wish that you could take my hand…and, you know, at this time of the night, I'm on the floor dancing to Kate again.

Your girl,
Aurora

P.S. My mother taught me that "all the best dreams are slow." Go to sleep and share a slow dream with me. We are in sync.

☆ 51 ☆

I grab a bottle of 99 cent store silver glitter hair spray and spray it all over my head. I stare into the mirror.

"Y2K bitches. Let's fucking go!" I kiss my reflection. "I would bone the fuck out of me right now."

I turn on my TV, flip to the news, and a blonde woman with a dyke haircut says, "This Y2K bug, as we have been reporting, is a line of computer code unable to recognize dates beyond 1999. Is it a reason to panic?"

I turn her off and replay the answering machine message from Lu. "Cancel your plans! The world ends at midnight. We're going to an end-of-the-world Y2K rager and, fuck, this seems like this is it. I've been waiting my whole fucking life for something to happen, and this historic event will reveal to everyone the power of doom. I'll pick you up around eight, baby."

I peek out my window to see if Lu has pulled up before putting on my leather trench coat, black Levi's, and Docs. There's honking from the street, headlights on the driveway.

I run out the front door, lock it, and put my keys under the mat. Lu, smoking, rolls down the window. "Oh my fucking God! Where did you get your trench coat? Get in, you sexy beast."

We back out and speed off.

"I went to Goodwill like you told me."

"Who is this man? Look at this sexy guy!"

"Awww, our little blink-182 fanboy is all grown up," Shane adds.

"I look like a computer hacker in a horror movie. Isn't this the apocalypse dress code for the night?"

Lu laughs. "People are either going to think you're Neo from *The Matrix* or you're trying to look like a member of the Trenchcoat Mafia."

"Everyone better associate this look with danger. Do you think I'm going to get a lot of attention?"

"Definitely. I'm proud of you. This is a good marketing move! Big publicity. You're thinking like a mogul, n****."

"Sometimes you gotta make the big boy moves to get all eyes on you."

Lu smiles. "Bitches love fun and danger."

Shane puts down the Silly Putty he's been playing with, grabs a plastic liquor store bag from under the seat, and holds up a bottle. "Look what we got!"

"What is it?"

"Aftershock. Rum. Coke."

"Did you get me a bottle of Captain like I wanted?"

"We got you the Captain." He holds out the bottle.

"I'm so pumped to get wasted."

"I love that we're going to an actual apocalypse party, just like in *Nowhere*. We're the generation that will get to see the end of everything. I'm so ready!"

"I hope by midnight, the faucets in my house will spout some anime water, toxic purple slime from another dimension," Shane says.

"How do you guys know about this party?"

"This goth girl, PiracyPrincess, posted the invite on the internet. Her parents are in Palm Springs, so we can fuck up the entire place, do whatever we want."

Shane looks over to Lu. "Is there really going to be a transsexual DJ?"

"According to her... plus fucked up lights, and all the drugs you can think of. It's going to be fun as fuck."

Shane passes me the flier, and I smile at the weird graphics. "How will we get home?" I ask.

"You'll just have to walk like the rest of us."

"We can't cab?"

"Cabs will be so fucking busy tonight. It's New Year's, retard."

Shane turns the radio on and LFO's "Girl on TV" plays. Out the window, the rows of houses, trees, and streetlights blur. I stick my tongue out and lick the wind.

"Ew, turn this off!"

"Fuck LFO. This is a reminder of why this useless fucking decade needs to end right now."

Shane spoofs the lyrics. "Shoo-dee-hop and Scooby Snacks, I like to do drugs and cut myself to relax!"

I laugh. "I bet at sleepovers the guys in LFO stick Scooby Snacks up their buttholes while their managers rape them."

Lu hits the steering wheel. "I hope there's heroin there. That would be so chopped if I could shoot up for the first time tonight."

Shane responds, "We are in the Pacific Northwest in the nineties. Of course you're going to find heroin."

"Change the station. I can't listen to this gay shit anymore."

"I would rather drink bleach and die than listen to this."

"See if I have the *Nowhere* soundtrack in the console."

I lean over, open it, and look through: a Tool CD, Autechre, the *Natural Born Killers* soundtrack. "Not here."

"Fuck! It's in my Discman. I always forget to bring it in the fucking car before I leave the house. God, I'm so fucking dumb."

"We're almost there. Chill."

I close my eyes and try to imagine who I could be at this party, what could happen, who I will become. I see flashes of ABC's coverage of Times Square, people screaming into the camera with "rock on" hands, and I think of recording blink on MTV's *New Year's Eve Live*. *Did I remember to set my VCR? I should have double-checked that.* I fantasize about walking into a private club with Leo DiCaprio, a bouncer lifting a velvet rope. "Leo's Pussy Posse gets in first." Gwyneth Paltrow, movie stars, paparazzi outside, flashes bursting.

Lu's voice snaps me out of it. "We're here!"

Lu finds a spot in the long row of cars along the street. I step out and take in the huge brick house, the massive lawn, and the driveway crowded with people. Techno rumbles from the house. A brunette in a white miniskirt and a shiny, gold bikini top crouches down with a huge lollipop, mimics slutty Lil' Kim poses, and throws gang signs against the garage. A guy in a Nike visor grabs the hips of a girl in a velvet checkered skirt and tied-up white button down. A guy lies on the grass as someone in an "orgasm donor" shirt spits into his mouth. A girl in gold glitter makeup covers her face while talking to a guy in a Hilfiger polo wearing "2000" party glasses. Above the enormous porch, a banner says, "WELCOME TO THE END OF THE WORLD. ~*LET'S GET... Y2Kinky~*."

I walk through the open door. The house is crowded, laser lights and smoke hover above everyone's heads. Everyone is shouting. The bass from this trance remix of Janet Jackson's "Together Again" vibrates through my body. I look behind for Lu and Shane but can't find them in the crowd. I don't recognize anybody. A dizziness hits. I hold onto the wall and look for a bathroom to lock myself into for a few minutes to chill the fuck out. I push through the crowd and check the doorknobs of the two bathrooms downstairs, both locked. I move upstairs, passing a bookcase in the hallway, and watch a guy with Bulbasaur on the back of his tank top fuck a girl against the wall. The girl is grabbing and pulling on his glitter weed chain, his hands up her shirt. He smiles at me as he grabs her tits, "rage" in white letters on his trucker hat. I turn the knob to the bathroom and walk in. A guy with bleach blonde hair and black roots, an orange puffy coat, khaki pants, a D.A.R.E. shirt, and a halo made of plastic bag handles

148

on his head leans against the wall, smoking a cigarette and videotaping himself. He pulls his eyelids down, jaw jumping, a smiley face plastic backpack at his feet.

I open the door. "Sorry!"

"No, stay. Why are you sorry?"

"I didn't want to interrupt you videotaping yourself. Seems like serious business."

He puts the camera on the floor. "Why are you saying sorry? Tell me, why do you keep apologizing?"

"I don't know. I don't know where my friends are."

"How old are you?"

"Um, seventeen. How old are you?"

"Twenty-one. So, you like *The Matrix*?"

"No."

"But your outfit."

"I just wanted to look cool. I don't actually give a shit."

"Do you think that we're living in a simulation?"

"What? You can't be serious."

"So, you agree?"

"Huh?"

"Are you friends with Jolly Rancher?"

"What?"

"It's Jolly Rancher's party. We're here right now."

"I thought this was a goth party hosted by some super rich girl, PiracyPrincess."

"No, we're at Jolly Rancher's party."

"Uh, okay? Cool."

"Do you think your reality is a projection of your consciousness?"

"Are you one of those enlightened cyber-occult fuckos? Keep your bullshit in the new age section with the rest of the Oprah moms at Borders where it belongs."

"Listen... Think of this mirror in this bathroom. We can look into it and think we see reality, but it's a warped view, a warped reality. Think of how many warped views we have of reality when we reflect on our experiences."

"Look, dude, if I wanted to listen to strung-out raver bullshit, I'd be at home watching *True Life*. I came here to have fun."

"But what if fun is just a construct, an illusory destination that can't be reached?"

"Are you tripping? What kind of magic mushrooms did you eat?"

He takes a pill out of his bag and holds it in his fingers. "Mitsubishi X."

"Good for you."

"Do you roll?"

"No."

"What kind of drugs do you do if you are here and you don't roll?"

"Meth."

"Are you serious? Do you want dexys? I can get my buddy to drop some off. We just need to walk up to the village and get to a payphone, 'cause there's no way that we'll be able to make a call here. I forgot my pager."

"I don't want to do drugs. I'm gonna go look for my friends."

He pulls out his arm and shows me his track marks. He starts kissing up and down his skin. "This is what true love does to you."

I'm about to walk out when he stands against the door. "You aren't going anywhere, little boy."

"What?"

"We could just stay here, bring the party inside."

"Can you stop being weird?"

He covers my mouth. I scream and spit into his hand. He unzips his jeans and grabs my hand, puts it on his crotch. "Haha! I'm just fucking with you, rock star."

I push his chest. "You're one fucking freakshow. I should stab you in the fucking throat or choke you with that plastic 2Pac band that's tied to your skull."

"You have to recognize the laws of the universe. You have to sexualize chaos, sexualize destruction, become one with it. Just fucking do it. You have to bring order to chaos."

"What other drugs do you have?"

"Why are you so against trying X?"

"On MTV, they said it'll burn holes in your brain."

"If you believe what you see on MTV, you could use some holes in your brain."

He holds up a mini plastic bag with cartoon hearts printed on it. It's filled with a small pile of white powder. He puts it on the counter and gets on his knees, takes out a card, makes a mini alpine of coke, cuts the lines, and rolls up a dollar bill. He tilts his head back. "Oh, fuck me. Fuck yeah, baby." I watch him sniff another line and fantasize about what it'd be like to be somewhere glamorous, like the 1998 VMAs, in a private room sitting on a Versace blow-up couch with movie stars, rock stars, and models doing drugs. I start to see the tagline from Go spinning like a computer text graphic in my head, over and over again: *Life begins at 3 AM.*

I slap his back. "I want to try it."

"It's coke."

"Okay. Like, what do I do? Don't you have to hold one side of your nose? I swear Uma Thurman holds one side of her nose when she does coke in *Pulp Fiction.*"

"Buckle up."

"Can you eat it?"

"No, you sniff it."

"Okay. So do I just roll up the bill? Is it going to make my nose bleed?"

"You need to make a promise to me."

"What?"

"You have to submit and totally forget any relationship you have with a higher power before we do this."

"Oh, trust me, I will never believe in the immaterial."

I push the bill into my right nostril. I sniff a line and my nostrils burn: a jolt, a zing, a hit, and a rush all at once—a hot blonde with the best rack at the school dance coming up to me and telling me she wants to grind; a PlayStation level-up notification; a new blink-182 sticker appearing in their online store; someone I met at Tower Records leaving a message saying they want to hang. I do another, and the feeling loops. I wave "come here" to the boy and we drop to our knees, taking turns doing lines. I look up at my reflection and think about myself posing during a photoshoot. I notice his chain link choker and want to rub my fingers on it. I almost touch it, but I don't, because now I think of myself being eight feet tall inside of a video game with no human flesh: holographic, a god.

He knocks on my forehead as I turn around. He's taping me. I look into the lens. "Do not tape me. Get the camera out of my face!"

"You don't want Mom and Dad to see their little boy?"

"Shut the fuck up, dude. I'm going to break that video camera, I swear to God."

"You need to do enough to make it to the countdown."

"Fuck off!"

"Make a tongue in a V for the camera."

"No!"

"Just do it. Move your tongue in a V. It'd look bling."

He's twisting the screen. "You have to look at yourself while doing drugs. That's the only way to do them. You'll want to see this tomorrow. It's so much fun to sit in bed and watch tapes of yourself fucked up on drugs."

"I don't want evidence this ever happened."

"You don't even want to know my name?"

"No, and I don't want you to know my name!"

"True party friends never reveal their names to each other." He makes a pile of coke. "Look at the little glacier."

He keeps trying to film me. "I said I don't want this on tape."

He powders some coke under his nose. "Got Milk? Let me get a close-up."

I swat away the camera. "Stop taping me!"

"Dude, chill! I'm fucking kidding around." He does more blow. "Am I high yet? Stop laughing! Fuck Tony Montana. This is how you do blow. Am I high yet?"

"Whatever." I do another line.

He puts the camera down, takes the headband halo off his head, and puts it on mine. "This is an initiation. Bring order to chaos."

"Wait! What did you just say?"

"Bring order to chaos?"

"Stop saying that. You're freaking me out."

He opens a stick of Juicy Fruit and puts it in his mouth. The silver wrapper is blinding. He's clenching his jaw. Thump, bounce, thump, bounce. He jogs his knees up and down, slobbering. Now he's humping the air, biting his lips and rubbing his fingers on his face. He's fucking the wall: "Fuckah! Thumpah! Oh, fuck. Fuckah! Fuckah. Fuckah Thumpa. Fuckah." The porn moaning continues as he slobbers his tongue in the mirror. I look at the empty plastic anime heart drug bag. A commercial plays in my mind of groovy futuristic graphics: lime green, yellow, baby blue, hot pink, and burning flame text with a voiceover: *"y-y-y2k is all about…fucking hype…"* Then a shot of a girl smiling, kicking her platforms into the screen: *"R-r-right in your face!"* A guy by a pool chair: *"This is not about bling, b-l-in-g-g-g, or the b-b-bi-itches, you got."* And then a girl in a mystical purple slutty top, holding a crystal: *"This is what you see through your eyes, and who you are as a person, and what, what, you, you, ex-x-x-xpress as a person."*

He puts his shit back into his mini bag and holds the straps in his mouth as he crouches down. I jump on his back and he piggybacks me out of the bathroom and down the stairs. He's screaming, "AOL pussay is the future!"

I jump off at the bottom of the staircase. *Calm your jaw. Calm your fucking jaw. Calm your fuuuuucking jaw.*

A guy in a ski mask approaches. My coke buddy middle fingers him and tells me to bite his hair. I feel it in my mouth as he asks, "Doesn't it taste like a Klondike bar?"

I search for the living room and notice a half-open door illuminated by red lights on the other side. I look in and a girl is naked on a bed, spread eagle with lit candles on her stomach. Two guys in alien head masks are holding dildos, while one of them holds a video camera. I shut the door, but the red light stays with me. It's inside of my body, injected somehow from that one look. Total arousal.

"I've been trying to get scouted, you know, at the mall, to get in the movies and maybe a commercial. Sometimes I look at myself and I just don't understand why I'm not on MTV. So, you were saying that you have parents, you know, who work in the biz? Is it true that your dad is in the biz?" A girl in a Ty heart shirt holding a red cup touches my arm. I'm in the hall and don't remember how I got here, but I've lost my balance. I think of being in *Go*, someone taking my hand and leading me to the dancefloor. Spliced montage of me dancing in an LA warehouse, smiling, jumping up and down to Underworld.

I open my eyes, look down the hall, and see everyone walking toward the living room.

"Do you remember Krista Jade's older brother? He was bisexual."

"What?"

"He was bisexual during his rave phase."

"Do I know you?"

"I was gay too, for a minute. Anyone can be gay if you're enough of an attention whore. You can keep up the role for as long as you want. Guys think it's fucking hot when two sexy girls kiss."

I find a closet near the entrance, open the sliding mirror door, and look at the pile of shoes and jackets. I throw on my trench and look at my reflection as the silver foil biohazard symbol shines on my shirt. I put my hand on the back of my head, pose, and turn to walk around.

A remix of Fatboy Slim's "Praise You" heats up as a guy in a *Cat in the Hat* striped hat and a "100% PURE" cutoff sits on a kitchen island. His padlock chain flickers as he shoots up, a tourniquet around his bicep. A guy in a Tool shirt videotapes him. I look into the LCD screen and watch him zoom in on the needle as it finds a vein. He zooms out to his face, dark circles around his eyes as they roll back. He bites his lip and moans.

A shirtless guy in Strawberry Shortcake boxers is on his knees licking the combat boots of a girl in a black wedding veil sitting on the countertop above him. She cracks a whip along his back. I look at the butterfly tattoo above his ass crack. Black guys with nose piercings in red and blue bandannas tied across their heads and matching Sean John hoodies are passing an alien head bouncy ball back and forth by a table stacked with soda bottles, beer cans, and red cups.

A group of Asian girls in matching *Blue's Clues* slutty strap tank tops feed me Slurpee cup Jello shots and ask to take a Polaroid with me holding a box of strawberry Pocky sticks. I turn my head, stick my tongue out, make a peace sign, and the flash bursts. I go into the kitchen and rearrange the magnets on the fridge: "Dairy Bitch," "If there's such a thing as karma, I am fucked!" Kate Moss's face, a Nine Inch Nails logo.

Suddenly, someone is behind me, dragging their fingers down my back. They grab my waist and rub my stomach. I turn around to see a guy in a *Powerpuff Girls* tank top, a dangling butterfly belly ring and silver belly chain, and an o-ring choker.

"I'm so horny. I just slammed. I need to suck dick right now. I need to get railed. Can I please suck your dick? We can go outside. I'll get you out before anyone sees. I do it with straight guys all the time. I love straight guys. You can fuck my hot tight Barbie pussy."

"Fuck off, you fucking faggot."

I push him away but he tugs at my shirt. "I'm serious. I want you to soak my throat. I need straight cock. I'm so fucking horny right now. I'm so starved. Please, pwetty, pweety please, dom me."

I punch him in the face and he falls to the floor, nose bleeding. The guy in the Tool shirt leans over my shoulder. "Dude! Do what the guy in *Nowhere* does to him. Oh my god, this is your big *Nowhere* moment." The guy in the Tool shirt opens the fridge as I look down at the fag. I think of jumping on his stomach for touching me, curbstomping him. Tool shirt hands me a Heinz ketchup bottle. "Squirt it on his face. Give that cumpig twinkie a blood facial. Fuck his face in."

I squirt the ketchup on his face and he squirms. I hit the bottle over the side of his head and spit on him to cheers and guys chanting. "Fuck his face! Fuck his face!" I kick him. A girl in purple-tinted sunglasses is cry-laughing.

Tool shirt slaps him and says, "I'm gonna bitch slap you 'cause you're a fucking bitch."

I cheer. "Check his pockets, boys. See if he has any goodies we can jack."

Tool shirt opens his pockets and takes out a little baggie. He holds up a pill and flips it over. "Dude, it's the Mitsubishi X!"

Strawberry Shortcake boxers snaps a Polaroid. The flash bursts, the image spits out. "Wow, this is going to look so Gregg Araki vibes."

"I know, dude. This is so fucking Araki! This is *my* aesthetic."

The homo pulls himself up and steadies himself against the kitchen counter. He bursts into tears and runs off into the crowd.

A Taco Bell dog balloon bounces across the dance floor as I turn and see a group of high girls in saran wrap tops stick bindis all over each other's faces. I scan around and see two shirtless guys feeling each other up with Windows 98 stickers stuck to their bodies. One gets on his knees and begins to zip and unzip the other dude's tearaways. Temporary "2000" glow-in-the-dark tattoos. A girl with crimped hair in a CD necklace lifts up her shirt, flashes her boobs, and smiles for a camera as the flash bursts. "Orgasm Donor" guy's jaw is on the floor. He smiles. "That's a great last pic to have on my roll." Baggies of shrooms, X, coke. A group of guys in backwards Nike caps huddle around a *Playboy*, unfolding the centerfold: a blonde with huge tits and a shaved pussy. The sound of my teeth grinding, drinks spilling over me.

A hardcore techno mix of Cher's "Believe" pumps as I fight through the crowd. Two lesbians in Sky Dancers belly shirts that I saw making out are now fingering each other. The transsexual DJ with pink and blue dreads draped over a Sony MiniDisc cutoff tank stands in front of a projection screen with flashing computer-generated graphics. Merkabahs, kaleidoscopes, fire suns, pill logos, Y2K logos, smiley faces, all spinning into oblivion. I look at her twisting the knobs of the silver Pioneer equipment.

"Hey, he/she DJ. How do you stay up all night?"

"I pretend that I'm playing *Half-Life*." I look at her manly shoulders, then up to her silver metallic lipstick and blue eyeliner. She grabs my head and whispers in my ear. "Do you ever feel like we have the souls of people who were once alive and we're finishing off their biddings?"

I look at the crowd, the jumping bodies flashing in the strobe lights. Everyone is in sync. A voiceover above a shot of me behind the DJ booth, banging my head, punching the air: *I'm wide awake, weaving a dream inside my head and living it at the exact same time. The longing to go as far as a person can push themselves is hidden in the internal tears of every dancing body in this room. This one hundred percent purity, one hundred percent happiness I have right now, I didn't even know existed. I didn't know you could feel this close to strangers. I didn't know you could be this in sync. Right here, right now, we are all a broken, immortal family reuniting for one night only. Never have I been so synced.*

I stay close to the speaker, spinning, dancing, vibrating, shaking. I think of how badly I want time to move faster, for everyone to move quicker, and what it'd be like to control the will of the party to be at my speed, to sync them up to my BPM. I claw at my face as it goes numb. The song sounds like Madonna. Lyrics about kissing and dying. It fades into a harder sound that I've never heard before. The feeling of drinking cold water with ice after having a popsicle pulsates through me as I land on a girl in a hot pink miniskirt and cut-off top. She grinds her ass on him, eyes rolling back. I look down her legs and back up to her tits. I fantasize about her against the wall upstairs, my tongue down her throat, fingering her pussy. A Black guy in a Raptors jersey, a big dollar sign chain, and a backwards cap comes from behind her and puts his arm around her. He moves his hands on her belly. I get up, go to the booze table, and grab a bottle of vodka. I chug it and pull my hair. *Who the fuck are all of these people? Where the fuck are my friends? Why have I not seen my friends the whole fucking night?*

A guy in a blink-182 shirt crouches while he videotapes two blonde twins with huge fake tits sitting on a couch in white bras, miniskirts, and angel wings. Holographic tears streak down their faces as they kiss an orange Creamsicle and sing along to Britney's "(You Drive Me) Crazy." One deepthroats the stick as her spit drips down. I watch them make out on the camera's LCD screen, timestamp: "DEC 31 1999." One says to the camera, "I bet this is your *Varsity Blues* fantasy. I bet you didn't think this happens in real life. Well, it does." Her sister undoes her bra, takes it off, and a guy in a ski mask hands them a glow stick as he chants, "*Girls Gone Wild!* Y2K Edition." The LCD screen zooms in on her nipples. "Take it off." The girls rub crushed glow sticks all over each other's tits. I watch them massage each other's boobs. I'm so hard. I think of locking myself in the bathroom to jerk off.

The lights turn on. The DJ turns off the music and the crowd rushes toward the living room. I see my coke buddy standing on a table holding a wireless mic. Everyone puts their hands on each other's shoulders.

"What's up, motherfuckers? This is the last night of the millennium. Nobody in this room is ever going to feel this way again. I know you all may think that you came here for an end-of-the-world party, but nah, I'm going to tell you some shit. Listen up: it's not the end of our world, it's the end of *their* world. We are the new generation that is going to change the fucking world. Uranus is in Aquarius and they cannot stop us. We are the online kids. We don't need *Newsweek* to tell us shit about ourselves. For the first time in world history, we have control over our own lives. We get to curate our own reality. We get to choose what we simulate, what we see. We connect on message boards, in chat rooms. We can burn our own CDs, make our own fuckin music, our own brands, *be* our own brands, and share our visions with the whole world. I get DJ tips from dudes in London. The possibilities are endless now that we have the passwords to culture. We are hacking the planet. We are the fucking illuminati."

"Yeah!" The crowd chants, pumps their fists.

"And we don't need the Prada."

"Yeah!" The crowd chants, pumps their fists.

"And we don't need the Benz."

"Yeah!" The crowd chants, pumps their fists.

"We won't be slaves for corporations."

"Yeah!" The crowd chants, pumps their fists.

"We all look fucking cool because we are all ourselves. Everyone here is their own person. Our souls are ascending to levels that can't be reached by being home alone in your underwear, staring at your computer. We are not regular people! This is alien technology. This is hardcore. Fuck the little teenyboppers in Hilfiger trying to get into our parties, trying to get our X pills, trying to be a part of our world. Fuck that culture-vulture coolhunter old bitch Madonna trying to co-opt our shit, talking about The Prodigy and thinking she fuckin knows techno. We don't need that bullshit. We don't fucking need no Maverick fuckin Records. We collect call to the gods, to the angels in the upper worlds. That's who we fuckin do our deals with."

A guy in an "arrest madonna. stop ray of light." shirt loses his shit. "Fuck yeah!"

"We only have one hour left of this decade, and if we don't explode into nuclear waste at midnight, I'll be around with my business cards. I got stacks if you wanna book me to DJ your next groove. You may now return to your regularly scheduled programming."

He jumps off the table and the lights go dark, replaced by the strobes and lasers. Everyone returns to grinding on the dance floor and this kind of unending molasses, heaviness, and rage washes over me as I move through the kitchen. A remix of Vengaboys's "Boom, Boom, Boom, Boom!!" cuts into "100% Pure Love." I look for more booze and see Shane standing shirtless, sweating, taking Polaroids, arm over the guy who was shooting heroin. I grab his hand.

"Shane! What the fuck are you doing? I've been looking for you. You're sweating balls. Holy shit."

He pushes me away. "Dude, what the fuck? I've been selling drugs. You should see how much cash I've made. I'm having a blast, like everyone else here. Ever heard of that? A fun time?"

"Don't be a dick. Real drugs?"

"RealPlayer, real drugs."

"What?"

"No. I told you that I did what the girl in *Go* did. I sold my antidepressants to these computer nerds and told them that it was a new drug my dealer got that everyone is going to be on. They believed it."

I turn to Shane. "Stay away from this guy. This guy is fucking white trash. You were shooting heroin and your friend was taping it. I saw you guys."

The *Cat in the Hat* dude pushes me. "Buddy, who are you calling white trash? Take a look around you. Look at the people you chose to ring in 2000 with. Try self-awareness. You're at this party. You're no better. I don't care what you fucking think of me, kid. You don't fucking think that I've been called every fucking name in the book by my fuckin parents?"

I push him harder. "Stay away from my fucking friend before I Björk the fuck out of you."

Shane holds me back. "Brad, you aren't being cool right now. Stop."

I push him back, harder. "Don't fucking give my friend heroin. I'll fucking fuck you up. He's only seventeen, you know."

"Stop."

"Shane, you aren't on heroin right now, right?"

He shakes his head. "No."

The guy makes an evil smile. "He was about to go shoot up with me. He said he doesn't give a shit about his life. We are going to an afterhours after this. You can roll through if you want."

I grab Shane's hand. "Fucking come with me right now."

He pushes me away. "Dude, you're not my fucking mom. I can do whatever the fuck I want. Leave me alone. If I want to fucking try it, I can. This is my life, not yours."

"Why are we at a party where there's heroin? Shouldn't we be fucking doing like, I don't know, Doritos and root beer?"

"Don't play dumb. It's so annoying when you do this. You think because you do such a good job of controlling yourself that you somehow have the power to control whatever the fuck I want to do tonight? Get out of my fucking face."

"That was so fucking low, Shane. I can't believe you fucking just said that."

I go through the door to the back deck. Some guys are passing around a glass pipe filled with weed. I look out and see people in small groups smoking cigarettes, holding red cups, bottles, smoking joints. One of them: "Yo, buddy. Do you wanna buy some crack?"

I have a vision of myself in anime trying to climb out the bottom of a temple, a Silly Putty monster pushing me down. I bang my head against the sliding deck doors. I flash back to my family huddled around the TV watching CNN two years ago, to President Clinton making an announcement: "The glorification of heroin is not creative, it's destructive. It's not beautiful; it's ugly. And this is not about art; it's about life and death." This loops in my mind over the footage of the guy in the *Cat in the Hat* hat shooting up across montages of Angelina Jolie's character in that HBO movie we all watched last week, running from a fashion shoot to Skid Row to score. I look over near the end of the fence to a guy making out with a plastic angel statue. *Every boy here is becoming the person their father warned them about.*

I go back inside and see an ice cream cake on the table, people grabbing pieces of it with their hands. Glazed on top in green icing is "HACK Y2K."

Scratching down my cheeks, walking over to the kitchen sink, I look at my warped reflection in the silver knob. *You are one of those calculated types, those good-boy types. You are one of those control freak boys.* My fingers are in my mouth as I dry heave. In my mind, nothing is making any sense: the sound of the *Inspector Gadget* "now available on VHS/DVD" commercial, the ad for the Sound Bites radio lollipop sticks, "bite down your teeth and the sound will transmit into your ear," the "move over Mario!" *40 Winks* PlayStation ad, the Virgin poster on the telephone pole by Subway: Everything But The Girl, Savage Garden, *Hotel LaChapelle*, "all now twenty-five percent off." Ending with the woman's voice that I heard on TV this week. "Wear your money on your sleeve with this new Prada strap-on pouch. Isn't that so 1999? We Americans love our bling!" I look at a girl pushing a guy off of her. He keeps pushing her back into his arm, headlocking her. These sounds and images are splitting, spinning, repeating fast as I fight my way through the crowd. I've never felt so sick. A girl in a pink wig, braces, and a light-up soother hanging from her neck stops me and grabs my arm. "Do you think it's true?"

"What?"

"That Freddie Prinze Jr. is here. Everyone is talking about it. He went upstairs with this girl I know."

"Huh?"

"Do you know about Jolly Rancher?"

"What?"

"It's true, right? You must be tripping. Do you know about the new *Media 100* software? You know, to make your own commercials?"

"I'm not into computers."

She takes out a Bart Simpson Nestlé Butterfinger, half unwrapped. "You want some?"

I rip off the silver stick-on earring that some girl in pink put on me and run upstairs, head against the wall in a fetal position, sucking my thumb. Pushing up onto my knees, I look down the row of family pictures in frames. I look into the eyes of the father of this home in a tuxedo on the deck of a cruise ship. I lift my shirt up, look down at my boxers' waistband, and bite down on my thumb. I think of myself at six years old, the feeling of going to a friend's birthday party, noticing their shoes on the welcome mat, and running downstairs to see them, feeling the safety that they were there. I felt a part of something. Now, there's nothing. I have a vision of myself in a Versace suit, a shot of me in between burning palm trees and burning crosses, spinning and dancing between them. *There is no time, only Hollywood hours. How do I not get to tomorrow? Why is tonight, how it feels right now, never going to exist again?*

I get up to the sound of Marilyn Manson's voice screaming through a jungle remix of "I Don't Like the Drugs (But the Drugs Like Me)" and run down the stairs. Shane is looking at himself in the sliding door mirror, pulling down his eyelids, fake screaming, and covering his ears. He's posing, twisting his body, running his fingers through his hair. The poses mimic a mix of MJ's "Scream" video and a model I saw in a Sony commercial last week.

I push him. "Look, I know you don't fuck with me right now, but do you know where Lu is?"

"He said he was going down to the point. He was like, 'I'm gonna end it all. It's zero day.'"

"Shane, what the fuck!"

I open the sliding door, rummage around, and grab my trench coat. I head outside.

Under the streetlight, guys in Canucks jerseys and Juggalo makeup are checking car doors. A guy with fucked-up piercings pours Gatorade into a baby bottle on the sidewalk. Another pulls out his dick, puts a glow bracelet around it, and spins it. A shirtless guy holding a triton dressed in platform sneakers and weed leaf underwear smokes a bong.

I head into the trees, run down the path, and see Lu lying on the grass field with a video camera pointed at his face. He's chugging Aftershock and watching himself on the LCD screen.

"You can't finish a bottle of Aftershock by yourself!"

"Watch me, faggot," he slurs. "I can do whatever the fuck I want."

"MM was on. I wanted to mosh with you. Shane told me you were out here." I wave my hand in front of his face. "Hello? Earth to Lu! Why are you fucking ignoring me? You won't believe this shit. I beat up this fag and squirted a bottle of ketchup on his face! He was bleeding so much. It was so damn cool. Everyone kept saying that it was like *Nowhere*. I'm sure someone got it on video. Everyone has Handycams at this party. I know that we live in a rich neighborhood, but Jesus, I've been partying like a rock star. You'd be proud."

He puts his camera down. "What did you honestly think? I was going to take you to a party where you'd sit around and play spin the fucking bottle? House parties in the real world aren't like they are in *Can't Hardly Wait*. Don't fucking insult me."

"Wow, that's low."

"Alert! Someone call *Entertainment Tonight*! Brad made his super naughty Y2K Party Boy debut. Why don't you go to the mall tomorrow and get a chain that says 'filthy' to celebrate?"

"You're supposed to be happy for me. I was having fun. Why are you acting this way?"

"Fuck you and your bullshit night with your fabricated good feelings and all of the rest of the idiots in this house."

"You're being a dick. Fuck you."

"You don't deserve recognition for losing control. You did something PG-13 for once. So what? Get over it."

"This is deeper. I'm making memories and creating experiences. These are about good fucking times in my life right now, you bitch!"

"What are you going to have from tonight? Home videos? Polaroids? Who gives a shit? Footage means fucking nothing because no one here cares about each other. No one gives a shit. You think that you're making memories tonight? You're wrong. You aren't even going to remember any of this or any of these people. None of these people are going to remember this night."

"Shut the fuck up! I don't want to hear it! Tell me what's wrong. Who pissed you off? I want to know why you're being this way."

"I disappoint myself more than I could ever disappoint anyone else, and that's just the truth. I'm not interested in giving you a fucking victim sob story after-school-special bullshit. I don't want to be alive right now. There's so much hate inside of me."

"Why the fuck do you want to be dead? You were so excited for this party. You were so fucking happy at the beginning of the night."

"Ever since sophomore year, when I saw *Nowhere* for the first time, I was like, 'One day, one fucking day, I am going to get to go to an end-of-the-world party with freaks and queers and it's going to be so fucking cool, so fuck-the-system,' and now I'm here and it just doesn't fit how it felt in my head, and I'm fucking pissed off."

"But you know that no guy we know is ever gonna be the guy in the American Eagle ad, jumping up and down, snowboarding through the air, in that perfect moment. Advertisements are fucking lies. They're scams to make us think that we feel good so we buy more shit."

"No, no, no! I'm so fucking sick of being disappointed by my own expectations of how I think things are going to feel. I'm let down every single fucking time."

"So what? Maybe that's just life."

"What is the fucking point of being alive if my life doesn't fit the vision I have of myself in my mind?"

"You're being stupid right now. Stop it. I don't know what to fucking tell you. It's not like we're going to wake up tomorrow and somehow become friends with someone who's been on *Celebrity Deathmatch*. That's not fucking real."

"I don't want to go into 2000 and not be famous. You don't understand that and nobody here understands. I didn't ask to be born. I didn't ask to experience the pain of how unfair life is. People in this world judge you by the people that you know and the places that you've been. Who do I know? Where have I been?"

"You're being pathetic."

"Do you even know how powerful it'd be to one hundred percent know that you're living on the other side of people's fantasies of you? I want to be the superstar of the new satanic age. What is the point of being alive if nobody can see me?" Lu gets down on the grass, opens his camera bag, pulls out a gun, and puts it to his head.

"That gun is not loaded."

"Fuck yeah, it's loaded!"

"Put the gun down."

"No! No, no, no."

"You're only doing this because you want me to videotape you. You aren't serious."

"I'm one hundred percent serious! Look at my finger! It's on the trigger."

"You don't know how badly I wish that gun was a Happy Meal toy right now."

"I'm tired of standing in the waiting line. I want to live in the fast lane."

"I can see you! Why is that not enough?"

"Ew, not you! I want cameras. I want a studio audience." He puts the gun to his lips, then in his mouth. Sucking on the gun, he pulls it out and tongue-twists the barrel, then deepthroats it. "Have you ever tasted metal before? Metal is pretty yummy. This is crazy, but gunmetal and blood kind of have the same taste. All of this psychosexual gameplay is getting me horny!" He pulls his jeans, rubs the gun on his crotch, pulls it in and out of his pants, and sucks on the gun again.

"Oh, okay. I get it. That's when you become real, right? That's when life becomes meaningful? When you shoot yourself in the face? That's when you'll achieve the shock that you're chasing?"

He puts the gun to his throat. "So? Come on, why don't you push the gun into my mouth and pull the trigger for me? Come on, do it."

I push him down. The gun falls. I headlock him and grab the camera and the gun. I flip the screen over, looking at ourselves via LCD, the battery indicator light flashing. I put the gun to his cheek and spit on him. "Let's do it then. I know how to make you famous. I'll give you everything you ever wanted. I'll shoot you in the head on camera and run. It'll look like you did it to yourself. How about I go inside, find someone in a Manson shirt, get you to put it on, and then kill you? The media will eat that up! 'Kid in the suburbs in MM shirt shoots himself in the head on tape, found in a field.' Can't you see it now? That's *USA Today*! That's Fox News! That's the front page of AOL.com. You'll be a star. Don't you want it? Come on! Let me shoot you in the fucking head right here. Should I hit play?" I push the gun into his cheek.

"Let me out! Let me go!"

"No! You fuckin think that you can get out of your seat and leave all because this is a scene that you don't want to see? It's going to happen right now, live. So, you want me to? I'll fucking shoot you in the fucking head. Let's make a snuff movie right fucking now."

"Ple—"

I cock the gun. It clicks. "Should I hit play? How does it feel to know what could happen when someone makes your 24/7 straight-to-home-video-goth-bullshit performance into something real? I'm sick of this shit." I let him out of the headlock, then drop the camera and the pistol.

Lu bursts into laughter. "Want to know what I was thinking about? That Diesel campaign from five years ago with that car accident. So chopped."

"You were acting?"

"I knew you were too much of a pussy to do it!"

"This is what I don't understand. What makes you any better than Shane? At least he knows this world is bullshit. You try so hard to make everything seem so much more dramatic, so much more intense. It's not like that."

"You want to know the truth? All night I've had this haunt in the back of my mind, like, 'Today is another night of your life. You'll be out of the house, trying to know yourself, trying to become yourself, and you will fail at it.'"

"Dude, I was feeling exactly the same. You aren't alone."

"No one feels the way I do, and no one feels as much. So you couldn't have ever felt that."

I sit on the ground, head on my knees, picking the grass. "You don't think I feel stupid trying so hard to unlock myself all the time? We don't even have real adult responsibilities. Yet here we are, fucking feeling all of this retarded bullshit."

Lu kicks the air. "Do you understand how unfair it is that everything I experience, every memory I make, amounts to nothing? You think all of this is so fragile because we're seventeen? Well it's not, because it doesn't matter."

I tear up. "We're just kids."

"Why are you fucking crying? Fucking stop it."

"I would lose my best friend if you did anything to yourself."

"Did you just call me your best friend?"

"I shouldn't have done that. I'm just so weird right now. I'm so overwhelmed. It's the drugs."

"Yeah, do you want to go to Claire's and get matching necklaces now to make us BFF official? Like, fuck off."

"My mom is always like, 'You're a baby, seventeen is a baby,' and I didn't get what that meant until I came here tonight. If this is how the world is, and it's this intense, it's too much. Is tonight not allowed to be a lot for me?"

"I don't want you to care about me, ever."

"Oh right. You hate that I care about you because it means you have a responsibility to another person who doesn't want you to fucking do all of the stupid shit you do."

Lu sits beside me. "There are so many versions of me that used to exist, that I've lost, that I don't know anymore. I like who I am right now so much, I've never been so in love with myself. I don't want to change. I don't want to evolve or know anything about who I could be in the future."

"What are you so afraid of changing?"

"What if I'm not this evil forever? I don't want to grow out of having this much hatred in my heart."

I shrug. "Maybe you won't."

Lu puts his arm over my shoulder. I lean my head into his arm as he takes a cig out, lights it, and twirls my hair. I look up and see fireworks bursting in the sky. Lu puts his hand in my jeans pocket, scratching and tickling my thigh. "Who is going to be my year 2000 kiss?"

"Kiss one of your demons. I'm sure they're always down to hook up."

Lu starts kissing, slobbering the air, and putting his hands down his jeans. He puts the gun and Handycam back in the camera bag, closes the buckle, and slings it on.

"Can you just drive me home right now? Everyone's going to be partying until six a.m., so the streets won't be busy. You can just drop me off."

"Yeah, let's leave now."

"Getting in a car with a drunk driver, oh no, what would D.A.R.E. think? And what about Shane? He was talking to these guys who were shooting up heroin and going to an afterhours on the Eastside. I was freaking out. There's no way he could—there's gonna be so much traffic into the city tonight."

Lu eyerolls. "If Shane is stupid enough to still be stuck in heroin chic '96, then maybe he deserves to overdose."

"But you always talk about how you wish you could try heroin? I'm confused?"

"That's one of my many stunts to get people's faces to melt."

Fuzzy bubblegum techno comes from the house. I walk up to Lu's car. Under the streetlight, a shirtless guy in a *Scream* mask punches the air, screaming, "Does anyone know how I can get my fuckin dick sucked?" I try to read the brown lipstick written on his chest. It looks like "Mein Kampf Slut."

I open the door to Lu's car as he revs the engine. I rub my fingers down the passenger window. The radio comes on. I turn up the knob. "Remember, we're playing the best songs of the last decade nonstop, all morning. Matthew Sweet's 'Sick of Myself' coming right up…"

I look out as soundbites from the night skip and glitch. "The world is just one big costume party, don't you know?" "How else will I know if what we're doing right now is happening if we don't tape it?" "Yo! If she's showing her shoulders and belly button, she wants to fuuuuck!" "I trip face, I trip face, off the bass, off the bass…"

We reach my street. Lu stops the car and turns the headlights off. I get out, walk up the steps, take the key from under the mat, and open the door. My mom greets me. "Happy New Year, sweetheart! Did you have fun at Kev's house?"

I hug her. "Happy New Year, Mom. Yeah, it was fun. We just watched the countdown on MTV, ate chips, had Pizza Rolls, and stuff."

"What's with the leather jacket? Fill me in."

"Oh, it was just a costume party."

"Nice. Well, we're going to bed."

As I walk down the hallway, my dad calls out, "You good, kiddo?"

"Yeah, I'm good."

I open my bedroom door, turn the lights on, take my clothes off, throw them on the floor, and put on one of my dad's baggy shirts. The sound of fireworks pulsates through my window and vibrates my body under the blankets.

How can you lose something that you didn't even know you had? Party boys only know how to hurt.

I turn my night light on and grab a piece of paper and a pen off my table.

"There are no such things as fantasies. There never was an American dream. Life was, and always will be, a never-ending nightmare."

☆ 52 ☆

"Never Let You Go" by Third Eye Blind is ending as we walk into McDonald's. As I look at the line by the register, a guy with spiked hair and an "Internet Killed the Video Star" shirt in plaid pajamas and Docs grabs his order. He puts his headphones on as we make eye contact. Children are staring into the Barbie and Hot Wheels Happy Meal displays as I look across to the entrance of the birthday party room.

Lu puts a fry in his mouth. "What do you think of Michael Alig?"

"Who is he again? You talk about serial killers so much that I'm starting to lose track."

"The club kid who chopped up his friend, taped him in a box, and threw him into the river because he thought he was an uncool try-hard. Talk about impressive life accomplishments."

"Oh, him! I want to read the book his friend James St. James wrote. I heard about it on E!"

"Are you still bumming over the Shane heroin fiasco last night?"

"I mean, did you even go to a party in the nineties if your depressed friend didn't threaten to shoot up drugs for attention? Isn't that his whole shtick, being the miserable boy?"

"Well, we made it, we're here. And in the first few hours, I still don't feel any different."

"Let's face it, bro, new millennium or not, the world is always going to feel like random chaos."

"It's so corny to me how every movie trailer right now has a narrator teasing us about some promise to enter an underworld happening beneath the surface."

"I was thinking that the other night! What could we be on the verge of? What will be revealed in 2000? What is going to be exposed?"

Lu plays with his straw. "Something and nothing is coming, all at the same time."

I nod. "Why do people act shocked over how boring and depressing reality actually is?"

"Right? Big fucking deal. News flash: it's been sad for centuries."

I grab his drink and take a sip. "Have you done any cool stuff on your computer lately?"

"I've been killing it with these phishing programs to get passwords from people, like stealing people's credit card numbers and stuff."

"That's so chopped."

"Hacking is going to be part of my aesthetic this year. This year for me is going to be about, like, realizing stuff."

"I keep thinking about all of the bad shit that goes down when you don't know how to tolerate yourself." I hold my stomach. "Seriously. I feel like I'm going to vomit out Flubber every time I fucking move."

Lu rolls his eyes. "You embarrass me. I had my first hangover at twelve."

"We can't all be child stars, okay? I'm going to hurl."

"You still managed to gangbang those nuggets."

"You just went down on that double cheeseburger."

Lu pulls out his Polaroid and tells me to smile. I shoot a middle finger instead.

"Special moments. Our first hangover at McDonald's." The picture spits out and he puts it in his bag.

I look over to the ball pit and the playhouse and watch little kids hold onto the netting. My mind goes back to last night. "Word of advice: you need to stop sucking on guns."

"I can't help myself. I love the taste of gunmetal. Ruger feels so good in the back of my throat."

"What's your New Year's resolution?"

"To be the first unhinged sex-obsessed male on a *Jenny Jones* 'Extreme Teens' episode."

I laugh. "You would love five minutes of trashy talk show TV *Jerry Springer* fame."

Lu slams the table. "Cut, calculate, destroy, clawing people to shreds on the road to my goals. That's what my 2000 is all about."

I eyeroll. "Where did you learn that one?"

"Madonna's *Behind the Music*."

"Good riddance."

"One week of people talking about me on CNN, one week of fame. I'll figure it out. My life is going to amount to something huge."

"Paramount Pictures presents a new story about the desperate, empty, fame-driven school shooter that never was. In theaters, fall 2000."

"Oh, and you guys! The movie was made with all found footage from handheld cameras. How realistic! How scary!"

"Tell me something funny that will make me laugh."

"I just found out they call fags 'poofters' in the UK."

I start choking. "*Poofters?*"

He fakes a British accent. "Yeah, you fuckin poofter." We laugh hard.

The beginning of Hole's "Celebrity Skin" plays. Lu gets up and does a freeze-pose. I stand up and play air guitar, humming "Na-Na-Duh-Duh-Na-Na." I look at our ketchup packets, sweet and sour sauces, trays, wrappers, and bags. I turn to Lu. "We have to throw out our garbage."

Lu looks over at the overweight Black women in McDonald's polos cleaning up. "Let's let the McMammy slaves handle it."

I put my hand over my mouth. "You can't say that! My family sponsors starving Africans!"

He winks. "I just did, bitch."

I push open the door. "I will say this… can you imagine being so poor that you have to work at McDicks and wear a headset and those visors? Ew."

Lu runs over to the Ronald McDonald bench out front and puts his arm over it. "Did somebody say…murder?"

I sit beside him as he starts fake sucking Ronald's dick. I push his head down. "Fuck yeah!" We get up and Lu lights a cigarette. I look at my reflection in the windows beside him. *We can say nothing to each other, but I always know what he's thinking. I am different with him—stronger, faster, extreme. Hardcore. I'm more handsome. There are feelings and worlds that can only exist when I'm with him. Some of us cannot outrun our desires for others to access the violence within us. I am not a nice boy.*

☆ 53 ☆

Shane and I sit on the fountain in the school courtyard as we drink Surge and Pepsi. Shane is in a Joni Mitchell shirt tucked into mustard pants, wearing red Converse. A group of football players pelt us with Pez and fries.

"Sup queers?" one in a silver tech vest shouts. "Where's your Satan-worshipping boyfriend today? Is he the head of your fag cult? Your little goth superstar clique?"

Another jock elbows him. "Maybe he's at home with pinkeye. I heard that can happen when you get jizz in your eye."

"Maybe his dick missed his mouth when he was shooting his fucking load into it."

I get up. "Can you guys just fucking not right now?"

"Whatever, fags." They make "L" signs in unison then walk away.

Shane passes me a handful of gummy bears. "Are you honestly shocked they didn't all just start busting into some gay-ass dance sequence? When yuh clit goes owtttttttt!"

"Does he know how ugly his haircut looks? I saw Tyson make fun of this dude in my math class who had a No Doubt CD. Fuck that Nick Carter I-like-it-backway faggot."

"Why is it that everyone that shops at Old Navy is the worst?"

"The tech vest is brutal."

"Your Starter jacket works for you."

"What is that supposed to mean? Are you saying I'm like them?"

"I mean, you wear Starter."

"Why the fuck can't I wear Starter? Also, I left my hoody at your house and told you to bring it. Why didn't you bring it yet? I've been waiting all week. That's my favorite fucking hoodie."

"Shut up. I'll bring it to you. Chill. Do your Morpheus, but do it good. Do your ultra uber-deep voice."

"Are you sure?"

"Please, please, please! Do it like the Movie Awards parodies."

I pick up my Surge. "But Neo…is this all real? Is this Surge bottle real?"

"That movie was so fucking retarded. Try-hard cyberpunk end-of-the-century fashion trend marketing bullshit. I know actual goths who wear those leather jackets and they aren't hip or trendy."

Lu arrives in a Baphomet hoodie, silver beaded chain, and baggy black jeans.

Shane jokes, "We were just talking about the time I found a 'Backstreet's Back' video in your VCR."

"Lu loves the Fagstreet Boys! Na na na na boo boo!"

Lu starts humping the air, making orgasm faces. "Am I fuckableeeeee? Yeahhhhhhh."

I fist pump. "Oh yeah, Nick! Yeah, Nick! Sit on my face! Fart on me, Nick!"

Shane jumps up and makes an "S" with his fingers in the air. "*Sexxx Clubbbb 7 in Miami.*"

A group of freshman guys across from us are freestyle rapping in a circle, making gangsta hands to their own beats: "Optimus Ebonics, all the new bitches love my hydraulics."

Lu goes up to a Black kid in the circle wearing a *Chronic 2001* shirt and pushes him. "Oh, I bet you think you're so fucking cool in your Lugz and your baggy fucking Dre shirt? You think you're so hard because you shop at gangsta stores? You fucking try-hard lil tar baby."

The kid puts his head down and turns away.

☆ 54 ☆

I grab the Costco groceries from the trunk of Mom's car.

"I want to tell you something."

"Before you do, I want to share something I learned on *Oprah* today—"

I cut her off. "Maybe later. Can I tell you what I was going to say now?"

"What is it, honey?"

"I've joined the student council. I'm going to be super busy doing a lot of after-school projects. I might stay out late some nights too, so if I'm not around, I'm working or I'm studying. You don't have to worry about me."

"That's great! Congratulations, Brad." She touches my cheek. "Another good thing you can put on your applications."

"You said someone at Dad's office has connects with the admissions guy at Berkeley, so I should be fine."

She pats my shoulder. "Connections don't guarantee that you'll get in, honey."

"I'm a fierce competitor, Mom. All that volunteer work I've been doing at the senior center? I have a lot of great references, too."

"Maybe you should take a shift at that soup kitchen Brenda told me about. She said it really stood out on her daughter's applications."

☆ 55 ☆

A whiff of his whiskey mouth makes me dizzy. Lu has his video camera in my face. I finish a line of Ritalin off his palms. He flicks on the cam light and it beams on me. His cat, Thorazine, jumps into my lap. "I want you and T to make out."

I stick my tongue out. "Are we redefining the gross-out genre?"

Lu winks. "Tom Green can't compete with these sick teenage minds."

I put my thumbs up, my tone goes super fast. "Fuck it all, I'm going to do it. I'm going to put on the sicko crown. I'm a tragic ex-child star! I'm Drew fucking Barrymore! No rules. That shit wasn't laced, right?" I hold Thorazine's mouth open by his teeth and spit into his throat.

"You're nasty! Keep going!"

I slobber the cat's tongue on my tongue and shut my eyes. We're kissing. I look back into the lens. "I bet you all didn't see that coming."

☆ 56 ☆

"Being a woman in America today is like, 'If you're going to get raped at a party next weekend, just make sure you're wearing the new Lancôme lipstick that Salma Hayek was talking about in *Vogue* last week.'"

Parked in the Walgreens lot, Kristen applies brown lipliner in her rearview mirror. Garbage's "Push It" drizzles from her stereo as I try to hide staring at her rack in a slutty leopard print top under a plastic raincoat. In the backseat: a dELiA*s catalog, textbooks, a Mantrap clothing flier, copies of *The Ethical Slut* and *Paradoxia*, *Gia* and *200 Cigarettes* VHS tapes, a Shirley Manson CK ad taped to her school binder, a purple boa, and temporary tattoo packages of cherries. The internet poll I saw yesterday comes into my mind: "What current issue is the most important to you? Climate change? Torture and government conspiracy? The military industrial complex? Immigration? Overuse of chemicals and plastics?"

I return. "Lana-what-a? English, please."

I turn to a guy in a Comedy Central hat in a Volvo parked beside us licking his lips, making a tongue-in-the-V gesture.

"Did you see that? Men are disgusting. Guys think that if women wear halter tops, get their belly buttons pierced, or, God forbid, show their shoulders, it's for them. It's not. It's for the girls. This is for us. If I have the opportunity to go out in public with my tits bouncing everywhere and be absolutely fabulous, I'm going to take it! There are no rules. Who made the rules anyway? Some dumb guy!"

"This is what I don't understand about chicks. You ask for this attention and then freak out when you get it. It's ridiculous to me."

"This is why I loved when Lil' Kim had her boobs out on the red carpet. We need role models like Lil' Kim and Madonna to remind the stupid men on this planet that, shocker, women have their own sexual fantasies and desires."

"You would get dirty with Vanilla Ice?"

"No, but Naomi Campbell, yes. Women at least know what to do with a pussy. Most of my girlfriends have never even orgasmed. They fake it all the time. Men are clueless."

"Why do you think so many girls love playing the victim?"

"It's the easiest role. It requires no responsibility, no agency, and you get lots of attention. A lot of chicks scream rape and like to rewrite history. Like, ladies, you can't return what you've offered. I mean, we all saw *Wild Things*."

"Oh yes, we all did see *Wild Things*."

"As a feminist, I'm allowed to say this. Look, if I ever got raped by a guy I was attracted to and he was hot, I wouldn't report it to the cops because if he didn't tie me up or whatever, and I wanted to fuck him anyways, I don't feel like it's a big deal. I would just try to enjoy it, like, you know, if it's inevitable and things didn't get all Cronenberg. That's pussy power."

"I have...no words."

"Why don't I just put on a turtleneck, get a Bikini Kill tattoo, and read Gloria Steinem? Maybe that'll make me more acceptable. I want to live my truth. You can be a hot girl and still care about women's rights."

"Yeah, I don't know." I grab the Walgreens photo envelope.

"Don't touch that!"

"Ooh. You have naughty pics in there? I can't imagine the crazy shit that photo lab techs get to see."

"No, I was just wasted this weekend. I don't look good. Pics are like the only evidence that the night even happened. The drunker I get, the blurrier the pictures become."

"You should talk about that with your therapist."

"How do you know I have one?"

"Don't all women?"

"You're so sexist and clueless."

"What's wrong with being sexy?"

"Point proven!"

"Are you still getting your tramp stamp this week?"

"It's a dillemz. I can't choose between the cherries or 'feminist' in henna looking Indian text."

"Tramp stamps are hot."

"So hot."

I gulp. "Okay, so I wanted to ask you about this. When you go and get an STD test, is it like in *Kids* with the whole taking-a-number thing?"

"You just reminded me… I know this girl, Ashley, who got chlamydia. She used to have the *best* eyebrows. The *best*, but last thing I heard was that she's on Wellbutrin and fat now."

"Do any of your gay friends have AIDS?"

"Not yet, but soon. I'm sure that's coming up next summer for at least one of them. I mean, it has to, right? It's so fated, but they bring it upon themselves. Cruising is so dangerous."

"Some gay guy was trying to get with me at a party the other week. It was disgusting. I had to protect myself."

"Super normal. All of my straight friends get molested by gay guys. Try fighting with one. It's like, no, I don't want to watch reruns of *The RuPaul Show* with you and talk about Cher when you go behind my back and tell everyone I know that I need to hit the StairMaster. Spineless losers."

"Creepy. Maybe because they all feel like women inside, they think they can talk that kind of shit."

"Two facts of life: fags are all clones of each other and fags hate women."

"That's been my only experience. It's like, stop acting like a stereotype and maybe people will stop typecasting you. Ever think of that?"

I pick up the booklet for *MTV's Amp 2* comp on the dashboard, flip through it, then put it back in its case. Kristen goes through her CD wallet and grabs a disc. She hits play. Aphex Twin's "Windowlicker" blares.

I cringe. "This music video is so weird."

"Aphex Twin is my god right now. I go somewhere else when I dance to his music."

"The music is too digital. It's not like rock. It's the void."

"Have you ever watched *Amp* on MTV?"

"No."

"You have to try it sometime. It usually starts at eleven p.m. They play techno music videos from all over the world. Sometimes I'll go on the *MTV Amp* AOL chatroom and stay up with other net-heads discussing the new music we've discovered. People understand things in cyberspace that people in the real world don't."

"Would you ever make your own music?"

"I'm not creative, I just have obsessions, and obsession doesn't produce anything. I'm always the only girl in the techno section at Virgin. Guys find it so hot that I love Underworld." She closes her eyes and waves her arms to the music, flicking the cherry-shaped air freshener dangling from the mirror. She pets her neck and I think of the anime movie that I watched at Shane's with the scene that featured an Aphex Twin logo sticker on a door. "What was the last cool video you saw?"

"My buddy and I watched *Paradise Lost* about that child murderer guy, Damien Echols."

"You have creepy friends! I can't stomach that stuff. I could barely get through *Urban Legend* when my ex took me."

"Why did you two break up again?"

"Dick size, but you could say that the real breaking point was when he was sobbing in a packed theater during *Jerry Maguire*. What a pussy!"

"Hilarious. I love it."

"Tell me about your new friends! I'm not a total consummate narcissist."

"You're in luck. I'm keeping that private."

"Shut up. I've seen *Swingers*. I know men are obsessed with each other."

"I'll give them letters. S. Let's just say that Pearl Jam writes songs about people like him. He's a drama queen."

"And what about the guy you were calling off my line and acting super sketch about when your mom was over?"

"That's L. You know when someone new comes into your life and you don't feel invisible anymore? That's how I describe him."

"That's so sad. I didn't know you felt that way, Brad."

"I can be in a crowded room with all the friends I've grown up with and there's always this clawing feeling of being superior to them. With L, he's the first person to take that feeling away."

"Doesn't that freak you out?"

"No, when we're together we enter these strange dream worlds and come out with something new about ourselves, some kind of shared understanding, a feeling that's hard to explain unless you're with us."

"Aw, how cute. He's your hero or your boyfriend?"

"Hero! That's so corny! I love that we're the opposite of heroes. There's no path ahead of us. All three of us, we aren't trying to save anyone or make the world a better place. We just do what we want when we want to, and we know our generation is going to shit."

She pinches my cheek. "That's called being immature, sweetheart."

"I don't know where to go from here. I still don't know who I am. Sometimes I think that I mirror the worst parts of my friends on a daily basis. I don't know what I'm going to exchange for the person that I'm going to become. It's a very scary in-between place to be."

"I still have no idea what I'm doing. Sometimes I think I'm no different than the disposable Kodak I just dropped off. I nicknamed myself 'Kodak girl.' I should just wear a shirt that says, 'Use me once and throw me out.' Sorry, we should go. I just love staying parked in a lot and talking to people when I'm bored. It's nice."

"Come on, don't say that about yourself."

"Sharing this with you doesn't change that you don't know how I feel."

"Maybe it's way easier to be delusional than having to accept the fact we aren't perfect."

"Everyone does that. We all try to convince ourselves we are who we think we are."

"Yeah, it's almost like we make things up about ourselves so we have something to talk about and then we're left empty. The real goes unseen."

"Something I realized last year is it's not ever the things we can see about a person that make us obsessive and haunted, it's what we aren't allowed access to. Fantasies. Mysteries. Curiosities. Those are the things that linger."

"You look so sad right now."

"You don't want to be like me in your twenties, going out every night, trying to discover a love that you know deep down inside doesn't exist. It is impossible for someone to give me back the level of love I've given to them. It must be a Scorpio thing. I just hope you don't grow up to be like all the other men in my life, convinced that your incapacity to be vulnerable is a strength."

"Fair."

She digs into her purse, grabs a bottle of Clinique Happy, and sprays me down. "I don't want your mom calling my mom saying you smell like smoke."

A long pause, a deep breath. "K…"

"Yeah."

"How do you know when your life is getting out of control?"

"It's not like one moment. It's several that become this never-ending chain reaction. You'll start to feel like there are these concealed places inside of you that you keep returning to. These feelings will keep repeating, spinning, and you'll notice nothing is changing. It sucks, but sometimes you have to get lost to remember who you are."

I smile. "I'm not lost."

☆ 57 ☆

I close the blinds and undress as my parents drive away. Shirtless in Hanes boxer briefs with a turbo hard dick, I grab my shoebox of Aurora's letters from under my bed and open it. I grab my dick, lie on the floor, close my eyes, lick her handwriting, and jerk up and down. I think of us fucking in the woods, my hot fingers in her warm pussy. I look down at my dick. *Yeah, no. I'm bored.* I think of what I read in a magazine I flipped through at 7-Eleven yesterday: "Eating a Kit Kat while jerking off makes you cum faster."

I go to the stack of videotapes on my windowsill, grab *Wild Things,* put it in the VCR, and hit play. I grab the remote and rewind to the threesome. Leaning against my bed, I grab my dick and watch Neve Campbell holding the champagne bottle. I spit on my dick, spit on my hand, and jerk my dick up and down so fast. My other hand around my neck, Matt Dillon kissing Denise Richards, knees shaking, my voice drops seven octaves. "Oh, fuck yeah. Come on, Kelly Van Ryan, give it to me. Give it to me. Come on! Kelly Van Ryan! Fuck yeah!" Matt Dillion pulls up Denise Richards's gray skirt, her ass in a white thong. I look down at my belly, hardcore moaning, sticky cum on my treasure trail. I don't want to get up to get a sock to wipe it off. *No matter how hard things get, no matter how out of control the outside world becomes, I know that Denise Richards's ass will always be there for me. She never changes.*

♡ L9 ♡

Aurora,

You're totally right. I can be so damn consumed by my own sadness and emotions sometimes I forget how other people are experiencing the world around them. First off: thank you for sharing all of those beautiful memories of your mother. At first, I was angry with myself for only being able to imagine the pain that you feel as an abstract idea in my head. If I had the power to never make you feel pain or to prevent any future chaos in your life, I would use it. The idea that I can't stop you from ever feeling sad or hurt is excruciating to me. Also, I'm so happy that you dig the necklace!

I loved reading what your mom said about this "place in our hearts." I can't live without the kindness of strangers. I love quick conversations and compliments from people on my walks around the neighborhood. I love charming people, leaving an impression on them. Missing people that you'll never meet is a poetic concept that fascinates me.

I have this friend, Shane, he's so miserable. I mean, Pearl Jam writes songs about people like him, but I know that I hate myself as much as he hates himself, even though I'd never tell him that. I pretend I'm okay, or that I'm more stable than him in some twisted way. I guess there's some comfort in pretending I don't feel as pathetic as I see him. I feel nervous writing this, but I just wish that you could hold me in your arms during the times I feel so worthless, just so I could know everything is going to be okay.

Something I don't understand in this world is the amount of hate and intolerance others have against people who are different. I witnessed a brutal act of homophobic violence at a Y2K party with my friends and I kind of want to join the GSA my school just started. I'm comfortable enough with my sexuality and fighting for human rights is something I'm passionate about. Remember when you told me about your friend Talia's gay brother getting bullied, how you all marched for his rights? I want to achieve your level of virtuousness.

I feel like I'm such an empathetic person. I just feel so different from most people. It's not normal how much time I spend wondering how other people are feeling. Most of the time I forget how I even feel. I don't know what belongs to me or what is just me thinking of someone else's feelings. Maybe that's a state of enchantment? How do I expect someone to understand me if I'm not even enough to figure myself out?

The moment I met you, I felt this safety. I knew that you could give me the space to be who I am. I didn't have to be strong, to put on this image I maintain for all of my friends. I could just be me. I think that's the beauty of girls. You give us boys a place to be ourselves. It's really fucking cool.

Now that I'm back in a place where everyone knows who I am, I crave this anonymity all over again.

If I were to tell my friends any of this stuff, they'd laugh right in my face and call me a "sensitive little flower." You want to know how I know that? I've been making fun of sensitive boys since I was a little kid. I'm fucking awful.

Yours truly,
Brad Sela

♡ LIO ♡

Brad!

I'm just grateful that you're a sympathetic listener and let me express this pain in my soul. Sometimes that's all I really need—a shoulder to lean on. I haven't had an easy life, but I still somehow believe in something beyond myself. Maybe our purpose in this material realm is to recover something that was lost, to return to a part of ourselves that seemed gone forever.

You should understand something: you don't ever have to be any stronger than you actually are. I mean, it's not rocket science! It makes sense. It's easy for you to hang out with groups of guys because it's a predestined script that you've been practicing ever since you were a kid. You never have to reveal anything real about yourself around other boys.

Please be nice to yourself. As much as you want to prevent me from feeling pain, just know that I feel the exact same way about you. Hearing you talk about hating yourself is so heartbreaking.

I'm so proud of you for understanding the importance of protecting people who are different from you. Me and the girls always talk about how that's such an attractive attribute in a guy. Is there anything more ridiculous than nonsensical hate? I totally support you joining the GSA even if your friends make fun of you for it. Screw them! Be your own man.

I'm sure this will look great on your application to Berkeley. I'm so happy to know I've inspired you!

It's so sweet that you can write to me about your doubts and fears. I think often of how you'd give the girls in my cabin love notes to hide on my bed. That's the good guy you are! I remember you telling me that the only way you felt you could ever feel safe just being who you really are was in a hotel room hours away from your neighborhood with me. Maybe privacy is your thing.

At camp, I recall there were moments where I felt like Daniel and I were having a lot of fun and then we'd look over and find you quiet, deep in your own head, contemplating too much. It made me wonder what was happening in there, what was entangling you. I thought maybe, for you, life felt like one long, sad song. I got hooked into the mystery of your world.

I wish I could hold you too when you're feeling lonely. The recurring daydream of the week is me laying on your chest, us on a couch in a basement as you play your video games.

Can you tell me all about your dreams?

Your girl,
Aurora

☆ 58 ☆

In Sam Goody, Shane is moving pop CDs into the metal section. I can't keep my eyes off a blonde girl with decent-sized tits in a tight Dawls belly top and cargo pants at *The Virgin Suicides* soundtrack listening station. She sways her body as I approach, then takes her headphones off.

"What's up?"

I make a suave voice. "Do you like that album? My dad put it out on his record label."

She gasps. "I love Air! Your family is in the biz?"

185

"Oh yeah, I've gone to video awards afterparties and stuff. I've met Mandy Moore. You know, you're beautiful. You kind of look like Anna Nicole Smith."

She blushes. "That's so cool! I can't believe I'm talking to someone who knows people in the biz!" She takes out a pen. "Would you want to hang sometime? What's your number?"

I write a fake number down on her arm and wink. "Call me sometime."

☆ 59 ☆

I study the stickers on the payphone windows in front of the school: House Intruder, LIT, blink-182, Eminem. Eric and Kev appear through the front doors. I avoid eye contact and check my pocket for cigs. Lu's voice plays in my head: "Never care about your reputation. The people at our school are the press. The media is supposed to get you wrong. This is the whole point of celebrity."

I try to dodge them, but they get up in my face. "You aren't going anywhere…"

"What do you guys want?"

Eric's spastic. "We've left messages. We've called a hundred times. We invited you to Marissa Weiss's pool party and you fucking ignore us at school? What the fuck is going on with you?"

"Nothing is going on with me! Beat it, chode sauce!"

Kev pokes my chest. "It's the Satanist you've been hanging out with. Did he put a hex on you? I should kill that guy."

"You don't think people talk? Everyone thinks something is going on with you and that creepy psycho motherfucker."

"That's my fucking friend, asswipe, and you have no idea what the fuck you're talking about. You guys really wanna do this? You think this is some fucking teen movie where I'm the spiraling main character and everything is just *Black Circle Boys*? News flash: that doesn't happen in real life."

"What is wrong with you? We've been friends your whole life."

"You can't drop us like that. And the lies you've been telling your mom? We saw her at Food Front and she was talking about how proud she is that you're on the student council. My little sister is on the student council."

"You need to eat shit."

"You don't even want to hear about me losing my virginity?"

"You don't want to hear about how that chick, Ashley, I was hanging out with's best friend sucked my dick last weekend? Maybe *that's* what this is about."

"You aren't getting any bitches. You're jealous."

"We're going to get our dicks sucked by these Glencoe girls we met at the pool."

"Well, we're gonna *try* to get our dicks sucked. You could come with us."

"No, no. Not try. We *will.*"

"I'm fucking busy."

"Why are you fucking shaking and shit? We're your real friends, your brothers."

"Fuck off. I've not changed, okay? I'm just hanging out with different people this year."

I take off to the student lot, Kev and Eric screaming behind me. "But we've seen your dick. You can't just cut us out!"

I find Lu standing near the tennis court. "Can I please have your keys? I need to be alone. I don't know where else to go right now."

"Uh, sure." He throws me his keys and I run to his car, unlock the door, and fall into the front seat. I rev the engine as I rest my head on the steering wheel. The radio comes on and I shiver to the sound of Collective Soul's "Heavy" as it serenades my tears.

☆ 60 ☆

The dull sound of the freeway beyond the trees. I lift my shirt, rub my stomach, stretch, and stare out at the ramps and rails. I imagine a shot of me in *Rolling Stone* in a bathroom stall, sitting on the toilet, smiling, my thumbs up, a porno mag in my lap, my jeans below my knees. I think of the feature—teen heartthrob in a new WB show. Headphones in hand, I take off my Discman and lean down. A guy in a Shorty's devil head Play-Doh shirt beside a matching backpack is moving his board back and forth with his feet as he sits on the ramp drinking a Bud and smoking a Phillie.

I walk over and sit beside him. "Whassup buddy? Do you go to ND?"

"Whassssup? Yeah, I do." I notice his Joe Boxer waistband poking out of his cargo pants.

"Isn't there a winter dance tonight?"

"How do you know that?"

"My little sister was selling tickets. She does the student store or some shit."

"Sick."

He holds out his cigar. "Want one? Grape flavor."

"Nah."

"Do you skate, bro?"

"In *Tony Hawk*, I can nosegrind. In real life, I can barely olly. The world doesn't need another poser skater."

"Fuck, man. There are so many fag poser skaters who shop at trendy spots like Mr. Rags. It's actually fucked how many dumb sloots wear skater clothes thinking they're cool, like the Porn Star track pants with the little snap buttons on the side."

"Sloots?"

"Like turbo-sluts who sit and watch the boys skate." He pretends to grab tits. Then he holds his deck up to show me a sticker of a busty anime nurse girl holding a syringe. "Check this Hook-Ups sticker that my buddy got me yesterday."

"Sick."

"So fucking sick."

"Yeah, man. Do you know about the haunted pink sofa in the woods? The legendary one?"

"Are you fucking kidding? My girlfriend gave me head on it every lunch period in junior year. The memories, man, reading *Big Brother* and shit."

"Wait. You were flipping *Big Brother* while she was sucking your dick?"

"Fuck yeah, bud."

"That's insane."

"The suburban legend or whatever is the Theta Xi Frat left the couch in the woods in the late eighties. No one wanted to move it. There are all of these creepy stains on it and people try to make it into some real-life *Blair Witch*–type shit. Gross."

"What?"

"Any time I hear *Blair Witch*, I flashback to when my buddy Colby barfed all over me in the theater."

"Fuck that."

"Ever see the Rosa chick from the Shorty's ads in *Big Brother*?"

"Never heard of her."

"You should go look under the cushions. There's some dirty pics of her. Legs open and shit. If you're going to take 'em to beat your meat, make sure to put them back. It's the rule of the legacy to put the porno mags back under the cushion for our fellow North Douglas men to find and initiate themselves."

"Come on, man. A porno mag curse?"

"You laugh now but there are consequences from the natural energy in the universe if you don't return those mags."

"Sela!" Shane calls out. I fistbump the skater and walk down the grass curve to meet him. He is walking toward me in a Cibo Matto shirt with a bag of Doritos in his hand.

"Can I have some? Cool Ranch gives me a boner."

"Just crumbs left." He crumples the bag and throws it in the air. "Self-induced house arrest is so fun."

"You should graffiti 'feed me' on your forehead, male Kate Moss."

"Suck it."

"Your balls are going to turn yellow and fungi are going to start growing on your dick if you don't shower soon."

He lifts his hair. "I got all these matted clumps."

"You are so G-ross sometimes."

"The prince of G-ross."

"Don't be proud of that. It's disgusting."

"Do you not understand what it's like to be suicidal? You don't know what it's like to not have enough energy to brush your teeth or get out of bed. I'm so fucking sorry. I have, I don't know, other things on my mind, like killing myself. I don't have time to think about hygiene."

"Do you ever change out of those fucking 501s?"

"Do you ever change out of those Kmart khakis?"

"You've been wearing those clothes for a week. You look homeless."

"I look how I feel."

"You look like a toy that was dropped off at Goodwill. Major welfare vibes."

"I guess that's my look: toy dropped off at Goodwill."

"Yo, fags!" Lu's voice carries through the air as he appears, his padlock silver chain bouncing on a black t-shirt with "I'M A VIRGIN" in large white letters. Something is moving in the Food Front plastic bag under his arm.

"Is it in there?" I ask.

Lu rolls his eyes. "I'm bored to death, so let's just do it."

"Do what?" Shane asks.

"Shane, you don't even want to know what we're planning to do with this rat."

"You…aren't serious."

Lu clutches the bag and the rat squeals.

I turn to him. "Is it going to lose oxygen?"

"Well, that would fucking suck, retard. It's our job to suffocate the rat."

"Shane, why are you standing like that? You look so fucking angry."

"Why else? The Fiona Apple obsession is getting to his little sad boy head. Now he has his arms crossed like a whiny bitch."

"You didn't tell him?"

"Huh?"

"The reason Shane's eyes are so black is because he stayed up all night watching the *Undressed* marathon again."

"Really, Shane? A girl putting a banana on a condom is hot enough for you?"

"The scenarios are so stupid and mind-numbing that I just can't stop when I start. *Undressed* relaxes my brain."

"I know something else that relaxes your brain. Do you want me to tell him, Shane? You want me to tell Lu what I saw in your room?"

"Don't fucking do it. If you fucking tell him, I'll leave right now and won't come to Pizza Hut."

"We didn't meet up to go to Pizza Hut. We met up to murder, retard."

"Stop fucking with me. Hit me with the 411. Are we going to go eat or not? *Gummo* is on IFC at ten thirty and I want to get a nap in before."

Lu pushes him. "You wouldn't even know about Harmony Korine if it wasn't for me. Fake fan."

"You're just jealous that Manson loves him."

"Oh, look, the LittleBitch.com homepage just finished loading and there's a pic of Shane."

"Pisces." I joke. "Pisces Iscariot."

Shane pushes me. "Did you just fucking say 'Pisces Iscariot' to me?" He Indian burns my wrist.

"What the fuck?"

"Only Lu says that. What is your fucking problem? What is happening to you? Why do you think you can call me that?"

"Lu, say it."

"Shane, we don't fucking need you and your politically correct Pearl Jam, R.E.M.-listening pussy-ass here. Go back to your room and jerk off to RuPaul, tranny fucker." Shane's mouth opens like he might scream. Lu continues. "Did you hear me, tranny fucker? Go back to alt.trannys and read more sick sex stories about RuPaul. I'm sure all the other tranny-fuckers on the internet will circle jerk over it."

"How do you—"

"You left the window open on your computer when you were in the shower, tranny fucker."

Shane points his finger at me. "You don't look like yourself right now. Your eyes are going black." He shakes his head, rubs his eyes, and runs off.

Lu hugs me from behind and leans into my ear. I remember Aurora saying, "If you want to do something bad, you go into the woods."

I push him with my elbow and walk into the trees to find the pink sofa, which sits in a little clearing surrounded by empty beer cans, burned wood, and hundreds of cigarette butts. I lift a cushion and see a brunette on the cover of *Juggs*, a blonde on the cover of *Big Butt*, a redhead on the cover of *Voluptuous*, and a torn-out Shorty's ad of a girl leaning back and spreading with stockings on.

"This must be Rosa. God, she's fucking sexy." I pick up *Juggs*, flip through it, and show Lu. "This is the legendary porn collection that North Douglas men have been keeping here since, like, a hundred years ago."

"A hundred years ago?"

"The eighties."

"Well, you can look at pictures of naked chicks another fucking day. Right now, you need to focus. Every man knows that pussy is a distraction."

Lu and I sit on the sofa. I grab the plastic bag with the rat as it squeaks like it's having a panic attack and zip it into my backpack. "Now there's no way for the little fucker to get out." Lu laughs. "I think I'm in love." I pick up *Big Butt* and flip through it until Lu grabs it.

"No!" He puts it back under the cushion. "Focus!" Lu slaps my knee, then slaps my face. "Fucking focus. You're about to get hazed. This is serious shit."

I hit Lu on the shoulder. "Don't you think this is wrong? There's no cooler older guy who gives enough of a shit to indoctrinate us. We have to haze ourselves. We're making up the rituals. There's no tradition. No older dude fucking cares about us. That hurts."

"Stop being a pussy. Step your cock up. We're about to do what man came to do—take control of nature and abuse it at our will."

"You're right. What's the point of power if you don't abuse it?"

"The intensity of this shared experience you and I are about to have cannot be replicated. No one will ever be able to have what we have together. Brotherhood. We have to be the ones to create the myths we want others to hear about our town. No one else is going to do that for us. You know how I always talk about evoking demons for fun and you never believe me?"

"I'm not doing magick. I told you, I don't believe in it. I don't need to call on demons. I know where evil exists within myself. I know how to access it all on my own. I don't need outside assistance."

"Imagine a world where magick and demons are real, just for one second. I know you think it's bullshit, but just pretend for one second with me."

"Fuck you, fine. I fucking hate you."

"Okay, so this is full-on one hundred percent serious: demons love something called loosh... Shame... Humiliation. Risk. Reward. That's all, loosh."

"Huh? What is loosh?

"Loosh is an energetic substance. It's when you put yourself into a state of fear or lust because demons feed off of fear. If you are in the frequency of lust or fear, you can let one into your body."

"It's like a drug?"

"It's an extremely addictive chemical energy. There is nothing like it, better than any erotic high that exists. You know when you feel so much fucking pleasure that you want to figure out how you can make it last longer? There is an unlimited supply of loosh and you can tap into it all the time."

"I want to try it. I want to try loosh."

He pats me on the back. "That's my boy. This is our circle, our circle of chaos. It's a reality within reality that we can control, that only we are a part of."

I nod. "We are not in control of anything outside of our circle. Anything happening outside of the woods doesn't matter. But what we are doing here right now, in this moment, we are in total fucking control."

"Fuck yeah!" He grabs my hand. "I need you to think of something that makes you feel hatred."

"Like when I want to rent a movie at Blockbuster and someone else has it so I have to go to Hollywood Video, only the video is out there, too? And then I go to Sam Goody to try to buy it and it's sold out?"

"No, no, no. You need to go darker, deeper. Think of something that makes you feel ashamed. Demons *love* shame. Close your eyes."

I'm tied to a chair in my underwear in a frat house surrounded by shirtless men in hoods holding black candles. They're dripping candle wax onto my chest. "Mark him!" A branding iron with their insignia is pressed into my shoulder and burns my skin. Splice. Home alone and someone is pounding on the door. I grab a steak knife and hide upstairs. I peer out my bedroom window and a shirtless muscular man in a Scream *mask is staring back at me. Splice. On a locker room floor, men standing over me, feet near my face. An Oreo stuffed with the cum of the whole football team is pushed into my mouth. "Eat it, fag. You want to be on the team, don't you?"*

I open my eyes. "My body feels…so heavy…so low…"

"That's good, but we're going to need you to be hyped up."

"Huh?"

"Close your eyes again, but listen to me. Think of me as a guided-audio CD." I close my eyes. "Imagine yourself at the 2000 MTV Movie Awards about to win Best Villain. Think of the excitement. Think of the feeling of watching yourself on MTV. Think of the adrenaline of hearing your name announced. Work yourself up into total fucking euphoria. Build the energy up. Feel the feeling of everyone talking about your big win tomorrow all across America."

I open my eyes, look at him, and chant. "Immaterial, no flesh, no blood, immaterial, no flesh, no blood, immaterial, no flesh, no blood."

He grabs my face and pushes it to the side, thumb pressing into my cheek. "Listen. Satan is not something you believe in; Satan is not something that exists outside of you. Satan is something you create within yourself."

"Satan is a celebrity! That's the only reason you want to be him so bad."

"The loosh is activated and working."

"How do you know?"

'How do you *not* know?" Lu hands me a pocket knife. "Welcome to your snuff-tape-satanic-hazing-initiation. Class of 2000, bitch."

I grab the knife, put it to my mouth, lick and kiss the blade, then put it above my forehead.

"Pull up your shirt." Lu gets on his knees and writes in Sharpie on my stomach "666." He pulls up his shirt, showing me his matching "666."

He hands me a pair of plastic gloves. "Where did you get these?"

"The pharmacy? Duh." Lu pulls out a dollar store mirror and poses. "I want to make sure I look hot. This is my first murder."

He flips the mirror over. I pull down my eyelids and look at myself. "If we're going to kill, we might as well look good." I hold up my Jan and toss it back and forth in my hands as the rat screams. "Tonight, on The WB New Tuesday..."

"Motherfucker, you can't find us on The WB Spring 2000 lineup."

"Wait. What do they say in the *Popular* commercial again?"

"'The new show about how everyone wants to be popular.'"

"Fuck that. This is the new show about how everyone wants to be a murderer."

"You could never find this on FOX."

"Sorry, but you aren't going to find this coming up next after *Ally McBeal*."

"Who wants to sit at home watching another rerun of *Angel* when you could be having a ceremonial satanic ritual sacrifice with your best friend?"

"There isn't even anything good on TV this time of day. Everything sucks."

"The channel has flipped. We're inside the TV."

"This isn't *The Craft*."

"This isn't *Dawson's Creek*."

"This is our fucking lives, baby. Uncensored, uncut, never-before-seen footage."

"Our too-horny, too-violent, too-hot-for-MTV lives. Only our brothers get to see this. The Nine Inch Nails *Broken* tape, Stile Project, and rotten.com don't have shit compared to us."

"No suit would ever put this on MTV. That's exactly why we have to do it."

"I wish I brought my video camera."

"In our heads, we get to watch things the way we wanted them to happen, and I'm not willing to let go of that for this memory."

"You don't remember what I told you? Nothing becomes real until it's on camera."

My voice is rising. "No. No videos, no cameras, no Polaroids, no footage, no evidence."

"What the fuck is wrong with you? What's the fucking point of doing this if we don't do it on camera?"

"I don't want to see this again."

"How will we have proof?"

"We don't have to remember anything."

"You think that not taping us will make the experience last longer, but zero footage will only make us lose the memory faster."

"This is an original moment, airing once, live in real-time."

"Shut the fuck up. Come on, I wanna kill."

Lu grabs my hand, flips over my palm, and stabs it with a black thumbtack. I'm bleeding fast. He flips over his palm and hands me the tack. "Hurry. Do it to me." I push it into his palm and his blood bubbles. He puts his palm in the air, then I follow. We push our hands together and close our eyes as Lu speaks.

"Now, repeat after me. Belial. Your fallen sons give you permission to defile."

"Belial. Your fallen sons give you permission to defile."

We open our eyes to clouds of smoke surrounding Lu's face. "What the fuck is that smell?"

Lu sniffs. "Sulfur, baby! Our ritual worked! He's here! Real witches do real things!"

The sulfur fills my mouth and makes me cough. "No fucking way! Are you fucking serious? Oh my fucking God! How the fuck?"

Lu licks the blood off his palm. "There is no such thing as coincidence, only magick."

I grab my Jan and unzip it, take out the plastic bag, and rip the knot with my teeth. I take the rat out and pin it to the couch. I hold up Lu's knife. "We're going to rape the fucking fuck out of you."

Lu is biting his shirt, rubbing his stomach, putting a hand down his pants, and moaning. "I swear my dick is never going to be soft again."

"Hold up! Let's name the rat."

"What?"

"We should name the rat before we murder it."

"Huh?"

"Let's call him Ben Affleck."

"Let the execution of Buttman begin."

I hold Ben against the sofa. Lu etches a smiley face on his cheek. Ben's fur falls onto the sofa as he squirms. The metallic scent of blood fills my sinuses as Ben thrusts and tries to bite my fingers. Lu grabs Ben's head, forces his mouth open, and shoves the blade down its throat.

"Did you just fucking hear that? That sounded like a grape bursting. That was so fucked. Oh my God."

"It stopped screaming. Oh my God! Oh my God!"

"I swear, I have a fucking semi right now. This is so fucking hot."

I go to Lu's bag and pull out a Gillette razor. I watch the blood appear fast as I move the razor across the side of Ben's body. I moan. I grab the knife and flip the rat over. I stab its stomach and blood splatters on my face.

Lu smiles. "Your face right now is my aesthetic. I wish I had my camera."

"Instant gratification is not fast enough for me."

Lu leans down and stabs Ben's stomach, dragging the knife across its fur. He starts jumping up and down. "This is so much fucking fun! Do not go off-script! I want to see more hate in your eyes." Lu is air-jerking as I hold the rat down. "This is my kind of porn. I'm so fuckin hard over this."

I high-five him and look at the rat squirming. "It's not fucking dead yet." A voice enters my head, dragged-out, sluggish: *Boys feed on the lust of other boys*. I look around the trees and up to the sky. "Did you hear that?"

"What are you talking about?"

Boys feed on the lust of other boys. "Did you hear that?" I look down at the rat, bleeding out, its feet twitching.

Lu grabs a balloon out of his bag and sucks in helium. "Aren't you having so much fun?"

"Oh my fucking God. Don't you wish Nine Inch Nails was playing in the background right now?"

I look at him, then back to the rat, grab the knife, and stab Ben in the stomach again. I drop the knife, make a fist, and punch Ben in the face. Lu is MGM lion roaring, banging on his chest. "Woo fucking hoo!" Breathing heavy, I grab the dollar store mirror and look at my reflection. This multiple-reward, multiple-high, multiple-orgasm brain freeze pulsates through me, like a DJ telling me I've just won a VIP sweepstakes, biting into a McChicken with six nuggets in the middle, or the claw crane landing on the Beanie Baby I want.

Lu holds Ben upside down by his tail. "What do you think? Should I bite its head off?"

I smile. "Nah!"

"Give me that broken glass over there."

I pick a shard off the ground, but instead of handing it to Lu, I draw "666'" into Ben's stomach. It's hard to see the numbers beneath the blood. *You are controlling this. You are directing this. You are producing this. You decide each and every moment.* I hold up the rat. "Why won't this fucking thing die?"

I stand on the couch and look out to the trees.

Lu jumps up and down. "Fuck yeah!"

I lift my Doc high in the air and stomp. The final sound of bones crushing.

Lu approaches with McDicks ketchup packets, rips them open with his teeth, and squirts them onto the remains. "Take that, you fuckin whore."

"Well, that's not cherry Kool-Aid."

"What do you feel?"

I shrug. "Nothing."

"Don't you fucking love us? I'm fucking obsessed with us right now." Lu grabs his bag, takes out a piece of Tupperware, and places the corpse inside.

"Oh, you fucking *would* do that."

"Tupperware and animal mutilation are my aesthetic."

I envision Lu holding a new Barbie Polaroid i-Zone camera, taking a sticker Polaroid of me, blood splattered on my face, thumbs up, smiling.

Lu unzips his jeans, cherry boxers showing.

I laugh. "What the fuck are you doing?"

"Should I bust a nut on the corpse? Suck on that, alt.bestiality."

"Come on, man. You need to chill."

Lu is going through his bag. He takes out a face towel and water bottle. He tosses me the mirror. I grab the face towel, dab water on it, look in the mirror, and wipe the blood off my face.

"Haven't you heard? Killing cleans your pores." Lu makes jazz hands.

"It's fifty times more effective than your average Clearasil brand! I'm saving my gloves, taping them in a scrapbook. Senior memories." I take them off and throw them to Lu.

"These are the gory years." Lu holds up the Tupperware. "This is not about causing a scene. This is about leaving one behind, totally fucking scarring someone's mind, like some kid who comes into the woods and finds this."

I nod. "No one else did this, only us. We created this. This myth belongs to you and me."

"Nothing turns me on more than people never being able to unsee something."

"How do we one hundred percent know that we aren't on live TV right now? Do you ever live off-camera?"

"Oh, I'll never live off-camera."

"You are behind the scenes of your own life right now."

"Image is more important than how you feel."

I stare at the dead rat and try to think of a song to match the moment, but no feeling, no intensity, nothing arrives. Lu sits beside me on the sofa. I lean my head on his shoulder. He starts scratching my neck, rubbing on my arms, before leaning in to hug me.

The more I expose, the more invisible I become.

☆ 61 ☆

I stare into the half-drunk Surge in my Burger King cup until visions emerge. I think of myself walking past an electronics store downtown. The city is empty. Silver TVs are stacked in the store window, all playing a clip of me ripping off the top of a Strawberry Splash Go-Gurt tube with my teeth, sucking on it, and leaning back on the couch, before cutting to the bloody remains of the rat hung by an AV cable from a tree. Lu pushes it back and forth. "Aww, it's like a little Beanie Baby." *Do I only ever get to watch things the way that I wanted them to happen? Where does the real experience exist?*

I think of the poll I saw on AOL.com: "Is Britney's racy style a bad influence on young girls? Would your daughter dress like Britney? Do you think schools should have dress codes?" I flash to the *Teen People* at the grocery store. On the cover: "Drug tests, dress codes, curfews… Do you know your rights?" I lean down and bite on the strings of my Starter hoodie and grab my remote. I turn the TV on to the TV Guide Channel: *Moesha* at 8 p.m. on UPN, *Ally McBeal* at 9 p.m. on FOX, *Alanis Morissette Storytellers* at 10 p.m. on VH1, then *George Michael's Video Hour* at 11 p.m. I turn it off and get on my knees, put my fingers inside

200

the VCR flap, get up, and nosedive onto my bed. I scream into my pillow. *I can promise you. This neighborhood is never going to let you live.*

I crawl on the floor to my bathroom and turn on the radio to 94.2 FM. "Ex-Girlfriend" by No Doubt plays at max volume. I lean over the toilet and put my fingers down my throat. My eyes water as I throw up. I look at the chunks of Cool Ranch Doritos mixed with Surge before standing in front of my mirror. *You beg for it. You want to be so far gone more than anything. You want this world to violate you, to hurt you, so something real can happen.* I run to my phone and dial Shane. "Come on. Pick up, Shane. Pick up, pick up, pick up."

Someone picks up. "Hello?"

"Shane?"

"No, this is his mother. I'm just cleaning his room right now."

"Oh, I'm sorry. Do you know where Shane is?"

"He's playing video games."

"Do you think you could get him for me? I'm in his English class and I just need to ask him what the homework was."

"Sure, honey. One second."

I dig a plus sign into my arm.

Shane picks up. "Jesus fucking Christ. Hello?"

"I'm sorry, Shane. I'm so, so sorry about today."

"No, you're not."

"Fuck you. Why the fuck have you not been picking up my fucking calls? I'm tweaking out."

"I've been playing *Zelda.* I'm in Jabu-Jabu's belly right now, and that's much better than hanging out with an animal killer."

"You don't get it. The things I do when no cameras are around are never going to define me. I'm still me! I'm still your friend."

"You have such a hard-on for Lu's dark world and you don't even see it. You are so drugged up."

"Huh?"

"You're so dense. You're a bimbo. An idiot."

"Why are you fucking insulting me?"

"You're trying to play the victim, trying to get me to feel sorry for you, meanwhile you're the one who put yourself in this situation. Take some fucking responsibility."

"Why can't we just move on from this?"

"That's the thing with you two, right? It's always whatever vibes. 'Time to move on. I'm over it.' Well, I'm not going to forget this just because you want me to. I can't forget it. You two are on your way to becoming the next Columbine killers at the speed you're going at."

"You're just jealous. That's it. You're angry that Lu and I are getting closer than you guys ever could. Lu actually likes me. He loves me like a brother. We're best friends."

"Just admit why you did it. Be honest."

"I don't fucking know. Everyone's always calling guys our age evil, that we're tortured and messed up, abusing ADHD meds, and planning school shootings. I was curious, trying to have some fun while playing into the character, becoming a part of the panic."

"Bullshit. I know why you did it."

"Fuck you! There's something about winning the approval of another guy—it's intoxicating. You can't help it. No girl could ever give me this feeling. It's too powerful."

"This is your life you're gambling with. You can't even see that. And for what? Your obsession with someone?"

"I'm not obsessed with him."

"You're obsessed with who you become when you're with him. That's the truth."

Shane hangs up and I slam the phone down. I put on MTV. Maynard Keenan is in purple-lensed goth goggles and a "do what thou wilt" hoodie on a tour bus, holding up a copy of Bret Easton Ellis's *Glamorama*. "This is what I'm currently reading. Ellis captures how sick American society is, how desensitized, how numb, and how empty the youth are today. You talk to a teenager and he doesn't know the difference between violence in a movie and the violence he sees on the news." I turn the TV off, throw my remote across the bed, and press my finger down on my teeth. A voice in my head: *Murder is an act of sex, not an act of violence.* I dial Lu and scratch up my arms as the phone rings. He picks up.

"I'm like *this* close to overexposure. It's not normal who I become when I'm with you. It's not healthy."

"Hold on. Do you mind if I do a line?"

"Not at all."

Lu snorts. "What the fuck do you want?"

"Whoa. Pipe down."

"What? You won't stop calling and I'm busy. I was just with you three hours ago."

"You don't feel weird about what we did?"

"Uh, no? I already forgot about it. Did you see that Brian McFayden was talking about how celebrities are wearing Porn Star? They showed a clip of the girl from *American Pie* wearing it on *Buffy*. Also, what do you think about the new Fruit Gushers coming out? The Hawaiian Punch flavor? I can bring you a box from my job when they come in."

"We just murdered and you're talking about Fruit Gushers?"

"I've been thinking, maybe video games are real life and real life is a video game. I can't feel shit. It's not like there was anything good on TV while we were out there. This is super chill."

"But it's so empty being this numb. It's like I'm stuck in between with nowhere to go."

"I read on the Manson message board that this girl from Alabama's older brother is in a frat. He and all the guys impaled a dog and threw it into the river. They taped the whole thing and it was super chill. Oh, and you know that book I've been reading, *American Psycho*? Patrick Bateman, the serial killing stockbroker, sticks a rat up a girl's pussy. We could have been way, way worse."

"Yeah, you're right. And you know what? Why didn't we just put a 'You will die in ten days now that you've found this dead rat' sign in the Tupperware? Why didn't we get someone to call a news crew to catch us?"

"Why are you mocking me, dick munch? Have you ever gone to rotten.com? There's actual kiddie porn all over the internet. Compared to what I've seen online, what we did was tame. I've seen pretty much every gross image on the internet and thought that pushing myself, that creating the next crazy thing in real life rather than looking for it online, would make me feel good. And fuck yeah, I felt good for a second there, but the loosh wore off, and I'm over it. Onto the next."

"You don't think there's something wrong with me? I feel so fucking guilty."

"You need to zoom out, zone out, chill out, bleach what happened out of you. Put on MTV, maybe jerk off. Did you jerk off today?"

"Not yet?"

"Maybe you were so horny that you took it all out in murder. Now you have that post-nut clarity shit."

"But I didn't nut."

"You did, my friend, you did. Wait one sec. Mom, I can't fucking hear you from downstairs. Also, where the fuck are my goth boots with the buckles? I can't find them. Stop going through my room and touching all my shit. If you threw out my shirt, I will nuke this place. I fucking hate you!"

"Lu, I'm going to go."

"Look, before you hang up, remember this: caring makes you weak. One hundred percent of your problems will go away once you stop giving a shit. Nothing matters."

I hang up and flip onto my stomach in bed. Pushing my head into the pillow, a voice outside of me: *One day you will understand that your demons have been the ones looking out for you.*

☆ 62 ☆

Blurry-eyed in the hallway at Stephen's house party, I chug a bottle of Aftershock. OMC's "How Bizarre" blasts from the speakers, blissing me out as I stumble toward a bleach blonde, blue-streaked junior girl in a shiny foil belly top, *Playboy* sticker glowing on her stomach. A guy in a bandana and a Nautica polo lips a joint in the corner, laughing as he watches me.

Slurring my words, ready to grab her hips, I say, "Yo, wanna dance? You're fine, girl."

"Brad?"

"Corinna?" It's Eric's little sister, all grown up. She looks freaked out.

She grabs my new "filthy" chain. "You missed my brother's birthday! My mom was so upset. You haven't missed her cupcakes since you guys were like ten."

"Yo, girl. I'm fine. You feel me?"

"Is everything okay with you? You're wasted. My brother is freaked out about you. He was saying that he and Kev were going to go over to your house and plan an intervention. Rumor has it you're going off the rails."

"Fuck you, little bitch. No one's fucking coming to my fucking house, yo."

"Don't call me a bitch. You're not a wigger. Stop. Ew! We used to play Sega together! Who are you right now?"

"You don't fucking know me no more. Y'all think you know me? You have no idea!"

She shakes her head and walks away.

☆ 63 ☆

The chaotic pattern that appears on the screen when you point a video camera at a TV is all I'm thinking about as I stare into the car's rear-view mirror. The Texas song "Say What You Want" is fading out on the radio. We're parked in front of the duck pond. Lu passes me a cig. Shane is in a Roxy Music shirt in the backseat drinking Mountain Dew.

I tap Lu. "Do you know about this new thing, affluenza? It's a theory that teenagers who grow up wealthy are totally numbed out by the violence and immorality of the world around them."

Shane laughs. "Okay, so now having the free time to participate in satanic animal torture is a luxury of the upper class?"

Lu chimes in. "You need to stop watching Parents Bullshitting. This info is useless. Come on, high-class suburban psychosis? Next."

"Everyone thinks that to be a rich kid, you have to go to private school, but does anyone ever think that our parents put us in public school so we can be less obnoxious and more cultured? I think going to this school humbles and grounds me."

Lu nods. "I want to make something of myself on my own, even if it means working at a grocery store and blending in. I don't want that dependency and control."

"My dad could buy me a Prada raincoat right now and maybe I'd feel powerful for a second, but I think it's more powerful to not be excessive. It's way cooler."

Shane turns to me. "My grandfather calls being flashy *nouveau riche*."

"Shane, not everyone can say their grandfather is the founder of Avery paper. You're going to get a trust fund when you turn eighteen. You're going to be fine."

"Lu, you know all your cool older friends who live in cheap apartments downtown and protest gentrification with their 'Starbucks is evil!' chants would be horrified if they knew the kind of family you come from."

"That's crossing a line."

"That's interesting. You don't like being reminded that you aren't the only one in this circle who wears a few masks?"

Lu plugs his ears. "I'm not listening."

Shane pulls out the new issue of *Spin*. "The Miseducation of FIONA APPLE."

I tap Lu's shoulder. "You're going to want to see this."

Lu looks back and bangs the steering wheel. "Why couldn't we have left her where she belongs—in the last decade? Fiona Apple must be stopped. I hate that cunt!"

Shane laughs. "You never read the article where she was talking about how she knows that she's going to die young? Isn't that me?"

"That's all a lie. It's a character she's creating for the media."

I grab Lu's headrest. "*MTV News* had a clip of her performing the other night. She's got a new album out."

"She's just the girl in class who writes lowercase poetry and is trying so hard to be deep but is just a pretentious bitch. I mean, she ditched Manson at a red carpet event. Unforgivable." Lu leans over, grabs the mag out of Shane's hand, spits on Fiona's face, then throws it back to him.

"Oh man, what the fuck! I just got that in the mail."

I laugh. "We all knew that it was going to get wet at some point today. I bet you wish there was a scratch 'n sniff of Apple's pussy in there."

"Ugly-hot man. She's hard to resist."

"You need to go to fionaappleshoulddie.tripod.com. It's this amazing site where everyone writes all of the great ways that she should die. The *Mad TV* tape I have of them making fun of her 'Sleep to Dream' video is spot on."

"Shane! Your dick would kill her. That's how tiny she is."

Shane holds up the mag and points to an ad. "What's Helmut Lang?"

"I don't fucking know!"

Lu scoffs. "The spoiled girl stunt that she pulled at the VMAs was so desperate. We know this world is bullshit, Fiona. There was this gross clip I saw where she was complaining about being exploited, looking for sympathy."

I shake my head. "Exploited? All girls are victims who want attention. It must be so hard crawling around on MTV in your underwear. It's not like every other teenager in this country doesn't want that opportunity."

Shane bangs his head on the window and drags his fingers across the trim. "I have that clip on tape. That was so raw. She really spoke from the heart. Her *Unplugged* is so good. The Jimi Hendrix cover? Outstanding. You guys just don't get real music."

Lu lights another cig. "If your whole personality is defined by the fact that you got raped when you were twelve, then you're very boring."

I laugh. "Whenever a chick calls *Loveline* and starts going on about her emotional distress problems? Boner kill."

"I bet her label made up that story to sell records. Apple talks about the rape on Stern, her sob story shocks everyone, then she mentions the song about the incident, and boom, you're hooked. The miserable pouty bitch burns your pockets."

I nod. "Jewel and Fiona should star in *Vagisil: The Live Musical* sponsored by Lilith Fair, starring women who don't shave their legs."

"Alanis Morissette and Tori Amos can join them."

Shane raises his voice. "Something you two idiots share is being so negative about everything because you need to reinforce your fragile self-images. Two hateful, directionless cynics who think they're above everyone isn't exactly groundbreaking."

I tap his knee. "Thank you, Shane. Thank you for your weak-ass input. We really needed that."

"Glad to help." Shane shows us a picture of Christina Ricci. "What do you think of her?"

"Isn't she a compulsive liar who tells reporters she blows her brother?"

Lu laughs. "She and I should get married."

"By the way, Lu, what the fuck did you want to tell me about that you couldn't tell me in the halls earlier?"

"I sold the tape!"

"Which one?"

"The snuff movie we made during Xmas break. It's so Richard Kern, so Kembra Pfahler vibes. It belongs in an art gallery."

"*America's Scariest Home Videos*. What was the listing?"

"'Tape of two shirtless underage boys. Lots of real blood (not fake!) Industrial soundtrack. Forty dollars. Comes hidden in a *Bambi* case. *Underfed and Underage Pacific Northwest Fresh Teen Meat Vampires Vol. 1*.'"

I laugh. "And now, your feature presentation... So how the fuck did you meet this guy?"

"AOL chat room. Selling snuff tapes on the internet to old daddies is my new hobby. You would shit if you met this guy. He seemed so normal, like a regular suburban sports dad."

"Friends don't let net-head friends start a black-market snuff tape business on the internet."

Lu smiles. "Creating your own video ring online is the most revolutionary thing you can do in 2000."

"Why?"

"Blood and gore are sacred images. You never get to see them unless something is wrong, but violence is always lurking underneath, even when you can't see it. I don't want you to freak out, but the guy who bought the tape said that he recognized you from somewhere. He had this bracelet with this weird symbol on it."

I pause. "How on earth could this stranger see a photo of me?"

"Well, I put a picture of us hanging out on my website."

"Are you kidding me? You posted photos of me to cyberspace without asking? That's a huge violation."

"Take a chill pill. God, I'm so tired of your paranoia."

"Well, he's lying. There's no way he knows me. He's fucking lying, Lu."

☆ 64 ☆

Above the Quik Drop slot, the sign on the Blockbuster window reads "New February Releases—Top VHS Rentals of the Week: *Stigmata, Love Stinks, An Extremely Goofy Movie*. Coming Soon in March: *Body Shots, The Sixth Sense, Drive Me Crazy*." I put two tapes through the slot. In the parking lot, Shane is in a Led Zeppelin shirt I've never seen him wear before. He lifts up his shirt and rubs his stomach.

I hit his shoulder. "Want to know why you're a good friend?"

Shane looks away. "'Cause I forgave you for murdering a rat? No, I really don't. I'm in a bad fucking mood. I left my lollipop in my locker and my whole day is ruined. I swear, I'm fucking cursed. I hate having to do this whole being alive bullshit."

"'Cause when I wanna get out of the house, walk to Blockbuster, and drop off tapes, you come with me."

He pinches my cheeks. "If I had a life, I'd be doing other things."

"Did you ever play *Pogs* when you were a little kid, or eat Pizza Rolls at your friend's house? Did you have *G.I. Joe* sheets? Fuck, remember Crystal Pepsi?"

"I didn't have a fun childhood. I don't remember much."

I touch his shoulder. "Look, I've been wanting to ask this for a while. Why do you let Lu treat you the way he does? He's such a dick to you! He insults you in front of people. I can feel how uncomfortable it makes you."

He shrugs. "I've known him since I was twelve. He's the closest person to me. I don't know, I guess it's better than having no one around to talk to. He always does whatever he wants to me. I gave up on trying to control it a long time ago. He's shitty to me, but I'm shitty to myself too."

"And all the weird shit you guys do? Like making the snuff movies and all of that? You're okay with it?"

"I don't mind any of that because I'm just going to cut myself anyway. I might as well make something creative out of being a self-mutilator. What about you? You're obsessed with him."

"I'm not!"

"Sure you are. You're doing way worse shit with him than I ever did. Can I tell you something fucked?"

"Sure."

"You know, when we were, like, fifteen, he had this pet tarantula. We made this tape where I was in clown face paint and he filmed the spider going down my shorts like it was going to fuck me or something. Sometimes I get this weird feeling that if I piss him off, he'd use that as blackmail against me. Just don't be dumb. Don't let his video camera capture anything that can be taken out of context."

"Are you warning me about what he does with his video camera?"

He looks me in the eye. "I'm telling you to be careful."

"Well, you know, I always defend you in front of him when he's making fun of you. I know sometimes I can gang up on you around him but it's just in fun, you know? Like brothers. You make jokes about me too."

"Yeah, yeah. It's fine."

"Honestly, I'm really afraid that if I play it safe all the time, I'll be living my life for other people. Lu challenges that for me. It's like channel surfing and landing on the one thing you wanted—it's him."

"You think you'll miss out on something that you won't discover about yourself if you don't pursue the friendship."

"Exactly. How did you know?"

"I felt that way once. Now you're his biggest fan and he knows it. If he was a celebrity and there was a *Fanatic* episode about him, you'd be sending in your audition tape."

I knock Shane's shoulder. "Shush. You know, if he doesn't stop being a piece of shit to you, we can always team up and kill him."

"Do you mean that?"

"If there's a chance he could blackmail us, we might have to strike first."

"You're kidding, right?"

☆ 65 ☆

Shane and Lu are behind me in the photo booth. I pull the dark curtain behind us, lean in, and drop in a quarter. "HOLD STILL" is written above the camera lens. We stick our middle fingers up. *Flash.* We lift up our shirts and Lu bites my nipple. *Flash.* I cover Shane's eyes. *Flash.* Shane turns around, pulls down his jeans, and moons the camera. *Flash.* I get out and Lu follows as Shane waits for our pics to spit out. I watch a kid with frosted tips stick a "Satan Inside" decal sticker on the Pepsi machine across from us. I can hear a remix of Fuel's "Shimmer" drizzling out of PacSun. The bass rattles the store windows. Lu walks over to a gumball machine and finger-bangs the slot. "Oh, you like that? Yeah, I bet you do. You're welcome, you little bitch."

211

☆ 66 ☆

By the duck pond, a college guy in a red Adidas tracksuit and wraparound Oakleys stands in front of his car.

"You guys Lusif's friends?"

"Yeah. You're Jeremy?" I fist-bump him. "I thought there was gonna be some kind of secret porno salesman handshake. I was the one you were talking to on AIM on Shane's account."

"You made it in time."

"You said five-thirty. We bolted over here."

"You boys look how I thought you'd look."

"Uh, is that a good thing? How old are you?"

"Twenty-three. Me and my buddies do this to make money off of seniors on the side. You boys get your porn, we get our dollas."

"Okay."

"Yeah."

"So, can we have our porn now?"

Jeremy takes a plastic Disney Store bag from inside the car. I peek inside: *Buttman's Big Butt Euro Babes* and *Red Vibe Diaries* 2 starring Stacy Valentine. I hand him the cash and he counts it.

Shane smirks. "Do you know how we can get any pics or vids of girls our age? Or at least ones that might look like they go to our school but, you know, in porn? Any discs of junior girls?"

Jeremy smiles dirty. "Try the internet."

"We will be seeing you again. This won't be the last time. I want *High Society* next."

☆ 67 ☆

I bang on the door until my English teacher, Mrs. Caldwell, lets me in. "You smell like cigarettes," she says.

"The person who drove me to school smokes and so does everyone in this classroom."

"You're fifteen minutes late, so you need to stay outside."

"I can't do that."

"Go to the office then."

"What are you talking about? I've never been to the office."

"I don't want to deal with this today, Brad."

"*Deal* with what? I'm never late."

"I'm not letting you in my class, Brad. I'm sorry. You have to leave."

"Excuse me? Are you—"

"Are you high right now?"

"*What*? I'm not a druggie. You know I'm not a druggie."

"You are the last kid I would consider at-risk, but is something going on with you? Do you want to talk after class?"

"Is this about my grades dropping? Please don't call my parents. Can you just give me extra credit to get me back to an A? We've done it before. Please."

She sighs. "That's fine, but only because I know how good you can be when you want to be. Now please get your notes out and sit down."

As I walk to my seat, Jason cracks, "There are some wicked rumors going around about you."

"Why would anyone talk about me?" I snipe.

Alexis in a purple scarf: "Brad, is it true Lusif is a model from New York? I heard he has an agency and that he's been in *The Face*."

Madison in a Roxy shirt: "I heard his uncle is a Hollywood big shot and that he's going to be in *Scream 4*."

Matthew in a WWF hat: "Brad, I heard you were banging your head on your locker yesterday. Is it true that MTV is coming to document you for *True Life: Senior Heroin Head*?"

Philip in a WebTV shirt: "I heard that Brad is into black magick. He's part of The Church of Satan, yo, and Lusif is his boyfriend. They kidnap little boys and torture them on the pink sofa."

Brooks in a Taco Bell dog shirt: "Anyone who hangs out with Lusif is desperate for attention. He's the one scribbling those devil heads in fake blood in the boys' bathroom."

Christina in a pink tank top: "I heard—"

Before she finishes, I stomp. "Stop! Stop! Just stop! I've been at this school for four years and I have never even heard one rumor about me, but now because I have some new friends, you all think that I'm some kind of psychopath? I—"

I run out the door and down the hall.

☆ 68 ☆

I watch from the hallway through the half-open door: Lu's eyes are rolling back on the bed, hands down his pants, rubbing his dick. He's in a Coil shirt and black jeans. A magazine is on the bed, split open.

"I'm twenty-one, a hung top. A strict, total top. I'm not into dick at all. I just want to abuse you. Yeah, I'm straight. This is my first time calling. You said in your listing that you love jizz. Is that true? Good, 'cause I want to fuck your mouth like it's a hot tight pink pussy, and when I'm inside of your mouth, I'm going to think of a huge pair of jugs to cum. Does that turn you on? Yeah, I bet you want a hung, twenty-one-year-old down your throat. I bet it turns you on that Pam Anderson is going to be the one making me cum and not you. I'm curious, yeah. I'm curious, 'cause I don't know. I wanna feel more satanic. I don't know, gays are like cocksucking zombies so I thought, you know, you might as well treat a faggot like a cocksucking zombie. Yeah, keep calling your hole a pussy. Yeah. I'm going to come over and beat your face with my huge dick. I'm going to rape your mouth 'cause you're a pathetic little faggot. Yeah, you want me to call you a fag again? So is it true that you're a photographer for *Details* and friends with Peter, the editor at *XY*? Do you think you could take some pictures of me and get me in a magazine? There's no other way into the industry. I want to be a huge star. I'll fuck whoever I have to fuck. I'll fuck my way to the top, do the whole casting couch thing, I'm so down to do it if it means that I get to be a movie star."

I run down to the kitchen and pick the house phone up off the counter. "Oh yeah, baby! Yeah! Suck my dick! Oh, yeah!"

"Brad!"

I run back up to his room, sit on his bed, and look down at the "69 reasons to j/o to Eminem" on the open magazine page.

"How did you get in?"

"You told me to meet you here."

"How did you know I wasn't using my own line?"

"I know you'd only ever call a gay sex hotline using your mom's phone so AT&T can bill her and her Christian Fundamentalist Republican ass can be mortified. You aren't actually going to meet up with that guy, right?"

"Teasing fags is entertaining."

"Can we leave now? I want a Slurpee."

♡ L11 ♡

Aurora,

Thank you so much for this last letter. It's comforting to know that someone is paying attention to all of my details, just noticing me. I love the way that you perceive me. You remind me of how good of a person I am. I'm sorry for upsetting you with all of the self-hate talk, but it's just what's going on these days. This is just not my year.

I'm happy to let you know that I joined my school's GSA and it's been great learning how to spread tolerance. You aren't going to believe this, and if you have a soft stomach, maybe take a breath before you read on: a couple of seniors mutilated a rat in a Satanic ritual behind my local skate park. It's freaked a lot of people out. Some people think we've got Satanists lurking around, but I bet it's just a couple of boys doing dumb shit because they're bored. It seems like 2000 is bringing out the worst in people.

Dreams! A haunting topic. The whole idea of your mind being filled with significant images as you sleep is very strange to me. What do you think dreams are? Are they the places where we become nostalgic for something that has never happened to us? I wish that our shared dreams could be one movie, all cut up into pieces. You have some and I have some, and when we go to bed, we get different scenes on the screens in our minds. In our conversations together, we could try to bridge together the worlds being built for us within the multiplex of our dreams.

I don't know if you know this feeling, but do you know when you're in a dream taping something, you wake up thinking that the video exists somewhere in your room, but it doesn't? In reality, it never will, of course, but you still remember watching it with all of the feelings it gave you, but all that's left is a void?

Am I making any sense? I'm sorry if this was too much.

Yours truly,
Brad Sela

P.S. I wish I could be with you on your birthday. I guess my letters and this gift will have to do for now.

♡ L12 ♡

Brad!

There you are! You make sense to me! Thank you for mirroring all of the feelings I felt when my mom died. You could say it made me feel like a real crazy girl searching the house for something I thought I owned but never did.

I love the butterfly stickers and the ring. They are so pretty! Thank you for remembering my special day. I really miss you too.

That's so gross about the rat. I hate gore. That's why I can't watch horror movies. I'm too sensitive. How haunting it must feel to know that such a senseless act of violence has happened in a place so familiar. I hope they catch those guys and give them what they deserve. It's so cruel and disgusting. Only degenerate boys could do such a thing. Please keep yourself clear of boys like that. They're poison.

Sometimes I wish I could bring a video camera into my dreams and transfer them to tape just to show you all the beautiful things I see. I've craved this closeness for so long. I know that you have, too.

Oh! Oh! I wanted to tell you. My dad let my girl, Lizzy, come over. She and I were up on the bed eating starfish Dummy's Gummies and watching House of Style *and she asked me: "Have you ever dreamed in anime?" And God, I thought it was such a strange concept, I knew I'd have to ask you about this. I mean, seeing an entire dream in this format? It'd be so trippy. Has that ever happened to you?*

I have another question for you: do you think that when we expose something precious to sunlight, it loses its magic? Oh! I'd love to own an entire box set of your dreams on VHS, and I'm sure you'd love to watch a network playing mine. Memories, dreams, it's all the same to me.

Your girl,
Aurora

P.S. I'm not kidding! I have this written on a sticky note from a few months ago: "the feeling of being nostalgic for things that have never happened." I love that our minds are so in sync!

☆ 69 ☆

A little girl in a *Blue's Clues* shirt in front of me on the bus is spinning a Tamagotchi. I look at the Tinkerbell Band-Aid wrapped around her finger, then up at her elastic tattoo choker. *Innocence is so powerful. How could I ever look away? Was I ever this innocent? What would a conversation be like between her and me if I was her age right now? Sometimes I don't want to wonder who I'll become, I just want to be there. I want it now. The waiting, the expectation, is what will fucking kill me. How many times a day must we take our own innocence away?*

She turns to me. "What are you looking at, weird boy?"

"Cool Tamagotchi. You keeping it healthy?"

217

"I love my Tamagotchi so much. I feed it every day."

"It's like a digital pet or whatever?"

"Did you know that chameleons are omnivores? I have a whole book about them. People think they're slimy, but I like them. I wish I could have one of my own! You're a weird boy."

"Aren't you a little too young to be on the bus alone?"

"Weird boy, can I ask you a question?"

"Sure."

"Why do all the boys on the playground point at me and laugh, and tell me that girls are dumb and can't play Game Boy? Why don't they make a Game Girl? I love *Pokémon*. Boys drool! Girls rule!"

"Those boys are the dumb ones. Don't listen to them."

"*Small Soldiers* is my favorite. I've watched it one hundred times." I laugh. "Why are you giggling at me? When I get older, I want to be pretty. I want to be a really pretty girl."

The bus stops and she gets up.

"Where are you going?"

"I'm going to my Grandma's! One day you'll come to Grandma's too! We'll all go to Grandma's!" She sticks her tongue out at me as she is about to get off. "Did you know that whenever you fall asleep out of nowhere, it means a fairy has kissed the back of your ear?"

I look at a group of girls in the middle of the bus, all blondes with crimped hair, blue streaks, in the same "SIMULACRA SLUT" baby tees, patched hearts on their jeans, impressive tits, sucking on heart-shaped lollipops. "It's true! She did a total subway with Cody and Brody. I even heard that Cody's friends live streamed it on the internet. It was a total hidden webcam thing. She didn't even know."

"Chris is such a liar. He told everyone he fucked Lizzie at Jason's backyard rager."

"Chris is the one with the BMW? The one who goes to Earl Marriot?"

"No, that's Justin Bobby."

"Justin is the one who wears the Starter sweats every day? With the rich dad who works in radio?"

"No, that's Jeremy."

"Jeremy is the one who's Steve's friend?"

"No, Jeremy is the one who knows Luke."

"Luke is the one we hung out with who said that his dad is super rich but how could he be super rich when he wears those nasty Champion sweaters all the time? Ew! It's called Bloomingdale's. Get help."

I look out at a bus stop adorned with a poster of a cyber anime busty logo girl with purple skin and imagine rotating heart computer images flashing and spinning around her. In tattoo henna font: "Are you ready to bring order to the chaos?"

I take a cigarette out of my bag and put it into my mouth. I hold my wallet and look at my student ID, then put it back in the bag. I think about the people living in the houses we pass, the people my age who live in this neighborhood who I've never met, who I could connect to. The bus drives past the trees, then the skate park, my school, and the strip mall.

We hit the highway and I take out the Prodigy CD that Lu gave me by my locker yesterday. I open it, put it into my Discman, hit play, put the case away, then put on my headphones. I bang my head against the bus seat to "Smack My Bitch Up" and think of myself in the back of a minivan in Miami. There's a Latina chick with a big ass on all fours in a thong, ready to get destroyed doggystyle. A camera crew is with us. The guy behind the camcorder is flashing money and smacking me on the shoulder. "She's all yours, buddy. You own her." He hands me oil to rub all over her ass cheeks. "*Scream 3* is the best *Scream* of all." "An all-new *Malcolm in the Middle* starts 8/7 central on FOX Sunday." I hear this loop as I look out the window and realize that the bus is about to stop. I get up and wait for the people in front to get off. I jump down the stairs and into the parking lot. Leaning against the mall entrance wall, I light my cig, smoke, and put my Discman back into my bag.

☆ 70 ☆

Inside the auditorium, a senior pic photographer wears all black. "Are you ready?"

I'm in my cap and gown. A blue and purple backdrop is behind me. The flash bursts.

☆ 71 ☆

The rock station plays low as I sit on my bed with my history homework. VH1 shows a preview of *Behind the Music: Russell Simmons*. A song I've never heard before plays and something feels special about it. I run to my radio, turn up the volume, headbang, and circle around my room, jumping up and down. I look for a tape.

"Fuck, I'm out! It's about to finish. Fuck. Please say the name, DJ."

"That was 'Absolutely,' the new one from Nine Days on 106.9."

I fist pump. "Yes!" I write down "Absolutely—Nine Days / call rq it to record the full song, buy tapes" on a receipt beside my bed.

My mom yells, "Brad, dinner is ready!"

I walk downstairs and sit at the table.

My dad comes in. "How's school going, kiddo?"

"Fine. Senior year, keeping up the straight A's."

"I saw that on your report card. Awesome stuff, bud."

"Uh-huh."

The phone rings. I get up and answer it.

"Hi! This is AT&T. We'd like to talk to the head of the household about changing your long-distance plan."

"Can you please stop calling us during dinnertime? For the one hundredth time, we don't want to change our long-distance plan. Goodbye!" I hang up the phone and walk back to the table.

"Whoa! Letting some steam off there, kiddo?"

"Sorry, I'm just so annoyed." I twirl my spaghetti. "Can I ask you a question, Mom?"

"What is it, honey?"

"Why here? Why did you choose this place to raise me?"

"We just wanted you to be in the safest environment, the safest community, away from the city. It's so quiet here. We just wanted to give you the best life. It's like an empty island secluded by the river. There are good people, nice neighbors. Anyways!" She looks at my dad. "Brad has been so busy with all of his student council projects."

"Of course I have. That's why I haven't been home lately! We're planning how to get all of the funds for prom by May, staying up all night. Counting money, ticket sales…".

"Wow, that's great!"

"Yes, it is great. They have so many after-school projects! I'm so proud of him. He's never home anymore. He's really growing up!"

"Brad, remember when you used to scratch X's on the dinner table when you were a little boy?"

"There's no way that he could remember, he was so little! I can't believe it. You're seventeen!"

"Dad, can we go to the mall tomorrow and get a mini fridge for my room?"

Mom freaks. "No! Oprah just had someone on her show talking all about how all of the kids in this country are becoming addicts because of sugar and junk food. Candy can lead to heroin addiction. There's facts about it from doctors I saw on TV!"

"Okay, so I'm not allowed to have a new Windows computer in my room and now I can't even have a mini fridge? How is that fair? I have to hear everyone at school talk about their mini fridges and all of the stickers they're buying to decorate them. I want to put my Snapple Elements and Sobe in there!"

Dad agrees. "Brad, we will get you your mini fridge."

I smile. "Can you pass me the salad?"

☆ 72 ☆

"She's different, you don't understand. You weren't there last summer."

Lu and I are in black sweaters smoking underneath the bleachers at sundown, overlooking an empty field.

Lu smirks. "You have the post-virginity drought. You're only so attached to this Aurora chick because she was your first. This happens all the time."

"You have no idea what you're talking about. This is why I didn't want to tell you."

"You're writing letters to a girl you met at summer camp, creating a fantasy of her in your head because you're bored and horny. Do you have nothing else to do but delude yourself over some girl?"

"Can you, for the first time in your life, actually show up and be a supportive friend? You can't just nod, agree with me, be happy, and let me have a nice thing? I met someone. That's what friends are for."

"You're cybering and you don't even know it."

"Cybering?"

"You have an online flame. Sure, you guys started out in person, but everything about you now is virtual. The reason things feel so good is because there's no real-life work. You only have the good memories as the jumping-off point."

"Well, fuck. Are you saying that I'm no different than the chatroom freaks who have AOL girlfriends?"

Lu emphasizes, "You're about thiiiiiis close to being into *Final Fantasy* hentai."

"Fuck!"

"You'd be less interested in what sweater label Mark Hoppus is wearing this month if you fucked more."

"I thought when you like a girl, you aren't supposed to bang other chicks."

"That's a made-up rule."

"Wait, so you're telling me that having a cyber lover doesn't mean that I can't sleep with other girls?"

"You can't touch her, and until you can, she's not real. You're a free man."

"Why didn't you tell me this before? I could've gone to town on some drunk chick at the Y2K party."

"Shane gets more pussy than you, and that's plain sad. Think about that for a second."

"What about that Amber chick who blew you at the park the other night? She got some fine junior friends?"

"You're already set up. Tonight at three a.m. I told this slutty sophomore chick, Carly, that's got a huge crush on you that you want to meet up behind the gas station by NA."

"This isn't some Heidi Fleiss-type shit, is it?"

Lu slips his arm around my neck, puts me in a chokehold, and whispers in my ear, "What's that boy? Did you say, 'I want to fuck the hot sophomore chick behind the gas station tomorrow night?' Is that what I heard?"

"I'll do it, but under one condition."

"I'm listening." He lets me go.

"Hand over the Baphomet necklace."

He pulls on the chain. "There's dark sex magick infused in this. Are you sure?"

"Hand it over, big guy."

He undoes his chain. "Can I put it on you?"

"Sure."

I turn around. Hands on my skin, he locks it around my neck.

☆ 73 ☆

Behind the gas station, under the backlights by the dumpster, Carly is waving at me. She has purple hair, a zip-up sweater, an o-ring choker, a glow-in-the-dark heart ring, and blue jeans. I walk up to her.

"Brad? I can't believe it's you."

"Carly? Lusif told me you were looking forward to our little hangout."

"I can't believe you have a crush on me. I think you're one of the hottest guys at school. I was so happy when Lu told me."

"Um, yeah, I think you're super cute. How old are you?"

"I just turned fifteen. Are you eighteen yet?"

"Still seventeen. Why'd you want to meet up here?"

"Well, it's a dare between me and my friends regarding who can have the kinkiest public sex."

"It *is* pretty empty."

She nods. "Well, yeah. Let's do it then?" She unzips her sweater. I start sucking on her cleavage as she moans. I grab her tits, and she puts her hand on my dick. She giggles. "How did you get so hard so fast?"

"My dick is kind of like a rocket launcher. I'm horny all the time. Take your bra off."

She lifts up her sports bra and I motorboat her tits. "You like that?" I take a Trojan out of my wallet. She lies down. I lean over. "What are you doing?"

"I wanna look at you while I do it."

"I don't do missionary, sorry. If you want another guy to get your rocks off who is into that, find him."

"Sorry. I hope I'm not messing this up."

"I don't want you to look at me. I don't even know you. I just want you to feel good."

"I'm sorry. I shouldn't have said anything."

"We're good. Don't be sorry."

She gets on her knees, doggystyle. "Is this better?"

"Much." I push my jeans down to my thighs. I put on the condom and land inside right away, burning hot. "You've done this before, right? I'm uninterested in a cherry blaster on my dick tonight."

"I'm such a slut, I love sex. Don't worry."

My arms wrapped around her stomach, I thrust in and out, turn her o-ring choker around, pull it, and cover her mouth, fucking her with all my might.

"Call me Lusif."

"What?"

"Do it."

"Oh, fuck yeah, Lusif."

I squeeze the Baphomet necklace with one hand and a tit with the other. "Say, 'Fuck me harder, Lusif.'"

"Fuck me harder, Lusif."

"I'm about to blast."

"Already? That was so fast. Can you at least blast on my tits? Money shots are so cool!"

I pull out and throw the jizz-soaked condom onto the pavement. We put on our clothes. She goes to a payphone to call a friend to drive her home.

☆ 74 ☆

Before I left the house, I found a cassette from ninth grade of "The Freshmen" by The Verve Pipe that I recorded off the radio. It plays in my headphones as I arrive at Shane's back door. He comes out wearing a Slowdive shirt and black jean shorts.

"The AOL servers are down right now. I gotta update my away message and check my IMs. I'm pissed." Wind chimes ring as we sit on his back porch with a bottle of wine.

I shrug. "Oh no! What will all of the chatroom deviants in this country do? I'm still trying to wrap my head around how people can check their email more than once a day."

"I downloaded some video off the net. I thought it was gonna be an interview with Spike Jonze, but it ended up being this clip of a mutilated puppy. It's crazy, man. The internet can be like a dungeon. It's kind of like the things you look up on there reflect your subconscious throwing up all of your worst curiosities."

I reach for the bottle of wine and grab his Cool Ranch Doritos. "That must be a metaphor for what's going on in our lives."

"Everybody is so happy all the time, and then there's me, the miserable one. I've always been the miserable one. 'Let's not invite Shane, he's too weird, he never smiles. He's too sad, too sullen.'"

"You know I have cable, right? I saw the clip they've been playing all week from Fiona's MTV special. You can't rip it off right in front of me."

"Sorry. Sometimes I relate so hard to something that I forget if it's something I thought or something I saw."

"It's fine. You know whose CD I've been into these days? Fountains of Wayne. I love 'Sink to the Bottom.'"

"Did you hear that theory going around the internet about Tom Cruise? It's this full-on Scientologist thing where every movie he does is apparently him acting out all of his fears about dying."

"Let's not think about other people right now. You and I are sitting in your backyard, drinking wine, eating Cool Ranch Doritos. That's all we need in this world, at least for today." I pass him the bag.

Shane lies down. "Sometimes I like to come out here at night, lie on the grass, and look up at the sky. Everything looks like it's being shot through a fisheye lens."

I lean over him. "The first summer of a new century is right around the corner. Do you think there's any hope for our lives moving forward?"

He shrugs. "I think one of the greatest lessons from New Year's Eve 1999 is if you want the world to end badly enough, you have to do it yourself."

"Do you ever wonder what's being wasted when we spend so much time hiding? There's gotta be some kind of cost."

"Are you saying that you feel like when certain people get one version of you, they might be missing out on the concealed sides that you don't want them to see?"

"Yeah, I don't get it. Why the fuck do we reserve different parts of ourselves for certain people, then act all shocked when we don't ever feel fully seen by the people around us?"

"Here we are again, you and me, sitting around, talking about life, pretending we're having all these big discoveries and breakthroughs, but it doesn't change much. Everything remains the same after these short sparks of self-indulgent bullshit. How am I supposed to be okay with that?"

"Outside of talking about hating the world, chicks, drugs, sex, great food, conspiracies, music, and movies, what's left? What fills up the convo when you're hanging out with your friend? I don't know."

"For the past month, I've been in limbo, like I'm in between lives. Part ghost, part human."

"I know how that feels. Every day I look in the mirror and don't know what parts of myself to keep or release. It's too overwhelming trying to decide."

"I'm so depressed. I don't even feel the details anymore. It's all gone dark."

"No one gets it, dude. People don't know what it's like to wake up, look at your reflection, and feel like your life is happening to someone else. It's not apathy. It's not detachment. It's something way more mysterious."

"Dude, I can't even tell what you're chasing anymore. Consequence? Reward? Punishment? It seems like it might all be the same thing for you at this point."

"Most of the time I just feel stupid. I mean, why would anyone want to experience a feeling they can't return to, and yet, that happens all the fucking time. It's like a curse. You find something that feels good, and, just as the pleasure hits, it's gone. When we finally experience those moments that we convinced ourselves were so important, the times we thought we were missing out on, those are the most devastating."

"I always think that just by being born, we weren't given enough time for everything we want to happen in our lives. It's impossible. Maybe it's easier to desire nothing."

"I'm just so freaked about getting older, you know? I'm always going to be an unfinished version of myself."

"There's no reflection to look back at, I guess."

"Yeah, something like that."

"I've gotten so used to never letting myself go through anything. I just try to go around the pain. Avoid. I'll try to kill off any feeling before it gets the chance to eat at me."

"Bill Hicks says, 'Life is a ride.' He must be onto something."

"Well, call up Mr. Hicks and tell him I never asked to get on the carousel."

"He's dead, Shane."

"Right. What else were you saying?"

"Don't you think it's unfair? We're supposed to grow up and move through life giving away certain pieces of ourselves, yet all that will be left in the end is this empty space buzzing in the background, reminding you that you're never going to have what you gave away ever again."

"Okay. Do you think that someone you meet can be a reflection of your future self?"

"No, but I think people can mirror back what you haven't created yet."

"I think one of the saddest parts about being alive is that a moment never comes where you actually get to live."

"I'm so tired, Shane. Sometimes I just lose myself to these darker impulses, and I swear, it's one of the most haunting things that I've ever seen."

"I hate that in real life we can't just hit the remote when something we don't like comes on."

"Boys born in the eighties have it rough, I'm telling you! We're not a happy bunch."

"Do you ever feel that there's this place in your heart where all of these exciting feelings and emotions are happening, and then this fear comes? This fear that in a few years, all that's going to be left there is this lingering void where all of those sensations used to be?"

"All the time, dude. I'm loving this heart-to-heart stuff."

"Can I tell you a story about something that happened to me as a kid? I just need one moment of your time with no eye rolls, no jokes, no sarcastic remarks. Can you handle that?"

"What is it, Shane?"

"The first person I loved and trusted molested me. I was eight years old. I don't remember much, other than the fact that a Janet Jackson video was on during one of the times he did it. It was my babysitter."

"I don't know what to say. I don't know how to step into the kid version of yourself who got his world shattered, how to feel the pain you've felt. I can only support you by being here right now and listening. Is that chill?"

"Picture this little kid carrying this huge secret around and I can't tell anyone about it. I don't know how to speak about it, but I know that I've been violated, and it has followed me ever since. I remember standing behind him while he played *Street Fighter* at the arcade. I'd hug him so tight. He was just my whole world. I can even smell his cologne right now. You can't explain what it feels like to get confirmation from the world so young that you're so completely worthless. It's such a dirty feeling."

"No kid should go through that."

"Even though he's not here, he is. He's a part of me. It's like that closeness we shared is something I'll be chasing for the rest of my life. It's how I started. It's where I'm going to end."

"Is he like a ghost now?"

"Not really. Sometimes I have dreams where we are at this dinner and I'm asking him all these questions, but his lips are zippers. I'll always be curious because out of all of the boys, why did he pick me? It's confusing because sometimes I feel like I'm making it all up, that it's just the big story I've created to try to make my life feel more tragic, but I swear…I remember the video, the smile on his face, the loneliness I felt as he touched me. It can't just be my imagination."

"I get that."

"Sometimes his face appears in my head like a possessed TV that I can't turn off. I get high and he still doesn't go away. I get it, a little kid shouldn't put that kind of blame on himself, but I still wonder if it was my fault."

I reach out. "Is it cool if I hug you?" We embrace. "Shane, I know that we've hung out hundreds of times, but this is the first day that I've felt like I understood you. I'm sorry. Does that make sense?"

"Sometimes my greatest wish is to go back to 1989 before I became totally engrossed in the darker side of my life so I could freeze myself there."

"Don't worry about it. Any dude would understand why you'd hold that secret in for so long. Being victimized is so embarrassing."

Shane rubs his arms. "Do you ever think that some people came into this world without innocence?"

"Maybe I'm one of them."

"How do we get out of this neighborhood?"

"In our dreams."

I stand and look over the wooden fence at the house next door: an empty trampoline, a sprinkler, hose, and a boombox on the deck. I put my hand in front of him. "Come with me…"

Shane gets up. We open his garden gate and walk to his neighbor's driveway. "How do you know they aren't home?"

"The van isn't parked out front. When I come here, the van is always out front."

I lift the lock to the wooden gate. Shane follows, closing the gate behind us. In the backyard, I grab the hose and sprinkler and crank the knob. The water flows. Shane crawls up on the trampoline and starts to bum drop. "I…can…feel…the wings…coming…in…on…my back…" I put the sprinkler underneath the trampoline so that the water shoots from under the net. I go to the boombox and turn the radio on. *The chorus of Eagle-Eye Cherry's "Save Tonight" sounds so beautiful right now.* Shane takes his shirt off and throws it on the grass. I lift myself up onto the trampoline, take my tee off, toss it, and jump in sync with Shane, wet, shirtless, singing along together.

I pick *Glamorama* up off Lu's floor and sigh. "I'm so sick and tired of hearing about this fucking book."

"I wish I was in that book!"

Shane shrugs. "I gave up on reading it. It makes no fucking sense."

"Someone online told me the reason it's so genius is because it doesn't make sense. Mariah Carey dies in it, some chink eats his own balls, terrorist models. It's got everything."

"Did you watch the VH1 documentary about the author this weekend? It was so annoying, all about how he grew up rich in L.A. and had an alcoholic father. Like, okay? Thanks for fucking sharing. Poor you. You're rich, you're famous, and there's a documentary about you. Fuck off and stop complaining."

"Maybe he's now on my hex list. I hate anyone who complains about being famous."

I sit on his bed. He's in a Manson "666" jersey, leaning over his clear answering machine with MM stickers on it. Shane picks his hair. I twirl my fingers through his curls.

"Okay. Are you ready?"

Lu hits a button on the machine: "Now recording." Beep.

"What's up? This is sexy Shane."

"And bone-worthy Brad."

"And loaded Lu. We are currently charging two thousand dollars per hangout, so if your wallet is packed and you're looking for some fresh meat teen cock, please leave us a message with a time and date that you'd like to hang out and we would be happy to accommodate you with all of our unforgettable, sexy, satanic services. We will get back to you as soon as possible. Hail Satan!"

Our voices in unison: "Thank you so much for calling Lusif's official teen sex ring triple six hotline." He hits another button. It ends.

"Oh my God, that was so fucking funny."

"I love that we're on your answering machine."

231

"People are going to be so disturbed by that!"

"I love it! Imagine if the school ever calls to check if you're sick?"

"They have my house phone, not my personal line."

"I love that you have your own voicemail."

"And I love that I'm in your North Douglas bus pass pic."

"And I fucking love that you boys are my best friends!"

☆ 76 ☆

Fake palm trees by the escalators. I go into Persephone's Pizza, "Better Off Alone" by Alice Deejay booming. I sit in a booth and start grabbing napkins, ripping them up. I think of taking out the *Disney Adventures* comic in my bag. I envision myself skateboarding at the park. I take off my helmet and shake my hair in slo-mo, pouring Gatorade all over my face. A hot girl comes up to me. A guy in a Strand Releasing shirt and an o-ring choker is bawling in the booth behind me. He goes through his messenger bag as the light reflects against his "R.I.P. Matthew Shepard" pin. He takes out a magazine. On the cover: a shirtless guy in a vest, holding a laptop in front of a school bus. "cYbER"—*XY Mag*. He starts smashing it against his head.

I hold onto the booth and look over. "Uh, what's wrong?"

"My boyfriend. Leave me alone. I don't want to talk right now. Scram!"

"Yikes."

"Oh, you *would* be making that face. Yeah, I like dick in my mouth and asshole. Deal with it."

"Look, I don't give a shit about what you do with your personal lifestyle choices. You're crying in public like those mental patients. Do you think this is *Boy, Interrupted*?"

"You better leave me alone. I have straight boy pepper spray in my bag."

"Calm the fuck down and have some respect. We're in public."

"Okay, do you really want to know why I'm so upset that I could hang myself?"

"Sure."

He folds his arms. "Do you promise you won't call me a fag or be mean if I tell you this?"

"No promises." I laugh.

"Oh, come on."

"I'm kidding. It's a joke. Like ha ha ha funny. God, do you gays not have a sense of humor?"

He smiles. "I met this guy, he's twenty-eight, a total daddy. I just turned sixteen so I got a fake and we met in the Village. He tells me that he's a top and we've been seeing each other for like three weeks, which is about six years in gay years."

"What's the point of this?"

"Well, I found out that he bottomed for my friend at the baths last Friday after Shower Power Thursdays. He lied to me. I wanted him to bottom for *me*. I'm so angry. I hate my life. I swear I'm going to meat cleaver my wrist in front of everyone. Nobody understands."

"How did you even find that out?"

"He left his email open when he was in the shower and I saw that he sent pics of his ass to him."

"Your life is *Drool Intentions*. Congratulations."

"What the fuck! You're not at the movies. I'm a person. I'm not a screen."

He grabs my cheeks and pushes my head toward his face. "Don't touch me, fag. I don't want to get AIDS. You sound Fiona Apple levels of psychotic right now. Try calling a hotline, you oversensitive loser. Maybe they'll care about your bullshit feelings."

"I knew that you'd do this. Do you know why you don't care? You're straight, white, and male. You're ignorant and privileged. God, this is exactly what we were talking about at our PFLAG meeting yesterday. This encounter is a sign from my higher power."

"Oh, yeah? Well, maybe you queers would actually get people to listen to you if you were less emotional, less angry."

"Would you look at that? The straightie is a genius. Why don't I just act like an obedient, kind, nice boy? That's the mindset that set off Stonewall, isn't it?"

"What the hell are you even talking about?"

"You would never have to know about gay rights because you have no history of oppression. The world never challenges your identity. Everything is always for you."

"Look around at all the cares that I have. Oh wait, there are none. You should apply for the victim Olympics. I have this gut feeling that you'd qualify."

"I don't understand why it's so hard for straight boys to be nice to me. I have to be this sexless little faggot every day, hiding in the background, getting pushed into lockers. You're never going to know what it's like to have your best friend call you saying that they got jumped by a bunch of straight guys at a party. You'll never know what it's like to not be allowed to bring your boyfriend to prom, what it's like to turn on the TV and re-experience the trauma Matthew Shepard went through every time someone gets gay bashed. A gay guy was beaten and tortured to death for no reason other than the same homophobia that you're displaying today."

I start clapping. "That was a real soapbox! Bravo! Are you thinking of auditioning for your school musical? Are you guys doing *Grease* this year?"

"Ugh! I never asked to be born on your disgusting, fascist, heterosexual planet."

"This is the last time that I'm ever going up to a homo to check if they're alright. The hysterics are unbearable."

"You sociopath. You total piece of shit! I'm not performing! You gotta be an Aquarius or something. How could you be so calm? You don't think I know from one look at you that your entire personality is boiled down to your wallet chain, liking blink-182, wearing hideous Champion sweats, and eating BBQ with your friends in the summer all because you have nothing else going for you but to be a boring straight boy?"

"Oh, you are going to regret calling me boring."

"See? Back to your ego. You don't give a shit. You're so selfish that you can't even take a break from your schedule of stroking your teeny little dick to fake tits to have the compassion to fight for the rights of the oppressed."

"You don't know a single thing about me. Watch it. Why do you think that you can say these things to a stranger? Your self-pity is getting my cock soft, and that's a shame for you, now isn't it?" I wink.

"I'm fucking scared, that's why. I'm sickened that this encounter is a normal occurrence for my queer friends who have to fight to survive every fucking day. I'm so tired of being quiet. I usually just walk away, but today I can't."

"Listen, dude. I'm not holding the weight of something about me that I can't control. Your problems with me are not my problems, they're *yours*. This isn't on me. I'm just chilling."

"Another slice of reality: You don't know how lonely it is to be in fear that a guy you picked up from Pulse could take off the condom while you're getting fucked. I'm scared, man. I want to grow old. One mistake could change everything."

"You need to stop. This is so uncomfortable. When are you going to realize that the things you go through on a daily basis mean nothing to me? You're just a statistic."

"Get uncomfortable! When are people going to wake up and start caring?"

"Why don't you go hang out with Pedro from *The Real World*, you flamer? Oh wait, you can't. He's fucking dead."

A waitress with huge tits looks at me. "Is this man causing you problems? I can call mall security."

"Why, yes, ma'am! He's sexually harassing me. He keeps asking to perform homosexual acts on me. He's also trying to sell me illegal drugs."

She glares at him. "You're one disgusting homo. I will be praying super hard for you. Mall security will be on their way."

"He also said he's been having sex in the mall bathrooms."

"He's lying! None of that is true! You… You are framing me right now. The leader of my PFLAG meeting said that straight boys would do this to us. He was right." He bursts into tears, rubbing his eyes with his shirt. The waitress pings mall security on her pager. I wink at him.

"How could you?"

A group of Black mall guards comes in. The waitress signals them to our table and points out the gay guy. I pout my lips, then blow a kiss.

"Ciao, Kermit the Fudge Packer."

"Come with us."

"No!"

The policeman grabs him. "Do you want to be charged with resisting arrest, you little fairy?"

"Fine, do it! Cuff the Scorpio homo who cries in public about his boyfriend. I'll just love jail, right? You know, my boy-hole getting raped? I don't want to be a part of your rules. I'm never going to be one of the boys! You can't beat the fag out of me. You've all tried, but you can't."

The gay guy follows them out but looks back at me, sobbing.

The waitress pulls out her pen and pad. "Those are the freaks who go to those HIV walks you hear about on TV. This is why we need Jesus Christ in this country."

"Do you think he'll be able to find out when the new *Will & Grace* episode is on in jail?" She laughs as I place an order.

"Three Dr Pepper milkshakes with whip coming right up."

I look at her ass as she walks away. Meh, a seven. I think about asking if I can use the phone to call Lu's house, but I see Lu and Shane walking in. Lu is in a black Baphomet shirt, a black fur coat, and red-lensed Briko sunglasses. Shane is in mustard jeans. A song I swear I've heard multiple times this month drifts from the diner speakers, Tal Bachman vibes.

The waitress walks over with our shakes and puts them down with the bill. "Thank you." I look at her ass again as she walks away. The scent of Gap's Dream lingers.

Shane looks at her, then looks back to me. "Wow. This is why I need some kind of pill to deflate awkward boners whenever I leave the fucking house."

We cheers with our milkshakes. Lu lights a cigarette and passes it to Shane. He hands it to me and I take a pull. "I know, her tits are ridiculous."

Lu slams the table. "You guys aren't going to believe this. I was walking to the 7-Eleven by school and this truck slowed down. It was filled with these old dude porn producers. They were looking around for 'real teen boys' to star in their videos and offered me five grand. I've never seen that much cash in my life. I said I wasn't eighteen yet and they were like 'So? Who cares? Most of the guys in our videos aren't.'"

"You were late for our hangout 'cause you were too busy trying to be the next Dirk Diggler?"

"I didn't tell you the best part. It was a gay porno studio, Falcon Studios."

"Come on. I've had enough gay shit for today. Can I catch a break from America's new homosexual agenda?"

"It's perfect timing. I'm reading this book right now about this group of friends who teamed up to murder this guy Bobby Kent in Florida back in the early nineties. He and his friend Marty went into business together making gay porn and were rolling in money. This is a thriving market. Instant big bucks."

"I don't think that you should model yourself off of that guy. He was probably a level-ten poofter."

"Both of them were straight. For those boys, everything was about money, humiliation, and power."

"I'm not helping anyone make skin flicks."

"I have something called class and morality. I'd never be as white trash as those losers. I bet those Florida killers come from a poor trailer park background."

"But going into the adult entertainment biz could start out my career in Hollywood as an upcoming movie star. Look at Traci Lords. She was a total pornstar before she started acting, and now she does movies with big stars like Rose McGowan. It's not fair."

"Yeah, but it's not like anyone gives a shit about her acting. Traci Lords is just a whore on camera. Once you get fucked on camera, and you're a woman, I have no respect for you. None."

"I wouldn't ever get fucked or put a dick in my ass."

"You are not considering this. Don't tell me you got his card."

Lu pulls it out. "FALCON ENTERTAINMENT—213-928-9307." "The producer was like, 'Just close your eyes and think of a chick. You won't know the difference. A mouth is a mouth, kid. A lot of straight guys work for us. A man's throat is full of surprises.'"

"I don't care if it's one milli in cash. Don't fucking do that shit."

"It's the worst, most disgusting thing that I could do. I would want my face in it just so I could show my mom. My 24/7 number-one target. I'm only here in 2000 to push the boundaries, to be controversial."

"Shane? What do you think?"

"I don't engage with retarded conversation, and besides, I can't stop thinking about our waitress's rack."

"Manson isn't gay. Sucking cock on stage is just entertainment, it's art. It's not being an actual faggot cocksucker. You've seen Rose McGowan's tits. You saw that dress. The man is engaged to the hottest chick alive."

"What about J.Lo's dress? Now, that's a whole other conversation. Latina knockers."

"Great dress."

"This is not like getting Ben & Jerry's instead of a Klondike bar. You're a man. You can never go back once you do that gay shit. It's irrevocable."

"Who cares? Today, anyone who owns a videocam can be their own pornstar, anyway. Look, sometimes I watch videos of myself jerking off, swing my dick in the mirror, and I'm like, 'That's a big veiny dick.' I love screaming my own name when I cum these days. I'm into *me*."

"But that's you. That's you being proud of your gun. That's not another man's dick."

"There was this quote page I was looking at, but I fucking forgot someone said it in a magazine. It was something like, 'No man has a dick under his belt. Only a gun.'"

"True."

"I need to become our neighborhood's Heidi Fleiss. Wouldn't that be such a chopped scandal? I want to start a prostitution ring and sell hot girls to businessmen, maybe rich college guys. I'll save up and be able to be like Diddy, have my own restaurant and clothing line. I just need a jumpstart before I become a worldwide brand. Young girls are going to get fucked at some point, they might as well be getting paid for it. I want to be a capital P Pimp."

"You need to get into *The Real World*."

"Are they doing auditions here?"

I look at our empty glasses, inspect the bill, and put cash on the table.

Shane takes out five dollar bills. "That's for the rack."

"You know, she wore that shirt for you to do that."

"Fuck it, I'm an idiot. Diner tits is going straight into the spank bank."

Madonna's "American Pie" is starting. I look over to Lu as we walk out. "Good time to leave!"

"Where are we going?"

"Hot Topic."

☆ 77 ☆

A sticker on the wall: "He who dies with the most toys wins." I'm in the employee bathroom looking at my reflection, gray Champion sweats and a hoodie. *My dick print looks fucking huge in these sweats.* I jump up and down, watching my cock swing around in circles. *Swing that shit! Dick's looking good.* I run the tap, flicking water onto the mirror, and watch myself drip while grabbing my silver beaded chain. *I look so fucking hot right now.* The Dreamworks logo of the boy fishing from a crescent moon appears in my mind.

In the grocery store stockroom, both boys are in matching Food Front uniforms. Lu is sitting on an inflatable Budweiser blow-up couch surrounded by stacked brown boxes: a Sobe bottle, a busty She-Devil Coopstuff action figure, Walgreens photo envelopes, a Lemon Fresh Pledge bottle, a half-cut Gatorade bottle ashtray, last March's issue of *Maxim* with Rose McGowan on the cover. "Hollywood's #1 Bad Girl!"

Ax is standing behind the couch, hugging Lu's neck, holding a gummy worm above his lips.

Lu licks it. "Being a lil slut is so fucking awesome. I just want to drop out of life and eat fifteen-year-old pussy all day."

Ax laughs. "I'm so obsessed with you. I can't believe you know who John Balance is."

"I can't believe that you know who Donald Tyson is."

"I fucking love when we have shifts together. It's so fucking awesome."

"I love that you love Sobe too. I'm so into drinking that right now."

"Nootropic drinks are the way of this new world, man. You don't know the endless potential of when we start modifying our supernatural abilities to the tenth degree. We could be capable of total world domination and annihilation at the same time."

"Ginseng, Guarana, Ginkgo."

Ax starts rubbing Lu's arms and stomach. "Once you've been as awakened as we are, where is there for us to go from there, you know?"

"Yeah."

"Tomorrow I've got an empty crib. You're coming over to watch *Doom Generation* and *Nowhere* back-to-back. I don't give a shit."

"Fuck yeah. I got this new Warp Records VHS. We can do the last fifteen mills of the Four-Pointed Crown I have left from last weekend. I'll go to Blockbuster after work and pick up those new sour Jolly Rancher lollipops that you're obsessed with."

Ax pulls Lu's cheeks. "That sounds so chopped."

"I'm so excited for 2001."

Lu and Ax high-five. "2001 is going to be all about ruining people's lives!"

Ax grabs the Sobe bottle off the side table and holds it as Lu drinks it. The smell of a cologne I don't recognize is in the air.

I walk over. "Did I seriously just fucking walk into an episode of *Undressed* or what? And what the hell is that scent? Get me out of here."

Ax takes a torso-shaped bottle out of his bag. "Uh, it's Gaultier Le Male. Duh." He changes the topic. "Wait, Brad. Have you ever seen *At Close Range*, the eighties movie with Sean Penn?"

"No."

"You kind of look like him right now. I just got it from a bin dive."

I suck on a Tic Tac. "Do you know that firecrotch twenty-year-old dude who works at Blockbuster?"

"Oh my God. The fag who won't shut the fuck up about his movie review website? Shouldn't he get fired for self-promotion?"

"I know. When he handed me his card, I was like, this must be illegal. PatriksMovieReviews.com? A place in my nightmares."

"Listen, pretentious film student fags offer nothing to the world. Like, I don't give a shit about how many Cronenberg movies you own or the Poppy Z. Brite novel you're trying to adapt into a screenplay, 'cause you're going to fail at it. You're never going to get an agent anyway, and besides, you're probably fucking poor. You work at Blockbuster. Like, pass me my five-day rental and shut the fuck up!"

Lu rolls his eyes. "Agents. Don't remind me."

Ax continues. "You can't believe a word that comes out of Harrison's mouth. He's a drugged-out, tweaked-out, social-climbing fucking homo. It was all a fluke."

"But he did land that Dockers ad. He got scouted at Burger King. Our Burger King, our mall! It's too close to home. It's unfair."

"Oh, yeah. You do one Dockers ad and now you think you're going to be the next VH1 Model of the Year. We know what he did to get that job. Do a hex so he stops getting modeling work. I'll kill myself if I ever see him in a Choose Denial campaign."

I grab a Lemon Fresh Pledge bottle and put it to my face. "If you guys don't shut the fuck up about Harrison, I am going to whippit OD right here, right now."

"Oh! Whatever. What do you want to talk about then?"

"I don't know. Something fucking cool and interesting?"

Ax leans into his bag, pulls out an issue of *Talk*, and holds it up: Gwyneth Paltrow in black lingerie. "Like sex?"

I grab the mag out of his hands. "Look how sexy she looks!"

Lu snatches it. "We were unboxing them and I had to save one 'cause goddamn, Paltrow looks insanely hot in this shot."

Ax puts his hands in front of his chest, cups fake tits in the air, and sticks his tongue out. "She looks like she's just begging to get fucked by a huge cock like mine. Dumb bitch."

"I nutted to the McGowan *Maxim* on my break. The things I'd do to get a chance to eat that pussy."

"Do you have the new issue of *Celebrity Skin*? The one with the pics of Amy Smart sunbathing?"

"Didn't *Celebrity Skin* publish those naked pics of Cameron Diaz?"

I shrug. "I haven't seen those yet."

Ax looks directly into my eyes. "What turns you on? Top kink."

"I'm not going to tell you that."

"Just say it out loud. You can't shock me. I've seen the craziest shit on the internet, like pic galleries of freshman girls passed out at parties naked, real fourteen-year-old chicks, spread-eagle. *And* I've read the most fucked-up incest stories on Usenet. I've even cammed with some hot chicks before who have done some fucked up sex shit for me."

I get ready to get up. "I'm going to head out. I gotta get a history report done."

Ax takes off his shirt and stands up in front of me. "What the fuck are you doing?"

I get halfway up and Lu pushes me down, a blade to my throat. Ax is holding me down with all of his force as I'm sitting on the couch. Lu takes out a roll of duct tape, grabs my hands, and tapes them up. He tapes my body to the seat. My throat is burning from my screams. Squirming, fighting back. Nothing. He pulls down my sweats.

Ax grins. "Awww! The seventeen-year-old is wearing Joe Boxers. I thought you'd be a Tommy briefs kind of guy. You have that look."

"This isn't funny anymore. Please stop. I know this is just a joke."

Lu pauses. "I told you I wanted to be the Heidi Fleiss of this neighborhood. We all have to start somewhere. No matter how hard you want to pause, fast-forward, or remote control this, it's happening. This is a live stream."

"Yeah, you can't call a 1-800 crisis hotline to get you out of this one. Sorry."

Lu presses on the knife. "I'm not moving the knife unless you want to go home with a blood-scar branded on the back of your neck. You might as well submit and enjoy this."

"This Spring 2000, cruelty is in fashion. Get into it!"

I gulp and look at Lu. "What kind of man are you to do this to your best fucking friend?"

Ax interjects, "You see, Brad, every taboo in my head has been explored online and now I'm bored. I want to try something new."

"There are worse things happening right now on this planet than hazing. Stop being a pussy! Besides, this isn't gay, this is a prank. There's a difference."

"You have to pretend you're in a chatroom. We're all not who we say we are, we're just anonymous strangers on the internet."

"No, I'll do anything. I'll lie to my dad about something and get him to write you a check for a thousand dollars if you stop this."

"Money can't buy the arousal that comes from putting someone else through fear, now can it?"

Lu taps Ax's shoulder. "This is way more entertaining than watching *Se7en*."

"This is scripted, but we're editing this as we go along, if that makes sense."

"Should we blindfold him or write on him in Sharpie?"

"It's better to make him suffer. The possibility that he could open his eyes and see his worst nightmare is just too good."

I try to get another word in, but my lips are sealed with duct tape.

Ax says, "Shhh, don't make this any harder than it needs to be. It'll be done soon. Sit still. Lu told me when I paid him that you're a good boy who likes to cooperate."

I hurl my body back and forth. I'm sweating, sent into a flashback of Lu and me bullying preteen girls the other night at the park, making threats, and having fun. Third Eye Blind's "Losing a Whole Year" plays on the radio, but it sounds remixed, droned, terrifying. A heavy molasses washes over me. Ax's cold hands on my dick rub me up and down. The blade on my skin. I can't lift my eyes. Ax is laughing. Lu's laughing. I can feel him watching me squirm. *This place does not exist inside of me.* I'm not able to create a pornographic fantasy of a woman with each pull on my cock. The amount of shame building in my body with each stroke makes me dizzy. Montages of the other choice: coming home cut up, unable to hide what happened. The weight of having to explain where I'd been, my parents hysterical. There are no words. No tears come. *This place does not exist inside of me.* Montages of shooting Lu in the throat. Up I go, outside of me, gone. I bite my lips as I can feel the orgasm coming. Billy Kincaid, the child abductor from *Spawn's* evil smile in my mind. Paranoid images of a hidden camera in the corner, guys at school seeing this footage, laughing, arms around each other, bonding over this humiliation. *This place does not exist inside of me.*

Ax's voice: "Should I suck on it?"

I'm moving around trying to say, "No, no, no." He spits on my dick. Biting on my lip, my knees shake. I orgasm. I don't know where my load is going because I won't open my eyes, but then I do. My jizz soaks his palms as he licks it off of his sticky fingers.

"Warm and young. My favorite flavor."

Lu comes over, rips the tape off my mouth. "See? That wasn't so bad."

"Thank you, guys, I enjoyed that. I feel like a new man. I'm even more comfortable in my straight sexuality."

Ax beams. "Really? Would you want to do more?"

"Ax, I'd actually like you to suck my dick, if you're down for another round. But do you think you could take off the tape?"

He comes over and starts ripping off the tape. I'm shaking. When it's off, I run up to Ax, put him in a chokehold, headbutt him, and push him against the wall. "I'll kill you! I'll fucking kill you! If I ever see you again, you're dead. I'll shoot you in the mouth for what you did to me, you butt-banger." I punch him in the mouth, the throat, then the stomach. He's coughing and spitting up blood.

Lu runs up behind me, trying to get me off of him. "Brad. Stop. What are you doing? I've never seen you like this."

Ax looks over to Lu. "Oh, you're done for, little Lu. You don't know what's coming for you now. Just wait for who I'm going to send after you." Ax covers his bleeding nose with his hands, exiting the back door.

Lu pushes me. "You're such a wimp. What are you going to do? Report him?"

"You sat there and watched me and laughed. And you had a great time. How could you?"

"A forced handjob? That's the créme de la créme of hazing. That was nothing. Some guys end up bleeding on the floor with broomsticks up their asses. You should be grateful. The world fucked up by giving you a dick, jeez."

"This isn't brotherhood, this is ultraviolence."

"Come on, you've never seen *Youngblood* on cable before? Patrick Swayze held down Rob Lowe as he got hazed. Spoiler: he lived. Lighten up."

"They were shaving his pubes. He didn't have unwanted sexual contact with another guy for the first time."

"You just made me a new enemy. This could potentially ruin the most important plan in my life right now. How could you be so selfish? You say you're my best friend, then go and make everything in my life fall apart?"

"What did you even get out of that?"

"It's complex. This was a serious business deal."

"A serious deal I never agreed to! You want to be honest 'cause it looks like I've got nothing to lose now. I'm in a shitty place 'cause if I say I couldn't handle it, I'm a weak pussy. If I say I liked it, I'm a homo. If I stop being friends with you over this, I break a fraternal code. I give up."

"This was good-natured fun, and, of course, being you, you had to ruin it. You could've gone home, been comfortable with yourself and your sexuality, and just laughed it off as another meaningless nut. You made something playful into something serious. I'm pissed."

"You sat there and watched me. You participated. I'm done this time for real."

"You will never be able to stay away from me."

"Watch me."

Lu lights a cigarette, rolls his eyes, and flips me off. "Fuck you, Brad Sela. Don't turn up the knob so loud and act all shocked when the speakers get blown."

☆ 78 ☆

Lu's in an Eminem shirt and baggy black jeans with hanging chains, sitting on Shane's couch watching MTV. Carson Daly is about to announce the "Forgot About Dre" video premiere. Shane sits on the floor, feet against the wall, tossing a bouncy ball between his hands. I pull on Lu's shirt as the video comes on. I look at a poster of Jenny McCarthy in a white bikini beside the TV. *Why isn't my cock that mustard bottle she's holding right now?*

Shane gets up. "Do you mind if we turn this off? I'm in the Water Temple right now and I've wanted to play all day. It's my eighteenth birthday today, I get to make the rules." Shane grabs the remote, ready to switch to his N64.

Lu starts. "Fuck off! You can play N64 whenever you want. This is a video premiere. This is way more important."

"You guys need to fuck off. Can't you just go home? This is *my* house and I want to play *Zelda*."

"I did not bolt all the way from my fucking house for you to fuck this up for me. I would have just stayed home and watched it there if I knew you were going to do this. Move away from the TV." Shane sits on the floor. Lu takes the remote and turns the volume up. "I fucking love Eminem so much!" He gets up and checks the VCR. "I want to record this. Give me a blank."

Shane shrugs, voice rising. "If you want to fucking watch it again, pay two-fifty to request it on *The Box* and record it off of there."

Lu turns to me. "You realize that I love Eminem because he's the rap version of Manson."

I eyeroll. "That's reaching."

"It's not a reach."

"It's a reach. Eminem's jock Jordan-licking fans aren't smart enough to understand that his work is a satire of the American mind and society."

"I know that, fucker. It makes it so much better because I'm smart enough to understand Em, you fucking monkey-brain-dead-retard bitch."

I throw a Tic Tac at him. "I bet Slim Shady wouldn't set his friend up in some weird torture stunt and then expect them to be hanging out watching music videos as if nothing ever happened."

He throws the fuzzy back at me. "Brad! Guys for a billion decades have gone through what you did yesterday, and, after the fact, gone for beers together. They laughed. They got the joke. They manned up and moved on."

Shane's confused. "What is he talking about?"

Lu and I in unison say, "Oh, nothing."

Shane goes to a shoebox on the other side of the basement and tosses Lu a blank tape. The video fades into Carson Daly's face.

Lu hits the TV. "Get pretty boy Carson Daly the fuck out of my face and get me back to Slim."

"I want to face-fuck Carson Daly so bad."

"I always knew you were a 'mo."

"With a screwdriver soaked in cyanide nails, of course."

"What do you think it'd be like to get that close to the MTV studios? Being in New York, in fucking Times Square."

"Fuck, fuck, fuck! We almost caught it."

"I'm sure someone in class taped it and has a copy."

"No, I wanted it right now."

"It's a Dr. Dre video, not a fucking limited edition collector's item. Just fucking calm down. They are probably going to play it tomorrow, as well as ten million more times this month."

"If the internet didn't take a million fucking years, I could stream the video. That'd be fucking great."

"Why don't you call and vote for your wifebeater boyfriend?"

"It's prank phone call time, bitches."

"Let's call a youth crisis hotline. There's a number on the newsletter in my bag. Get me it."

Shane stomps. "Do not do that in my house."

Lu pushes his shoulder. "Why? Stop being a fag."

"Don't joke about that kind of shit. Seriously Lu, do not fucking go there in my house."

"Awww, tender little tulip. You really are a Fiona Apple fan, Jesus."

"You're with me on this right now?"

"I just don't know."

"You just don't know? Wow. I want to kick your tits."

"Brad, you know what would be hilarious? Let's call the National Gay Youth Hotline. You could pretend that your baseball coach molested you when you were five or some shit or talk about how your uncle tried to fuck you when he was drunk. It would be funny as fuck."

"That's so funny. I'd do that."

"Do it on a payphone or something. Not at my house."

"If we star sixty-seven it, then they can't figure it out, retard."

Lu grabs the house phone off the table and puts it on speakerphone. He dials.

They pick up. "KGON FM!"

"Hi! Can you please play 'Fuck Me in the Ass One More Time' by Britney Spears?"

"She hung up. You do it now." He hits redial.

They pick up again. "KGON FM!"

I try to sound like an old man. "Can you play 'Die, Die, Die' by *NSYNC?"

"Don't you kids have anything better to do?"

☆ 79 ☆

I scratch plus signs into my arms, punch my shoulder, and slap my face. *Fuck yeah. Five-star hotel-type shit. Give me all of that silence. When you control hurting yourself, is this when you become real? Can you change the speed of how you feel?* I kick my legs, whirlpools form in the water. I lift the bottom of my balls, hard pinch, put my pinky in my mouth, and bite down on my skin. *Oh fuck...brain...numb...I fucking hate myself!* I drag my teeth on my tongue. *You love to watch yourself spiral. No one else cares. How can I ever win back the lost parts of me?*

I push my head underwater and scream. I get out, fill my mouth under the tap, and spit on the mirror, reflection dripping. *The more time I spend behind the scenes with myself, the more I learn I know nothing about who I am. All you are is a concept, a perception, an image, an idea. Does it hurt?*

☆ 80 ☆

Lu is wearing a backwards "Got Satan?" baseball cap, a chain link choker, and a Nothing Records shirt tucked into black jeans as he closes his locker. I bang my head against the locker beside him. "I don't...want...to fucking go...to fucking class." I rub my hands on the white square tiles, grab his hand, and look down at the chipped black nail polish. "Everyone's going to think I'm a faggot for hanging out with you."

"Stop trying to make shit into a problem when it's not a fucking problem all because you're bored with yourself, fag."

"Fuck you, fag."

"You're the one who just grabbed a dude's hand in public."

249

Hot blue eyeshadow, blue bandana top, belly button ring, big tits, blonde hair, heart jewels on her blue jeans, and thick thighs: Candice is walking down the hall to her locker.

I elbow Lu. "This girl is fucking ridiculous. She's our very own Jenna Jameson. I would let her sit on my face for seventy-two fucking hours. I'm not kidding." I imagine her as a juggy girl in a slutty nurse costume and garter belt, dancing in *The Man Show* cage. The camera moves up her legs as she shakes her hips.

Lu elbows me. "You're being a fucking retard. Sluts don't deserve to have that much power over you. Watch this."

Candice leans into her locker. I stare at her big ass. Before he can open his mouth, she taps him. "Hey, Luke! Is it true you kidnapped some Latino guy from your computer science class and fucked him at the lake in some satanic ritual?"

"Do not call me that. My name is Lusif. Who do you think you are to speak your nonsense to me, huh?" Lu slams her locker door. "Look at you, you fucking whore. I bet you think you're so powerful. You think you're Carmen fucking Electra with your big titties out like that? Every guy at this school knows you're asking for it."

"You don't hurt me with your angsty bullshit, fag boy. Don't you have somewhere to be? Like the five o'clock news?"

Lu slams her locker again. "Oh, that's it!" Lu makes claws and squeezes the air. "You won't be calling me a faggot when my big dick is down your fucking throat and you have no way out. Come on, if I'm the school's satanic kidnapper, why don't you get ready? Maybe you're next."

"You're disgusting. Leave me alone! Just wait till I tell my boyfriend and his football buddies about your little rape threat."

"You tell your boyfriend about it and I will shoot him in the head. Make your choice. I don't think you want to spend your prom without your prom king. Your image will never recover." Lu puts his forehead into hers. "I am going to hex the fucking fuck out of you. I will ruin your life. All it takes is one black candle."

"Well, at least I'm more popular than you and people are obsessed with me. You make me want to vom.com!" Candice closes her locker and walks away.

Lu screams from behind. "Satan will always be more famous and more popular than you. All you'll ever be is a whore." Lu flicks the zipper of his jeans up and down. "You are one nasty bitch." He turns his baseball cap around and punches the air, and shouts, "Fuuuuuuuck!" as he walks down the hall toward the student lot. I follow him.

Sucking on Skittles and spitting them out onto the pavement, Lu and I sit on the curb by the school dumpsters. Lu passes a pack of cigarettes back and forth in his hands.

"I forgot. Is it pronounced Bafamay, or Bafemet?" I ask him.

"Bah-fem-et."

"Got it."

Lu's eyes intensify. "You know what I hate the most about Candice? She has this stuck-up cunt bitchiness. Like, shut up, you slut. I want to disembowel your body. I'll smoke a bowl of your bones."

"Well…"

"No matter what any woman says to me, it'll never matter. I'll always be the one with the dick, the superior one. I'm going to go home and fantasize about raping the shit out of her for hours. Torturous situations."

I smile wide. "Pussy power, man. Pussy power."

"It's ridiculous the power that sexy women have. It's just not fucking normal. I just want to take it from her for what it fucking does to me." He picks up my Pepsi.

"Hot girls aren't going to stop being hot girls anytime soon. Who gives a shit? Let her be a hot girl."

"Are you on her side?

I slap his shoulder. "You hate her because you can't fuck her. Admit it. She kind of looks like—"

Lu cuts me off. "Wait. You know about Tyson's spring break rager tomorrow night? The invite with the palm trees?"

"I'm not invited. Why are you talking about this? I don't want to think about that party right now. I'm not shooting up spring break with

251

you. Why don't we just find Candice's number in the phone book and leave a message on her answering machine that there's a tape going around school of her getting gangbanged by the football team?"

Lu rolls his eyes. "That's weak. There's no physical damage. Do you know where Stupid Miss Dick Sucker Teen USA lives?"

"We used to take the same shortcut home. I know her house, yeah. Why? You aren't actually going to, like, you know, rape her, right?"

His eyes roll again. "No, retard. I have an idea. Candice is going to be at Tyson's spring break party tomorrow, so let's vandalize her house while she's out. Shane and I have *Scream* masks we bought from Spencer's last Halloween. We'll use them to hide our faces and we can cover my license plate with streamers. I'll get silly string, eggs, and red spray paint. We'll write 'CANDICE CUNT' on her garage. This is going to be insane. I need to go to Spencer's anyway. I have to get a blacklight and some strobe lights."

"You know that her little sister has Down's, right?"

Lu grins wide. "Even better. Let's hope the retard is home and we can super-soak her fucking face off. Wait, do Down's Syndrome people have seizures? Imagine being handicapped and your life sentence is being the 'Welcome to Kmart' guy."

"Pick me up at nine-thirty. We can buy some Mountain Dew and get amped up. I'll call Shane and let him know. It's going down like syndrome, n****."

"What mask will you use?"

I shrug. "I don't own a mask."

"You don't own a mask?"

"No."

"Let's skip and go to Spencer's and get you one."

I high-five Lu. "Now this is what I call spring break 2000, motherfuckers."

☆ 81 ☆

I pull the tag of the black shirt: a blue skateboard deck, "Porn Star www. pornstarclothing.com." I flip it up: "Must be 18 or over." I hear a honk outside my bedroom window and look between my blinds, nothing. *He's up the street.* I roll my shirt into a ball, put it in my hoodie pocket, go into the Mr. Rags plastic bag near my door, take out another red Porn Star shirt, and put it into my hoodie pocket as well. I go downstairs, pass the living room with *Entertainment Tonight* on in the background, splices of Angelina Jolie posing on the red carpet at the Oscars. My mom is sitting, folding laundry, glued to the screen. "Jolie, who snagged Best Supporting Actress for her performance in *Girl, Interrupted* last night at the Oscars, is keeping today's goth trend alive and well with this haunting look!"

"Where are you going, loverbug?"

"Student council meeting. We're just finalizing some stuff for a project."

"That's lovely, honey. Did you see the news? The Black kid who held the pregnant white girl at gunpoint at 7-Eleven?"

I wince. "What a disgusting thug!"

Mom nods. "I don't care if you're a Black kid or a white kid, that's thugging."

"Mom, not to go all CSPAN, but what in the world has gone wrong in American society?"

"It's hip-hop, and people like 2Pac and Biggie. Why do we need to see all of this gun violence? It influences the kids. They want to be gangster, they want to be Black, they want the cool. We need more peace."

"You're right, Mom. See ya! Leave the back door unlocked for me." She nods. "Okay."

I open the front door and run up the sidewalk. Lu's windows are fogged up. *Chronic 2001* is pounding from his new JL Audio subwoofer. Shane is shotgun, Lu at the wheel. I hit his window, middle fingers, open the back door, and jump inside. The bass shakes my body as the streetlight shines through the window. I take the black Porn Star shirt out of my hoodie pocket and put it on.

Lu whistles. "Look at this naughty new man!"

I smile. "This shirt is the perfect way to show the world that I'm not this wholesome little boy anymore."

"College guys are going to see you in that and think, 'Man, that guy *fucks*.'"

"This is who I am right now, what I'm going through. If people don't like it, then they can fuck off! If I want to wear a 'filthy' necklace, fuck who gets offended! I'm in control now!"

I take out the red "MASTURBATING IS NOT A CRIME—A Public Service Announcement brought to you by Porn Star" shirt and throw it to Shane. He holds it up and says, "It's so ridiculous to me that adults who have it so-called-figured-out try to make us ashamed for trying to figure out who we are. Meanwhile, it took them years to discover themselves."

I shake my head. "Trying to stop guys from doing what they want is the most backwards thing ever. Why can't people just accept that chaos goes down even if it means we hurt ourselves? Isn't that the whole point of growing up? You can't prevent mistakes."

Lu cuts in. "Not to interrupt your after-school special, but did you see that *MTV News: UNfiltered* break today where they were showing those political activist kids? 'Real American teens tell their stories.' Barf me out."

I shrug. "All I know about politics is what I see on SNL."

Shane hits my shoulder. "Presidents like to get their dicks sucked by fat chicks. Oral fixations."

"There is only one democracy I participate in. It's called…" Lu revs the engine hard. "*Total Request Live!*" He speeds down the empty street. "We need to go to 7-Eleven to fill up."

I blow fog on the back window and draw shapes in the condensation. *I wish I could be in this car forever and never have to know what happens after.*

I hear the sound of a two-liter Mountain Dew bottle being opened. Shane takes a swig, leans over, passes me the bottle.

I drink and hold it up. "You want some, Lu?"

"There's no vodka in it."

Shane grabs the bottle. "I'm down to do this drunk."

I cut in. "Wait. You guys heard about the Candice-S&M-Kraft Dinner fetish thing, right?"

Lu turns back. "I'm listening."

"Candice loves to get Kraft macaroni and cheese eaten out of her snatch. It's a sensitive topic for me—I would one hundred percent eat whatever out of her pussy."

Shane smiles. "I bet she likes to get gagged with Jawbreakers."

I reflect. "That only happens to girls in the movies. I rented that film, jerked off to it, then returned it."

Shane's eyes light up. "The big-titty bitch from *Charmed* in the nightgown, Rose McGowan. There's too many movie star sluts these days to keep track of. Yo, big question. Why do football dudes grab each other's asses and hump each other in the locker room? I bet they finger fuck each other."

I put three fingers in the air. "It's not gay, bro. It's just sportsmanship. Male bonding."

Lu laughs. "Oh, Tyson, pour Gatorade on me. Good game, you sexy fuckin meathead."

"I bleed Frost Gatorade."

Shane knocks my shoulder. "Holy fuck. You're not going to believe what I just remembered. *The Duckman Show.*"

"That was so long ago. Wow, I was like twelve."

Lu pulls up to a pump at the 7-Eleven. As he fills the car, I'm on my knees fiddling with the radio. Shane drags a key down the window. I turn the dial. "And we got Aaliyah's 'Try Again' coming up after this…" Knob turn. "So, Douglas, what do you think of the young men in this country?" "The young American men in this country are addicted to the MTV-driven consumerist society. One way or another, these boys are going to…" Knob turn. "Remember when Donald Trump was on CNBC's

Hardball last year, giving the scoop to Chris Matthews on why he thinks he'd be one of the most controversial American presidents…" Radio off.

Shane holds up his "AT-RISK" hospital bracelet. "Do you like it? I mean, nobody fucking understands me. Everything I do gets the opposite response, so I think I can be a little ironic."

I shake my head fast and think of Shane with his tongue stuck out, Prozac pills in his mouth. Lu is paying at the register. The glow of the green neon sign lights up the pavement. I look over at the payphone, *Slap*, Aphex Twin, DC logo stickers, and Sharpie scribbles all over the glass.

I turn to Shane. "It's so strange to think that right now, we are living inside of never-before-seen footage, uncut, uncensored, unaired moments of our lives."

"Sometimes, man, it's like I'm never experiencing anything. I'm wondering about the moment while it's still happening. I'm holding onto it in fear that it's going to, like, disappear forever."

"Totally. This is all just a deleted scene that comes after the credits."

Shane nods. "Yeah."

"I have this total haunt that right now has happened before, or that every scene in my life is being broadcasted live on a TV somewhere."

"Dude, I thought that I was the only one."

"Do you think we're the only guys on the entire planet who feel this way?"

Lu opens the door, falls into his seat, and punches the horn. "You gangster bitches ready to fuck up spring break 2000?"

Shane turns on the CD player. The bass vibrates the car and shakes my body. "You playas ready? Dr. Dre, mothafucka!"

Lu speeds off as "The Next Episode" plays, rapping every word.

I scream. "Turn it up! This song makes my dick hard!"

Lu looks back at me. "Slim Shady is a god. I can rap as fast as him, I swear. I've been practicing in the mirror."

"You should have worn the blue bandana tied with the fake gold chain. You would have looked so Black."

"What are you talking about? I am Black, playa."

"I don't know if these speakers are going to make it through this ride! I don't know if we're gonna survive this dirty bass."

Shane turns to Lu. "I'm so happy you got this car mod. It's sounding real nice."

Lu's eyes dart ahead. "We're almost there."

I yell. "Stop the car."

Lu ignores me. "Is this the one?"

I cut back in. "I'm HIV positive, champ."

Lu parks beneath a streetlight. I get out and look at the house across from us. A BMX bike and Razor scooters with blue and green handles on the lawn. Three freshman-looking boys in DC shoes and Spitfire shirts with green hair and blue tips sit in a circle with Big Gulps and plastic candy mix bags. Shane sits on the sidewalk, head on his knees, smoking a cigarette. Lu opens his trunk.

"What are you satanic fucking freakos doing on our street?" one of the boys asks. "You think you're so gangsta blasting *Chronic 2001* at this hour?"

"You guys look like a bunch of fags!" says another. "What's with the shirts? You guys a bunch of gay pornstars?" He taps his friend, who joins in.

"Yeah, do you give anal jobs to each other? Are you going to buttfuck right in front of us, creeps?"

I look at Lu. "Anal jobs? What the fuck?"

Lu goes over to the lawn. "It's simple, little boys. Do you want to change the channel? Get chopped up, tortured, and be missing preteens in this week's satanic ritual abuse FOX coverage? Or do you want to stick to your regularly scheduled programming, taking turns playing *Tony Hawk* in between circle jerks to the new issue of *Juggs* that you stole from your older brother? You guys ever heard of Anton LaVey, the reverend of the Satanic church?"

"You guys are fucked!" The boys run into the house and slam the door behind them.

I go to the open trunk: *Scream* masks, a Super Soaker, a carton of eggs, bottles of silly string, and three mini devil head bags of crushed Ritalin. "This is ultra-chopped."

Lu grabs one of the mini devil head bags and closes the trunk. He pulls on my shirt and I follow him underneath a tree. We stand, smoking. "I think there's something special about you and me that makes us more powerful than anyone on this scumbucket planet."

I nod. "I don't know what's wrong with me. It's like sometimes I have concepts in my mind about how I once felt, but I'm not experiencing real feelings anymore. It's like I've got no emotions. I just watch, numb."

"You only forget how you feel because you know how to assume a character, yet still remain yourself. You're so good at that."

"Do you want to know something I love about you? Your whole philosophy toward life. This idea that you can hurt yourself before life gets a chance to hurt you."

Lu shrugs. "How do you mean?"

"The world is going to fuck you up. It's inevitable, so you might as well be the one doing that destruction."

Lu takes out his BIC, lights the flame, and puts his finger over it. "Doesn't it look like the flame is blinking at us?"

"I could watch this for hours."

Lu's eyes light up. "You ever done a smiley?"

"No."

"You take your BIC, let the flame come out, and heat the wheel up. You push it onto your skin and it leaves a burn mark in the shape of a smiley face."

"Do it to me."

"Are you serious?"

"I want it right now. Fucking do it." I push my shirt sleeve down my shoulder, "Right here." Lu pushes the BIC wheel into my shoulder, burning skin, wet eyes. I bite my lip. *This feeling exists? Where has it been?* "That's some good shit. One more time."

"You sure?"

"Another."

Lu gets on his knees, pulls up my shirt, and dabs his BIC above my belly button. Burning skin, wet eyes, I bite my lip. *This feeling…where has it been…* "Wow, that was amazing."

Lu gets up, tilts his BIC, and lights it sideways in front of my eyes. I look at him. "They see scars. We see souvenirs."

He smiles. "You can smiley anywhere, too. 7-Eleven. Mall bathroom. McDonald's, the movies. School! Someone's house. Wherever there's a private room, you can lock yourself in where no one can see you. You're good to go." Lu grabs my hand, flips it over, brings me down to the grass, takes out the bag of crushed Ritalin, and pours a bit onto my palm. He takes out his keys, dabs the powder on my hand, and sniffs some off his key. "Woo-hoo! Fuck yeah!"

I grab Lu's hand and look down at his black Timex. "Yo, it's almost ten-fifty. She's definitely at the party."

"Spring break 2000, mothafuckas!"

I smile. "It's time to vandahhhhl. Let's put on our masks and piss the fuck into the Super Soaker."

Shane is lying on the sidewalk smoking, staring at a real estate sign.

Lu kicks Shane's side on his way to the trunk. "Uh don't hurt yourself there, James Duval."

I look into the side mirror, pulling down my eyelids. Shane comes behind me and wraps his arms around my stomach.

Lu puts on his mask and hands one to me. I put it on.

Shane picks up the Super Soaker and puts it to his temple. "Let me *Gummo* the fuck out. Blow my brains out."

Lu cuts him off. "Come get your mask, faggot."

Shane puts on the mask. "Where are the eggs?"

Lu puts the Polaroid camera on top of his car and activates the timer. "We're going to piss into the Super Soaker and throw the fucking eggs after we take a group Polaroid." We stand in frame, me in the middle, Shane and Lu's arms over me, *Scream* masks on, middle fingers up.

"Wait, what are some sick gang symbols?" I ask. The flash bursts. "This is how the new millennium boys roll!" I grab the undeveloped Polaroid, shake it, kiss it, open the car door, and put the Polaroid on the dashboard.

Lu laughs. "Meet the sickest crew in the hood."

I grab the Super Soaker and piss into the hole.

Lu taps my shoulder. "Nice aim."

"Don't look, you fruit. Would you look at that! Apple juice, freshly squeezed from my cock."

I pass it to Lu then turn and look at the bushes to the sound of Lu pissing into the hole. Lu passes it to Shane, pushing it into his stomach. "Piss, dick-boy."

Shane shrugs. "I'm not doing it."

"This is what happens when you look up to Cobain and Corgan, kids. You become soft."

I knock Lu's shoulder. "Yo! We should piss into spray bottles and make piss spray and spray 'em on freshman on the last day of school."

"Shouldn't we use duct tape to cover the license plate? Wouldn't that be so *Sopranos*?" Shane asks.

Lu goes to the car and comes back holding the carton of eggs. Shane and I goose-step behind him toward Candice's house, hugging silly string bottles. "Okay…just like we practiced! Would you rather be at the movies right now watching *Final Destination* or here?"

"Here!"

"Pretend that you're at home playing PlayStation. You're player one. No real people are getting hurt. This is a fun time."

I chuckle. "Well, it's not an ABC TV movie, that's for sure."

Lu nods. "This is crime! You know what they say? Crime is the highest form of sensuality. This is just an unforgettable night at the movies. Once I say one, two, three, run, we destroy."

Lu finishes the countdown as we run up the street to Candice's house. I look through the living room window. A reflection of *The Little Mermaid*. A redheaded babysitter, some college chick, is brushing Candice's sister's hair. I push the lever and silly string flies into the trees and all over the garden.

Shane silly strings the pebble stone driveway. "I'm keeping it PG-13 with the silly string."

"Fuck. I legit wish 'Forgot About Dre' was playing right now!"

Lu pulls out his BIC. "Should I give no fucking fucks and pull a straight up Left Eye?"

I take an egg out of the carton, throw it, and look at the yolk dripping down the garage door. "Revenge has never been this special...ed."

Shane grabs an egg and throws it at the circular window upstairs.

Lu grabs another egg. "Do you think that's the room where she puts Juggahoe makeup on while getting pounded by a pack of Black dudes?"

Shane laughs. "Imagine if we had done this in Klux hoods? It'd be so stupid."

"I want to shove her bloody bitch tampon into her mouth so she can choke on her own fucking blood!" Lu says as he goes up to the white garage door, pulls out a red Sharpie marker, and writes, "Your Daughter Is A Cunt. 666. Hail Satan!"

I run up to the front door, knock, say, "Ding dong ditch death!" then hide behind a bush.

Candice's sister opens the front door in a Bambi robe. She stands on the welcome mat as Lu aims the Super Soaker, pulls the trigger, and sprays our piss onto her face. "My eyes! My eyes! Whaa..." She drops to her knees, sobbing.

Shane runs back to the car. Lu jumps over the bushes and I bolt down the street. *Pretend this is a PlayStation game. You're player one.* The babysitter lifts Candice's sister up as I open the back door.

Lu lifts his mask and looks me in the eye. "I just put...the hot...in psychotic." Foot on the pedal, volume cranking. "The Next Episode" blares, bass shaking my body.

Speeding down the empty streets, I grab the Polaroid from the dashboard. *And there I am again, some version of me, watching an idea of myself, trying to rid myself of a force I can't recognize, I can't handle. That's the fear, isn't it? That maybe another hit of pleasure isn't going to come? Do you have to lose who you are in order to become who you want to be for a few hours at night? Why is tonight not on videotape?*

♡ L13 ♡

Aurora,

I don't think I've ever told you this, but the first time I saw you across the room in the mess hall, I had all these visions of us kissing in anime. It was like a sequence out of one of those music videos that they play late at night on MTV. I've never had an entire dream in anime, but what a cool concept your friend Lizzy mentioned to you. Maybe all three of us can watch the movie Perfect Blue sometime. I hope to meet her when I come to visit. She seems great, and any friend of yours is a friend of mine.

I just want to go out with you to a warehouse party in a secret location, us spinning on dance floors. Maybe we could make friends with an acid dealer DJ and listen to British techno. Underworld and Björk remixes slamming us around, you and me, up until sunrise. Can you see it? Can you feel it? It's like being homesick for an experience you know should be happening right now!

Things have been pretty heavy here lately. There is no one else in my life I can go to about what recently happened to me. I've been holding it inside so tight, it feels like I could explode. One of my friend's older brothers hazed me, tied me to a chair, and assaulted me. I seriously did nothing to deserve this. It's so fucked up how older guys always want to assert their dominance over us. It happened so fast…they put a bag over my head and tied me up. I'm really sad about this, Aurora. I feel different.

Yours truly,
Brad Sela

P.S. I really really like the heart you wrote around your initials on this one.

P.P.S. Oh, and I wanted to tell you…I saw Polaroids of you in my dream last night. I woke up in a panic looking all around my room but couldn't find anything. I thought I hid them in a slipcase, but no luck. What an empty feeling.

♡ L14 ♡

Brad,

There aren't words to match the magnitude of sympathy I'm feeling in my heart for you. I can't believe that you were attacked, that you became a victim like this. I'm sure there's an assault victim hotline that you could call to get more support anonymously, who can give you more help than I can. Please tell your friend's parents about what he did. I don't understand what makes boys so aggressive, so cruel. I hope he gets what's coming for him. I wish I could kiss you better.

Moving on to softer things! I would love to go out all night with you! Dance is my love language. I can see us at that party, spinning in the strobe lights to Aphex Twin. Lizzy loves his music, too, you know! I mean, God, Brad, she hears so much about you, she feels like she's already met you. I hope you let that one get to your head.

I know. Our neighborhoods can be so boring without each other and fantasizing all day can only take us so far, but I still do it all the time. I would love to lay in the grass on your sweater at your favorite field.

There's nothing new to write. You know, me and the girls, we've been going to the pool, biking around, watching our shows. We bought some stuff at this small spiritual shop in town. We lit cigarettes from the flame on the incense holder sitting on my friend Ashley's bedroom floor yesterday while her mom was out. After that, we washed out perfume bottles, filled them with her dad's vodka, then took them to the forest to drink. The things that we do when we're bored! It looked cool in the Polaroids. Ashley's been having boy troubles. She says that every girl our age's nightmare is "falling in love with the same boy again and again, just in different bodies." I never want to go looking for you in other people. I want you to be the only one who gets another one of my summers. The day I fear the most is when my world stops being beautiful to you.

Honestly, going to your school would be so awful for me. I would totally compare myself to every pretty girl I'd see talking to you in the halls. These are the benefits of being homeschooled!

Why don't you picture this? You and I on a week-long escape to a hidden house on the lake. We night swim for hours in cliffside river pools and walk through fresh air trails in the daylight. I write you love notes by candlelight in our bedroom. I'll make you dinner. I'll kiss you in places that only trees can witness.

I swear, falling for you feels like discovering a new color for the first time that only we can see.

Sometimes I look into my closet mirror when the lights go off before bed and I feel you there for a second, your hands wrapped around my stomach. And then right there, it's like I'm waiting for you to return to my room, even though you've never even been here...strange.

Your girl,
Aurora

☆ 82 ☆

I put my video camera on top of the TV, grab the remote, and hit the red button. I sit shirtless on my bed in my Fruit of the Loom boxer briefs, sipping a can of Surge.

"Yes, there is Dorito dust all over my fucking fingers right now. Sue me.

I want to talk about some deep, fucked-up shit that most people are too stupid to understand.

"I just lost thirty minutes of my life watching *Spring Break* 2000 footage on MTV. Look, I enjoy seeing Carmen Electra's huge tits just as much as the next guy. And her legs. And her ass. But when I looked up and realized I was sitting there watching the guy from Lit grind on her, I got fucking pissed. MTV is dangling all of these hot girls in our faces all the time. Society wants us to be thinking about sex constantly, just as we're raging with whoremones. It's torture. It's the biggest blue balls, and I'm finally realizing this shit. I've got a shoebox of *Spring Break* tapes and now, at seventeen, this is hitting me. It's all a lie. Everything means nothing. My life isn't a P. Diddy video, my life is 7-Eleven and Jergens.

"You see all these girls in *Score*, porn tapes, and on *The Man Show*, for what? They aren't going to come out of the TV and suck your dick. And I'm the target market. Do I want to be the target of a corporation? Of suits? Of boardroom calculations? All to get me to spend my dad's money?

"I'm probably not making any sense, but I'm trying to understand what the fuck is going on in this fucking fake society that I'm living in. It's like reality doesn't even exist anymore, so any type of reflection that we see that claims to be reality is just another deception, another myth. What is MTV trying to distract me from by making me believe that all I'm worthy to think about is Carmen Electra's rack?

"What if *Newsweek* is right? What if MTV is the one raising me? It's not like I'd listen to anything my parents say, especially if I thought something was cool, but it makes me so fucking angry because I think that everything I see in magazines and TV is cool. Where is my own individuality? Am I just another mindless drone? Like, I can buy the Tool album and listen to *Ænima*, but am I really living that anti-culture lifestyle, or am I just another poser? Searching for something real in this world might be the biggest mistake because nothing is real. Everyone is fake.

"I'm stuck in this giant feedback loop, watching a version of myself that I want to exist, a version of myself being sold back to me. Then I watch more of these images and try to be like that guy. It's like when blink-182 tour footage shows up on TV and I see a guy who looks like me in a Porn Star shirt I want to buy. I'm like, 'Shit. That's me.' But is it? What if corporations are watching me aspire to be what they created of me? What if they are crafting a new version of me? Everything is so fake, so corny, such bullshit. I'll be watching a movie about a guy who is supposed to be my age and they'll just put a hackysack in the movie to be *relatable*. I'm not fucking retarded. I see what you're doing. It's insulting.

"Everyone at school makes fun of the posers and try-hards, but what if everyone is a poser and a try-hard? What if there is no authenticity and we just want to put certain people on pedestals as the *real ones*? What if

265

that's just another fucking lie we tell ourselves for more bullshit false idol worship? How do people not want to throw up in their mouths when they're around someone bragging about knowing a band before they went mainstream or predicting trends before everyone follows them? News flash: everything you love, everything you think is yours, is going to get killed by MTV. MTV is going to take anything cool, every underground trend, expose it to sunlight, and ruin it. This is the secret of mass consumerism. Doesn't that sound so fucking depressing, chasing trends that are over by the time you catch up to them? The anti-marketing is bullshit too, like that one Grant Hill Sprite commercial. It's reverse brainwashing because the machine knows that being anti-culture is cool. How the fuck do you escape and be an individual? What the fuck do I have to do in order to do that? Motherfucking pretentious know-it-all social-climbing trend-clinging retards who think they're so ahead of everyone else have no idea that they've already fallen behind. Even in those hip scenes, it's common knowledge that as soon as you think you've found a place to belong, someone will take it away from you and tell you that you're being yourself in all of the wrong ways.

"People need to give the fuck up on thinking that they're better than anyone who wears Tommy or Abercrombie just because they wear a choker or satanic ring on their finger! You try so hard to look different but can't see that you all end up looking the same.

"Everyone in my generation is so obsessed with being cool, with climbing up the ranks of an image, but for what? Just so you can feel a part of something? What if you don't want that? Huh? What now? Look, I'm not trying to go all Limbaugh, but mainstream media is propaganda. The TV gives you nothing back and yet here the fuck I am every day, hoping this time it'll be different, that this time I'll feel good.

"People come to fucking assemblies trying to tell us to be ourselves. Fuck off. How the fuck can anyone be themselves when we don't even know who we are yet? Why do jocks think that they're better than goths? Why do preps think they're better than jocks?

"MTV plays all of the same songs, the same videos, the same commercials. Where can I go to see something different? Maybe the only way to see anything else is to live your life in a nonlinear way, to go with the flow, to be outside of the house. I love MTV, but I hate MTV. I can't stop using it. I can't stop looking at it. You know what? Fuck this. I'm not a statistic or an example.

"TV is full of false worlds, false images, false illusions, and yet we use our remotes to submit and numb the fuck out. We don't even know what we're distracting ourselves from. Everything is about image. It's pathetic, and yet I'm the number one victim. Ideas and images seem so much sexier than the reality of being in the moment you want to exist.

"What do I owe to this world? Nothing. I don't want to change the fucking world or stand for anything or be part of a protest, because the world doesn't ever change as long as piece-of-shit human beings are on this planet. And I'm a piece-of-shit human too. Nothing on the news shocks me because CNN never changes. The people in the stories they show us always ruin our days. Opinions are just the product of temporary feelings, so why have one at all? Why stand for anything?

"People stylize themselves as advertisements, selling who they want to be and who they think they are. Why do I care so much about the new t-shirt brands, new music videos, and useless info about celebrities' lives that I'll never get to live? Why the fuck does the machine have so much power over me? MTV says the things that we want to say before we even get a chance to form our own opinions or thoughts. They're controlled perspectives.

"I am living in a society that is one huge commercial trying to sell me Budweiser, Prozac, *Girls Gone Wild*, and Tool shirts, and yet I still can't feel anything other than not giving a fuck about anything. I'm part of a generation where everyone is robbed of their identities. Fuck that. The more delusional you are, the easier you are to control.

"What works best? What works fastest? What makes you the coolest? Buy it now! Get it now! Need it now! Up for grabs! Enter the sweepstakes. Click, click. Buy, buy. Faster, hotter, sexier. Whatever. It's called programming for a reason. You rip something off to be a rip-off of a rip-off.

"You are nobody because everybody is you! How the fuck does that feel? I'm a clone of a clone of a guy that was sold to me. No one is powerful enough to fight the disease that is wanting to be seen, wanting to be cool, wanting to be noticed, wanting to fit in.

"The lies we let ourselves believe in become our own versions of the truth and no one is willing to unlearn that."

☆ 83 ☆

The red light is blinking. I play the first message on my answering machine: "Brad! It's Kristen. Call me back. I wanted to see how you've been doing? You aren't picking up my calls anymore. My mom told me your mom said you were super busy with student council stuff, which seems a little suspect to me. You should come over and watch this movie *Fun* I taped off IFC last night. It's from the early nineties and is about these two girls who become obsessive best friends and end up killing some elderly person. Also, I stole you a bottle of Mugler's A*MEN from this guy I've been fucking. Anyways—" I hit delete.

The next message is from Shane. "Brad, are you there? I need to tell you about something that happened at the waterpark last summer. Just between us. Please call me back. I can't keep it inside anymore."

☆ 84 ☆

Tied Converse All Stars hang from the power line. Through the front window, I see Lu's mom watching TV. I open the door as she's pouring Absolut into a Holy Bible flask. *Oprah* is on TV. There's a cross-shaped ashtray on the coffee table and Sandra Bullock on the cover of *US Weekly*. A VHS slipcase: "Understanding the Devil in the Media Today."

"Are you here to see my son?" She gets up from the couch and grabs my hand. "Please help him. Please pray for him. My life has been a living hell since he started listening to Marilyn Manson. He's the reason Luke is obsessed with obscenity, anger, and self-mutilation."

I hold back my laughter. "Your son can't change from music."

She picks up the slipcase. "Satan puts subliminal messages in his music. Even Britney Spears is a tool of the devil. Hollywood is brainwashing all of you. He's just deceived. He can see the light. He can change. Please help my son see the light of Christ."

Lusif leans over the banister in plaid pajama bottoms and a Tool shirt as he hugs a shark Beanie Baby and licks on a Disney Store Hades swirl lollipop. "Leave Brad alone, Mom!"

She yells at him, "Why do you betray the Lord for people you don't even know? All the sex chokers, all of the homosexual posters, the Marilyn Manson shirts. I live through Judgment Day every hour because of you! You just wait until Christ returns."

Lu roars, "I'm surprised the authorities haven't taken you away for the child abuse that was taking me to church! How could you enforce such an oppressive, limited reality onto a child, Mom? You dumb, pro-life cunt!"

I shiver. "Don't speak to your mother that way."

Lu bites back. "Shut the fuck up! You don't get an opinion. You have no idea what she puts me through."

She grabs my hand again. "See what the devil is doing to him?"

I let go. Lu starts again. "You dumb bitch! Why doesn't your only friend Oprah do something useful for once and teach you how to not be such a fucking retard?"

"You're grounded, young man. I'm taking away your computer. This house is going to be empty. Do you hear me?"

"I fucking hate you, Mom. I hate you more than anyone in this whole wide world." Lu motions to me. "Brad, come up here now!"

Lu's mom points to the stairs. "You want to know who the antichrist is? The antichrist is a teenage boy, and do you know where he lives? In my house, up those stairs." Lu slams his door shut.

I rub my fingers on the wooden banister as I climb the stairs, the sound of Nine Inch Nails blaring from behind his bedroom door. Taped to it: an XY subscription card with images of shirtless men, red Sharpie dicks, and 666s drawn over it.

Inside, Lu is holding a black candle, lighting his cigarette with the flame and leaning against a wall plastered with Marilyn Manson pics.

"Welcome to the chamber, bitch!"

I look up at the shock bolt American flag hung up on the wall by his desk as I survey the room. A *Party Monster: The Shockumentary* VHS sits atop his TV. His mattress lies on the floor below a dartboard with a picture of Fiona Apple on it. On his black desk: a computer with a bikini-clad Heather Graham screensaver sits between two speakers, a *Half-Life* computer box, a CD mini tower, Walgreens twenty-four hour photo envelopes. Posters of Eminem in a wifebeater dot his walls alongside a half-naked Rose McGowan and Pam Anderson. There are torn out pictures of girls in thongs from *Score*, a 2000 *Playboy* calendar, *The Doom Generation* movie poster. Scrawled on the wall in marker: "Life is a red carpet, but paint it black." A magazine is open on his bed. I close it and flip it around: the *Time* cover with the Columbine killers. "The Monsters Next Door." There are hearts drawn all over it with glitter heart stickers. I hold it up.

"Are you serious? A shrine to the Columbine killers? You can troll-shock all you want in cyberspace, but that doesn't work on me here in the real world."

Lu holds up a bottle of Jergens. "I bust a fat nut to that cover every night. Look how badass they look holding their guns. This is more exciting than most movie posters these days. Can you blame me?"

"How could you live with yourself? We took a moment of silence for the victims at school today. Last year I helped make the mural to honor the victims."

"You sound handicapped! How does that make you a good person? Did you brag about your good little deed on *Ricki Lake* and forget to tell me about it?"

"Oh, I'm surprised you haven't been on *Lake* yet. An episode about upper-class kids who don't listen to their moms and pretend to act all mature and hard."

"You don't give a shit about the victims. You're just opportunistic. You only give a shit about yourself."

"That's not true! I feel pain for those families."

"This is just you doing what you always do, impressing yourself and satisfying your own self-image to the most important audience member: you!"

"How could you even think of supporting their hatred?"

"Eric Harris and Dylan Klebold are the most inspiring people in the world. This is a real movement, a true revolution for people like me, people who feel different, smarter than everyone else. I mean, I even love Kip Kinkel! Kinkel says, 'Guns are the only things that don't stab us in the back.' I want that unconditional love."

"The fact that we know these people's names makes me sick! All because of these self-indulgent pieces of shit, parents won't be able to kiss their kids goodnight. Empty houses. Years of future family memories robbed. No more birthdays. No more Christmas dinners. This is a real thing that happened, something that affected people's lives. This wasn't happening on TV. How can you not care?"

"I see mass murders as the ultimate symbol of American freedom. If you want worldwide fame, you go on a shooting spree and our country knows exactly what to do to make you a household name. You don't even have to hire a publicist. The media just gets to work."

"Name one of the victims' names. I know them. Ra—"

"That's like going to a show and watching the crowd instead of the rock stars on stage." Lu claps. "Someone just got raped!" Lu claps. "Someone just died from AIDS!" Lu claps. "Someone just got cancer."

"What's your fucking point?"

"You can't control anything that happens to the people in your life. This is a disgusting, unfair, bullshit planet and nature is going to get us all at some point. No one asked to be born. You might as well learn to become one with the chaos."

I look toward the door and get off the bed. Lu picks up the magazine and flips to a page with Eric Harris's face in the corner. "I look like Eric. I feel like he and I could be brothers. It's the whole Mickey and Mallory thing. I want to be a part of it, leave a lasting impact on the world, get infinite attention for decades to come. No one understands the feeling of seeing them for the first time. It was the closest thing I've had to true love."

"Wait a sec. Didn't Eric and Dylan go to McDonald's before the shooting?"

"I thought it was Burger King."

"And they went bowling, too, right?"

"Dude, there's all these theories online, and I go on this message board with all of these other fans. We all bond over our obsession."

"Do you ever get bored of being so fascinated with yourself?"

Lu starts making out with the cover, opens it up, and tongues the side-by-side pics of Eric and Dylan. "Never."

"I'm sick and tired of watching this show about you, starring you, directed by you, scripted by you."

"Call your cable provider and cancel the channel then. Get me off the monthly bill. No one is saying you have to be here."

"Real life isn't a movie set. It's not a stage. It must be so pathetic being you. I mean, look at you. You're only seventeen and you're already a parody of yourself."

"Oh, so that's how it's going to be? You don't even see the way you perceive yourself, how the way you act is so split. I know the real you. There's no going back from the things we've done. I bet you sit in your bedroom at night and try so hard to leave our experiences on the cutting room floor. Guess what? No amount of editing will change the truth of who you are."

"Do not—"

"Your parents would be horrified to know about the show that starts filming the second you leave the house. Do you want me to mention where you were last week?"

I hit his head with a Pringles container, push him onto the bed, and straddle him. He grabs a bottle of Jack Daniel's from beside his bed and chugs it. I hold down his chest. "Slap me! Do it. Slap me. Make me feel something." I slap him across the face. "Do it again. Harder!" I slap him again. "Come on, fucker. Harder! Bruise me."

I catch our reflection in the closet mirror. "You want me to be all the things you say I am? You want to see me take on the cold-blooded, calculating bad boy? That's what everyone's waiting for, the moment I go full-on villain mode. Well, I'll show you."

"Ooh, this is the episode that'll leave audiences wanting more."

"You've pushed me to the point where I've become someone so much worse than what you're capable of. You will never recover from this revenge."

"Tell me about it. You look sexy when you're this angry."

I get off of him. We sit on the bed. I get up in his grill. "I'll tell my parents that you coerced me into a friendship. I'll say the stress of senior year has caused me psychotic anxiety and you preyed on me. I'll get my parents to tell your mom about all the things that you've done. I'll set you up when you least expect it. I'll get a computer nerd to make a fake website where it looks like you're planning a school shooting. Everyone will believe me. Oh, and the best part? Everyone is going to look at me like I did nothing wrong. I'll be the sympathetic one. I'll win."

"She already knows!"

"Well, I've seen all the *Poison Ivy* movies. I'll figure something out."

"Anything more?"

"You've never watched me work a family dinner. Charisma oozes out of me. Everyone loves me. Everyone buys everything I'm selling. No one has any idea of who I really am."

"Cut! I'm going to need you to redo those lines. We need to see more passion."

"What are you talking about?" I look over to a videocam on top of Lu's dresser, pointing at us. "You didn't." My hand covers my mouth.

He takes a microcassette recorder out of his pocket. "Oh, and I also got it on my voice recorder just in case I lose the video. A beautiful deposition. Hot new trend alert: Blackmailing Your BFF Creates Eternal Bonds!" I can't speak. "See how you reacted as soon as I brought up something that can compromise your reputation? That's how weak you really are. That's what's so great about being a committed villain. You have no one to deceive and nothing to hide. You should try it sometime."

My body shakes. "So many scary things are happening in my life right now. I don't know why I do the things that I do. I just watch and end up there, and I know that I wanted it, but at the same time, I didn't. I can't stop." Tears threaten, but I hold them back. "I have no one to talk about this with. I'm so alone. People in my life have no idea how lonely I feel. The pain is invisible. It's like I only have you, and you're the one I learned all of this bullshit from. It's all your fault."

"Nope, that's not how it works. You don't get to blame other people when they don't recognize the parts of you that you choose to hide."

"Maybe I need more attention. Maybe if my parents cared to dig a little deeper and violated my private life, our friendship could've been prevented. You would've made a short cameo instead of being cast for another season."

"I'm a recurring role, no guest stars here. It's so sad how the second things don't go the way you want them to on your screen you resort to playing the victim. It's like you're so delusional, you can't even experience consequences."

"That's it. I'm asking my mom for a therapist tonight. They can help me figure out how to crawl out of this mess of a double life I've created."

"I wonder what your parents would feel if they learned the truth, that they could never protect their son from the greatest danger in the neighborhood: himself." I'm speechless. "Are you going to say anything? Retaliate. I want passion in the next shot."

"Who the fuck do you think you are? You don't get to just come into my life and dismantle an entire belief system I have about myself. I know I'm pure! I know I'm a good person! You know nothing!"

"I want you to say something cruel to me. Make me feel alive."

"Empty. Unfixable. Unwanted. Broken. Loveless. That's what I think of when I think of you. No one in this world will love you. Not even your own father could, so how could you expect anyone else to? You hold onto these fantasy versions of yourself to avoid the truth that you're completely empty inside. Nothing about you is special. Anyone who has to engineer scandals everywhere they go is just trying to run from their truth. You try so hard to come off as so evil, so satanic, but you're not. You're a terrified little boy."

"You saying all of that made me feel nothing. I'm the only person in your life you can't control. It makes you berserk!"

"What about me? I'm sick of you attacking my character all the time. Why is it so wrong that I crave excitement and danger? You want the honest truth about me? I *do* produce the world around me. I *do* pretend that my life is a scrapped MTV pilot about teenagers in a suburban wasteland. I *like* being the starring role. I *need* to be the main character. What's so wrong with that? The twisted scenarios are all coming from me, but you'll never understand the heart-ripping pain and confusion of not knowing why I do all of this shit."

"Good work. Admitting to being a self-obsessed delusional narcissist who will scheme and hurt anyone in the way of protecting their façade-good-boy-image is the first step on your way to becoming a real human being."

"Today, you exposed me to the number one person I try to keep from seeing who I really am."

"And who would that be?"

"Me!" I push him. "Stay the fuck away from me at school and don't fucking call me."

Lu flips over on his stomach, grabs his pillow, and screams into it at the top of his lungs. I walk down his stairs and see his mom leaning on the couch, sobbing into her hands. Upstairs, Lu screams along to the chorus of Hole's "Violet."

<h2 style="text-align:center">☆ 85 ☆</h2>

A Virgin Records commercial plays on my muted TV. A bag of sour keys and my blink-182 school binder lay open on my bed. Lu calls and I pick up.

I raise my voice. "Stop fucking calling me! I can't keep unplugging my phone. Some Asian has to tell me what bio notes I missed. I need to

275

fucking study. Whatever Aaron Spelling motherfucker is up in the sky pulling the strings on my life, could I please just have one normal weekend of banging hot chicks and doing drugs on a Saturday night spiral?"

Lu sighs. "You're making loving school shooters so much more dramatic than it needs to be! Stop trying to convince me that I'm a bad person! You're acting like every other person in my life who's abandoned me! You don't feel guilty for icing me out like this. This is disgusting! I'm such a good friend to you! You're so fucking sensitive, little Cancer bitch boy."

"No! My mind is not your playground anymore. Get used to it! What happened the other night is something I've never experienced. I'm not going back there."

"I bet you're doing nothing with your life. You're just being a pathetic piece of shit ignoring my calls."

"See? You spin me out. Bury yourself in a monkey grave and leave me out of the shit pits."

"How can you handle ignoring me in the halls? I'm your best friend!"

"If you and I had one of those Claire's BFF necklaces, I'd rip it apart right now."

"You probably went to that stupid get-together and played UNO in some loser's garage, talked about a bunch of bullshit that I know you don't care about."

"You hear this? This is the sound of me hanging up."

"Don't!"

"Why? Haven't you had enough entertainment at this point? Can you just try to be a normal friend to me without setting me up all the time?"

"I want to now. I really want to. Listen to me for one fucking second. You and I have something too special to give up. We need to do whippits together. I stole a can of Glade from work. Trust me, it'll be so fucking fun. My buddy was telling me about it and it sounds insane. I don't want to do it alone."

"This fucking sucks. I just want to get back to where we were."

"Please forgive me then, dude. Fuck it. Forget about the other day. Honestly, I don't care about Eric and Dylan. It was just another script, a game. Trust me. I can tone down the mind games for a while. We're going to have a blast."

"I've been bored out of my mind, Lu. I don't know what to do."

"Do whippits with me tomorrow night."

☆ 86 ☆

We sit on a bench as I look at engravings on the pebble stone beneath us: hearts, stars, devil heads. I pick up an empty beer bottle and whistle into it.

Lu screams, "Fuck off! That sound is so annoying!"

"Yo, Lu, check it. This is your brain!"

"Oh my fucking God."

"This is what happens to your brain when you snort heroin!" I smash the bottle on the pavement. "And your friends! And your family! Any questions?"

Lu claps his hands. "I have tears."

"I haven't laughed this hard in so long."

"Who is in that commercial again?"

"The firecrotch skank from *She's All That*."

"All that commercial made me want to do is run to the nearest crack house and shoot the fuck up!"

"'It takes one day! One day to get addicted for the rest of your life!'"

"One day! One day! *One* day!"

"D.A.R.E. school assemblies just make me want to do drugs even more." Lu puts his bag on the bench and takes out a bottle of Cinnamon Sticks Glade, a Ziploc bag with glitter heart stickers, a BIC, a flask with a D.A.R.E. sticker, and his Polaroid. "Can you snap a pic of me licking the Glade bottle? That would look so chopped. It's so my aesthetic right now."

I grab the Polaroid. Lu licks the bottle. "Make your eyes look more fucked."

"Yeah." He sticks his middle finger up and I hit the shutter. The flash bursts and the picture spits out. Lu grabs it and puts it into his bag. He takes off the lid of my Big Gulp and pours the flask into it.

I hold the cup steady. "Is that moonshine?"

"No, it's Smirnoff."

"Oh, dope."

Lu takes off the lid of his Big Gulp, crushes it, pours the vodka in, and chugs it.

"You look so dope when you drink your Big Gulp. I wish you could see what I see." I take off my lid, throw it to the ground, and start chugging. I put my Big Gulp under his lips, and he bites on the cup as I pour it down his throat.

Lu slaps his forehead. "Owie! Brainfreeze!"

"Put your tongue on the roof of your mouth. It helps."

"Where did you hear that one?"

"It's a suburban myth."

Lu laughs. "Take a look around, bitch. You're living in a suburban myth."

I swish the Slurpee in my mouth, then spit it onto the pavement. "Look how chopped that looks." Pink Slurpee glows in the streetlight.

Lu nods. "You know, this looks like demon blood."

"That's my vibe."

I lie on the basketball court, look up to the full moon, pull my shirt, and rub my fingers on my stomach. Lu stands over me and rubs his shoes up and down my legs. Our eyes lock. I flip myself over and lie on my stomach, looking over at the empty water park. Lu sprays the Cinnamon Sticks Glade into the Ziploc bag. He pushes his hand through the air.

"You just go zzzzzzzip… Zzzzzip when you do this shit. You go… gone." Lu puts his head into the Ziploc and starts inhaling. "Did you…" He huffs. "Know…this…can enter your bloodstream?" He huffs. "Immediately? And reach the…" He huffs. "Brain… sometimes, causing…irreversible… physical…" He huffs one more time. "Damage! Come, get some…"

I grab the Glade bottle. "*Newsweek*, we have your new story right here, baby. It only takes one huff to kill!" I open the Ziploc, hit the lever, and spray it in. "Like this, right? Am I being fucking retarded? Wait. We have finals next week."

Lu's slobbering over his mouth, touching his forehead, his eyes rolling back into his head. "Never mind. Brad, you know that huffing can kill you. Something in all of our houses has the power to kill us!"

I grab the Ziploc, put my face inside, and inhale. "Ah, fuck. Fuck yeah."

I put my hands over my eyes and lick my palm. The images around me are replicating, glitching: *A version of myself in anime. A hotel room in Japan. Looking through a View-Master at a schoolgirl in a black plaid skirt. She lifts it, moans, and puts an octopus on her pussy. I flip the View-Master and see myself in front of a well. I look at my reflection in the water and letters appear in blue glitter: "jump in." I jump. I look up at the sunlight reflecting on the surface and swim upwards. I look toward an island and see a mermaid sitting on a rock. "You've always wanted to ascend, to go further, to experience total perfection, unlimited bliss. You'll never want to retrieve or return to the feeling." The mermaid opens her hands to a sugar cube gummy shell. "Swallow for total psychick warfare."*

Lu slaps me in the face. I open my eyes and look up. I'm on the ground, fingers in the dirt over tree roots. I grab the chain link fence and look through the empty water park. "Huh? How the fuck did I get over here?"

Lu shakes the bottle. "Brad! You can't do the whole bottle, you fucking dick shit."

"I…feel…so lightheaded."

"Huh?"

"Did you see that? Did you see those pink orbs?"

"The orbs disappear quickly to trick you into thinking they're an illusion."

I hug the bottle. "When do I stop? What if I go through the whole bottle?"

"A little abuse could do you some use, baby."

Lu puts out his hand and pulls me up. "Everyone is so dumb. We should be the only people on this planet."

"I don't want anyone to protect me from the world. I want to hurt myself and get something out of it."

"Remember when Shane left us with his house keys and we slept all day in his room? The rain was so loud, and we just kept sleeping?"

"Do you know how fucked up my life would be if you moved away, how fucked up it would be for me to lose meeting up with you on the path every day? Or you parking your car up the street because I don't want my parents to see you picking me up?"

"We should fucking overdose together."

"I'm obsessed with you, dude."

"I'm serious. I want to die in the same hotel room as you."

"I love when you do that."

"What?"

"I don't know. I love when you try to impress yourself."

"You know what my biggest fear is? If you and I ever stop being friends, I'll never have a way to see what's happening in your life, the life without me. I never want to know what it's like to have to go looking for you in other people."

"You are my blood brother for eternity."

I rub his palm. "Shane asked me the other night: 'Do you want to be him? Do you want to look like him? Or do you want to fuck him?'"

Lu laughs. "I know what you answered."

"It's not about answering those questions. It's just about being so fucking happy that I get to experience such an intense bond with someone when I need it the most."

He grabs my shirt, twirls his fingers in it, puts his hands up my body, makes a fist, and knocks on my collarbones. "It's the sound of the gods."

"Fuck yeah! Fuck, that feels so fucking good."

I rub my fingers up and down my neck and lick my lips, running my fingers through my hair. Lu pushes me down onto the pavement. "Rub your fingers on my teeth." Lu lifts my lips and rubs his fingertips on my teeth. "Fuck. Fuck, that feels so fucking good."

Lu puts his legs over my legs. "When else does my body…ever…get to feel…all heavy?"

I look up to the full moon. I'm so high now, I don't know who is saying what. It's as if we have become one sound.

"I forget how life was before this. I don't want to remember who I was before."

"I want to disappear to certain people and only exist to a select few."

"Do you ever get afraid that you have felt all of the feelings that exist? That you are so numb now that there is nothing left to feel?"

"All…the…fucking…time."

"You're doing it again."

"Huh?"

"Angel cloning."

"Can…I…clone angels?"

"Those chain link fences are the gates."

"How can I touch endless light?"

"Our real selves exist nowhere. Give up."

"Maybe angels are the only ones who will ever know the truth about us."

"I'm happy that you didn't bring your video camera to the park tonight."

"Nothing about tonight is happening to be remembered."

"Once footage of you is made, it's like anyone can watch it and make up a million impressions of you in that moment. You are forever frozen, gone in an illusion, no control."

"I want to feel the moonlight in my veins. Inject me."

"The truth is, there…is…no…truth…"

He tickles under my chin. "Zim…zum…zim…zum…."

I tickle back. "You only hallucinate yourself when you're with me."

I rub my fingers on his jawline. I lick his cheeks. He licks my eyelids. I lick his forehead. He puts out his palm; I spit into it. He rubs the spit across his elbows. I hug him, his hair in my mouth. He rubs his thumbs across my lips and pushes them into my mouth. I bite them. He pulls my bottom lip down. He twirls his fingers in my hair. I tickle his armpit. He puts my thumb up to his face, bites on it, sucks on it, and looks into my eyes. I rub the back of his ears and turn my hand over. He leans his head on my shoulder.

"No more reason. No more logic. A restricted zone."

"I'm inside of it with you. No one can get to us. I'm right here. I can't even remember who I was before we became…brothers."

Lu pulls me in and presses his forehead against my forehead. "You are my other head, Hydra boy."

I grab his hands and rub his fingertips. "Your skin feels like velvet."

"Your hands…feel…like…suede…"

"I like this…I like it best when you're nice to me."

"In between highs and lows, where is there for us to go? What is there for us to do? This is the empty space."

"My eyes are so heavy."

"We are on the ground, so high that we can't walk, and no one cares. No one sees us."

♡ L15 ♡

Aurora,

I loved this letter! Everything about it, especially you and Ash drinking in the woods. I love what you said about how falling for me feels like seeing new colors for the first time… I know what you mean. I love your daydreams about us in a lake house together. I think of similar getaways. I mean, most of the time I pace around parking lots, just trying to figure out pilot plots for the comeback season of you and me.

282

Thank you for letting me speak my truth. I think when I'm ready to share my story, I might write a book about the dangers of violence against teenage boys. Maybe I can help victims so they can feel a little less alone.

I'm feeling so much shame right now. Instead of going to my GSA meeting, I hung out with my best friend and ended up huffing. I know, it's awful. I feel like those out-of-control kids in the ads, but I had so much fun. I just don't understand how doing something so contradictory to my own values could feel so exciting.

Tonight at dinner with my parents, I felt this deep shame knowing that they had no idea their son was doing drugs in the park last night. I know this next period of my life is supposed to be about making decisions for myself, but I still felt like a stupid, lost, shrinking little boy. I want to end up somewhere new instead of back in these same spaces with myself. I'm very scared of what college will be like and I don't know how to describe this feeling. It's a terror not knowing what's coming next. How did I become so destructive, so high voltage, in constant overload with my own thoughts all the time? Why can't I just let go and not care like everyone else?

I've been very paranoid. I think that everyone is thinking negative thoughts about me and projecting ideas onto me, but maybe it's just in my own head. Masochism. Is my life meaningless? When I prescribe a meaning to my existence, is that bullshit? I'm sad, Aurora. Every time I share an authentic piece of me I wish I could rip it back immediately to protect myself. I don't know why I'm like this.

I just want to go back to summer camp, where everything was okay.

The future memories we've lost from all of this time apart is life's cruelty at its finest.

Yours truly,
Brad Sela

♡ L16 ♡

Brad!

You don't need to apologize for having emotions or for sharing your feelings. If you want me to be honest, it was a bit hard receiving this letter, to know that someone I care so much about is feeling so dissatisfied with their life. I have this feeling that discovering who you are while pretending to be somebody else is not worth it in the end.

Maybe you aren't getting what you want out of life because you're searching for happiness in the wrong places. You want to go to those higher levels, but it's not at a party, or in dangerous pranks, or in trying new drugs or whatever you and your boys do together. Love is the only thing in this world that's worth it, and you have that with me. Why don't you try to be happy about that? So many people want that one magical moment of shared emotion, and you and I have that.

About the huffing stuff…peer pressure, Brad! It happens to the best of us. A lot of my girls talk about things they regret, but I try to remind them: it's all part of the learning curve! I don't judge you. It's normal to experiment and figure out what you like at this age as long as there aren't any crazy long-term consequences. It's not like you're hanging out with school shooter types or are being a bully!

I know something that might make you forget all that shame. Think of your head between my thighs, your hands slowly pulling down my pink panties, ocean waves crashing as you lick circles inside of me. I'm pushing your hair down. Maybe I'll put a Sweet Tart down there to make it extra sweet for you. Our bodies unlocking secrets in slow-motion, knotted in the dark again. A sleepover on the sand. Eyes pressed on your neck. I'm not done yet. A post-physical place with no logic and reason, totally transcendent, my whole body surrendered to you. I don't mind waiting to be around your sound. I want you to come fuck me in my new silk nightgown.

Tell me what you see when you desire me.

Your girl,
Aurora

P.S. Do you like the special red glitter pen I used for that note? I bet you didn't see that coming.

☆ 87 ☆

The video flash heats my face in the dark as I sit on an electrical box in my new Porn Star shirt tucked into my blue jeans, red Converse All Stars, and silver beaded chain. I hug an octopus carnival stuffy, light a cig, and lean into Lu's camera, twist over the screen, mirror mode: "Record."

Lu hits the red button.

"Why are you taping me?"

"We get taped all the time. You go into 7-Eleven, you get taped. You go to the mall, you get taped. So why can't I record everything in my life? Turn the cameras on the world that is constantly creating footage of me? Whoa, you are so fucked up. You look supermodel high right now."

"Maybe I *am* supermodel high."

"Why don't you lift up your shirt a little bit for the camera?"

I lift up my shirt. "Oh yeah, you want that?"

"Look at that belly button."

I make a fist, roll my eyes back, and pretend to suck a dick in the air.

"Lick it up! Pretend that you're famous. Pretend that you're a model at a photoshoot."

"Talk about my rise to success as the VH1 Fashion Awards Male Model of the Year."

"Don't hurt yourself there, Charley fucking Speed."

"Come on, do it."

"You've been on the cover of all of the big magazines. *The Face*! *Details*! *Detour*! *MTV News* is reporting that you're being considered for the lead in the film version of Bret Easton Ellis's *Glamorama*, joining the ranks of RDJ and Christian Bale."

"I've been looking over the script."

"Did you always want this for yourself?"

"I never planned for it. I was just standing in the Dairy Queen that me and my buddies go to and this agent came up to me and was like, 'No one has a face like yours. You are going to be a big star.' From there, it's just been crazy Hollywood parties, photoshoots, and trashing hotel rooms." I put the stuffy over my head and throw it onto the curb.

"We saw you sitting beside Mark Hoppus at the Teen Choice Awards."

"Yeah, Mark is cool. It's no big deal, you know."

I walk over to a metal gate, get on the ground, slide my body underneath, and rest my head between his shoes. "Are you still taping?"

"Try to look more strung out, like you've been partying all night with a bunch of celebs."

"Like this?"

"Yeah!"

"Try to look hurt, like a little boy who scraped his knees."

"Like this?"

"Try to look like you're in fear, like something super bad is about to happen."

"Wait, why?"

"The aesthetic is chopped, like torture vibes, like looking like you are being held hostage vibes. Look like you're on ketamine."

I get up, put up a peace sign and a middle finger, drool, pull my hair, make a thousand funny faces in under a second, choke myself, then put my tongue through the chain link fence.

"Suck your thumb."

"No."

"Just suck your thumb."

"No."

"Lift your shirt then."

"I'm not that character in *Nowhere*. I'm a real person, you know!"

"You are whoever I say you are when you're on my camera."

"This is weird and fucked up, but do you think it's normal to feel sexy when you look at other guys trying to look sexy? Ignore that. That's retarded."

"I mean…"

"Shut the fuck up."

"Oh yeah, right there. Keep doing that. Misery looks hot on you."

I lift my shirt, flip my middle finger, and cross my eyes. "I'm a fruit loop, dingus."

"Unbuckle those 501s."

"No!"

"Come on, you'll like it. Sell something to the camera."

"Sex."

"Sell sex."

"I feel like I'm in one of those banned Calvin Klein kiddie porn ads. Remember when *Beavis and Butthead* made fun of them a few years ago?"

"Who says that you aren't in one of those ads right now? Do you fucking like it?"

"I fucking love it."

"That's 'cause we're fucking making art. Now pull down the back of your pants a little bit."

"No!"

"Do you feel like the camera is trying to fuck you?"

"I'm the one fucking the camera! I'm the one in control. I could stick my big dick in your cam's warm, tight lens."

Lu moves his camera up and down my body, then flips the screen so I can't see myself.

"Why the fuck did you do that?"

"If you don't do what I say, you can't look at yourself."

"What the fuck was life before mirror mode? The more you get the hang of it, the more looking at yourself all the time becomes more natural."

"If Tommy Lee can pull his dick out on camera, why can't you? Are you too much of a pussy?"

"I'm not pulling my dick out on the sidewalk."

"Unbuckle those 501s. Open your mouth like a good boy. Show the camera how it all went down."

I lick my pinky, spit on it, stick my tongue out, and roll my eyes back. I take a gummy bear out of my pocket and spit on it.

Lu's eyes light up. "You're being dirty. Is this torture? I bet this is hard for you."

I lean back against the metal gate and play with my zipper.

"Before you do it, say something to the camera. Anything."

"If you don't like the reflection, don't look in the mirror. I don't care. I'm too wild to live, too deadly to die."

☆ 88 ☆

Shane is spinning in the desk chair as a 3D pipes screensaver plays in front of him. I'm in Lu's Nothing Records t-shirt. On the table, there's a CD-R case, Sharpied title: "getting over someone i never dated y2k." I take the Jan off my shoulder and drop it on the floor.

"Well, what is it? Why were you doing all of that 'I can't tell you on the phone, you have to get over here right now' bullshit? What the fuck is going on?"

He puts his hand up. "I have these Elliott Smith CDs I have to go pick up. Let's make this fast."

"Who the fuck is that?"

"You wouldn't get it."

"I still can't believe that you hang out with college creeps who listen to the *Magnolia* soundtrack."

"That's what I mean. It's not for you. It's too alternative. Oh, I forgot to show you." He reaches under the table and lifts up a House Intruder metal storage box. "I got this to put my magazines in."

My jaw drops. "Did I not tell you last fucking weekend at Mr. Rags that I wanted one of these? Did you get me one?"

"No, they sold out."

"That's so low of you, Shane."

"You're going to want to grab some popcorn. You need to see this."

The house line rings in the kitchen. "Don't pick that up. Let it ring. We'll get knocked."

"I wasn't going to, asshole." Shane clicks on Internet Explorer, takes a receipt out of his pocket, flips it over, and types "www.angelfire.com/band/reverendlusif666/plan.html" into the address bar. I lean over his shoulder and he looks back at me. "You ready for this?"

I hit the computer. Half of the homepage is loading so slow. "If the webpage ever…hurries—" I hit it again. "…the fuck up!" A burning flame text GIF, "Lu$if," between two Baphomet heads, red text on a black background:

"Let's start. People are fucking retarded. It's simple. As the philosopher Eric Harris once said, 'I am the law… Feel no remorse, no shame.' That in and of itself is a magickal thing for this iconic modern black magician to say who has affected the mainstream successfully and obtained eternal fame that I will, too, receive after the public ritual I will be performing for the whole world on prom night. I've performed rituals on every full moon. I've prepared my consciousness with the same Tetragrammaton book that Manson mentions in *The Long Hard Road Out of Hell*. Six New Moons. Six Full Moons. My magick will work.

Fox News, CNN, and MTV are going to be obsessed with me. God, it's going to be hilarious when Carson Daly and Oprah say my name and show the candlelight vigils around my neighborhood. This is going to be a real-time media circus, all about me. I'll be the star. They will spread my face all over the country and people will wonder 'Why did he do it?' It's simple. I want to be the Antichrist Superstar that Marilyn Manson told you about. I want to be famous. I want to be adored. I want to be an icon. I want newsgroups about me on the internet, books written about me, Lifetime movies, a Hollywood blockbuster. I want the covers of *US Weekly* and *People Magazine*. And with my demon-hoes, the entities I've been working with, it was so fucking easy because of y'all. The level of magickal coincidences that led to me getting my hands on the TEC-DC9 semi-automatic? Just fucking touching it makes me nut. And the junior girls I sold to these older beefcake gym rats I met outside of 7-Eleven, who thought they were going on dates with older guys who liked them? Sorry, I was pimping you the entire time.

I should shoot that compulsive liar Brad Sela in the face. He annoys the fuck out of me. I said that I wanted to be on some crazy Heidi Fleiss shit, and the universe delivered. Oh, and I love the aesthetic of buying 100 rounds from Kmart, just like Eric and Dylan did. I feel so close to them. The media has already bent to my will. I can feel it. Visualization works! Follow your fucking dreams.

I'm not shallow enough to want revenge against jocks or cheerleaders, I'm just into the vibe of shooting up this Hollywood-themed prom. It's cinematic, surreal, beautiful. I can't wait to hear what horrible song the tasteless DJ is playing when I come storming in. Aqua? Britney? Vengaboys? Anyone who gets in my way will be shot in the fucking face.

I love getting into my school shooter look and posing with my guns. It's so sexy, and it'll be even sexier when it's all over the news.

I can't wait until the media discovers this website and the hit count of this page gets to the millions. Everyone in the world will be thinking about me. You all thought I couldn't become a superstar from a neighborhood like this. Think again, bitches!

To my future fans, I love you so much, and I can't thank you enough for all of your support. Knowing how much you'll love me inspires me every day.

I AM THE MALEFIC NODE—LUSIF—SUPREME! MAGNIFICENT! GLORIOUS! TRANSCENDENT! DIVINE!!

'There are no consequences for falling in love with how you portray yourself to the world.'—Lusif (Please include this quote in every article and story!)

THE REVEREND

Lu$if

666-HAIL SATAN!"

I pull my hair. "Someone change the channel. Put in a different disc. Get me to the next level. This is not happening. This is a hidden camera prank, right? Adam and Jimmy are gonna come out and tell us we're on *The Man Show*? Unplug the console."

"Chill."

"Could we go to jail for looking at this? AOL monitors people's chats. Why wouldn't AT&T surveil what web pages we go to? What if they're watching us right now?" I grab Shane's shirt. "I'm fucking paranoid about AT&T, motherfucker."

"You think I understand the law? It took me like five minutes to figure out what twelve plus sixteen was yesterday. I'm like half retarded."

"We're calling 911."

"How many jokes a day does he make about how human beings are just non-player characters that he wishes he could wipe out? It's not like he'd ever do this."

"Are you done using the internet? I'm going to call 911."

"You're not calling 911 over some whacked-out Columbine fanfic. This is some *Tom Green Show* bullshit. It's staged. This is how he operates. He wants to freak us out. He knew exactly what he was doing by leaving this webpage open in my room when I was in the shower."

"Are you the other shooter? Are you going to kill me? Is that the next reveal? Is he in the house right now?"

"I don't know how to make reality appear any more real than what's happening right now."

"So, how do we make reality become real?"

"No, Morpheus. Not right now."

"Do you know the level of guilt I'll have to live with if I could've saved innocent people from being hurt? Knowing I ignored an opportunity to stop a mass murder from happening?"

"No one is going to die! I shouldn't even have told you. You don't think I know my best friend? I've known him longer than you. Don't forget that."

"He told me this morning that he was skipping prom."

"What's your point? He skips all school events."

"What about when he was flipping through gun magazines at 7-Eleven? What if this is all connected? Did we not just read the same manifesto? Lu is addicted to chaos and glamour. He lives in his own world. Do you understand how dangerous it is for someone as removed as him to love serial killers as much as he does? Read it! He's already talking about how the media is going to react. That's real."

"You should go home. I can't listen to this. I'm not in the fucking mood. I had a shit day flipping my room upside down looking for my *Empire Records* tape."

"Oh, of course, Shane! You somehow have to make this about your feelings. I'm so sorry you can't jerk off to Liv Tyler."

"What do you want me to tell you? The uncensored truth? You want to listen to me talk about slamming my body against the wall and cutting my stomach up with broken glass last night while no one was home? Punching myself to the point that I passed out? You want front-row tickets to my downward spiral?"

"This is so gross. Lu was right. Your whole depression thing is just a phony image."

"You know that's not true. I told you what happened."

"People might die in a bloodbath at our school courtesy of our shared BFF and you're talking about your mental health problems. Pop another Prozac and focus. The world does not—"

"No, the world *does* revolve around my feelings. I'm the only one who has to live with this pain. I'm sick of everyone older never shutting the fuck up about how 'we're going to fix our teen sons.' It's like, you can't fix us."

"Why do you have to make it so personal? Every guy our age has to deal with the media portraying us like we deserve to be in mental institutions. Why do you give a shit?"

"I'm tired of everyone thinking that my existence is a joke. I get it: I'm a joke, my pain is a joke, everything is a joke because I'm a teenage boy. So, it's like what? When I turn twenty-one my pain is suddenly not going to be 'angst?' I just don't know how to make my pain real to the world. This isn't a phase."

"Teen angst is not real. That term is just a way for out-of-touch retards to reduce the magnitude of what we go through and discredit us. It's impossible for anyone older to get this."

"This is my point. It's why we shouldn't go to the cops. No one gives a shit. No one is looking out for us. No one fucking cares. I don't care that I don't exist to the world. I'm fine with that."

"How the fuck are you so sure you can't change other people?"

"'Cause I can't even change myself."

♡ L17 ♡

Screw all my whiny, existential bullshit. Fuck. This letter is all I can think about and it's exactly what I needed to hear from you. I've been so horny since I got it. I may have even licked the glitter ink a few times. I can't wait for you to feel my arms wrapped around your stomach as I thrust into you so hard. I need your warm pussy on my lips. Call it stupid teenage lust, but thinking of the possibility of waking up to your legs wrapped around mine every morning this summer just makes me want to die. I'll kiss you slowly, suck on your tits. Fuck. I need you to feel me grow down your throat. I pocketed a Dr Pepper smacker at CVS this afternoon and have been smelling it, just thinking of your taste. I want to be locked inside of your body for eternity. I can't even think. There is so much that I want you to feel, every emotion that is moving through my body. I want to transfer it into you, make what I am feeling become yours. The chemicals rushing through my veins when we touch.

I need to read your fantasies about me, all the dirty unspeakable things. Being inside of you is the warmest place I've ever been.

Yours truly,
Brad Sela

P.S. As a girl who likes me a lot, I'm sure you want to turn me on. Send me a sexy Polaroid. It's not like the mailman is going to know what's inside the envelope. You shouldn't be afraid to. Come on, do it. Please?

♡ L18 ♡

Dear Brad Sela,

I'm ashamed of myself for writing the letters I have sent to you. My father is videotaping me as I write this as punishment for talking to boys behind his back. He trusted me to go to West Canyon and be a virtuous girl. I made a promise to stay away from boys but failed to keep my word. My father knows everything and is extremely disappointed. I need to tell you that he is disgusted by the language in your letters and is horrified by the way your brain works. You are a negative influence in my life.

Please do not write to me anymore. Any contact with you is forbidden. Just forget about me.

—Aurora

☆ 89 ☆

The front lights of the school shine on me. Sitting on the bars of a bike rack, I spit Twizzler pieces onto the pavement. Lu's car blares "My Fault" by Eminem as he pulls up. He bobs his head as he raps along, drinking a beer behind the wheel.

I jump off as Lu gets out of his car in a black "BANNED FROM THE OSCARS" shirt and black jeans. Shane gets out wearing a brown leather jacket.

I rush them, screaming. "What the fuck is your problem? We saw your Angelfire page and Shane printed it. I'm ready to report you to the authorities!"

Lu scoffs. "Is this why you were so weird with me at school today? I was just sitting on the grass with some friends and you guys came at me like fucking piranhas. Pipe down."

"What do you expect? Don't tell me what to feel when I just fucking found out my sicko, so-called BFF is planning a bloodbath for prom!"

"You're being insane. This isn't the ending of a cult teen movie, okay? Relax."

"It's not wrong for me to feel angry right now. You aren't going to do it. Stop trying to control my reaction."

"Shane didn't find my Angelfire. I left it open so that you two would find it and freak the fuck out."

"So this is just one of your morbid pranks? Well, that's a wrap then. Let's all get stoned and go to the IMAX theater."

"Oh, no, I'm def shooting up prom. Like, duh, of course. That's my whole aesthetic."

I start, "You see me and Shane? We're the good guys. We aren't afraid to go to the fucking cops tonight and shut down all your plans!"

Shane continues, "If you're serious, Lu, I want your ass locked in jail. I hope they put you on death row!"

I smile. "We're innocent by default. So if you're going to mess with Shane, then you're going to have to mess with me, too. You can make fun of us all you want, but we're like a vigilante duo now!"

Lu laughs. "An alliance of two inbred retards appearing against the villain to open up the third act. How groundbreaking."

My grin grows. "We're going to ruin you! You're threatening the safety of my community and my friend for what? Your sick narcissistic delusions?"

Lu darts at Shane. "Shane, do you really think this kid you've known for barely a year is really a loyal friend to you? If that's true, then why did he tell me your little secret about what happened at the water park?"

Shane gets red in the face and pushes me. "Brad, how could you do that? How could you betray me like this? I told you that he's the one person in the entire world who would use that against me."

Lu mocks him. "Totally, like, yeah, like, I'm Shane. I'm just so ashamed for squeezing a nine-year-old boy's balls in the waterpark bathroom while his mom was waiting outside!"

I swallow hard and grab his shoulders. "Shane, I'm so sorry. I blurted it out. I didn't know what to do with that secret. I wasn't judging you because I know what happened to you."

Lu rolls his eyes. "Blah, blah blah. Why don't you just get a room with this kid fucker?"

Shane stomps. "You don't get to do this. You both don't understand. I was just trying to figure out what it felt like. I just stepped into that place again. It was like I was in a trance. Honest to God. I didn't mean to hurt anyone. It kind of just happened."

"Listen to me. Our friendship and the private things you've shared with me mean a lot to me. I wouldn't ever try to hurt you. I was never judgmental when you told me that secret. How are you not recognizing that?"

Shane steps forward. "You're a liar. At least I am who I say I am! You'll always be the deceptive, lonely loser who can't stand to be honest with *anyone*. I've never met someone who is so committed to superficial impressions of themselves."

I rage. "What about you? You think your self-hate gives you access to special perspectives that others can't see, but it's not true. You're just miserable!"

"Enough! I'm not going to give you the perfect opportunity for you to play into your wholesome boy-next-door bullshit. You don't deserve anymore airtime. I'm done listening to you praise yourself and brag about everything you've been getting away with. This is *my* time to hurt."

Lu gets in Shane's face. "You're so sick."

I approach Lu. "News flash: once you post your school shooter manifesto to the internet, you lose the right to call anyone sick."

Shane's eyes tear. "You guys will never know how much it hurts knowing that I'm missing out on a version of myself that I can't ever become. What do I have to do to make my pain real to the world? Cut up my arm?"

"Here it comes." Lu sighs.

I continue, "Shane, do you want to know why you're never going to be happy? It's because happy people don't get the amount of fake sympathy and attention that sad people get."

"I'm sick of my pain being ignored by you guys. I don't care about what you two think of me anymore. One day I'm going to have friends who don't judge me, who know that I'm not perfect, and who love me despite how hard it is to love someone with a psychiatric disorder—friends who have interests other than themselves. That's why I hate you both! You two are so preoccupied with who you want to be that you don't even see who you really are."

I shake my head. "Get the fuck out of here. You don't know how exhausting it is being friends with someone who shares every thought and feeling that they're going through as if it's my job to take care of you. Your friends aren't your therapists."

Lu pushes Shane. "No one likes you, Shane! Are you excited for your new life of being even more of a loser? You're nothing without me. You'll get to see that when you have nothing."

Shane trembles. "I think I'm having a panic attack. I can't fucking breathe."

Lu knocks his shoulder. "Get out of here, Fiona Amos, before I call your mom and tell her that her son is a tranny fucker. Imagine giving birth to a tranny fucker and a kid fucker? A full-on sexual deviant. Shameful."

"If you ever think…that I'll forgive you two after tonight…I'm not forgiving you, I'm forgetting you." Shane runs off, bawling.

Lu pushes me in front of his car. "What the fuck is your problem, huh? You have no loyalty to me? How could you threaten me and try to ruin my dreams of world domination? How could you be so stupid to think that you'd ever get away with telling the cops about my big opening weekend?"

"I'm going to—"

"Oh, you want me to say it? Let's do it. There's no one around. I've got no recording equipment. Let's talk about the videotapes and what you did on camera, where you went, who was there. Let's talk about what you don't want out."

I grab an empty Sprite bottle off the ground and throw it at him. "Let me tell you something! Do not fucking mention the videotapes!"

Lu's lips pucker. "You mad? Awww."

I punch his car. "Fuck you!"

"If you cross me, I'll give you the public crucifixion of your nightmares. Remember: I'm the real version of who you try to be behind the scenes. Do not doubt what I can do. This is the most reputation-destroying, image-compromising footage of your lifetime!"

"How can you be my best friend and not even be able to see me for the good-hearted person that I am? I don't deserve this. I never did anything wrong."

"The yummiest part of this whole thing is in these clips. You're not method acting or modeling. This isn't a shoot. You could never make a statement to explain what you did. You can only lose. This is who you are and what you've done. You've spent your whole life being adored by all of the people around you. I can change that in a flash. Wouldn't that be quite the scandal? Our charming main character's illusion of himself getting destroyed in a second."

I put my hand through the half-open car window and look for a beer bottle to smash. "You're not going to get away with blackmailing me."

"I've already won. You can't wish the evidence away. No amount of self-denial has the power to change it."

"I trusted you when we made those."

Lu gets close and puts his mouth on my ear. "You never had my loyalty. I tricked you. Report me to the cops and I'll have one of my goons drop off copies that I've already made. They're ready to go. Can you see it? Your mom and dad, sitting on the couch, seeing their little boy revealed. There will be nothing left to discover about you, no more wondering what you've been up to. You'll be fully exposed."

"No one has seen them, right?"

"I haven't shown anyone."

"Thank you."

"I know where you went last week and I know what you did."

"Who told you that?"

"If only you could see yourself on video right now."

"How do you know?"

"You don't remember that guy with the Olympus camera around his neck in McDonald's last Tuesday? The one who said hi to me? He was showing me pics of you."

"I'll drag you across the pavement if you don't shut the fuck up right now."

"Didn't you tell me that you've always wanted your teen years to feel like a too-dangerous-to-be-aired MTV series? Well, here you go. Welcome to the season finale!"

"This is my life and the lives of others that you're messing with. This isn't happening on a screen, so stop with that. It's creeping me out."

"You've sacrificed and pushed down so much of who you are. Do you even know which parts of you are real and which you've made up? Footage is facts! Wouldn't it be so much easier if our most out-of-control moments were staged? Yet the reason so many people get filled up with shame and fear about their secrets getting out is because they're trying to protect something that is more real than any rumor or speculation about themselves. Me? I have nothing to hide or protect."

"How evil! You're so cruel to edit me, to take secret moments from my life, present one fragment of who I am out of context, come up with a spin, and say that it defines me. What happens in my private life is meant to stay private. The feeling of the people that I care about the most's perception of me being ruined because of one compilation tape? I've never felt this amount of terror."

"You deserve a bucket of golden popcorn for your Best Breakthrough Male Performance this year."

"You have such sick excitement in your eyes right now. This isn't a storyline. This isn't MTV. This is my life."

"This isn't reality, bitch, this is a studio backlot. We're always on MTV. Welcome to the twenty-first century."

"Last time I checked, I don't have a mic on. No cameras are rolling."

"Look around: Camera A, Camera B, Camera C. A shooting crew doesn't always have to be visible. Surveillance never stops."

"I honestly thought that I could get away with trying to figure out who I am in private. I thought this time in my life was to make mistakes. I believed I could pull this off, that this was just for fun and none of this would follow me."

"Okay, but you said this isn't MTV and that this is real life. In real life, you can't cut the footage you don't like. You can't splice and edit the parts of yourself that you can't control like you can with a VCR."

"The truth is bendable. I can spin facts. I can say that I was being kidnapped and drugged. This will work. Everyone will believe me. Every Christmas, I've always gotten what I wanted. Anytime I want money from my dad, he gives it to me. I can have anything in the world. I always get what I want, and if you think you'll break that streak, you're wrong."

"What are you going to do? Go into your confessional booth and tell everyone your delusional twist of how you think things happened?"

"How could I have been so stupid to risk everything for intensity that added up to nothing?"

"Right? All it's left you with is consequences, the number one thing you try to avoid. Funny how that works, isn't it?"

"So what? I like being seen how I want to be seen. I don't think managing the way people in my life perceive me makes me evil. I mean, it's every guy's job to be the charming, good son."

"You kept coming back to our little video shoots for the shame. Shame is where the euphoria is!"

"You gave me a place to relax. Who doesn't want that?"

"Why are you making it so hard on yourself? Why don't you accept that what you were feeding came from a pure place inside?"

"You'll never know what it's like to be a good person. I'm so sorry that you don't know how to function in this world without bloodlust."

"Look, I have to go. I have some pipe bombs I need to finish for opening weekend."

"Where'd you even learn how to make those?"

"The internet."

"You hear that, kids? Cyberspace is your new how-to guide for an instant massacre. Courtesy of your monthly dial-up fee."

"So chopped."

"What do you want from me?"

"I want you to admit that you're the boy in the videotapes. Admit that this is who you are."

"Never."

"What's it going to take to look at yourself without lies?"

"It was a 'shadow version' of me at those parties."

"You don't understand. There is no 'demon' you, no 'dark angel' you, no 'other' you. You can't just conceal the real parts of yourself and tuck them away into compartments."

"Ouch."

"How would I sell it to your parents? Your good little boy has now grown into a young man in this new video set of disturbing unspeakable situations, a compilation full of uncensored, unaired, uncut moments— the year of his life that you didn't get to see. Nine ninety-nine. Order today and I'll throw in a bonus mini journal!"

"Okay! Okay! What is the deal?"

"This is the final offer. You don't tell anyone about my Angelfire page and I won't put you on blast and ruin your image. I'll burn the tapes. Sure, innocent people will die because of you, and you'll have to live with the guilt, but you know how to hide that away. I'm sure *ABC News* will interview you. You'll be a part of my media circus for sure, but more on that later!"

"I've never felt so hopeless. Why can't you just be normal and cancel your plans? This is so fucked, you emotional terrorist."

"Delicious, you've admitted it. You don't want to show up and be good when life presents you with the opportunity. You just want to look innocent in the eyes of the public. You want it both ways. A noble person would sacrifice their image to save the lives of others. This is why I'll never need a private life. Unlike you, I take ownership of what I am. You get the same person behind the scenes *and* on camera."

"That's what gets you off. It's not about the possibility of everyone else finding out who I am, it's that *I* get to find out over and over again. It's torture to feel this overexposed."

"Remember, Brad. Being a good boy is an image, and images do not exist."

☆ 90 ☆

I grab my phone, ready to call 911. I put it down. I pace around in a panic. I look at my TV and imagine people I know crowding around screens to watch the tapes of me, a montage of security cameras directed at my face in CCTV: footage of me walking into Blockbuster, 7-Eleven, McDonald's, Kmart. I think of freeze frames being shared in photo galleries in cyberspace. I get ready to dial 911. *If I tell my mom and dad, then the videotapes are going to get out. If I tell the cops, then people are going to know what I did. I'm fucked. There's no way I can win. It's not worth it. I don't fucking care about saving anyone's life. This is my life.* I pace around, bite my nails, and think of turning on KROK. I go back to my phone, grab it, and get ready to dial. Another nightmare: the most private moments of this year being played on a huge screen outside of the Virgin megastore. I put my phone down.

☆ 91 ☆

A dream from last night returns. I'm standing at the entrance of a dive bar in NYC watching a guy in a white tank top take a goldfish out of a bowl. He throws it into a tank of turtles. They rip the fish apart as the tank fills with blood. The hot pink and baby blue neon lights glow up my face in the dark.

I'm walking across the overpass by North Academy when I pause to hold onto the chain link fence, looking down at the speeding cars beneath me. I catch my breath and walk through the trees to the path by the river. In the distance, Lu is crouched over, staring into the water. I bend down next to him and spin my finger in the slowly moving water. The whirlpool distorts his reflection. After a few long seconds of silence, Lu mocks *The Real World* opening.

"This is what happens when two best friends have to get real over the dilemma they got themselves into involving a high school massacre and scandalous videotapes."

We get up and walk.

"The storylines I let the producers assign to me… Big mistake, looking back now."

"Come on. Anyone who didn't tap out by now obviously would've seen the writers were setting me up to be a Columbine copycat."

"Remember the look on that Viacom suit when he got the tape of that rat mutilation scene?"

"Shane's coming-out scene shocked me. I mean, with how much the guy loves whiny male rock stars, I could see a homosexual, but a teenage child molester? Now *that's* too edgy for reality TV."

"I wish I had never gone in for that casting call. I'll never work with that director again."

"You should have turned it down when you got the callback. Maybe the day you and I met was audition day."

I point up. "There should be a little bubble on the corner of the screen that shows you watching a montage of all of our fights from the past year."

"I know."

"Something I wish I could change is the way the producers edited me to look like someone I'm not. I wish I could've been portrayed differently."

"Due to low ratings, it looks like the show about your life isn't getting picked up for another season. You aren't interesting enough to carry a narrative set in the suburbs."

"We won't get to see the reunion special."

Lu laughs. "Hey, what's the name of our show again?"

"*new millennium boyz*, but instead of an s, there'd be a z, all lowercase. Hip."

"That was fun. I'm going to miss doing sarcastic shit like that with you. Period."

"If a camera crew was following us around, MTV couldn't even do anything with all of the footage from this year. It'd be impossible to present a structured narrative of our lives."

"It's all about how you edit it. That's where the magic happens."

"I'm past being angry. I'm only numb, which is just where you want me to be. I hate myself for how hard making this decision was." I pull off my wallet and whip him with the chain in a playful way.

"We ran out of tropes. There was nothing left to show. We covered all of the taboo topics, though an ending where you and I express our repressed homosexual love for each other would've been a real scream." He pinches my nose. "The romance of the century is coming to an end."

"I'm talking about the deal."

"This isn't about bullying a little girl with Down's syndrome, it's not about a satanic animal mutilation ritual in the woods, it's not even about the slutty shirtless dancing that you do to Nine Inch Nails when you get super high. There's no videos of that stuff, so we don't even know if any of it really happened. This is about what you did on camera."

"I hate that you have videos of me that I don't own. It's warped. I know that stopping you won't reduce the evil in the world because I bet some idiot right now in Kansas is gearing up for his own April 20th, 1999 remake."

"I'm becoming a prophet, an icon, and I don't even have to move to Hollywood. My massacre masterpiece will be distributed and released worldwide in real-time through the media. I don't pay a dime, don't need a publicist. It's free twenty-four-hour coverage. Be honored. You are hanging out with the hot new face of teenage evil in the post-Columbine era. These are the final days before my stratospheric rise to immortal fame. Posterboy. Supreme. Glorious. Magnificent. Divine. Adored. Seventeen forever. Lusif. Never Forgotten! School Shooter of the Year 2000."

"When the Littleton tragedy happened, I thought that could never happen here. That could never happen to us. It wasn't even a question of whether or not I felt safe at school."

"This isn't about revenge, baby, this is about the making of a star."

"The worst part is that this isn't even shocking. It's not like you had any moments of character development where you could've had a turning point and changed."

"Deception is so nineties. Transparency is so much cooler."

"That doesn't upset you, satisfying everyone who has ever called you a Trenchcoat Mafia–type? Isn't it a better ending to rebel against your impulses and transform?"

"Here's the deal: after the massacre is over, people are going to ask you about it. You have to create an idea of what our friendship was like for the American public. Be very strategic with what you say to the media. You want to be as extreme as possible so I get more waves."

"A school shooting, all to be breaking news that interrupts a Juicy Fruit commercial? That's how much fame means to you?"

"People are too pussy to continue the legacy of Reb and Vodka. There was an apocalyptic coding left behind, a torch passed for every senior class after 1999 to hold, and I cracked it. Harris and Klebold are demons now, rooting for me."

"Do you think someone is going to play me in the Lifetime movie about the shooting? Do you think that my name will be in the credits? Nevermind. Forget that I said that."

"When they do the *Dateline* special, maybe they'll interview you too. You'll be the school shooter's best friend. Oh my God, Brad! You're going to get on TV too. You'll get a profile in *Rolling Stone*, I'm sure of it."

"Great."

"Fame for killing is much better than having to live with the unending terror of being invisible."

"That's bullshit."

"I'm going to write some messages in blood on the walls in my bedroom for when the police come to investigate after opening weekend. I've planned the celebrities and movies I mentioned in a scripted journal so I can attach to their fame and get them involved. That'll land me more headlines. A media orgy is coming. That's what this is. The live broadcast is going to go on for hours. I don't even have to move to Hollywood to become a star. I can create this entire spectacle from my hometown! Everyone is doing the camera work for me. It's too easy."

"I did an English paper on this. People are too stupid to understand that both presentations of violence, in the news or the movies, are all the same entertainment. Who do we blame?"

"Trent Reznor said in *Rolling Stone* that he always thinks about murder, so what's the big deal? What am I doing wrong?"

"He's Trent fucking Reznor! He can say those things. It's for shock. It's his job!"

"Take a page out of the man's playbook. You have to create as many lies as possible to tell the media—scandalous, delicious content that will keep people hooked to the story."

"You understand that our neighborhood will never recover, right? People I see every day in the halls are going to be dead because of you. You better not touch Eric or Kev, or their dates."

"No promises. When you play *Doom*, you don't premeditate who you're going to kill, right? You just go with the flow."

"So, that's what you're gonna be thinking about as you kill people? Playing *Doom*?"

"The media's conversation around the murderous disenfranchised youth of America's revengeful motives is so overdone and boring. You want to know the true motive of this year's hot new school shooter? What was going on in his sick twisted mind? Nothing. Fame is my motive. It's that vapid. I'm that hollow. Get into it!"

"Our prom night isn't a WB set."

"It's the perfect set. Limos, a red carpet, cameras flashing constantly. Critics will rave it's like the end of *Jawbreaker*, only with a bloodbath twist."

"Well, I'm going to laugh my ass off when someone at *ABC News* puts a mic in my face and tries to create a storyline that you were some bullied victim of jock culture."

"Tell all of the news networks how badly I wanted to be famous, and if you get to meet Manson, tell him I love him. I really wonder what Manson is going to think. Oh my God, this is so exciting. Marilyn Manson is going to know who I am by the end of this month! My idol is going to be looking right into this face."

"This might be the last time I see you, and that makes me wish that I could die with you because I don't know if I can live with the guilt for the rest of my life."

"Join me. You don't know how much we're going to be loved and immortalized. Be part of something historic. We don't know what this world is going to become. Our generation could be the ones to witness the end of everything. If we kill ourselves after opening weekend, we get to escape all of the anxieties of getting older and die superstars. We never have to grow up. We never have to face consequences, be rejected, get our hearts broken, watch our friends die. No more room left in our lives to face any more pain than we already have. All the interruptions, all of the chaos, will come to a close. All it takes is you and me joining forces."

"Why can't we just have an ending where we run away to California as we cut to a Moby song?"

"It's still hilarious to me. You've been so strategic for so long and all of that chilling calculation still couldn't save you from these events unfolding. This is the problem with believing in the lie of your public image: you always end up representing the exact thing that you're against in private."

"People are going to need to stock up on tissue boxes for the memorial service they don't know is coming up. It's so sad."

"Why don't you be a supportive friend for the first time in your life and help me decide what outfit to wear? What would look good with my TEC-9?"

"You're right. High school massacres are so glamorous! Why don't I just pull up the 'Spring/Summer 2000' mass murder outfit suggestions on Details.com?"

"I'm thinking my black fur coat with some chains and black platform sneakers, but the media ate up Dylan Klebold's 'Wrath' shirt, so I might need something like that. I want reporters trying to decode my outfit. We gotta feed the conspiracy theorists on the internet! The front page of AOL.com. CNN! FOX! MTV! Weeks of coverage. My face plastered on every magazine in the country. A new outbreak of hybristophilia! Ugh! *Time* better use a good photo of me."

"You're murdering people's kids."

"No, I'm killing teenagers who probably want to die anyway."

I pull out a list from my back pocket. "Look, I want to read you this list of all the things I'm going to miss about you."

"This manipulative attempt to get me to change my plans is pathetic, but sure, I'll listen."

"This is your last week on the planet. Can you at least try to be a little nicer?"

"Whatever."

"I'm going to miss walking around and doing nothing, pouring Aftershock in our Slurpees at the park. I'll miss when you pick me up, your car parked up my street so my parents can't see you. I'll miss bullying losers at the mall with you. If I could, I'd rewatch all of our good times to the point the tape starts to skip. I miss—"

"Stop. I don't want to hear this."

I stomp the ground. "I hate that I'm not powerful enough to change you. Don't you care? That makes me feel like a piece of shit. More than anything, I wish I had the power to fix you. This isn't fair."

"Irreversible eternal damage. This is the shit I live for."

"Stop."

"I'll keep going. Do you want to know something else that's pathetic about you? The only reason you became an actor is because you hated being yourself."

"Please, enough. That's not fair. There's gotta be a limit, even for psychopaths."

"You're a victim of your own hoax. Your life was so meaningless that not even your own manufactured storylines could save you from the emptiness that consumes you." I shiver as Lu grins. "Why do villains these days have to have redeeming qualities? Why do I have to have that watershed moment where I become relatable and human, all so people can look at themselves for a second? Why can't I just do what I do best? Be pure evil."

"What about what I'm going through? Did you ever think for a second that I'm unhappy with my life? The pressure? You don't know how devastated I am that denial and shame aren't powerful enough to change the truth. The impossible expectations. I think the pressure of having to be a fantasy for everyone in your life is so debilitating. That's what kills you. That's what created this."

"You'll never be who you were before you met me, and I'll never apologize for the damage I've done."

"I can't ever go back."

"One thing I hope you learned from me is that reality is a horror show. It's worse than anything you could imagine. It's too gruesome to be portrayed in art. You have to be there for it. Alive. It's all around us. It's beautiful. It's going down, right now."

"This wasn't supposed to happen. In this friendship, I was supposed to feel different than this. I thought by now I'd discover who I am, and everything about who I used to be is gone. It's like I'm torn between two worlds and now I don't belong to either one of them. Where does that leave me? I can't go back. It hurts."

"Big mistake. The novelty of new surroundings doesn't ever bring something unexpected and life-changing. Those false expectations are just another part of the war within yourself."

"Why do you think those videotapes even exist? Happy people don't go to those places. I like certain scenarios to take place, then have them disappear forever. I told you, I'm not a fan of evidence. I like to be there. I like it to end."

"I'm not fighting with you about this. It's a done deal. Accept this: in today's world, once someone owns footage of you, it's over. You belong to the public. Anyone can do anything with it. There is no such thing as privacy and trust anymore. It's just something that people make up to feel a false sense of safety. It's nonexistent."

"All I wanted was a day without life feeling like the end of the world. I've been searching for that one magical person on this scumbucket planet, that one special moment when what you want to give is finally given back to you. The bubble wasn't supposed to burst. It's so fucked up. You have no way to break out of your artificial obsessions, to connect to something real, and I'm so sorry that you are…you."

"I don't care who gets hurt as long as I become the vision that I have of myself to the world in the end. I don't want to be human anymore. I want to be a myth."

I kneel down, hug his legs, and sob. "I wanted to grow up with you. I wanted to change with you. I wanted to see who we'd become together. I wanted to watch the next season of our lives, to see how we'd evolve, and you want to put a stop to that?"

Lu chuckles. "And scene."

☆ 92 ☆

In the student lot, I lean on Lu's car. He walks over to me to the sound of the morning announcements on the PA. "One lucky gal and pal could win the North Douglas High's Hollywood prom sweepstakes that includes the ultimate VIP star treatment."

I touch his arm. "I need you to do me a favor."

"Oh God, what is it? I'm not interested in blowing you. I've told you, I don't want to experiment. You need to find someone else."

"A mix CD. I need you to burn me a mix CD. Four songs. You told me you know how to download MP3 files and do all of that shit. I can't even begin to understand Napster or Gnutella."

I take out a receipt with a list written on the back and hand it to him. He flips it over. "I fucking hate you sometimes! Marcy Playground? Kate Bush?"

"Please. Just do it."

He shrugs. "Twenty bucks."

"Whatever."

I hand him a twenty and he puts the receipt in his pocket. "See ya around?"

"See ya around."

I hold him back. "Wait, I want to talk to you. I know that this is going to be one of the last moments we spend together."

"Talk then."

"I got a new DVD player."

Lu hits his sarcastic tone. "I got one too. I like the chapter selection and the menu and stuff. It's super weird and futuristic. It's exciting, a much more fun interactive experience than VHS tapes."

"Time is changing. I don't like it. I still can't believe that you called me a 'compulsive liar.'"

"Well, I'm only going to be able to use my DVD player for a few more days. Can you imagine knowing that this is your last week on earth? Strange."

I open my arms. "Can I have a hug? This is the last time that I'm going to see you."

He's dead-eyed. "No."

♡ L19 ♡

Aurora,

Your dad shouldn't have the power to keep us apart. I'm so sorry that I got you in trouble and that I've activated his rage. It must've felt so humiliating being taped and having to write that letter in front of him. I hope you receive my mix CD and this letter. I don't want to be a shoebox of letters you laugh at when you're twenty-three. I really thought that we would see each other again, that we would go the distance. You've unlocked a deep love that exists within me.

There are some people in this world who are open and vocal about their destructive ways and then there are those who move people around and align them in their grand design in total secrecy. I am one of those people. Yes, I have felt so loveless behaving this way, but I can no longer lie. My friend Lusif is going to shoot up my high school. I found out from a webpage he left open for me and my friend Shane to find. I wanted to go to the police but he's been blackmailing me with videotapes he has of me. He got me into all of this stuff. It's all his fault. I can't even explain to you the amount of manipulation that this person has done to me.

All before the year 2001. I have mutilated a rat in a satanic ritual. I made a snuff film that he sold to creepy men on the internet. I've done cocaine at parties. I've come home high and lied to my parents. I pissed in a Super Soaker and squirted it onto a retarded girl. I huffed whippits. I know you won't want to hear this, but I had sex with a junior girl who paid my friend so he could get more money for his massacre fund. I got hazed in a violent way that I can't even describe to you. It was the worst thing that ever happened to me. It was totally unfair, but also somehow my fault for being involved with these types of people in the first place.

Mostly, all of these things happened off-camera, but then there are the videotapes. The possibility of my family huddled around our living room TV watching these tapes of me in such unspeakable scenarios fills me with shame. I don't even know if living to see the possibility of these images of me being exposed is worth it. I don't want to be seen in fragments, I want to be seen for all of me. I feel like with you, I can be everything that I am. But if you saw this footage, you would see someone that isn't me, moments where I just couldn't control myself. It's so unfair to freeze one moment from someone's life and say, "this is him," but I know that no one will listen to what I have to say. I can't defend myself. I did what I did. I'm so nervous right now. My thoughts aren't together. I watched myself do it. I knew it was wrong and yet I couldn't stop. I wish no photos or videos of me existed. I want them all gone.

You don't think that this is fucking hard for me? Realizing I've changed something about myself little by little every single day? Waking up to learn I have no reflection? I can't even recognize myself. I never wanted to give up my friendship with Lu because of the confidence he gave me, but why would I trust him? Maybe it's because the validation of being accepted by him felt like the warmest, longest hug I never got as a child. It's almost like I was trying to manipulate time, speeding up the pace of my life by doing the most shocking things I could think of. I still don't know what I was looking for. I guess I've spent my nights trying to recreate feelings that shouldn't have existed in the first place and going to places that I should never have gone.

Yes, I'm Brad, the selfish motherfucker who would prefer kids at my school get murdered rather than have my image destroyed. I can't know what it feels like to have people's perceptions of me so compromised. It's like I put all of this work into being seen a certain way my whole life and now all of that effort means fucking nothing. I don't even know if it's going to be worth it, because knowing how much of an emotional terrorist Lu is, I just know he's going to give these tapes to my parents and ruin my life. I know this is another fake deal. He's making me think my silence about the shooting means he won't show anyone the tapes.

I know what he's planning. You don't know how obsessed with fame he is. He saw what happened with the Columbine killers, all of the media coverage and mythology about the basement tapes. He's going to leave everything in this room for the cops to find. He'll bring my image down with him. I can't bear to live to see my media crucifixion. By the time this letter arrives, I'm probably already going to be national news. My face will be everywhere. Maybe there's this sick part of me that wishes my parents paid more attention to my life, that they looked deeper, tried to stop what's been happening with me.

I'm so sad about my life. It's this kind of pain that shapeshifts and looks like something new every morning, and yet when you recognize it, it's never not shocking—lingering endlessly. It's so hopeless. I can't wish away what I've done. Maybe I was born without innocence. Maybe I never had any to lose. Maybe I truly hate myself to the point that I don't even care what happens to me, which is why I took so many stupid risks.

You have brought out a part of me that only you could, and it's what I wish I could be all of the time, free in a place of uncorrupted joy. What you gave me and taught me, I'll keep forever. You know me, Aurora. You know that I'm a good person. You know the kind, sweet, innocent boy I really am. I know you're the girl who knows things about me that other people will never be able to discover. You have shown me an image of myself that is closest to my soul. I love that I didn't have to be the starring role on a movie set when I was with you. I could relax and be myself. You are going to miss seeing the color that can only exist when we're together. Please. The purity. The halcyon. I need it.

I'm in so much pain. I will never understand why you and I couldn't end in a beautiful way after we started with so much magic.

Angels may love me, but it's not enough to save me. Sometimes, I swear, when I look down at my body, where there should be skin, there is only plastic...

Yours truly,
Brad Sela

☆ 93 ☆

I sit in my underwear, crying as Mazzy Star's "Fade into You" plays low. Aurora's letters are scattered on the floor. *You never knew if it happened because you can't see the proof. You keep thinking you're making the memory right now.*

☆ 94 ☆

Dad watches ESPN highlights on the couch as mom whips up blueberry pancakes. I think of going over to grab a Virgin Records flier on the kitchen counter but don't. I approach my mom and take a deep breath. "You know, I'm not really feeling like going to prom. I think I might have the stomach flu or something."

She looks concerned. "But your Armani suit is already being tailored! Don't you want to see the payoff from all of the hard work you've put into the student council? Brad, I wanted to ask you something. Are you guys planning a candlelight vigil?"

"Huh? I don't follow, Mom."

"You know, for Shane Avery, the North Douglas senior who hung himself last night? That poor mother, finding her little boy hanging in his closet. It's all over the radio."

Before I can say anything, Dad comes in. "That Avery kid could've had anything he wanted. What a waste. I'm just happy our son isn't as

314

messed up as that kid. Could you imagine if he had lived to see the day his grandfather croaked and he got some of that inheritance? Ridiculous."

My mom smiles. "Did you know him? I'm sure you saw him at school. He must've felt so lonely." She holds her heart.

My voice cracks. "Yeah, I saw him around. You know what, Mom? I have to call Cody, this guy on the student council. We have to meet up to lock down some last-minute details about prom."

She grabs my arm before I head upstairs. "Maybe the virtuous thing to do would be to prepare a little memorial speech. You can read it at prom. It'll make you look really good."

I bolt to my room, roll up a t-shirt, and scream into it. My throat is burning. I open my bag and grab a Polaroid of Shane and me at 7-Eleven last Friday, hug it tight as tears roll down my cheeks. I find the friendship necklace we pocketed together and squeeze it in my palm. I talk under my breath. "I'm so sorry, Shane. I'm…so…sorry." Through blurry eyes, I grab a bottle of King Cobra from my bag and chug it. I dial Lu and he picks up. I scream, "This is all my fault. I can't believe this. This isn't real. I've never experienced a real loss like this. You hear about it on the shows and think, 'That's never gonna happen to me,' but it just fucking did. I can't escape his ache. I'm falling apart. Somebody hit eject."

Lu sighs. "It's almost a relief. He always talked about doing it and he finally got what he wanted. Next scene."

"A relief?! You—"

"Oh, are you going to call me evil? A sociopath? He decided on this ending long before he met you."

"I should be on trial for his manslaughter. He would still be here right now if I hadn't sent him over the edge. Friends fight all the time. People say stupid shit. You get angry. You fight. Why did you tell him that I told you about his waterpark secret? He asked me to take it to the grave. We wouldn't be in this mess! I'm never going to reconcile with him. I'm never going to be able to apologize."

"The reason you're so upset is because now he can't forgive you so that both you and your little savior complex can feel good about yourself.

Wah wah wah. You're left with all of these, like, boring-ass post-bff-just-shot-himself-in-the-head unresolved feelings and it's so lame."

"You don't know how badly I feel for his mom. I mean, the guilt I have right now, thinking she's got this perfect image of me? Just last week, Shane was telling me how his mom was so happy that we're friends."

"Sorry if I'm mistaken, but is that not your whole gig? The whole 'getting away with it' thing? Shane's mom is going to think you were some good friend, that you were a great influence in his life. She'll never know the truth. Why are you upset? Isn't this what you always wanted? To never face consequences? I'm sure now you'll get to say some fake-ass speech at his funeral all about how you were such a close and loving friend to him, all while none of the people in attendance will know that it was actually your nasty betrayal that led to his flame out! You did him in! Is that what you want me to say?"

"Stop all this cruel bullshit. I'm so sad. What are you going to miss about him? There must be something."

"I'm going to miss when he'd do shit for me, like pick up my film rolls or bring me food or a video when I was too lazy to leave the house. I'm going to miss teasing him and calling him a tranny fucker and Pisces Iscariot. Face it, the kid was a good bottom bitch lapdog."

"How can you not be grieving? I feel this ache in my stomach screaming at me. Where do I put all that's left in me to give to my friend? Where do I put the love I have for him now? Where does it go? Did I give enough while he was here?"

"You're incapable of loving anyone but yourself."

"This is your fault, too! I should have never become friends with you. I wanted to grow up so badly and have all of this freedom and now I just wish that I could be a little kid a little bit longer. I just want Shane back. I just want to go back to before I met you. I feel like I'm being strangled by Hades or something."

"If that was true, then why did I just finish destroying the videotapes?"

"You did?"

"Burned them. Ripped out the tape. Destroyed them. And yes, Miss Paranoia, there were no copies. I mean, wouldn't that be the most boring obvious plot twist if I, the school shooter psychopath, ended up going against his word right before the movie fades to black?"

"It was only your camera that was there that night, right? No one else's?"

"Only my camera."

"That's the best news."

"So, what are you going to say in your *20/20* interview when they ask you about Shane? I can see it already. You're going to do a great job as the martyr who survived, the friend of the murderer whose life was spared. The last one standing with Lusif's secret. The reporters will eat you up."

"Can you just shut up? Can we meet up by the woods near your house? I want you to come cut me some dabs."

"Oh, yeah?"

"Please. I like it better when you do it for me. I need it so bad right now. Just some small slices on my back. It'll help ease the pain. I don't want to feel this."

"No."

"You've been doing it almost once every week over the past month. Why the sudden fucking change? Come on, man."

Lu's voice loudens. "Later…" He pauses, then shouts. "Firewire!" He hangs up. I shout into the phone. "What are you talking about?"

☆ 95 ☆

I catch myself on the security monitor as I walk into 7-Eleven. "Mirror, Mirror" by M2M glides through the store, calming me down and scaring me at the same time. I walk up to the fridge and grab an A&W Cream Soda, Shane's favorite. I shut my eyes as I squeeze the can, quick cuts explode in my mind. Doing shrooms in the mini park by his house two weeks ago. Listening to him complain about failing to get to the Shadow Temple in *Zelda*. Watching him draw dragons with his milky gel pen inside my binders when he zoned out in math class. Laughing till our bellies hurt watching our favorite George Carlin tape. The voicemail he left me about the nightmare he had where he was chased by vampires in the Virgin Megastore. Flipping through the photo album beside his bed that had just pictures of him as a child with his dad. The feeling of delaying my plans just in case he called and wanted to chill. All week I've been locking myself in my bathroom blasting CDs so my parents can't hear my wailing. *Why didn't I call him to apologize? Things could've been so much different if I had kept my mouth shut. He just wanted to be happy. Was this his only way to escape? Maybe I wasn't there enough for him. He lost the battle with himself, and I had a front-row ticket. I didn't do enough. I didn't do anything.* I look at the "Smile Shoplifters! You Are On Camera" sticker, and I'm hit with a kind of demonic déjà vu.

I put the soda back into the fridge as the M2M song fades and feel a panic attack coming on. The security cam feels like it's zooming in on me, tracking me. I'm staring into a live trial for bullying Shane Avery to death. My heart is pounding. My mind races. My nightmares terrorize me. All week I've been on movie sets with morphing faces, studio lights, rolling monitors, voices from directors and producers. I haven't slept since he hanged himself.

I run out and am about to light a cig when I see Eric and Kev in matching Planet Hollywood hoodies, laughing their asses off.

Eric says, "Would you look at that? North Douglas's biggest internet star out at 7-Eleven like the rest of us normal people."

I push him. "What the fuck are you talking about? You guys didn't even call me about Shane. You saw us at school every day! You knew how close we were."

Kev's mouth drops. "Wow, Eric. He doesn't know."

"He has no idea." Eric laughs. "GoodBoyBradExposed.com. Everyone in the neighborhood is talking about it."

I panic. "What's on the website? Tell me right now."

Kev says, "You're a—"

Kev gets closer. "You're right, it's more fun to tease the kid, but you did some sick shit in those clips, you know that? Actually, fuck it! Who were those boys? Was that real blood? Why were you cuffing up that guy? Did you get off on that shit?"

Eric continues, "Oh yeah, and that sexy little modeling video. 'Come on, Brad. Lift up your shirt a little for the camera. Suck your thumb for us, sexyyyyy.' Are you a fucking scumbag drug addict or what? You looked blitzed out of your mind. You're definitely not getting into Berkeley now. You're out of control."

Kev shoulders Eric. "Dude, that one guy looked like he was in a lot of pain. My buddy said it might be some kind of satanic ritual. Did your boyfriend Lusif tape them? People are saying he's the one behind the website. It makes total fucking sense."

Eric cuts in, "People are having viewing parties. My baseball buddies are coming over later to watch it. People can't believe we know you. The site is being passed around all over the net."

Kev laughs. "I'd hit a web browser if I were you."

Eric continues, "The site says if you pay for a membership, you can get bonus content. I even signed the guestbook."

Kev teases, "Yeah, the guy who made the website said he's selling limited-edition copies for twenty bucks. I think I'll snag one."

I'm sweating. "It's fake. There are fake images all over the internet. Come on, guys, that's not real."

"It's definitely you. You can't fake a video like this."

I stutter, "Computer wizards can. I'm sure they can. It's fake, okay?"

Kev sighs. "You know, buddy? The worst part of seeing you on that website is realizing you've been lying to all of the people who cared about you the most. Before you fell in love with that guy, you really had us all convinced that you were just one of the boys. You aren't."

☆ 96 ☆

I call Kristen from a payphone by Pan's Burgers but get her machine.

"Hey girlfriend, I'm not in right now, but you know what to do at the beep!"

"It's Brad. I did some bad things, and I don't know who to talk to. I know I haven't been answering your calls and I'm acting super weird these days, but I really hate my life and the situations I've gotten myself into. It's really bad. You know Lu, the guy I've been hanging out with? He's got some stuff and is blackmailing me. He made a website. I just feel so hopeless. Losing you, my mom and dad, everyone that I love the most and care about would kill me. I don't know if my life is worth living anymore. I wish I came to you sooner. You would have known how to help me. I'm sorry, Kristen."

☆ 97 ☆

The piercing sound of my mom screaming my name at the top of her lungs. I leave my bedroom and go to the kitchen where she's standing, arms folded. She grabs the remote and turns off the TV.

"Do you know what Rosalie said in the voicemail she just left? 'What on earth did you do wrong in your life to create such an unwell child?' Do you know how this makes me feel as a mother? Tell me what's going on right now. Explain yourself!"

I pick up the phone and throw it against the wall. "Oh, so this is all about you now! That's such a shock, isn't it? The most messed up thing that has ever happened to me in my entire life is unfolding right now and this is somehow all about your role as a mother?"

"Brad, I've never seen this rage before. What is going on with you? This is scaring me!"

I scream, "It's so fucked up! Just because you can't see my life, you assume you know what's happening! You think I have no experiences! You think that me being alive and happy is sitting in a basement watching MTV, eating pizza, and drinking Slurpees with my childhood friends after a shift of volunteer work that'll help me get into Berkeley? That's being dead!"

My mom's lips shake. "When I called back, she said that it has something to do with you and the internet. We told you to stay away from

320

the net and I did my best to teach you about its negative potential! An expert on *Oprah* said teenagers are being corrupted by the cyber world each and every second, and now my own son is a victim."

I kick the cabinet. "I'm not even going to try to give you an alibi or sell you some bullshit. I'm too exhausted! Go over there and find out for yourself. I don't care anymore."

"She told me I should come right away. What did you do?"

"See? That look. This is what I've been trying to avoid my whole life."

"What look?"

"The disappointment. I couldn't live up to your standards. I guess I could've been a bit more careful—that's the truth I know you need to go to sleep every night, that it was all my fault and you have no responsibility. Don't you get it? I'm not enough, I'm never going to be, and I'm done trying to keep your love and everyone else's by performing! I'm tired of scheming. I'm tired of lying. I'm tired of pretending. I'm tired of calculating. I'm tired of being an actor, okay? I can't do it anymore."

She leans over to touch me. I swat her off. "You're not making sense."

I tear up. "I feel like even when I'm alone, I can't relax because I'm thinking of how you and Dad will perceive what I'm doing and I'm sick of being so paranoid. I can't live up to the expectations that you and Dad have created of me in your heads. I can't keep trying."

She grabs my arms. "Tell me what you did."

"I want you to go over to Rosalie's house, huddle around the computer with her and her husband, and see for yourself! Leave! Go see the website that someone made about me. Go see the video clips. Go see the scenarios I got myself into. Go watch 'the real me' being exposed. There's going to be nothing past this point." I sob. "I'm loveless, Mom. I'm a broken person. I'm empty and I'm tired of hiding it."

She slams the counter. "I'm going to throw up. I can feel it. I'm about to become one of those PBS moms. Oh my God. Can you imagine the judgment from all of the moms at the grocery store, knowing that my son was involved in some lurid cyber scandal? I can already see the camera crew in our driveway!" She sobs into her hands.

"Stop fucking crying! You just don't get it, do you? You couldn't control any of the things that have happened in my private life over the last year. Stop making this about you! It's a me thing! This is *my* life. I'm eighteen in a week, and I'm responsible for those videos of me circulating, as much as I don't want to accept that. You want to know why? It's fucking easier to be a baby. It's easier to be a victim and to blame everyone else. I've done it my whole fucking life, but now that this has happened, I can clearly see that everything is my fucking fault. I'm the enabler of all of the chaos. I'm the problem! I don't want your sympathy. I hate myself more than I could ever hate anyone else!" She struggles to say something, but I cut her off as she cries. "You want me to keep going?"

"Please stop."

"You know Shane Avery? I basically killed him. He was one of my best friends and I humiliated him to the point of hanging himself. He told me a secret and I shared it with someone who ended up using it against him and the shame was too much. I caused the shame. I'm basically a murderer by proxy."

She screams. "What? You knew Shane and you never invited him over? How could you do this to your own parents? I can't believe this! You were friends with the Averys and never told us? Brad! Your father could have benefited from networking with them. Our family's net worth would have gone up dramatically. They could've been investors in your father's company."

I scream, "He was a totally fucked up dude, Mom. He's not who you think he was, all because of who his family is. You wouldn't have wanted me hanging around him!"

She backs away. "You're a stranger to me right now. You can't be my son. You can't be. I need evidence from God that the kid I raised wouldn't ever put me in this position. Why would you do this to us?"

"I wanted to be in control! For the first time ever I got to make decisions outside of your bubble of protection that you worked so hard to build for me. Maybe I destroyed my reputation by being a part of those videotapes, but do you know what I got out of it? Freedom. When you watch those clips of me, you're going to learn all of the things that you worked so hard to keep me from. I ended up chasing them. Are you proud of yourself? You did a bang-up job, Mom, because now I'm part of a neighborhood-wide scandal, and you'll be the one to blame."

She grabs her purse from the counter. "I have to leave. I'm going over there right now."

I grab her arm. "You need to accept that I'm not who you tell your friends I am. I want you to take that in. The real me is a miserable person who hates his life. I'm a compulsive liar who creates make-believe storylines about himself just to cope with this meaningless fucking existence." I cry, tapping my heart. "I've tried everything to take away this constant pain. Nothing fixes these aches."

She's about to make her way to the garage but pauses. She grabs my arm. "Promise me it's not that bad, that I won't have to listen to Rosalie and John judge the kind of parent I am and discredit all of the years I spent putting you together. You're still the gracious and sweet boy that we know under this roof. That's who you are to me, Brad, and I don't want to lose him."

"You've already lost him, Mom. It *is* that bad. You don't know what you're about to see. Your whole image of me is going to be altered forever. Things are never going to be the same between me, you, and Dad. Everything is about to change. Do you understand that? So go! Go over to their house and discover the truth about your son!"

She fakes a smile and tilts her head. "We will figure this out. You can recover from this, sweetie. If it's a home movie of you doing drugs, we can afford rehab. We can shove it under the rug. We can say you're visiting family in California. Don't you worry. I can handle this. I'm prepared for an image crisis."

"No, Mom, you don't get it. There's no lawyer, no money in the world, no connection that Dad has that can send this away. This is irreversible."

She screams to herself, "I can't believe this is my life. This is every mother's nightmare. What did I do to deserve this?"

I grab her arm again, my voice breaking. "One more thing. I was never part of the student council. You've been so zoned out that you just believed all my lies. Are you braindead? It's like, God, is all that primetime seriously frying you out?" I scream, then stop to take a deep breath. "Before you go, I've wanted to tell you this for so long. I wish I could've just talked to you and told you before everything got out of control. I wish I could've stood up for myself, made your opinion of me less important. I wish I could've just asked you nicely to stop trying to micromanage my life all because you can't control your own, for you to ease off the pressure of me being a 'good son.'"

She looks shocked and disgusted. I walk away. The garage door opens. She pulls out of the driveway and heads to Kev's house. I go back into the kitchen, grab a box of Oreo O's off the counter, and crush it, throwing it all over the floor as I wail. I get a bottle of Pepsi from the fridge and pour it all over the couch.

"I...fucking hate...everyone! I'm going to do it! No one is going to stop me! There is no point in living through this humiliation, this shame, this embarrassment. My whole life is over. The pain is too much."

I run into my bedroom in a sweat and pace around. I stare at the flashing red light on my answering machine and hit play.

"I'm sure you've seen the website by now. You really are fucking stupid, huh? You thought I'd destroy those videotapes? Nothing gives me more satisfaction than destroying your image and exposing you to all of the people you've spent this year lying to. Before I met you, I always fantasized about what it'd be like to corrupt an innocent boy-next-door type. Blast him on the internet. This was an honor. Well, thank God for *Studio DV* software. Anyways, toodles from the sexiest school shooter this country will ever see! Oh, and say nice things when they ask you about me on MTV! ABC! *Entertainment Tonight*! Whatever. Suck on that, Eric and Dylan, there's a new American prince of mass murder, and his name is Lusif."

I grab a Polaroid of me and Shane and sob. I run to my closet and take out the Ruger pistol I got a hold of after I last saw Eric and Kev. My video camera is on top of my TV as I sit on the edge of my bed and play "Adam's Song" low on my CD player.

I look into the lens and hit record.

"Um, I never wanted to be one of those boys who kills themselves to 'Adam's Song,' but fuck. I really wanted to turn eighteen. I really wanted to do that, you guys. Also, if Tom and Mark watch this, blink was the only thing keeping me alive all of this time. I'm not kidding. I couldn't have gotten through high school without you guys. I never thought that I'd have to make this statement, but now, in the last two weeks: a website damaging my reputation has been passed around my neighborhood, the love of my life has completely disappeared and stopped writing me, my best friend is shooting up my high school, and my depressed friend just hanged himself after threatening suicide ever since I met him. I don't know the point of going on, and I definitely don't want to live through all the media that Lu is going to get. I don't want to see the shame of our videos and pictures plastered all over the news. I don't want to see my face everywhere, to be known as the best friend of someone so evil. The one good thing I had, the one pure thing in my world, Aurora, was taken from me. I'm numb. At least now I'm going to a place where I can see Shane and apologize for being such a bad friend.

I never asked for this! I never knew that I was going to be blackmailed! I trusted Lu!

I have no desire to see that part of myself. That version of me doesn't even exist. It's insane. You can spend your whole life obsessing over yourself and then realize you don't even exist, that you've been dreaming up someone else the entire time. All you've ever known is a series of images you designed.

To know right now that my mom is with her friends watching these videotapes is too painful. I have too much shame. I can't believe I'm losing being America's sweetheart to everyone in this neighborhood. How could I ever show my face at a party again? Everything and anything disgusting, horrible, evil, you don't even have to imagine it, because it's already happening somewhere out there. What's the point of being alive in a world where you can't control anything you see? A world where you can't control the people around you? A world where you can't even control what fucking happens to you or how people think of you?

The number one fucking thing that wasn't supposed to happen did! I got caught not being who I am. The hours I've spent not being who I was, was ironically how I became myself. But please, all I ask is to not be defined by the videotapes…Mom and Dad and anyone who loves me.

I'm sorry to the Avery family for murdering your son by humiliating Shane to death and I'm sorry for what my parents are going to have to live through knowing that they will be judged for raising a monster. Maybe there is a solution and maybe the shame could go away but I just don't see it happening anytime soon. It's not worth living through this pain.

I never fucking knew that anyone would see them. I thought they were private. The worlds that we create as we try to become ourselves…I'll never understand. How stupid am I to think that privacy exists in a world where everyone owns a video camera?

Please remember me as the guy you knew, not by snapshots, not by moments. I am not defined by this website. I am not defined by these tapes."

I put the gun to my temple.

"The more you expose, the more invisible you become."

About the Author

Alex Kazemi lives in Vancouver. This is his first novel.